GEORGIA

KEYS

OF

TIME

SOUL DOMINION / ONE

Keys of Time

KEYMASTER CHRONICLES

Soul Dominion / One

by
GEORGIANA KENT

Copyright

Keys of Time
Book One of the Soul Dominion series

Cover by: GetCovers

First Edition: August 2021
10 9 8 7 6 5 4 3 2 1

Also by Georgiana Kent

KEYMASTER CHRONICLES

Soul Dominion (I – III)
Keys of Time

Coming Soon!
Keys of Fate
Keys of Death

KeyMaster Origins
Inner Demons

Dedications

To my parents – for providing a home of love, support and books
To my brother – for inspiring me in so many ways
To my husband – for being my best friend and believing in me
To my Tata Chip – for being my miracle

Dear Reader

In the *KeyMaster Chronicles* you will find everyone: humans, Lost Souls, KeyMasters, Soul Gatherers, Færies, Fæ, Dæmons, Angels and Demons. Overall, they are self-explanatory, and I don't wish to spoil the experience for you (so I won't!) But my Færies might puzzle you as they are referred to as 'it'. This is purposeful as they are Elemental Beings and do not consider themselves male or female. They simply adopt their chosen appearance when with humans on Earth, but they can freely take on other guises. In their elemental world, they are elements and, as such, aren't limited to genders. Furthermore, inspired by J. R. R. Tolkien's Elvish languages from *The Lord of the Rings*, I have also developed a language for my Færies. A taste of which you will find here.

Being British, I should point out that spelling, grammar and turns of phrase are all British and some pertain to my home, the Midlands. So, mobile phones, not cell phones, torches not flashlights, pavements not sidewalks, flats not apartments, etc. Though, I'm sure this won't stop you enjoying the story! If there's anything you're not familiar with, please feel free to email and ask.

One of my many jobs is a language teacher. I teach Mandarin Chinese, French and Spanish and have lived and travelled China, Japan, Taiwan and Malaysia. I love the world and all its wonderful sights, countries, cultures and people and this comes through in my writing. I wanted to create a universe as diverse as ours, and then some.

Names are particularly important to me. Some just came to me, like the names of Michael, Erica, Ashayla, Christian and Nathaniel (dear old Nathaniel), some have been inspired by films or found on the sides of lorries (ask and I might tell you!), some have personal significance, but others required research. Generally, when researching names, I looked initially at the character's nationality then meaning. For example, the werewolf Lunita is Peruvian and her name comes from the Spanish 'little moon'. Whilst Lizzie's middle name is Gráinne which was the name of the Irish grain goddess and is often associated with *gráidh* meaning 'love'. For Xerxes, I wanted a strong name of an ancient king who might have been able to command the Færie's respect. Then there's Anatole's Færie, Vozdukha. Since Anatole is Russian, I wanted a Russian name, or word, for his Færie. As Vozdukha's element is air, I chose the Russian word for 'air'.

Michael's London is influenced by my morning commute from my lodgings on Lexham Gardens to High Street Kensington where I either caught the No. 9 bus for work or the Tube for university. I counted myself lucky to live in such an amazing neighbourhood, it really fired my imagination. His house, with no front door, actually exists! I walked past it every day and it was the catalyst that sparked off the whole *KeyMaster Chronicles*!

But I reveal more in my bi-monthly newsletters. If you're interested, you can sign up on my website. For now, I'll leave you to enjoy *Keys of Time*. Let me know what you think! If you loved the book and have a moment to spare, I would really appreciate it if you could leave a short review on the store front you bought the book or on Goodreads (https://bit.ly/InnerDemonsGoodreads). Your help in spreading the word is really appreciated and reviews make a huge difference to helping new readers find future books.

Ever yours,
Georgiana

PS – Sign up to my mailing list here:
http://bit.ly/keymasterchronicles

*PPS – Get your **FREE** prequel novella here:*
https://bit.ly/GeorgianaKent

PPPS - Find me on Facebook and Instagram!
@authorgeorgianakent

PPPPS – Find me on TikTok!
@georgianakent_books

#georgianakent #keymasterchronicles #souldominion #keysoftime #souldominionkeysoftime #souldominionseries #keymasterorigins

Notes:

Chocolate Hobnob biscuit – crunchy, chocolate-coated cookies that are very scrummy and particularly good at surviving being dunked in tea or coffee.

Crisps - wafer-thin slice of potato fried or baked until crisp and eaten as a snack, a potato chip.

Yorkshire Pudding - a popover made of baked unsweetened egg batter, typically eaten with roast beef.

Soul Dominion / One

Keys of Time

Prologue

~ London, present day ~

It was late as Verity Parker walked Fluffy, her aptly named Pomeranian, wincing against the cold wind. She'd fought with her boyfriend and had stormed out of their flat to get some space: how could he think having dinner with his ex was okay?!

She walked blindly, seething with rage that boiled so much within her that she couldn't stay still let alone think straight. Blood pounded in her ears, dulling the sounds of the evening traffic. As she stepped out to cross De Vere Gardens she was greeted by the glare of headlights and screech of tyres; the driver gestured colourfully at her carelessness, blasting the horn for good measure. Heart thumping, she stumbled across to the other side and found herself on the outskirts of Hyde Park. It was a clear November evening and bitterly cold. The night sky was ablaze with stars that shone icily down upon the open green space of the Park. Cars, taxis and buses rumbled noisily along Kensington Road, west towards the High Street and east towards the City.

Lights from offices and flats illuminated the edge of the park where Verity walked. She had stupidly not changed and only wore a onesie and Ugg boots and was freezing. Thank God it was dark, or else she'd be embarrassed *and* freezing. She swore under her breath: this was all Josh's fault. She felt hollow, tears stung her eyes and it hurt to breathe.

Refusing to give in, Verity turned down one of Hyde Parks' many dimly lit walkways that led to The Serpentine lake at its heart. There was the odd dog walker even at this late hour.

Her mobile phone sounded. Looking at the bright screen she saw Josh's face smiling up at her and viciously swiped it, cutting him off. The ass! He was the last person she wanted to talk to right now. Betrayal tasted bitter upon her tongue. She continued to stomp along the path, fists clenched, nails digging deep, muttering as she went; Fluffy happily trotting by her side.

A howl disturbed the quiet of the night.

Verity looked up with a frown.

A responding howl echoed across the green lawns and trees. Then another and another. Glancing down, Verity noticed Fluffy's fur was now on end. An extra long, extra loud howl reverberated across the park and Fluffy began to growl. Not a light-hearted growl, but a deep guttural one that came from her belly.

"What's going on, girl?" Verity asked, scooping her up and cradling her. Fluffy's growls grew more and more pronounced. Verity could feel their vibrations and the *thud-thud* of her tiny heart beating wildly against her ribcage.

In the near-distance Verity could hear the rustle of grass and splashing of water as something, many things, made their way across the lake.

There was an uneasy silence.

Then, a nearby yelp of a dog and a series of bloodcurdling screams shattered it.

Jumping out of her skin, she scanned the dark trees before her, heart in her throat. Fluffy's growls reached a whole new octave as the hackles on the back of her neck stood on end.

Hurriedly backing away, she hadn't gone far when she saw the silhouette of a small dog emerge about ten metres from her. It looked like a Chihuahua. That wasn't so bad, maybe she was over-reacting.

"Hello gorgeous! What are you doing out here all on your own? Are you lost?" Her voice was shrill, even to her ears. There were no signs of any owners. She really ought to take a look at its collar.

Licking her lips, she took a tentative step forwards and Fluffy immediately started pawing at her, barking frantically.

Flinching, Verity hesitated.

Just then, the silhouette of another dog appeared next to the Chihuahua, and another, and another and another. Strays?

"Alright, sweetie, it's alright." She soothed as Fluffy continued to bark. "Shh. It's okay, we'll go home."

Gripping the little dog tightly, she slowly backed away, throat dry. Bravely turning, it was as they began walking that Verity heard the howl.

Looking over her shoulder, she saw the Chihuahua with its head thrown back howling loudly. The other dogs copied and within seconds more dogs appeared, big and small, until thirty or more dogs were gathered.

In the darkness she couldn't make out their features but the fetor that came off them was unreal: a heady cocktail of putrid flesh and rotten blood. Dread and nausea overwhelmed her as she turned and ran; though her legs refused to work properly, and she lost her footing more than once.

Behind her, a growl erupted from the Chihuahua and was picked up by the rest of the pack until they hummed in frightful unison. Glancing back, Verity saw the Chihuahua lurch forward, the rest of the pack behind it. Screaming, she ran as fast as she could with Fluffy cradled in her arms.

Within seconds the dogs were upon them bringing her to her knees with an almighty crash. Rolling over to shield Fluffy, she screamed in agony as teeth gorged her arms and legs, face and body. The pain was so intense she wailed as everything went black. Their stench smothered her. Despite her efforts to fight them off, there were too many and they were too strong; she was overpowered within seconds. Howling, she cried as they savaged her, lacerating her stomach, scattering her innards and tearing her limbs.

It was only when she lay dismembered and bleary eyed in a pool of growing blood, that the Chihuahua approached her. Gasping for breath, blood bubbling at her mouth, she noticed it to be a dark swirling mass of shadows, darker than the night. It bent down to sniff her, casually licking her blood from her face. Verity let out a whimper, tears trickling down her mutilated cheeks. Looking at her, it formed eyes of the deepest, darkest red, filled with loathing. Then, lowering its head, it gently, teasingly, nibbled through her jugular.

When the convulsions had finished and her soul lost its grip on her body, it was expulsed, a shimmering shower of black petals. The Chihuahua watched in satisfaction as they swirled and drifted away, lost and confused.

They would find their way, they all did.

Only then did the Alpha Blood Hound step aside, allowing its pack to feed.

A new member, a Pomeranian-shaped mass of shadows, approached the Alpha Hound, bending before it, paws extended. The Chihuahua welcomed it, licking one of its paws and inviting it to enjoy the feast: the more the merrier.

It had been a profitable night.

Sire would be pleased.

1

Wrathful

"Are you still here?!"

Nineteen-year-old Erica Shylocke poked her head up over her barricade of books at the sound of the Library Technician's voice as he entered the reading room. It was deserted apart from her.

"You know I was thinking of moving in. I could pitch up camp over there, get the kettle on and I'd be well away, wouldn't I?" She smiled wickedly, and he laughed. She began to gather her things into her bag.

"The day you do that is the day I go and get you help!" The Library Technician said as he went about straightening up chairs, tidying up scraps of paper and stacking his trolley with discarded books.

"Spoilsport!" Erica joked as she stood up. Flinging on her scarf, coat and rucksack, she stopped to eye the pile of books.

"If you're planning on borrowing any of those the desk'll be closing in ten minutes."

"If?"

He then watched as she stacked the books up. "You can't be seriously thinking of borrowing them all?!"

"Needs must. My tutor wants blood, so I've got to finish this essay double-quick!" She lifted the pile and grimaced under their weight: *maybe he could kill her after all?*

The Library Technician held open the door for her and she bid him goodnight before stumbling downstairs and joining the other book-laden students at the front desk. Once she'd all her books stamped, she exited the library.

She was in the second year of her BA History course at University College London. Whilst things were more than familiar, she still had to pinch herself as she walked along its Art Deco corridors, with its lavish marble flooring and glamour-drenched buildings. When she'd first arrived as a Fresher last year she'd been totally overwhelmed and, even after all this time, it still made tingles run down her spine. It couldn't be more different to home.

Walking out into the chilly November evening, the white tower of Senate House loomed overhead like some mighty guardian angel keeping its watchful eye over the City. The night sky was clear and the moon bathed her in its light. Stars sparkled high in their heavens: the bitter cold having already encouraged ice to glisten on the pavements.

Re-adjusting her books, Erica walked across Russell Square, towards the Underground station and home.

***

The train thundered into the station and stopped with a squeal of brakes and a screech of metal. Erica woke with a jerk and looked blearily out of the window: it was her station. Gathering up her books once more she braced herself against the inevitable cold as the doors clattered open. Shivering, she made her way up the stairs to the exit and noticed she was joined by some of her 'regulars'. The young lawyer, dark-eyed and sporting a stubble; the middle-aged man with a comb-over, buried deep in his newspaper; the singer dressed for another night's work. London was such a huge city where anonymity and indifference reigned that Erica was glad to 'know' these people—even if it was only by sight.

Erica and the singer smiled at each other as they swiped their passes at the ticket barriers. It was then that Erica noticed another one of her 'regulars'.

He was African, with skin the shade of ochre, and tall. Wrapped up in a smart three-quarter jacket, lined silk muffler, top hat and leather gloves, he looked as if he'd stepped straight out of a Victorian photoshoot for Giorgio Armani. She slowed as she walked by, surreptitiously studying him out of the corner of her eye. He appeared to be in his mid-twenties but there was a sense of agedness about him that fascinated her. Not to mention his good looks. What with his broad shoulders, chiselled jawline, full lips and aquamarine eyes, she felt weak at the knees.

He stood to one side of the circular entrance to High Street Kensington's Underground station, bathed in the gloomy evening light that filtered through the vaulted glass ceiling. As usual, he was keenly watching the embellished date carved high up on the frieze. He'd been standing in this same spot this past week, night after night, waiting for something. But what?

Slowing, Erica let her gaze follow his. Sure enough, the carved date read '1960' just-as-it-always-*did?!*

For, just then, the embossed numbers quivered and warped; morphing soundlessly to read '1781'. After a few moments, just as quietly, they shuddered and returned to their original date.

Stunned, Erica came to an abrupt stop, mouth agape, eyes wide in disbelief. She felt someone approach and found herself looking into those bright aquamarine eyes. Her stomach fluttered.

"How much did you see?" he asked, his voice euphonic.

Quickly composing herself she gave a shrug. "Not much." Anyway, she had to be mistaken. Buildings don't just change. She was tired, that was all.

Just then the lawyer pushed past her, giving her a look as if she'd lost her mind. He shook his head, muttering something about 'nutters' before continuing up the Arcade.

"Meaning everything," the man quipped, watching the lawyer leave thoughtfully.

"It's late and I'm tired. Please, leave me alone." She shifted the weight of the books onto her hips.

"Allow me, Miss…" he said, reaching for her books.

"Thanks, but no thanks. I wasn't born yesterday!" She scoffed, dodging round him to continue down the Arcade towards the lights of the High Street beyond. She'd met way too many weirdos during her time in London to be taken in by another. Even if he was hot.

Staggering on to the quiet High Street, she turned left, straining under the weight of the books. *Why, oh, why, hadn't they invented teleportation already?*

Scarcely halfway down the street her mobile sounded. Cursing she stopped by a shop window, precariously balancing the pile of books as she fished for her phone in her pocket. It was Lizzie Brennan, her best friend.

"Erica! You took ages. Am I interrupting?" Her friend's voice asked hopefully.

"Yes, I'm trying to navigate London with a pile of books," Erica said, setting off with the phone tucked under her chin.

"Get a life, Erica! You should be out partying!" On cue, loud music filtered down the phone.

"I know, I can hear. But I'm not you, Lizzie. Plus, I've got a deadline. This essay won't write itself."

"Screw deadlines! You only live once! Man, Erica, your brother's fit," Lizzie said suddenly, swooning.

"Is he playing?" she asked, turning left onto Wrights Lane and walking wobbly past a café. It was still busy; comforting chatter spilled out onto the pavement as the door opened. She breathed in the warm coffee aromas with an appreciative sigh. Maybe she'd have a latte when she got home. Better yet, a Bailey's latte! Or maybe even a Bailey's hot chocolate! With a marshmallow. Or three.

"Yeah, they're so good! He's asked me to join them backstage later."

"Well, call me when you get home, I'll be up."

"Okay. If I don't, it's because we're 'busy'! If you know what I mean!"

"Please, I don't want to bring up dinner. I can't afford another."

Hanging up, Erica gazed at her phone worrying her lip with a furrowed brow. *What if Lizzie did get together with Guy?*

Shaking herself, she continued down the road, cursing in between her huffs and puffs. She was so unfit.

The sound of dried leaves skittering along the road filtered through into her thoughts. Ears pricking up, she glanced back the way she'd come. There was no breeze; the night was quiet and the leaves gathering in the gutters remained still.

She scanned the street and its shadows. Some shadows seemed to warp, yet, if she focused on them, they looked nothing more than shadows.

Chiding herself, she carried on past a hotel and round past a block of Edwardian flats. She dreamt of the hot chocolate she'd make once she got home, ignoring the ache in her shoulders. Not far now.

There was a fizzle as the streetlights flickered once and died, plunging her into total darkness.

She froze, instinctively rooted to the spot. She couldn't see more than a few feet in any direction, though the shadows seemed to undulate and quiver every few seconds. She looked up and frowned; it had been a clear night but now it was pitch black, as if someone had blanketed the moon and its heavens. Fear gripped her. She suddenly felt massively disoriented as if all clarity had gone. Her chest tightening, she fumbled with her mobile and turned on the torch. Its beam of light, normally so bright, failed to pierce the churning blackness. Her heart sank: not good.

The skittering sound echoed somewhere to her left. This time it sounded like dried bones being dragged along the tarmac. And close.

She took a tentative step away. Nothing.

She took another step and another until she found herself running blindly in the darkness. A face with blank eyes lurched out of nowhere, its sharp teeth snapping at her. Screaming, she flinched as another dove at her. Then, the next instant, the darkness lifted, though the streetlights failed to turn on.

Gingerly she looked around the dimness, eyes coming to a stop on a writhing lump of shadows which swelled and oozed in the middle of the road. Erica watched in horror as it gathered within it the remaining darkness and shadows nearby, bulging further as it devoured their mass, growing larger by the second.

She remembered her books. The thought of throwing them at the weird shadow-monster crossed her mind. Taking aim, she grimaced. Nope. She couldn't bear damaging them. Cursing, she ripped open her rucksack and stuffed the books inside, its straps straining with their weight. Then, using both hands, she proceeded to swing it at the thing which hissed with each blow. She was encouraged to see some of its matter disperse in thin tendrils when struck but, despite her efforts, the thing continued to grow; bloating grotesquely until it heaved with blackness. Her gaze was now transfixed. Because, as it grew it took on a shape and, as if watching through a camera lens being brought into focus, the shape became more and more defined, until a shadowy face full of foulness and loathing bore down on her, malicious red eyes blazing.

She tried to tear her gaze from it but couldn't: it wouldn't let her. It wanted to see her suffer.

With the weight of its wrath pressing down heavily upon her, she felt her spine crunch as she tried to resist, then her knees buckled and she felt the cool tarmac slam against them. Her grip on her bag slackened and it tumbled to the floor. She became aware of a choir of shadows emerging from its bulk to encircle her. Her vision flashing red as they whispered in persistent, fierce unison. An overwhelming rage swelled within her, strangling her heart. Hot tears fell from her eyes, scalding them, making them bleed: *how dare they?! How dare they doubt her! She'd make them pay, even if it killed her, she'd make them pay!*

The choir of voices whispered to her soul: *join us, sister... Together we can make them pay.*

Unable to resist any longer, her body bowed in submission.

Together... Her soul replied.

As one, the blank eyes of the shadowy choir snapped open and smirked at her knelt form, baring teeth as sharp as needles. An air of malevolent satisfaction settled on the monstrous mass as it bent to feed.

There was the sound of running feet, a whispered command and an explosion of light, so bright and pure that it engulfed all shadows, bleaching the world.

The choir that encircled her jolted as one, withdrawing back within the monster, hands raised; their cries of rage following in their wake.

Erica gasped for breath as the creature's hold on her broke and immediately threw up. Wiping her mouth, she blinked against the glare, shielding her face with her arm. The massive body of shadows towered above her, but it was contorted in pain and trying to wriggle free from its assailant. For upon its shoulders, small and elfin, was a form of brilliant blue-white light. Its surface crackling and swirling with energy: it was from this that the bright light pulsed and glowed, leaving the world scratchy and drawn.

The shadows screeched and writhed as one, trying to buck the thing off. Its screeches turned to screams of pain as the form plunged a tiny fist into it.

Twisting and turning, the engorged mass screamed in rage as it diminished, drowning in the light that filled it from within. It made a final violent attempt to claw at Erica before succumbing, erupting in a blinding flash; its howl of rage echoed into the night.

All that remained as Erica looked up, was a swirling flurry of black petals, which drifted as one into the night, bewildered and lost.

The brightness subdued, and the little figure landed nimbly before her, cocking its head with interest. Pulses of energy flared across its skin and upon its head were fine wisps of light, resembling hair. A command was spoken and with a flash it streaked to where the gentleman from the station stood, vanishing within a medallion: the stone in its centre shimmered once.

Pocketing the medallion, the man ran over to where Erica was slumped on her knees, gasping for breath.

Shock then catching up with her, she began to cry. Tears gushed down her blood-streaked face. "What the hell was that"—she tried to think of a word to describe the creature that had tried to kill her and failed—"That *thing*?!"

"A Lost Soul, but first, let us attend to you," he said, reaching into his jacket pocket to produce a red vial. Uncorking it, he wafted the salts gently under her nose. Her eyes widened as soon as the bitter odour hit her nostrils and she began to sneeze violently. The tightness in her chest then melted away as air filled her lungs.

"And this is for your eyes," he said gently once she'd finished, handing her a handkerchief.

"Thank you." Taking it, she wiped her eyes and face. Traces of watery blood stained it. She shuddered.

Trying to stand, she trembled involuntarily, knees buckling. She fell back to the ground. Offering her a gloved hand, he helped her to her feet, steadying her.

"I am truly sorry that you should have had such an ordeal tonight," he said. "I noticed the blackness on my way home and came as soon as possible."

"It was real?" she replied dully.

"I'm afraid so. Most nightmares are… Pray, which direction to your house?"

She hesitated, folding her arms around her protectively.

"I'm *not* going to hurt you. I should like to ensure you get home safely."

She looked at him, eyes raw. "How do I know?" she asked, her voice breaking.

He regarded her tenderly. "You have my word."

A tremor ran down her spine and she took a deep breath. She noticed the concern on his face. Sniffing, Erica looked around her, trying to get her bearings. She must have run down Abingdon Villas in her panic. She indicated to the left turning at the mini roundabout.

Taking her bag, he offered her his free arm. Steering her forwards, they walked in time, their shadows elongating then shortening as they passed under the orange glare of the streetlights. The cool air was helping, her head felt clearer and she was no longer trembling. Although she found her heart still beat fast and wondered whether he could feel it also.

"What was that thing?" she asked, finding her voice at last.

"It was a Wrathful, a Lost Soul, a soul that died with vengeance in its heart and, consequently, with wrath for its demise—its revenge pulls it back to earth." He paused. When he spoke again, sadness coloured his tone. "All Wrathful are deadly," he continued, "some more so. The one you were unfortunate enough to encounter was particularly vile due to its large Choir. If a Wrathful reaches earth, those out in the field should be notified immediately, regardless of their station, they are that dangerous; but we were not." He finished darkly, eyes glinting under his brow.

"'Those in the field'?"

"People like me," he said cautiously.

Erica looked at him, thinking back to the little creature that had plunged its fist into the Wrathful. "And what are you?"

Nice, Erica. Real subtle.

"Someone who wanted to help."

"And I'm really grateful, but it still doesn't answer my question: what are you?"

"I cannot say. Contact is strictly prohibited."

Contact? She yanked her arm free and rounded on him. "You're the one who started it!"

"And you would be dead if I had not," he said bluntly. "Sometimes, rules are worth breaking."

She stopped short, guilt pinching her. "Fine," she said, bottom lip sticking out. "But I will get it out of you, you and your little glow bug! You can't expect something this weird to just happen and me to be okay with it."

He doffed his top hat in acceptance of the challenge.

"What did it want? Or can't you tell me that either?" she said, reaching for her rucksack. It weighed a tonne but at least she could swing it at him if he tried anything funny.

"Your most valuable commodity: your soul. For without it, what would you be?"

She shuddered as a chill ran through her and pulled her jacket closer for comfort. "How many are there?"

"Thousands and growing."

"Growing? How?"

He caught her eye then and she saw grief there, grief that had hardened over the years but remained grief, nonetheless. "Any person that falls victim to a Wrathful does in turn become one of its Choir, those with a grudge are targeted first since they are easy prey.

As part of its Choir, they then seek revenge on those they believe failed it and brought about its demise. The number of Wrathful is not measured by their single form but by their Choir: the larger their number, the stronger they are."

Erica stopped abruptly: *the voices...*

"You saw them?"

She blushed and nodded. She'd forgotten the malignant group, cajoling her in her revenge. She was glad when he didn't press the matter. She herself hadn't realised the depth of her resentment until the Wrathful bore down on her: to be honest, it shocked her.

"I arrived just as you attacked it—that was very brave," he said warmly.

"A fat lot of good it did though. How do you kill those things?" She swiped away her tears.

"Light. You must fill it from within with light."

"Not exactly easy for people who don't have glow bugs," she scoffed, blinking against her sore eyes.

"No, it's not. And it's not a 'glow bug', it's a Færie," he said, hiding an amused smile.

"Of course, it is," she said, her voice weary. At this rate, her Bailey's hot chocolate would be more Bailey's than hot chocolate.

She hesitated, voice suddenly dry. "Do many die?"

"Not as many as before—security is tight. Well, it was..." Anger crept back into his voice.

"I've never heard of any; and I'm positive the media would never pass up on a story like that!"

"There are security measures in place, so such things are not reported—for people's safety."

"Ignorance is bliss, right?"

"It does appear to be the best way to avoid pandemonium."

They walked past quaint mews and down windy cobbled lanes. They were not far from her flat now. Passing under a grand stone archway they found themselves on a wide street lined with white stucco houses.

"Well, we're here," she said, coming to a stop. "I'm just over the road."

She turned to find him quickly masking a look of shock.

"Thank you… Sorry, I don't know your name, or is that something else you can't tell me?" she said with a crooked smile.

"Michael, Michael Nicholas."

"Nice to meet you, Michael. I'm Erica Shylocke."

"The pleasure is all mine, Miss Shylocke. Please accept my profoundest apologies once more." And he gave a little bow.

"If you hadn't found me, I'd probably be dead or, or worse…" She stopped, voice fading to a hoarse whisper.

He bowed even more deeply. "You are too kind."

She extended her hand. Smiling, he shook it.

"Well, goodbye. It was…" Her voice drifted off as she felt him place something cold against her palm. Looking, she saw his medallion. In its centre was a precious stone that winked iridescently at her. It was tear-shaped and encased in silver filigree, its edging intricate and tactile. Within the filigree was a tiny key-shaped relief. It was beautiful.

"It's a periapt. Keep it for now. It's talismanic; it will help keep you safe. Tap it and Ashayla will notify me. Ashayla is my 'glow bug'," he explained on seeing her confusion.

"I couldn't!" She looked up in shock.

"I would feel happier knowing you had it," he insisted. And with that he closed her hand gently over it.

Crossing the road, he watched as she got out her keys and entered the building.

Once inside, she breathed a sigh of relief, depositing her bag to walk over to the window. She could still make him out in the glow of the streetlight, looking up at her.

Just then, her mobile rang. She waved nervously as she answered Lizzie's call and drew the curtains firmly shut.

"I gave up waiting," whined her best friend. "What took you so long?"

2

The Actualle

Erica had a penchant for all things vintage, amassing an outlandish collection over her years of trawling markets and sales. Lizzie described her preference for skirts and pretty tops 'frumpy', whereas Erica preferred the term 'eclectic', especially as they hid her thighs so well. Provided there was an element of purple, she considered her outfit complete and made a quirky sight on most days. As a rule, she avoided wearing black (it reminded her too much of death), only wearing it for work.

Sadly, today was such a day and her black uniform of skirt and blouse smothered her petite pale frame. Black hair framed her face, setting off her emerald-green eyes. Though at this precise moment, they were bloodshot and bleary: dull shadows hung heavily beneath them—she hadn't slept well.

Admittedly, her encounter with the Wrathful had left her plagued by dreams of snapping teeth and malevolent shadows eager to feed on her soul. But she'd been disturbed several times during the night… She glanced down at the burns on her forearms, where fresh, unsightly blisters pocked the skin. There was a bluish tinge to them…

Fetching a glass jar from her kitchenette, she slathered on the pungent ointment, sneezing as the oils tickled her nose. Ensuring the burns were well covered, she bandaged them deftly, wincing as she tugged on a baggy cardigan. She pulled down the cuffs. Perfect, no one would know.

Just then, Lizzie video called her. She was back home in Bonsall opening The Bonsall Tea Rooms, her parents' business.

"Erica! Come on! You've not even left yet!"

"I know, I know," she said, fetching her coat and winter woollies.

"You look rough. Bad night?" Lizzie was peering into the screen. The morning sun dancing across her auburn hair. "What's wrong with your eyes?"

"Thanks. You know you're a little too honest sometimes, Lizzie," Erica said, rubbing them—they were still sore.

"Sorry! Guess what!" Lizzie's face suddenly alight with excitement.

"You're going to have lunch with Guy."

Her excitement fizzled away. "How did you know?"

"It's Saturday. He always eats lunch at the Tea Rooms on Saturdays."

"He does? I made him his favourite: Chocolate Dandelion and Burdock cake," she admitted, blushing. She was wearing one of her favourite slogan t-shirts with IN MY DEFENCE I WAS LEFT UNSUPERVISED emblazoned across her bosom. Paired with her signature leather jacket and skinny jeans, she was rocking it. Definitely dressed for Saturday lunch with Guy.

"Will you just ask him out already!" Erica moaned, grabbing her bag and locking the front door to her flat behind her.

"No way! He should ask me out. That way I'll know for sure."

"Okay, yeah, you'll know he likes you, but you already know that. We all do," she said. "But isn't loving someone about opening yourself up and being vulnerable? Letting them know they're loved even if you risk not having the same feelings returned?"

"Erica, this is all a bit heavy for a Saturday morning. Why don't you—"

"I'm not getting involved."

"He is your brother," Lizzie pointed out, turning on the till.

"Exactly my point! Anyhow, I'll call you later."

"Are you going to run?"

"I don't think I've got a choice." Erica sighed, bracing herself.

"Wish I was there. You always make me laugh when—"

Erica hung up.

What followed was the usual mad dash to the Underground station, weaving in and out of people and dodging traffic. She found the Tube a cheerless place full of Londoners too glum to smile, who shot laughing tourists accusatory looks over the tops of their newspapers. What's more, the airless tunnels and compressed darkness reminded her of catacombs twisting deep below the city. The one good thing was that these deep tunnels provided some respite from the chilly winter's morning above ground. Plus, no one spoke to you, so you could read in peace.

As the train clattered from station-to-station Erica took the opportunity to continue reading one of the books for her essay; reluctantly stowing it away when she finally reached her stop.

She worked in Piccadilly, at the flagship store of a major book chain near to some of London's most popular tourist attractions and theatres. As a result, her station was always busy with people coming and going and tourists ambling along with their noses buried in guidebooks.

"Excuse me!" she apologised, squeezing past an excited gaggle in matching hats.

Climbing the stairs up into the bright winter sun she was momentarily blown away by the grandeur of the buildings that greeted her. Not to mention the chaos as Piccadilly, Regent Street and Shaftsbury Avenue collided in a whirl of neon and noise. She doubted she would ever get used to it.

It was then she noticed a young girl frantically handing out fliers to passers-by—her older sister had gone missing.

"She'd never leave without telling us!" The girl insisted, as Erica accepted a flier. A smiling face beamed up at her as she scanned it: she'd failed to return home last night from walking her dog. Unbidden, the Wrathful leapt from the shadows of her mind. A chill ran down her spine: *could it be?*

It was then she noticed the time on her wristwatch. Cursing, Erica ran pell-mell up the street, arriving in a panting heap at the doors of the store.

"You're late, Shylocke. Again."

Breathing heavily, Erica smiled weakly up at Hincks Percival, the Store Manager, who was patrolling the doors. A short man with balding hair and a protruding neck, he resembled an over-angst vulture as he paced back and forth in his black waistcoat. A garish handkerchief peeped out of his breast pocket. He ran the store with military precision and abhorred lateness.

She slipped through the doors he held open and, under his beady gaze, half-walked, half-ran to the service stairs.

The amazing irony of working in a high street monopoly was the people who tended to work there were so individual. Erica knew at least two amateur directors, five writers, six actors, three musicians, two photographers, seven dancers and one animator. (Not to mention all the other students, the communist-in-training and the clown who worked part-time in the Crime department.) Nowhere else had she met so many creative and genuinely nice people under one roof. They'd put it down to the books, or maybe some illegal substance publishers laced their books with to keep sales high. It certainly wasn't the pay.

Reaching the staffroom, she opened her locker and hung up her things.

"Glad to see you're as colourful as ever."

Looking over her shoulder, Erica smiled at her friend Marc Deveril who was looking pointedly at her purple tartan tights. "You know I don't like black."

"And is that eye makeup to complete the punk look or dark shadows under your eyes?" he teased. "Wait, what happened to your eyes?" His tone turning serious.

"Marc! You are *so* rude!" Joslin Singer said, coming over. He attempted a look of indignation and failed miserably; instead, resorting to a broad grin.

"But loveable, right?" he said, leaning against the lockers, a twinkle in his green eyes, his brown hair tousled.

"She never said that!" Erica pointed out.

"Cruel, that's what you are! And it's not even half eight," he said woefully. He then paused and glanced at his mobile, catching her

eye mischievously. "Oh, wait, it is! '*You're late, Shylocke. Again.* '"
Putting on his best impersonation of Hincks.

Erica flicked him playfully.

Marc was a little older than Erica and a PhD student of history,
specialising in the Sepoy Mutiny of 1857. Whilst Joslin was the
same age as Marc and the tallest girl Erica had ever met, easily
dwarfing her modest 5'3". As an actress, Joslin had been warned
that she might have to ditch her lavender hair dye and nose ring for
certain roles. But she was determined to keep them for as long as
possible.

Waving hurried greetings to fellow colleagues, they closed their
lockers and made their way to the service stairs, signing for their
cash floats before leaving. All three of them worked on the same
floor but in different departments: Marc in 'Film & TV' and Erica
and Joslin in 'Mind, Body & Spirit'. As a result, they'd become
good friends over the last year and a bit, especially as they shared
the same shifts.

"How did your audition go?" Marc asked Joslin, holding the
doors open for them.

"Terrible!" she groaned, "I'd rather not talk about it."

"That bad, huh?" Marc raised his eyebrows. A grin erupted on
his face. "Go on! Tell us. We'll be really sympathetic."

"I bet," she snarled.

Erica chuckled. "Well, we could do with something uplifting to
start the day. Hincks is going to be down our throats what with
everything to do for Christmas."

Joslin looked at Marc's doggy eyes and sighed. "Okay! It's
actually quite funny." She smiled to herself. "They got me to
imagine I was a fish."

"Come again? Since when did *The Tempest* feature fish?!" Marc
looked at her in disbelief, stepping aside to let someone pass.

"They're doing a modern interpretation."

"Not enough humiliation in the original?"

They caught each other's eyes before bursting into fits of
laughter.

"And the best bit is," Joslin continued as they reached the door to their floor. "I got through!"

"You obviously make a damn fine fish." Marc winked as he opened the door.

Laughing, all three walked through only to be met by Hincks and his most icy stare. They came to an abrupt halt, hurriedly stifling their laughter.

"Nice to see you're all getting into the festive spirit. Marc, I want you to make more room for Christmas stock. I'll see you about displays later."

"Right you are, Mr Percival," Marc replied jovially, saluting.

Hincks eyed them impatiently before walking down the large marble staircase that was the focal point of the 1920s building. They heard his nasal voice echoing up as he reprimanded the chatter of the Children's department.

"Wow. You've got yourself a barrel of fun later, haven't you?" Joslin said, as they closed the door to the service stairs.

"Yeah, as if I need it. My supervisor's on my case at the moment; the last thing I need is extra stress here," he muttered, running a hand through his hair.

Erica nodded sympathetically. "Same. My tutor's giving me a hard time too. My essay needs finishing for Monday…"

They looked at each other glumly.

"Well, you've kind of asked for it, haven't you, going to uni. And you're paying for it too!" Joslin said brightly.

"*This Is Your Life* presented by Joslin," Marc chuckled, eyes twinkling once more. "Right, best go and make merry. I shall pester you forthwith, my beauties." He bowed with a flourish before leaving for his own department.

"Maybe we could tell him not to bother?" Joslin joked.

"Tried that one, remember?"

"Maybe a restraining order…." she murmured thoughtfully as she turned on their till. It wasn't long before they heard the footfall of customers on the stairs.

"What did you get up to last night?" Joslin asked as they finished tidying up the counter.

"Nothing much. I was at the library, although the journey home was interesting."

"Oh?"

Erica hesitated. She had wondered how much to reveal and had decided a drastically tamed down version would be best. She didn't want people to think she was losing her grip on reality.

Joslin's silky brown eyes looked at her expectantly.

"Oh, I was attacked by the usual weirdoes, nothing much. He was just extra weird!"

Joslin flashed her a knowing look.

After playing paper, scissors, stone to decide who would do the morning's shelving (and losing), Erica proceeded to restock and tidy up the shelves and island displays; rushing over to help Joslin whenever she had one too many people to serve. Deenesh would start at eleven which would help.

It wasn't a challenging job, but she enjoyed it. It was quite relaxing, and she loved being surrounded by books. The only downside was that, as they were based in the city centre, there was a constant onslaught of customers, tourists and people seeking refuge from the elements, so it was a never-ending battle to keep everything in order. And with Christmas looming things were set to get busier; as well as people becoming more impatient the longer Christmas shopping dragged on. She felt her spirits dampen at the thought of Christmas—she should go home.

"Penny for your thoughts, luv?" Deenesh asked, approaching her and her trolley of books.

She'd been standing staring across the room, muttering herself, apparently lost in thought, a copy of *Know Your Inner You for a Better You* in her hands.

"Funky tights, man, as always."

"Very smooth. What are you after?" She winked, subconsciously adjusting the sleeves of her cardigan.

Deenesh Sihota hadn't worked long at the shop and unusually, in comparison to most staff, he was a scientist studying Astrophysics at Imperial. Most people thought him slightly mad, which was probably why he fitted in.

"Busy, innit?" he said, casting wide eyes over the milling crowds.

"Ooo! You haven't had the pleasure of 'Christmasageddon' yet! That's when the fun really starts," Erica teased, as he started to help with the shelving.

"Can't wait," he muttered. "More, 'I'm looking for a book' queries, innit?"

"I keep telling them they've come to the right place." Erica said, smiling.

"I need food!" Joslin moaned, clutching her stomach as she approached.

"Go take your break. I'll cover," said Deenesh.

"You're a legend!" she replied, grabbing Erica by the wrist and leading her away. "You're gonna take your break too, right, Erica?"

"Does she have a choice?" Marc laughed, coming through from his department to take his break also. "Our stomach's must be synchronised; I was just getting hungry myself. Hey, what did you do to your wrists?"

There was silence.

Joslin spun round and looked down at Erica's wrists. Some of the bandages were peeking out from under the black cardigan, now exposed. Joslin let go.

"They're just burns—hot water from the tap. Way too hot! I think the boiler's on the blink." Erica waved her hand dismissively.

"Again?! That's like the tenth time in two months!"

"I know, I've told my landlord. He says I should be grateful I have any hot water at all." She lied.

"Do you want me to have a word with him?" he asked, ignoring Joslin yanking at his arm.

"No, he'll get around to it in his own time. Thanks anyway!" She smiled brightly.

"Well, if you're sure…" He looked unconvinced.

Erica blushed. She hated lying to Marc.

"Now that's sorted, can we please get some food? I'm going to die of hunger!" Joslin moaned, now tugging violently at Marc's arm and dragging him to the service stairs.

"And that would be a problem how?" Marc's voice floated back.

Pausing, Erica tugged the sleeves of her cardigan down so that her bandages were once again concealed before joining them.

***

He didn't know how long he stood there after he'd watched her enter her flat. He knew the area like the back of his hand; he'd lived there long enough. But he'd purposefully avoided this street. Ever since her…

Was this all just coincidence?

Memories flooded in on all sides, almost overwhelming him. They were never far away but he was used to opening the floodgates whenever he wanted, not having them opened for him. For a moment, it was too much…

Breathing deeply, he steadied himself.

He looked up at the lit windows of Erica's flat with mixed feelings. It had been a long time since he'd spoken with an Actualle and it surprised him how much he'd missed it. Though it did complicate things. And then there was the Wrathful…

"Well, she was different." A rich voice said, speaking softly in his ear. *"'Glow bug'!"* It scoffed.

"Are you ill?" The voice asked when no reply came.

"No, just thinking…"

"That is the second Wrathful they have failed to warn us of." The voice remarked, reading his mind.

He nodded grimly. "It could, of course, be an accident."

"Of course." Agreed the voice, indulging him though they both knew the likelihood of an 'accident' happening once let alone twice.

The voice's agreement with his own suspicions, though unspoken, unnerved him even more. Cold panic began to chill his bones. He had to go and see Christian—he'd know for sure.

Casting one last look up at Erica's flat, now dark like all the others on the street, Michael Nicholas thrust his hands deep within his pockets and set off: his mind preoccupied and his heart full.

38

3

Christian Blake II

It was gone one o'clock when he finally arrived. At this late hour he didn't expect the hallway light to be on, let alone to be bumping into the short Asian man on the doorstep. He wore a leather jacket, black jeans and sported an undercut hairstyle.

"Nathaniel, what are you doing here?" Michael asked warily, stepping aside.

The man looked at him with his pitch-black eyes and hair and smiled, teeth flashing. "Nice to see you're as direct as ever. It's been a while, Michael."

"Indeed. Where's Christian?"

"He's inside with Lunita—we've just come back from a hunt. I'll see you around. I've got places to go and people to—"

"Eat?"

Nathaniel Lee glanced over his shoulder in annoyance, meeting Michael's stony gaze. "I do not 'eat' people!" He snarled, turning abruptly to set off down the dark street. After a few moments, there was a whooshing sound and the shadows nearby wobbled.

"Oh, not another one."

Michael looked up at the vexed voice of Biggleswade, the butler, who was studying him as if he were something he'd just scraped off the bottom of his shoe. "It is late, Mr Nicholas and the master of the house is already detained."

"Please can you tell him it's urgent?"

"When is it not?" Came the tart reply.

"I know he's just come back from a hunt. He shan't sleep for hours," Michael reasoned, trying to hit the happy medium between requesting and grovelling. He watched the butler contemplate his appeal, unable to garner anything from his indifferent countenance. Just as he deliberated diving past Biggleswade, the butler stepped aside.

"Thank you!" Michael said, rushing past before Biggleswade changed his mind.

Shoes squeaking on the herringbone flooring, Michael made a beeline for Christian's study door pausing briefly when he heard stunned voices.

"It worked…"

"It worked? It worked! *¡Querido, lo hiciste!* You did it!"

There was an excited whoop and Michael pushed open the door to find a man twirling a woman in an ecstatic embrace. They were still dressed in their combat gear, jackets, breeches and boots. A fire burned low in the grate and an electric lamp cast its yellow glow over the desk closest to them. A bottle was upon it.

Stopping, the man set the petite lady down, his eyes wide with disbelief. He wore a pair of bulky goggles on his head. "I can't believe it worked!"

"I had every faith in you, *cariño*." The lady said sultrily, standing on tiptoe to kiss him. Her long dark hair flowing down her back in luscious waves.

"Did what?"

The couple broke apart in surprise, instinctively reaching for the knives in their utility belts.

"Good golly, Michael! You gave us a fright!" The man said, sheathing his blade. "I didn't hear Biggleswade announce you."

"He didn't," Michael said, entering the library-cum-study: it was a large room with three of its four walls covered in bookcases. The other wall housed a large display cabinet filled with Christian's weapons and contraptions.

"Oh. Like that, was it?"

"I think I was the metaphorical nail in his metaphorical coffin."

"Dash it, that's us eating porridge for breakfast then," Christian said, looking glumly at the lady.

"I can cook," she soothed, patting his arm.

"I wouldn't. Biggleswade would be furious if he finds you in the kitchens then we'd have porridge every day." His voice despondent.

"Perish the thought," said Michael, warming himself by the fire. "So, what did you do?"

Christian and the woman shared an excited look. She nodded encouragingly and Christian pulled the goggles over his eyes. "Ta-da!"

"If that is a Dæmon detector it looks like it is broken." Michael looked pointedly at the woman.

The woman scowled at him, a low growl starting at the back of her throat. Her pitch-black eyes flashing copper.

Christian placed a reassuring hand on her waist. "Why don't you head up to bed, *querida*. I won't be long."

"*Por supuesto,*" she said, giving Michael a look of daggers on her way out.

Christian Blake II, acclaimed Soul Gatherer and expert on Lost Soul Psychology, rounded on him. "Blast it, Nicholas, get off her case!"

Michael looked up in surprise.

"It's been almost a year and you *still* can't be civil with her. Not even for a minute. Can't you just pretend to like her?" he asked, controlling his voice with difficulty.

"*It* is a quondam, a Dæmon. You cannot 'be civil' with a Dæmon," Michael said coolly.

"Lycanthrope if you will, or werewolf. And *she* is more amenable than you think. She's assisting me with some research. If you were interested, you might regard her differently."

Michael ignored him. "What if *she* turned on you?"

Christian took his goggles off impatiently. "She is mature enough to control her Connate. I trust her, she's not a pup. In any case, my blades are silver," he added.

"Glad to hear your senses haven't totally escaped you."

Christian glowered at him. "I doubt you came all this way to lecture me on my bed fellows. *Again.*"

"No. So, what did you do? What is in that bottle?" Michael said, glancing at the bottle on the desk. It seemed to be full of black petals.

"It hardly matters now, Nicholas. The moment's gone," said Christian, folding his arms.

"But I am interested."

"I'd rather you be interested in Lunita! I love her, don't you know what that's like?"

"Of course, I do!" He couldn't help the sharpness in his voice. He knew the bittersweet taste of love all too well.

Christian looked at him, eyes pained. "Look, I'm sorry I—"

"No, it is I who am sorry..." Michael slumped his shoulders in defeat. "I was rude to Lunita, I shall apologise next time I see her. You're my friend; I just worry about you. Anyway, I should go, it's late. Good night."

A wolf made up of copper light strands appeared from the shadows.

Michael watched in shock as it padded over to sit in front of him, offering him a paw. "Is that a—"

"Connate. It'll pass on your apologies," Christian said.

Gingerly, Michael took the paw in his hand. The wolf regarded him carefully before bending to lick it. Its tongue felt rough against his skin and real. Far too real. He shuddered.

The wolf then continued out the door, leaving them alone.

Michael looked across to Christian. "I had no idea she could do that…"

"There's a lot you don't know about her," he said bluntly.

"Well, I'm sorry. I shall do better from now," Michael said, making for the door.

"You look like a rat's arse. Aren't you going to tell me what happened?"

Michael stopped in his tracks, hand on the door. He turned round to find Christian walking over to the fire using the poker to freshen its flames. There was a hiss of anticipation as he threw on a log, sparks dancing cheerily. He took that as a sign he was forgiven.

"I was attacked, rather, my companion was attacked, this evening by a Wrathful."

"A Wrathful? Did it use *Ombre Totalus*?"

"Yes," Michael replied.

"And how long did it take the Wrathful to define itself? I have a theory that the more there are in its Choir, the less time it takes," he explained as he lowered himself into one of the armchairs clustered round the fire, its glow illuminating his fair hair.

Michael moved away from the door to join him.

"Eight or nine? I was not the one who heard them, to be truthful."

"You weren't? And how did Ashayla dispel it? *Lumínate*?"

Michael nodded, sinking into the chair opposite him.

"Interesting." Christian steepled his fingers as he gazed into the renewed flames of the fire. "And when was this, dear chap?"

"Some time before eleven."

"Impossible," he said at once. "I was still here and my alarm didn't sound."

"Pardon?"

"The bell," Christian said, indicating to a small black bell hanging on the wall behind his desk. "It didn't sound, so you must be mistaken, my dear fellow. Couldn't have happened around eleven, I was still at my desk; didn't hear a ding dong or a bell."

Michael looked at him, speechless.

"You're sure it happened tonight, or last night, rather? There was an attack just before midnight. Though that was Blood Hounds, that's the hunt we'd just returned from. Most of the pack eluded us, dash it. A right mess they made; at least five human casualties, not to mention their dogs."

Michael turned a sickly shade of green. "So many in one night?"

Christian nodded grimly.

He let out a shaky sigh: *Erica had been lucky*. Dread smothered him—he could hardly breathe. "Is there any chance that a Lost Soul might reach Earth undetected?" he asked hoarsely.

"None whatsoever." Christian eyed Michael. "You said you were with someone—can he vouch it was this evening?"

"I was with a young lady, and she can't, well, she can, it's just that she's, erm, an, an Actualle." He found himself blushing—it was forbidden to have anything to do with someone from the present.

Christian raised his eyebrows before a smug smile settled on his lips. "I see. And there you were nagging me about my involvement with Lunita. You do realise what The Guild will say if they hear of this Actualle?"

Michael hesitated despite himself; he'd hoped not to mention Erica as he knew exactly what people would say. Although, it wasn't as if he'd intended for her to see him.

"You were using the Ignorant Charm?"

"She saw through it," Michael snapped. "Not that she realised…"

"The standard one?" Christian looked stunned.

Michael nodded.

"Good Lord!" Christian sank back in his chair. A look of excitement suddenly erupted on his face and he looked at Michael, his eyes shining. "You should've brought her along! I've never heard anything like it! Someone who can perceive Ignorant Charms—I could've run some tests!"

"I think encountering a Lost Soul was enough for one evening without having to travel here also," Michael responded dryly. "And, as you said, The Guild wouldn't be pleased."

"Ah. Yes, true, very true," he muttered, staring into the fire, a faraway look in his eyes. "Astounding…"

When he next spoke, his tone was suddenly solemn. "This is rather serious, isn't it, old chap?" Their eyes met, and relief flooded Michael's chest.

"Do you think you could make enquiries? Subtle ones, naturally."

"Of course, dear boy. Can't let something like this happen! I'll pop and see Yophiel tomorrow, well, today!" He chuckled.

"Thank you, Christian, I knew I could rely on you," said Michael, getting to his feet.

"Not at all. Oh, and this Actualle girl," Christian began, also getting to his feet, "I shouldn't have anything more to do with her. It'll only complicate things."

By now the fire had once again reduced to embers. The room was dim, even the moon, visible through the window, did little to illuminate its interior.

Michael looked at Christian, now obscured by harsh shadows. "Of course."

***

"Earth to Erica!"

Erica started and looked up from the book nestled in her lap.

Using the pretext of preparing stock for the new Christmas displays, Marc had enlisted Joslin and Erica's help, so they could legitimately sit around and natter.

They were seated in the Film section, surrounded by all manner of books to entice Christmas shoppers. There had been the usual mad rush at lunchtime, but it was a lot quieter now, with only a few tourists and the odd student lurking amongst the shelves.

Marc wrinkled his nose at yet another celebrity's biography for display. "What can they have done that's interesting in only sixteen years of life?"

"Just because you have the life experience of a gnat, doesn't mean other people have," Joslin said from where she sat, her feet tucked under her, flicking through: *Christmas? Bah Humbug!*

Ignoring her, Marc threw the book aside and looked up at Erica. "Well?"

Erica blushed and looked back down at the book in her hands. She had in fact been thinking of her encounter with the Wrathful. Her journey to the station hadn't concerned her at all this morning, the looming journey home in the dark on the other hand was. Her thoughts had then drifted to the choir of voices she'd heard and her own grudge. She'd never openly admitted it, but she couldn't deny it was there. Whilst her parents had been proud at the thought of her going to university, the reality had been quite different…

45

"Erica?" Marc was watching her closely.

"Well, I was just wondering, do you think someone could hold a grudge without knowing it?" Trying to sound light-hearted as she straightened up the pile of books at her side.

"What a random question!" Marc exclaimed, a hint of relief in his voice. He sat and pondered. Joslin observed them over the top of her book.

"I suppose it would be possible," he paused as he thought for a moment. "Such as, if you didn't get to finish something you really wanted to."

"Like a PhD?" Joslin teased.

Marc laughed. "Like a PhD, or maybe if someone treated you badly or didn't believe in you or—"

"Didn't hire you to perform in a popular musical!" Joslin piped up enthusiastically. "I'd love to haunt that Mr Tatlow, you know, that guy who didn't hire me for *The Lion King*."

"Joslin, you can't blame him. You were the one who wanted a selfie with Mufasa after the antelopes concussed him. Maybe lending a hand would've got you the role?"

Joslin gave a blasé shrug.

"Anyhow, revenge isn't the answer, Miss Singer," he continued, wagging his finger. "They may deserve it, but it solves nothing. Love, that is the answer!" He clutched at his heart.

Joslin gave a snort. "Whatever. So glad you're not an actor. You're way too cheesy."

"Hey!"

***

Erica had been eyeing the sky with apprehension for hours, watching the blue-green heavens slowly darken to a cold blue-black. Then, in an instant, it was dark; even the twinkling Christmas lights did little to lighten its black depths. The panic that seized her was like no other she had ever experienced. It was as if an icy hand had emerged from within to grasp her chest, twisting her lungs until spots blurred her vision. By the time her shift ended she was a nervous wreck—her heart was beating so loudly against her chest she was shaking. Her hands were clammy, and her stomach was a can of worms. Clumsiness took on a whole new meaning and whenever she tried to speak her words came out a garbled mess. Joslin ended up shooing her away from the tills as customers began to give her a wide berth.

So, it was with dread when six o'clock finally came and she was standing outside wrapped up in her scarf and coat. Her legs had turned to jelly, and her eyes kept darting around her, scanning the shadows for malicious eyes and snapping teeth.

Marc and Joslin had also finished their shifts and parted ways with her at the Underground station, with Marc telling her to call him if she had any problems. They were both concerned about her sudden nervousness, though she shrugged it off whenever they mentioned it, blaming tiredness. She wouldn't risk other lives.

The steps to the Underground station at Piccadilly opened below her, a gaping hole stretching far into the black earth. Taking a deep breath, she stepped down and was immediately swept away by the tide of tourists and commuters.

The train roared to a stop at the station and she stepped into the carriage, jumping as the doors clattered shut behind her. Keeping her back to the walls of the carriage she stared out at the sea of faces before her: *don't be silly! With all these people around no Wrathful would dare attack!*

The darkness of the tunnels didn't help; as she watched through the windows the tunnels whizzed by, their gloom seeming to warp to reveal hidden faces contorted in rage. She blinked and turned away, concentrating instead on her hands that were gripping the safety bars, her knuckles white. She was breathing far too quickly. Head reeling, she leaned against the wall of the cabin and tried to calm herself.

Commuters and tourists filed on and off at each station, their faces drawn from a long day at work or delighted by the sights they had seen. A young boy got on with his mother; he watched in excitement as the doors closed behind them and they pulled away from the station which was now a blur of white and green tiles.

It was nearly her stop.

She bit her lip and looked at her reflection in the window beside her, she was deathly pale and there was a wildness about her eyes, she could feel the adrenaline pumping through her veins, her muscles tensing against the encroaching walk home; the possible dangers that lurked in the shadows... Why didn't she have an umbrella or something? Remembering the periapt, she felt for it in her pocket and let out a sigh of relief on touching its intricate coolness. She wasn't totally defenceless.

Something twitched to her left and she spun round, blood pounding in her ears. Nothing. Just an old man. He clicked his tongue at her and settled back to his newspaper.

As the doors opened, she could feel cold sweat break out upon her back. It was her station. Bracing herself she took a deep breath and stepped off the train with a wobble.

It was eerily quiet. No one else alighted and she watched the train trundle away with dull resignation. *Of all the times for it to be quiet!*

She could avoid it no longer. Mustering her courage, she crept up the stairs, peering round corners as she went. Passing through the ticket barriers, she took in the darkness awaiting her at the end of the long Arcade with a moan.

Hand over the periapt, she set her shoulders back: *let's do this!*

Something flickered in the shadows to her left. Rooted to the spot, her heart lurched painfully, sheer terror overwhelming her. *Move, Erica! Move!* Why couldn't she move?! Fumbling, she began tapping the periapt frantically.

Why wasn't this thing working?

The shadows warped.

Had anyone escaped a Wrathful more than once?!

She braced herself for the worst, letting out a loud sob when Michael Nicholas materialised before her.

"I thought I would make a habit of it." He smiled. "Ashayla says you have activated the periapt. Is anything amiss?"

He stopped then, seeing her wide eyes and hunched shoulders, and rushed forwards as tears spilled over and she fell to her knees.

4
The House with No Door

He caught her with ease, helping her to her feet as she clutched at him. At first, he'd patted her on the shoulder, but, as she began to shake and the sobs took over, tears streaming down her face, he, despite everything, reached for her and held her close, if a little awkwardly—Christian's admonishments echoing in his head.

She wept uncontrollably onto his shoulder. When her senses finally returned, she breathed deeply, calming her hammering heart. She then fell silent, with only an occasional whimper blubbering through. The reality of having sobbed her eyes out on the shoulder of a virtual stranger struck her and she felt herself blush hotly. If only it were Marc, she wouldn't have felt embarrassed drenching his jacket in tears! Finally calm, a scent reached her nose: a warm blend of bergamot and spices. She felt her blood rush at the fragrant cologne. It was like incense to her soul, soothing yet invigorating at the same time.

"You're still in shock, as you have every right to be. I was worried about you walking alone after such an ordeal," his voice said softly into her ear. His warm breath sent a tingle through her.

"Sorry to trouble you." She pulled away, avoiding his eyes, her cheeks still red. She brushed herself down and wiped her face.

"Nonsense!" He smiled, looking down into her green eyes and wishing he hadn't because he suddenly lost all train of thought and, before he knew what he was doing, he was saying… "Would you like to partake of some tea, Miss Shylocke? It's the least I can offer. I would have offered last night but the hour was indecent, half past six is much more acceptable."

She looked up shyly and nodded. "Yes please."

***

He said his house was only a short walk from the station, so they left the Arcade and he led them towards Cheniston Gardens. Walking past white stucco terraces, some of which needed repair, he stopped outside one which had steps leading to a blank wall. It looked like two houses had been merged into one. Yet one of the front doors had been bricked up and rendered to blend in, leaving its steps as a memento.

He began to walk up the steps, fishing in his pocket for a key. Erica looked at the wall with raised eyebrows and started to feel irritated: she didn't have the time to waste! It was all very well him inviting her to 'partake' of some tea but when someone starts walking into walls there's got to be something wrong.

On his approach, dissolving out of thin air, appeared a handsome black door with a brass knocker. Reaching the top step, he placed a large copper key into its lock. The door unlocked with a neat *click*, swinging open with ease. He stepped over the threshold and into the hallway.

Erica swore in a most unladylike way as he vanished from sight. She couldn't move for shock. *What the actual hell?*

First, the Wrathful, then his Færie and now this: doors appearing out of walls? She glanced up the street. Maybe she should make a run for it? Or maybe, just maybe, someone *this* weird might know someone like her…

Then, his voice drifted out onto the street. "Ashayla! We have a guest!"

Wrestling with her better judgement, Erica finally came to a decision. Tightening her fists, she walked up the steps. Stopping just outside the door, she placed a hand upon its frame; it felt real enough. The hallway before her had a smart tiled floor; its walls were painted in a dark purple; luxurious velvet curtains framed mirrors and portraits. Michael was standing just to her right, holding a periapt—identical to the one he'd given her—close to a fitting on the wall, a gilded pentacle. The pentacle, sensing the presence of the periapt, shimmered. He then proceeded to take off his jacket, top hat, muffler and gloves.

"Do come in, Miss Shylocke. It's quite safe, I assure you. Please, make yourself comfortable." Hanging up his jacket and muffler, he placed his gloves and top hat on a wooden table, revealing himself to be wearing a dark suit and a white shirt with stiff lapels complete with black cravat, set off by a silk waistcoat, the same blue as his eyes. He wore a signet ring on his left index finger and a jade bracelet round his right wrist.

He deposited his periapt within his waistcoat pocket and turned to look at her: she'd yet to enter.

"Just what are you? You know *this*"—she gestured around her— "isn't normal. Are you like some eloquent existential hippy who likes suits?"

"Not exactly. Whatever a 'hippy' is." He gave a disarming smile before beckoning her in.

"I will get it out of you," she said, wagging a finger.

"So, you say, Miss Shylocke."

Chin up, Erica stepped over the threshold. Once inside, the front door swung silently shut behind her. She gulped. What had she done?

Assisting her with her jacket, he frowned and looked at a door to the left of the hall.

"Ashayla! I said we have a guest! Ready to meet my 'glow bug'?" he said, turning to her with a smile.

He placed her jacket alongside his and walked towards the room with Erica following close behind. This room acted as a living room-cum-study and had a selection of comfy chairs and sofas in front of the fire. By the window was a large desk with pieces of parchment, newspapers and large tomes scattered upon it. A violin case rested to one side. Floor-to-ceiling bookcases covered several walls, providing room for his vast library and a collection of exotic artefacts. A trinket box had pride of place on the mantel. A well-worn Persian carpet lay in front of the three-seater sofa before the large fireplace, the fire within unlit. It was upon this carpet that a young lady sat, legs crossed, glowing palms facing upwards in its lap, eyes closed. Despite the late hour, the velvet curtains had not been drawn and the glow from the streetlights flooded the room.

"Ashayla!" Michael called impatiently.

The Færie's eyes snapped open and flashed blue-white in the gloom. They turned to look at the two humans, narrowing as they rested on Erica.

"We have a guest. This is Miss Erica Shylocke. Pupils, Ashayla."

Erica looked at Michael in confusion. *Pupils?*

The Færie rose gracefully to its feet. It was slender and, despite the cool November weather, wore a leather bodice, harem trousers and a long waistcoat, both in light cotton. Its long fine hair spilled over its shoulders, shimmering silver in the darkness whilst a glow emanated from its skin. A crescent moon tattoo decorated the centre of its forehead and glowed with an ethereal light; whilst a gleaming streak marked the bridge of its nose. It turned its bright blue-white eyes to Erica and regarded her. Meeting its eyes, Erica noticed the middles shrink and darken until pupils appeared. The Færie walked to Michael's side. It was barefoot with bells about its ankles which tinkled with every movement. An ornate slave bracelet adorned its left hand.

"Welcome, Miss Shylocke." Its voice was rich and soothing, as if it had been mellowed by time. *"I shall go and make some tea, Michael. Earl Grey?"*

Michael nodded. It gestured casually to the grate where a pile of kindling, logs and paper waited. The glow of a fire began to flicker down through the veins in its arm until a flame sprung to life within its palm. With a flick of its wrist, it directed the flame to the fireplace and the awaiting fuel. Greedily consuming the kindling and paper, the growing fire then licked contentedly at the logs. Satisfied with the result, the Færie padded past them and out into the hallway, its bells tinkling in its wake. Erica watched it leave in awe. Not noticing anything out of the ordinary, Michael proceeded to draw the curtains and turn on some ancient gas lamps.

"Please, make yourself comfortable, Miss Shylocke. I apologise, I seldom have guests so rarely use the parlour; I do find it less comfortable than here and since we're already acquaintances—of a sort—I do not think it unseemly to sit comfortably, do you?"

Erica was still rooted to the spot, taking in her surroundings. "Not at all! It's fascinating! Do you mind if I look at your books? I can't resist!"

He nodded, and she wandered over to the large bookcases. "You share a weakness for books also, Miss Shylocke?"

"Call me Erica, Michael." He inclined his head graciously. "Yeah, I'm a book fiend! I work in a bookstore, spend all my other days in libraries and read myself to sleep. In other words, I'm sad, or wildly intelligent, but most likely sad." She smiled good-naturedly and went back to pouring over the book spines.

Michael looked puzzled. "'Sad'? Books make you sad?"

"I mean sad as in boring or dull."

"I see. Interesting turn of phrase." And, producing a notebook and pen, noted it down. "Why would reading make you sad?"

Erica looked at him smugly. "Well, it's safe to say you're not from around here. I'm getting closer."

His scowled. Maybe this had been a bad idea.

She studied him for a moment before continuing to peruse the shelves. "Let me see… Can I guess what you are?" He looked up sharply, nervously tugging at his shirt cuffs, covering scars that peeked through. "You can tell a lot about a person from their library… From your collection I would say you were either an Anthropologist or a Historian, maybe both. Though, obviously, not a normal one."

He smiled. "Obviously. You're correct on both accounts! I'm not sure whether the fact my collection belays my interests so much is a good or bad thing."

Erica shrugged her shoulders. "But it is natural. If you're interested in something, you naturally enjoy reading about it." She looked up to find him watching her, his blue eyes bright.

Just then a bell rang from the hall.

"Please excuse me, I must go and help Ashayla." And, giving a quick bow, he walked out and down towards the kitchen, his shoes echoing on the tiled floor. Waiting until she heard the kitchen door shut, she tiptoed over to his desk and picked up some loose sheets of parchment. She skimmed them with a frown; she saw nothing but records of the day's news and weather. She was just about to open one of the leather-bound tomes when she heard a door opening and footfall in the hallway accompanied by the gentle jingling of bells. Quickly replacing the parchment, she returned to the bookcase and opened a book at random.

Moments later, Michael entered carrying a silver tray bearing a teapot, two cups with saucers, milk, sugar and a plate of homemade biscuits. Ashayla followed. Once he'd placed the tray on the table beside the sofa, the Færie set about pulling on a pair of white cotton gloves before pouring the tea, touching the china cups gingerly, vestiges of discomfort upon its fine features.

"Would you like sugar in your tea, Miss Shylocke?"

"No thank you and I won't take milk either." The Færie turned its blue-white eyes on her in surprise. "Would you like some help?" Erica asked, returning the book and walking over to the sofas in front of the fire.

The Færie surveyed her.

"No, thank you, Miss Shylocke, this is my duty. Manmade products cause discomfort to us Færies, that's all. Please make yourself comfortable."

"Thank you for saving me… Are there many of you? Can you all do magic?"

"It was my pleasure, Miss Shylocke. We Færies are innumerable and, yes, as elemental beings we can all do magic."

"Why do manmade products hurt you?"

"Because they have been befouled."

"'Befouled'?" Erica looked mystified.

Michael quickly changed the subject. "Why do you not take milk with your tea, Miss Shylocke? I mean, Erica." He corrected, looking flustered on saying her name.

"Not everyone does nowadays. Some people have allergies; I just prefer to drink it without milk. Milk and sugar were initially added for their nutritional benefits and as a display of wealth.

Though, as an Anthropologist, you probably already know that."
She took the cup Ashayla offered her and regarded him shrewdly.

"You presume I'm an Anthropologist of British people," he said, accepting another cup from Ashayla with a nod of thanks.

"Yes, especially as all the newspapers on your desk are local ones."

He looked momentarily stumped. Then he gave a broad smile. "*Touché*."

"And one that's invisible too. Were you invisible yesterday at the station? Is that why people were looking at me like I was a looney?"

He took a nervous sip of his tea.

"Well, if that is the case, you're not a particularly good 'Anthropologist', are you? Watching from the sidelines, invisible, making presumptions and observations without really knowing us, our language and our habits." Erica chided, taking a sip of her own tea. Ashayla looked at her with renewed interest and knelt down on the floor near her.

He was lost for words, his cheeks flushed. "Are you suggesting that I walk around, *un*-invisible?"

"You mean visible? Yes."

He noted her defiant chin and sipped his tea ponderously.

Erica helped herself to a biscuit before offering the plate to Ashayla who declined and then to Michael.

"And you're well? After last night?" He took one, nodding his thanks. "How are your eyes?"

Erica reached involuntarily for the silver chain round her neck; a small magnifying glass held safe by a slender hand. "Sore but otherwise fine. Thank you…" she paused for the briefest of moments, "I'm glad you were there tonight. At the station, I mean. I was dreading the walk home in the dark."

"I could not let you walk alone, not after your ordeal."

"Thank you, for tonight, for last night, for saving my life. I wouldn't be here if it weren't for the two of you…" Michael looked at her with compassion as she quickly took a swig of her drink.

"Which is exactly why we shall meet you from now on, until you have properly recovered from your shock."

Ashayla looked at him in surprise.

"I appreciate the sentiment, but you're not responsible for me: I'm not a child."

"True, but I would feel happier knowing that you were safe. Also, rather selfishly, I enjoy the company. I do not get to meet people from this ti… from this town often." He recovered himself quickly.

She raised an eyebrow, measuring him up. "On one condition. You're to be visible. I can't walk home talking to thin air."

"As you wish," he said, blushing.

Her eyes lit up suddenly. "Why don't we meet up tomorrow after my shift? I'd like to buy you dinner, to say 'thank you'. Plus, it'll give you opportunity to conduct some 'anthropological' research." She added, seeing his hesitation.

"Visible?"

"Of course."

His hesitation lasted a second more before being replaced with a wide smile. "That would be most kind, thank you."

Ashayla looked askance at him, eyebrows raised.

***

The two men met in the shadows, where their business belonged.

"This is a risky rendezvous," one commented, surveying the battlements.

"On the contrary, this is the safest of places." The other replied. "I summoned you to pass on our latest progress report. Since the barriers were altered, Bloodlings have announced a three-hundred-fold increase, Bog Dwellers and Virvatuli a seventy-fold. Arbolis Noir claim to have a hundred-fold increase. Shadowlings two hundred-and-fifty-fold and Strigoi a hundred-fold. Wrathful have a forty-fold, though their Choirs have increased by two hundred percent."

"That is… remarkable, given the short space of time they've had." The thought did cross his mind that each number was a person's soul, now lost for all eternity. But only fleetingly.

"What can I say? Where there's a will, there's a way."

"Well, if you're in agreement, then I shall begin."

"No, the time is not right. Await my word."

"As you wish."

***

"Do you know what The Guild would say?" The voice said as they waited for Erica to enter her flat.

He turned to leave, walking quickly, his mind a whirl. He dug his hands deep within his jacket pockets: of course, he knew what The Guild would say, he knew what everyone would say, but had her words not made sense? Had they not voiced what he'd felt for so many years? What was the point of observing people if you did not live amongst them? How could you accurately record them and their lives without knowing them, their hopes and their dreams? How could you judge them without understanding them? He'd land himself in a lot of trouble if it were known that he'd deliberately walked around Actualle London without using the Ignorant Charm, let alone in the company of an Actualle. Not that it had done any good; Erica had perceived him despite it. But how? That was a question, one of many, that remained unanswered.

"Are you sure this is a good idea, Michael?"

"Truth be told, no."

"You gave her one of my own." The voice said after a moment's pause, its tone accusatory. Michael glanced at his pocket where his periapt was safely stowed.

"Only temporarily, remember? It's for the best, Ashayla."

"Whose? Hers, or yours?"

He didn't answer. His head was spinning; he didn't need this on top of everything else—he had a busy night before him. He was behind with his Loggias and he still needed to see her.

He'd have to work quickly.

5
Cleopatra's Needle

She'd had a productive evening and had managed to finish her essay. She'd also had a better night's sleep with fewer disturbances. As such, she had donned her bold flowery tights with gusto and was buzzing around the third floor with a skip in her step.

"What *is* wrong with you? You're making me dizzy." Joslin growled as Erica fluttered around shelving books and serving customers.

"I just had a really good night. I finished my essay and it's not rubbish either!"

"You sound surprised, dear pea," Marc said, approaching them. He leaned against their counter and sighed. "Man, I'm beat. It's been crazy busy."

"You haven't had to watch Miss Sugar Rush buzz around all day."

"You have been more up-beat, little Miss Shylocke. A good night?"

"A productive night."

"Aye aye!" He raised his eyebrows.

"Meanie, you know I'm talking about my essay!" she said blushing.

"That I do. Better than me, I ended up needing the one book I didn't have which is why I've ordered this!" And with a flourish he typed in a code on their computer and details of a book appeared on the screen.

Joslin and Erica leaned forwards.

"*The Sepoy Mutiny and the East India Company*. Wow, you've got yourself a barrel of laughs there." Joslin read out its title, a look of utter boredom on her face.

Marc ignored her. "It's not released until the New Year, but without it I can't finish this chapter as it's got new sources. So, I'm just going to start the next one. Do you think my Supervisor will buy that?" he asked, checking with Erica.

"Maybe, you'll have to really prove it's worth it though."

"Oi, Tight Queen, there's a geezer waiting downstairs for you— Ground Floor," said Deenesh, appearing.

Joslin and Marc looked at Erica questioningly. She held her hands up in defence. "I'm not expecting anyone."

"Slick dude with blue eyes, said he wasn't sure if you were finishing yet or not."

Erica froze: *it couldn't be?*

***

Walking down the marble staircase Erica scanned the crowds but couldn't see any sign of Michael anywhere. Maybe Deenesh was having her on? Then a young man in fitted jeans, trainers, reefer jacket and striped scarf emerged from out of the crowds, smiling broadly.

"Ha! It worked! Marvellous!" He looked incredibly pleased with himself. Erica barely recognised him; she'd expected him to be wearing his usual smart, if rather formal, getup. The modern clothing, however, suited him. A lot. The jacket showed off his broad shoulders and the jeans fitted him *perfectly*. Erica quickly looked away.

"Michael, what are you...? Why are you...?" She failed to finish her questions, too stunned for words.

He beamed, blue eyes dancing. "Well, I was going to come in my usual apparel, but Ashayla dogmatically declared it would draw too much attention, so insisted on purchasing Actualle clothing for myself to wear. You like it, do you? I was unsure whether its choice was adequate. The trainers feel odd," he said, eyeing them suspiciously.

Erica could find no fault whatsoever in Ashayla's choice and gave him the thumbs up. He looked at her puzzled.

"Like at the Coliseum? Intriguing. No gladiators though?" He grinned.

"No, they're too busy." She grinned back.

"I like the tights—purple again." He noted with interest, studying the flowers on her tights.

"Thanks, it's actually my—"

"Who's your friend?" Marc asked, appearing at her side.

Erica blushed. "Oh, Marc, meet Michael Nicholas. Michael, this is my good friend Marc Deveril. He's doing a PhD, researching the Sepoy Mutiny."

Michael visibly stiffened. The two men shook hands, eyeing each other coolly. Marc cast Erica a questioning look.

"We're at uni together. Michael's an Anthropologist."

"Lucky him. You don't get off shift for another couple of hours."

Erica looked flustered. "I know, I hadn't yet told Michael."

"Yes, my fault, apologies, we'd not arranged to meet until later, but I thought to surprise Erica. I shall be quite happy perusing books to pass the time." He smiled reassuringly. "Which floor do you work on?"

"Third," Marc said shortly, replying for her.

"Then I shall peruse the delights of the third floor."

"Wonderful." Marc growled.

***

The rest of her shift was spent with her trying to keep her attention from wandering over to the sofas where Michael sat flicking his way through a stack of books. She found him massively distracting, particularly when his t-shirt lifted up to reveal his lean chest as he removed his jacket. The tight material hugged the contours of his shoulders and chest oh so well.

"Not that I'm into guys, but your friend is hot! Where've you been hiding him?!" Joslin said as she finished serving a customer.

Erica joined her at the till, fanning herself. She opened her mouth but was unable to string anything coherent together. She'd seen him in his formal 'apparel' and found him handsome but the fact that he looked drop dead gorgeous like this was another thing altogether.

"I don't think Marc's impressed." Joslin observed with a grin.

Indeed, Marc had been keeping a close eye on Michael, often stalking past him with books to shelve or glaring up at him from his till. Marc looked across to Joslin and Erica's till and the two girls quickly bent over the screen, trying to look serious.

"I'm going to offer him a drink, he must be thirsty. Do you want one?" Erica asked.

"Yeah, mocha please."

Erica walked over to where Marc was pacing near Michael. They both looked up as she approached: Marc with a look of annoyance, Michael with one of relief. "I'm going to go to the café, do you guys want anything?"

"I'll have a latte," Marc said.

Michael looked confused.

Ha! She crossed her arms triumphantly as he began to squirm. *Serves him right for not telling her the truth.*

She decided enough was enough. "Since Marc's got to cover for Deenesh whilst he takes his break, do you mind helping me carry the drinks, Michael? Then you can choose what you want."

Michael got to his feet gladly. "Certainly."

Marc watched them walk down the marble stairs, his brows furrowed.

"Your friend seems displeased with my arrival. Have I inconvenienced you?" Michael asked as soon as they were out of earshot.

Erica smiled and shook her head. "No, it's just Marc being protective, overprotective, that's all."

"Are you courting?"

She laughed. "No, I'm not dating anyone."

"'Dating' as in courting?"

"Yeah, but we say 'dating' or 'going out with' or 'seeing'."

"Quite evasive terminology." Michael observed as they reached the café in the basement. "Why are you not courting?"

Erica blushed, tearing her gaze from the line of his pectorals visible through the t-shirt. "I don't see why we have to start discussing my love life!"

"Shall we discuss coffee instead?" He offered with a half-smile.

"Yes, far more useful for your 'anthropological' research." As they queued, she explained the different types of coffee, as well as why some people drank their coffee from straws.

"And which would you recommend?" he asked, studying the menu on the wall.

"I'm a chocoholic, so I always have mochas."

"It's comforting to know women's tastes have changed little. In that case, I shall partake of one also."

"There's another condition," she said after she'd given the baristas their order. "If you're going to be 'un-invisible' you're going to have to start using your 'can'ts', 'won'ts', 'ain'ts' and 'innits'. No 'partakes', okay?"

"Understood. But 'innit'?" he asked looking confused—he'd been watching the baristas prepare their drinks.

"You know, like it's well warm, innit?"

"Indeed, it is…" He replied carefully, looking to her for clarification.

"You don't need to reply."

"So, it's a rhetorical question, innit?"

"Got it in one! High-five!" she said, raising her hand. He looked at her blankly. "Never mind."

Carrying the drinks between them, Michael followed her up the stairs back to their floor. Marc looked up from where he was standing with Joslin. He reluctantly accepted his drink from Michael and stomped back to his till. Michael gave Erica one last knowing look before returning to his sofa and books.

The rest of the afternoon passed quickly, and Erica was glad when she finally stood next to Michael in her jacket, scarf and gloves. "Sorry about that!"

"No worries, innit." He offered her his arm. Taking it, they walked out onto the busy street. "Jesting aside, it's not a problem, it was nice to see you in the environs of work. In any case, it was my fault, I should have found out at what time you finished work."

"Well, we hadn't actually arranged… Wait! How did you know I'd even be here?!"

"I followed you this morning before buying these garments. Apologies," he added. "I meant no offense. I just wanted to surprise you. I presumed that we would need to be in town to have dinner."

"Forgiven." She smiled.

"Where to?"

They'd stopped outside Lillywhites which was busy with shoppers and tourists. At that moment, Erica's attention was focused on the steps of the Shaftesbury Memorial Fountain, a look of sorrow on her face. She composed herself quickly to smile brightly at him—he was watching her keenly.

"Where to? Well, I was thinking I would take you for some dim sum, before showing you the London Eye by night; how does that sound?" she said, navigating the busy pavement.

"Sounds delightful. Lead on, I'm all yours."

She wished! Erica laughed nervously before leading him towards China Town.

After eating an extortionate amount of dim sum, Erica suggested wandering the small shops and lanes around Gerrard Street before seeing the bright lights of Leicester Square where Erica introduced him to her favourite 'pick-me-up': ice cream. It was whilst they sat and ate their sundaes that Erica answered Michael's questions on wi-fi, smart phones, Harry Potter and bling. Amongst other things.

"Could you describe that as bling?" he asked indicating to a young man sitting close by with diamanté earrings and multiple gold chains round his neck.

"Most definitely."

He scrutinised the man's glimmering jewels with interest.

"But not you," Erica said, eating the last of her Forest Fruit ice cream.

"You wouldn't recommend it?"

"Definitely not. You don't strike me as someone who'd wear that either," she said indicating the jade bracelet on his wrist.

He glanced down at the pale green band with a crooked smile. "No, but a friend gave it to me and she'd be offended if I took it off."

"I feel the same about my friendship ring. And how was your Tiramisu sundae?"

"Delicious. Although, I don't think I will be able to finish it all." He eyed the remains ruefully. Looking up, he noted her doleful eyes and offered her the bowl. "Would you care to help?"

"I'm really greedy when it comes to ice cream." She apologised, helping herself to a large spoonful.

"The problem now is that I feel cold."

"Fear not, dear Nicholas, my plan was now to let you 'partake' of some speciality lattes—they're typical in cafés at wintertime. My favourite is the Gingerbread flavour," she explained when she saw his confusion.

As they waited for the bill, he settled down to watch people cross the Square, a faraway look in his eyes. Light from the coloured fairy lights fractured upon his ochre skin, almost staining it: hot pink, electric blue, lurid green. Erica watched him out of the corner of her eye, noticing his sudden sadness.

Picking up an extra hot Gingerbread Latte each they walked along the Thames, holding their cups tightly against the keen wind. The ornate streetlights flanked the river on either side, casting their orbs of light into the water.

Michael stopped in surprise when he saw the London Eye lit up on the opposite side of the river, its neon lights reflecting brilliantly on the inky black waters.

"I've read about it, but this is the first time I've seen it… I'm rarely down here these days: the river's changed so much."

Erica noticed the same faraway look in his eyes. He scanned the river, with its bobbing boats and glistening waves. He seemed lost in some other world.

She drank her latte, giving him a moment.

"How has it changed?" she asked tentatively at last.

"In every conceivable way. Everything has," he replied wistfully, voice faint; a great wave of melancholy swept over him.

"Are you okay? We can walk another way if that helps?"

"I can't hide from it, not anymore. I cannot remain invisible forever; it's as you so astutely said, how can we study you without knowing you. Even if we're exposed, even if it hurts…"

They walked on in silence, Michael looking out at the river, the pain he spoke of plain to see, it was so tangible she could feel it burning her. Tears pricked her eyes: she felt awful, she didn't know how, but bringing him here had hurt him.

She couldn't stand it.

It was then that something happened, something that would change everything.

***

They were just walking past Cleopatra's Needle and its sphinxes on the Victoria Embankment when there was a bright flash and a crack of light cut its way up through the air above the great monument. Erica cried out in shock, shielding her eyes with her arm and spilling her Gingerbread Latte down her in the process. The glare of the light lessened and, blinking quickly, she peered to find a doorway before her. It was made of light that crackled and pulsed like electricity. Through it Erica could see London, but a different London, one with horses and carriages upon its cobbled streets and men and women walking about in smart jackets and top hats, long dresses and warm shawls: the crack that had opened the doorway started at her footfall. Taking her foot away, the light crackled anew. She walked slowly around the side of the monument to look at the street behind it, but there were no horses or carriages or smartly dressed people, just the deserted Embankment. She walked back round to the front of the monument where the doorway persisted to flicker brightly.

Recalling herself, she spun round. "Oh no…"

Michael was standing stock-still and his eyes were no longer sad but wide with shock.

She twisted her hands. "I didn't… I don't know…" She trailed off, unable to comprehend what was happening let alone defend herself.

Then, without another word, he took out a set of ancient keys from the inside of his jacket and stepped forwards. Selecting an ornate bronze key, he placed it into the crackling light of the doorway and, giving it a turn, the ladies and gentlemen, the horses and carriages, the doorway vanished.

***

Sitting down heavily on a nearby bench she knocked back the remains of her latte, staring into space.

"I had my suspicions." Michael sat down beside her and pocketed his keys, his expression weary.

"'Suspicions'?" Erica repeated dully.

"That you might be a KeyMaster-in-Waiting. I thought I was mistaken. No, I wanted myself to be mistaken…" He corrected himself, shaking his head.

"That I was a *what*?"

"A KeyMaster-in-Waiting."

"Whatever. You know you're not helping me here! What was that?!"

"That was a Temporal Gateway and what you saw was 1870s London, based on the people's attire. Most likely 1878, after the Needle was erected."

Erica looked at him in disbelief.

"KeyMasters are able to open up Gateways. It's what we do so that we can travel through Time to document and protect you Actualles, people from the present. A bit like a PhD, but one for life."

"I need a drink." Erica moaned. He offered her the rest of his latte but she shook her head. "I meant something stronger."

They sat in silence; her lost in her own thoughts, him watching her with concern—finding out was always the most difficult. It had been no different for him.

"This is it, isn't it? This is what you are. This is why you're so weird."

"I shall take that as a compliment."

"I think I preferred you as an existential hippy." She licked her dry lips. "How did that Gateway-thing open anyway?"

"When you are undiscovered you have less control, so, if you feel strong emotions, you can sometimes open Gateways; some are weaker than others. This particular Gateway isn't as it's in such a prominent position."

"Meaning?"

"You are strong, but then I already knew that." Erica looked at him perplexed. "You perceived me though I wore the Ignorant Charm at the Arcade. I was invisible to everyone, yet you saw me. That is no small feat; I have met no KeyMaster who can do that. You can also see spirits." He added.

Erica's heart skipped a beat and she froze.

He studied her. "You're a Medium, aren't you?"

She looked down at her gloved hands unable to speak. She felt cold to the core: *she was always so careful. How did he know?!*

"I saw you looking at a spirit on the Memorial Fountain at Piccadilly Circus, there's also one at your place of work that enjoys your company; and the burns on your wrists are from a spirit touching you..."

There was a pause.

She finally cleared her throat. "You can see them too?" Her voice barely a whisper; eyes full of longing.

He shook his head. "No, not unless they've chosen to reveal themselves to me. I know of spirits through my friend's research with Lost Souls, though their matter differs. Only a few can perceive them. I merely recognise some signs."

"What does this mean?"

He sighed then, heavily. "It means you're my heir: I'm to train you up. Then, you take my place and I retire."

"You can't retire, you're too young! And what if I don't want to become a KeyMaster? I've got plans, you know!"

"I was the same when I first found out, but my plans were taken away from me… So, I became a KeyMaster. I've never heard of anyone declining."

"Well, I can show them how it's done, can't I? I'm not going to just abandon all my plans. It's taken me years to get this far, I'm not going to toss them aside like *that*." She snapped her fingers, emphasising her point. "Not when I'm so close to achieving them."

"You're refusing to take up the mantle?"

She glared at him. "Too right! I haven't asked for it; find someone else to carry on your crazy work."

"Time has chosen you—you cannot deny it."

"I can, and I am! I want a normal life with a normal job and a normal home and a normal family doing normal stuff! I don't want to go Time Travelling, or whatever it is you do. I don't want to have to live invisible, watching the world go by without me!" She leapt to her feet, tears stinging her eyes, her fists clenched.

He got to his feet also, reaching for her. "Erica…"

"NO! I won't! I don't want anything to do with KeyMasters, Time Travel or you! Leave me alone!" She roared, shaking him off, running blindly back down the Embankment.

He recoiled as if he'd been slapped and watched her leave, eyes pained.

6
The Intermundus Club

She didn't see him the following week or the week after that.
Part of her was glad. The other part wasn't.

Unsurprisingly, the fact that she'd somehow managed to open a Gateway that cut through Space and Time to reveal Victorian England unnerved her a great deal. She was on tenterhooks for days.

Sometimes she thought someone was playing a practical joke on her. That Marc would jump out from behind his till one day and shout: "Fooled you!" and life would return to normal. Then she'd feel the periapt in her jacket pocket and realise Michael did exist and so had the Wrathful and the Gateway.

She wished it were a dream that she would wake from, leave behind forever and remember only as some distant, vague memory. But it wasn't, so what did it mean? Was she finally going mad?

She'd thought she'd lost her mind when she first found out she could see and talk with spirits. Maybe this was the next level up? She'd mastered her medium skills enough to now open Time portals? Yeah, whatever. She was so confused! She wished she could go and see Michael and ask him to explain things, but she didn't dare. She felt awful at how she'd spoken to him. Though, he hadn't feared her when he found out she could see spirits… He hadn't thought her a freak.

She smiled weakly to herself.

That was something at least.

***

He was in no mood for the meeting, but he had no valid excuse not to attend—especially with the AGM fast approaching. So, it was that Michael Nicholas found himself outside 50 Berkeley Square, Mayfair, on Tuesday morning Actualle, umbrella up against the glory of Great Britain: rain.

Despite the appalling weather, the late-Georgian townhouses that paraded round the oval gardens still maintained their dignity. Each shared common features: stone casings and sills stood out proud against the stucco or brickwork, ornate stone pediments topped each grand door and iron railings fronted each house like guards on patrol.

It was quiet, with only a few smartly dressed Actualle businessmen walking along its pavements. One such Actualle unknowingly walked through Michael despite the Ignorant Charm's best efforts.

It was a horrid sensation to be walked through: almost as if you had been turned to a jelly that was in the process of being mashed to a pulp by an over-excited toddler. Whilst, for the Actualle, a cold chill fell upon him and the hairs on the back of his neck stood on end. He looked up, wide-eyed, saw that he'd passed Number 50 and hastily walked away.

50 Berkeley Square had garnered a reputation of the paranormal, and rightly so. Besides many KeyMasters having been walked through and the chills becoming the hushed gossip of the Square and beyond. Some unlucky (*i.e.,* inebriated) KeyMasters had even been spotted disappearing as they belatedly applied the Ignorant Charm, having forgotten to do so before stumbling out from its doors. For it was here, at 50 Berkeley Square, that The Guild's Intermundus Club could be found. But only to those who knew of it. To the people of Actualle London all they would see was what currently lay before Michael: Millward Bros, the antiquarian book dealers. One of London's most haunted buildings.

Michael sighed. He would much rather peruse Millward Bros than attend the meeting.

The black front door lay before him; overhead a highly decorative iron arch that formerly housed a gaslight arose from the railings. Closing his umbrella sharply, he shook off the rain before removing a large silver Time Piece from his jacket pocket. On opening it, he began turning a series of dials this way and that. "1781…" he muttered, brow furrowed. Once happy with their configuration, he placed it inside a niche within the ironwork and the whole building convulsed before shattering like a mirror. Sharp shards fell to the ground with a tinkling crescendo.

***

Stripped of its disguise, in front of him now stood the Intermundus Club: grand, sober, imposing. Michael sighed even more heavily—he hated coming here. It certainly lacked the relaxed atmosphere of the Hunters Club. But the others would meet nowhere else.

Shoulders slumped, he mounted the steps, the shards of reality dissolving beneath his footfall. The main doors were opened with ease by Cid Wilkes, the Head Butler, who bowed reluctantly on seeing him, before snatching his umbrella from him.

"Dreadful weather, Mr Nicholas." He sneered.

"Yes, awful, Wilkes. Have the others arrived yet?"

"All but Signore Olea and Miss Ebadi." He gave an indignant sniff on saying her name; he was still offended that the fairer sex was now permitted within his precious Club. Michael chose to ignore this and proceeded to take off his outer garments with Wilkes' assistance. "Is your Færie with you, sir? Shall I take it to the back parlour?" A Færie Footman appeared at the click of Wilkes' fingers to take the garments away.

"No, thank you. It'll remain with me."

"Very well, sir," he said, further disdain in his voice. "And what refreshment can I get for you?"

"A cup of Earl Grey without milk, thank you, Wilkes."

"Without milk! Like the savages?! Missing home, sir?"

Michael chose to ignore his comment. "I've found the flavours greatly enhanced without milk. After all, it was only added for its nutritional benefits, nothing to do with taste."

Wilkes bowed deeply. Nodding over to a bartend, he proceeded to show Michael through the main sitting area.

The room was high ceilinged with ornate covings and a grand chandelier that shimmered splendidly. Its walls were panelled and polished so much they gleamed even in the dim grey light that seeped through four tall windows. Oak floorboards peeped through rich Persian rugs underfoot. There were already a few gentlemen sitting in the comfy armchairs scattered around the room, either alone or in pairs, reading the morning's paper and discussing its news. A couple were tucking into a hearty cooked breakfast at a table to the right. An elderly gentleman in the armchair closest to the fire snored dully from under the journal that covered his head much to the amusement of the young men playing cards around the club fender. Most of the patrons looked up in interest at the new arrival, though few returned his greeting.

"The others are gathering in the Blue Room, sir—the room facing you." Wilkes said, opening a pair of doors to reveal a grand foyer.

"Thank you. If you could ask Bill to have my tea served in there that'd be greatly appreciated."

"Of course, sir," Wilkes replied, closing the double doors behind him.

Michael proceeded to walk across the foyer, a balustraded viewing gallery encircled him on the first floor, accessible by a staircase to the right. A rug dominated the floor, upon which stood a circular table with newspapers and journals for members to help themselves to; as well as cigars, displayed in exotic lacquer boxes. In its centre was a tall flower arrangement, its heady fragrance filled the air, and, hanging high up from the ceiling, was a crystal chandelier that oozed opulence.

Checking that he was alone, Michael took out his periapt and touched its stone.

"We have arrived, Ashayla."

***

72

Holding the periapt in his palm, the stone pulsed once, and a tiny streak escaped from it, whizzing around the central table merrily, its brilliance struck the chandelier and lit up the foyer as if with fireworks. The small elfin figure landed gracefully upon the rug, pirouetted, and grew, until Ashayla stood before Michael in human-form.

"Thank you, Michael."

"Not at all, saves you getting wet," he said, pocketing the periapt.

Taking in its surroundings it scowled, causing its moon tattoo to crease. *"I dislike this Club."*

"You and me the same," he replied, though in softer tones than it had used. He opened a smart leather briefcase and produced a pair of white cotton gloves. Ashayla looked at them and then at Michael. "You know how they are towards Færies here. Do as you must but wear these, this way you won't hurt so."

"Thank you for your thoughtfulness," it said, accepting the gloves before donning them.

Snapping the briefcase shut Michael crossed the foyer with Ashayla beside him. Knocking smartly on the door, he pushed it open and walked into the aptly named Blue Room.

Its walls were decorated in patterned blue silk, brocaded curtains in dark blue velvet hung from the windows, draping lavishly onto the blue carpet. A large, gilded mirror hung over the mantelpiece, upon which stood a clock that whirled softly. One wall was lined with leather books of various heights and in the centre of the room was a large circular oak table polished to a high sheen; around which were seven chairs upholstered in blue leather.

The people already in the room looked up as he entered, taking him and his Færie in.

"Welcome, dear Nicholas! Welcome! I trust you had a good journey here this morning?"

"I did, thank you, Joe. And you? You're in good health I hope?" Michael asked Joe King, a middle-aged KeyMaster with a dark moustache and keen eyes. They shook hands.

"Not bad, my dear fellow, not bad. Appalling business with the markets, what? They just keep on getting worse… Wish I could advise them, save everyone a lot of pain, you know. But then, we're here to observe, not advise, are we not?"

Michael nodded uneasily.

"If the government were more forthright, British industry would be stronger," chipped in Urban Bunkins, a rotund KeyMaster who was sitting to Joe's right and chomping on a cigar.

"Hear, hear! British industry is rather lacking in Actualle England, is it not? I find it all jolly awful. It affects one's mood so…." Edward Quigley said at Joe's left, leaning forwards, his Adam's apple moving energetically.

"Ind'd, but if thae government cannae protect its ohn peple wit'thae maust suitable lores, then thae peple'e gonnae suffer." A warm Scottish lilt interjected from the corner of the room. September Morris replaced the book he had been perusing and returned to his seat beside Urban.

At that moment, the door opened and Mahin Ebadi walked in. The men all rose to their feet and bowed politely at her, whilst she inclined her head gracefully in reply. Her luscious dark hair was piled upon her head, held in place with gold slides of Achaemenid style; a small bonnet sat smartly on its peak. She sat down in the seat offered by September and smiled her thanks. A young boy with pale skin that glowed and luscious golden locks followed her into the room wearing the robes and tunics befitting those of the Achaemenid Empire, a large gold chain hung about its neck and golden cuffs adorned its wrists.

Once it had helped to rearrange the deep plum skirts of its mistress' dress, the young boy bowed and placed in front of her a document file bound in leather that she unwrapped to produce pen and ink and several sheets of parchment. She nodded, and the boy moved to the edge of the room where Ashayla had taken its position, in the shadow of the bookcases, away from the KeyMasters. It eyed Ashayla's human form with envy.

The men seated themselves, producing leather tomes and writing tools from their briefcases.

"Madame Ebadi, it's'a delaeght t'see yer. Ah trust yer've bin keepin' well?" September purred, leaning forwards in his chair.

She smiled and turned her almond-shaped eyes on him. "I have, dear sir. Thank you for your kind enquiry. Though I'm afraid the Head Butler is still displeased with my successful petitioning for gender equality within this establishment. His manner is quite appalling! I have a good mind to get Faridoon to compose a letter to the High KeyMaster!" she nodded in her Færie's direction, her lips trembling.

"Ah cannae agree wit'yer more, m'lady. Ah have long appreciated thae benefits o'equal rights in lore. Yer must be patient. Yer've campaigned long an'hard an' brought aboot great changes, but it'll tyke tym for peple t'accept these changes," September comforted.

Edward leaned forwards and guffawed. "Especially that Wilkes, what!"

Everyone chuckled.

"If it helps, Miss Ebadi, I have similar issues, though admittedly not regarding my gender," Michael offered.

The party smiled awkwardly.

The time piece on the mantel chimed. They looked at it and noted its many hands whirling around its centre, moving from one point to another before continuing to another. Occasionally they returned to the midday point before starting upon their merry, random, way.

"There's a lot of to-ing and fro-ing in Time," commented Urban, puffing on his cigar.

"People rushing to their meetings, no doubt. So, without further ado, I declare this meeting of the District Council of 21st Century London open," Joe King said, rustling his sheets of parchment importantly.

"Steady on, dear chap, Justus has still yet to show up," Edward reminded him.

Joe frowned with annoyance. "Has anyone received apologies from Signore Olea?"

Just then the door burst open and a short man in an elegant suit strode into the room. "*Bonjorno, Signores*! I am so sorry that I am'a late'a!" He surveyed the seated KeyMasters, his eyes finally coming to rest on Mahin. He bowed reluctantly and added sulkily. "And *Signora…*" She inclined her head in greeting, though her eyes remained watchful. He took his seat between Michael and Edward.

"As I was saying, now all are present, I declare this meeting of the District Council of 21st Century London open," Joe King repeated with a second rustling of his parchment.

"Now," continued Joe, "since the AGM is approaching, we need to audit our Loggias, as well as any Lost Soul encounters and any other matters of import that you wish to be passed on to The Guild. However, first there're a couple of amendments to the Minutes from the last meeting."

There was a sudden loud snapping of fingers and everyone turned to Olea, who was trying to get the attention of Ashayla.

"Eh! Færie! I am'a thirsty! A glass of *vino rosso, grazie!*"

Ashayla looked at him in surprise and then at Michael. Michael nodded, and it left the shadows sulkily.

"And come back with *gli occhi*, Færie, eyes!" Olea said, shaking his head in disbelief and pointing at his own eyes. Ashayla stopped as it opened the door and turned to look at Olea, pupils forming to reveal a look of utter disdain with a sprinkling of loathing. Michael indicated for it to leave quickly and it stalked out of the room, bells roaring in its wake. "You have problems with dat one, eh, *signore*?" Olea said in tones of commiseration.

"Not as you think."

September smiled over his steepled fingers.

Joe cleared his throat. "The amendments are as follows: there was heavy rain from 28th July through to August 29th—nice to know nothing ever changes." He gave a lopsided smile. "There was indeed a streaker at this year's Wimbledon and the Prime Minister was assaulted by a tetchy Shadowling and not angry pensioners armed with tomatoes as the media reported." There were open chuckles at this news as Joe placed his parchment to one side.

"Thank you all for being so prompt with your Loggias—The Guild are very pleased with this District Councils' organisation, saying we're far more prompt than 19th Century London who appear to have a hectic social calendar; probably because they can afford to," Joe muttered in an undertone.

Michael looked at him sympathetically. It was general knowledge that Joe, being so interested in economics, had dabbled too much on Actualle's unpredictable markets, resulting in the loss of a small fortune.

People averted their eyes politely apart from Olea who leaned forwards and complained that thanks was all very good, but a little extra credit wouldn't come amiss.

Joe nodded in acknowledgement before going on to ask whether there were any objections to the amendments to the last meeting. Since there were none, he went on to request all to confirm their Loggias for the past two months.

Whilst each consulted their leather tomes the door opened to admit Bill followed by Ashayla bearing the drinks. Coffee was deposited in small porcelain cups to all but Michael who received his tea (without milk) from Bill; and Olea, whose wine was plonked down unceremoniously by Ashayla. Mahin had simply requested boiling water, to which her Færie, Faridoon, added a spoonful of fragrant spices.

Once Bill had left, the KeyMasters resumed their consultation of their Loggias.

"Oh yes, I had a rather odd incident late September," Edward began chuckling as he read his notes. "Probably some mix up at the Sonnastry, although Yophiel was awfully peeved when I said so."

"Go on," prompted Urban.

"Well, it's just that, on September twenty-third, my wife and I had a run in with an Arbolis Noir."

7
The Plot Thickens

The KeyMasters all looked up aghast.

"Yer were boh'th well, Ah horp?" September enquired, concern furrowing his brow.

Arbolis Noir were Lost Souls that possessed trees, attacking from above. They were particularly notorious for their ferocity and had caused the downfall of many a respected Soul Gatherer and KeyMaster.

"We were, thank you, September. Thankfully Uliall, our Færie, managed to vanquish it. Although, my good wife did lose her favourite bonnet to the foul tree!"

Mahin gasped, reaching up to her own bonnet.

"And, wat was de problem, *signore*?" Olea asked.

"Oh, just that the Sonnastry had no record of the attack."

Michael choked on his tea. He looked up sharply: *surely not?*

"I know, Michael! Totally unheard of! Uliall and myself hadn't received any warning, you see, so I was frightfully angry. Stormed right up to the front desk at the Sonnastry and told them it wasn't on! Told them to buck their ideas up! I was nearly arrested! They thought I was out of my mind, trying it on so. Of course, they would've heard if a Lost Soul had reached earth, let alone warn people. Very bizarre, what?"

"Quite. And how was it resolved?" Joe enquired, his voice thin.

"Oh, I just noted it in my Loggia with a question mark and carried on as normal, old chap. Not much more I could do. My wife did purchase a new bonnet though, it's really rather fetching."

"It's plausible that there was a glitch in the system. Some of the bells have been known to stick," Urban said.

Michael caught Ashayla's eyes from across the table. It knew he was battling the urge to mention their encounter with the Wrathful.

It shook its head, its voice low in his ears. *Be-ye! Wait for news from Christian.*

He let out a shaky sigh. It was right. There'd be time soon enough. In any case, Erica had made it extremely clear she didn't wish to be involved.

The meeting was adjourned forty agonisingly slow minutes later, after all Loggias were approved. The AGM was to be held early January, so any final reports would be required no later than the end of November. Michael was more than happy to end the meeting. He had to find Christian, and fast.

"Ashayla, find Christian for me please. Tell him that I need to speak with him urgently," Michael said in hushed tones when it reached his side.

Ashayla nodded and closed its eyes before dissolving in a cloud of glittering mist. Olea clucked his tongue disapprovingly as he walked out the door. Michael ignored him. He knew the use of Færies was frowned upon in public, particularly in Clubs, but this was of the utmost importance. If the Sonnastry had revealed they had no record of the Erica's attack that could not be mere coincidence. Could it?

"Michael, he's here!"

Turning at the sound of its voice, Michael saw Christian rushing towards him as the Færie re-materialised.

"Finally!" Christian exclaimed.

Several of Michael's colleagues looked up in surprise at the Soul Gatherer's entrance.

"How did you gain admittance?" he said, pulling him aside.

"Old Burnside vouched for me. I've been looking for you everywhere! I called by Sunday afternoon—where were you?"

Michael blushed, that'd been the day he'd met Erica at work. The day she'd opened the Gateway at Cleopatra's Needle… "Apologies, my friend. I was detained. What did Yophiel say?"

"Gave me a right earful, it did, old boy! Said it was getting rather sick of people implying it couldn't do its job properly."

"I fail to follow."

"Although the Sonnastry has no record of them, there've been attacks reported by other KeyMasters, old boy. Yours was one of several."

***

Together Christian and Michael went to the Sonnastry to talk with the Færie Yophiel which was still disgruntled at its professional capabilities being brought into question. Reassuring the Færie that no blame was being laid at its feet, they asked for the names of the other KeyMasters who had also reported such attacks, promising to research quietly. On seeing the male Færie hesitate, Michael watched as Christian leaned in close and whispered into its ear. With a laugh it rolled its eyes and quickly wrote the names of three other KeyMasters on a piece of scrap paper, hiding it from the beady eyes of Mildrew Sterner, the overly keen receptionist.

Over the next week, Michael paid a visit to all those on the list—excluding Edward Quigley whose account he knew of—enquiring after their health following the attacks. Once they discovered that his attack had also been unknown to the Sonnastry, they were more than willing to recount their own, all of which had occurred over the last few months; one with a particularly malicious Wistful and one with a pack of Blood Hounds. Both KeyMasters had survived with minor injuries. Nonetheless, Thomas Pyke and Gregory Fletcher had taken their queries no further than mentioning them to Yophiel. After all it was probably a glitch, some bells sticking. Nothing more.

No one had died, had they?

***

She'd come to a decision. It'd been too long. And each time she walked past where his house was, invisible to all, her words echoed back. *"I don't want anything to do with KeyMasters, Time Travel or you!"*

80

How wrong had she been? She couldn't get him or the Gateway out of her mind. So, she'd decided to apologise.

Yet, despite the rush of adrenaline she'd had after reaching her decision, going along with it was proving difficult. She was a bag of nerves by the time she reached the end of Cheniston Gardens.

Taking a deep breath, she walked up the steps leading to the house with no front door.

She had hoped that the black door would materialise when it sensed her approach, just as it had for Michael, but it didn't, and she found herself staring at a blank wall. She frowned. How could she get it to appear?

Turning to walk back down the steps, she froze. At the bottom stood Michael, a look of the utmost surprise across his face.

Her heart lurched painfully against her chest. He had dark shadows under his eyes and was sporting a stubble. He looked terrible. And sexy. Could terrible be sexy? She bit her lip. She didn't know and didn't care. He was gorgeous.

"Michael! I, erh… I… hi…" She ended lamely.

"Good evening," he replied, a slight edge to his voice.

Come on! This was it, a chance to apologise! She braced herself. "I came by just to say how sorry I was. I was caught off guard by everything. It was all a bit of a shock. I'm sorry. I didn't mean what I said."

His blue eyes locked with her green. "Apology accepted," he said, giving a bow.

She blushed and bobbed clumsily in reply. "I'll get going then, it's late."

He stopped her as she made to walk past him, catching her arm. "No, stay. Please. You're more than welcome. How about that drink you mentioned, Miss Shylocke?"

She hesitated, unsure whether she'd be overstaying her welcome, saw the warmth in his eyes and nodded her acceptance. "It was lucky you came by—I was just trying to figure out how to find your door."

He looked at her sheepishly. "It was more than luck. I hope you don't find this offensive, but I've been accompanying you on your walk home every evening, as I promised. Consequently, I knew that you were here because I'd followed you; though I was surprised when you stopped, I thought you'd walk on by as before…"

It was her turn to be surprised. "You've been walking me home? Invisible?" *Was she stupid in thinking it sweet rather than freaky?*

"There are other planes of invisibility. I said it was turning into a habit, did I not?" He gave a crooked smile.

Michael produced the same large copper key as before, lips moving in a quiet charm. By the time they'd reached the top step, the front door had materialised. Unlocking the door, he swiped his periapt in front of the pentacle.

"What would you like to drink? I can offer sherry, cognac, whisky or gin. I'm partial to cognac."

Erica was hovering on the threshold. "A gin and tonic, please."

He hung up his jacket, taking off his hat, muffler and gloves. "Please, do come in. You're most welcome."

She stepped into the hallway and watched the door shut magically behind her.

She had expected him to call for Ashayla but instead he motioned her to follow him into his living room-cum-study where embers burned dimly in their grate. Michael added some extra kindling and logs. After a few moments, the embers sparked, and the fire burned once more, growing from strength to strength. She sat down happily on the sofa and stretched out her hands towards its warmth.

Crossing over to a collection of crystal decanters on a side table, Michael proceeded to pour out their drinks. There was a shadow of a frown upon his brow. His eyes were laced with worry. He looked up then and she quickly turned to the fire, assuming the air of one in thought.

He walked over with their glasses and she accepted hers with thanks.

He sat wearily down in the comfy armchair next to the sofa. There was a silence as they soaked in the fire's warmth. Its light casting fractures across the rug. There was a sweet aroma to the wood: apple?

"So," she said, taking a sip of her drink, "how's it going?"

"Very well, thank you," he replied with a smile, though it failed to reach his eyes.

"You're very bad at lying," she remarked, and he looked away. "What's happened?"

"You wouldn't understand so there's little point," he said bitterly, taking a large swig of his cognac.

"I can be an objective sounding board, so there is a point. And in any case," she added, "I want to understand, so there is definitely a point."

He looked at her, his eyes softening.

"I cannot, sorry. You're an Actualle, someone from this Time; I should really have no contact with you, if The Guild found—"

"I'd tell them they were fools. How can you observe, how can you live without truly being in the thick of life?" She interrupted stoutly.

Michael gazed into the fire. "You have a point," he sighed after a while, running a hand through his short hair. He took a deep breath and cleared his throat. "More Lost Souls have been found to have attacked KeyMasters, people like me. All the attacks were unknown by the Sonnastry, an office of The Guild which monitors travel through Time. No one has been killed yet, so The Guild is unaware. Or, if they are aware, they've given no indication that they are and have not yet acted. I don't know what it means, let alone what to do. Am I worrying unnecessarily? It cannot be coincidence, not with so many unreported attacks…"

There was a pause as she processed the information. "It means we've been lucky so far, haven't we? But that luck won't last forever. What happens if someone is killed by a Lost Soul? Do they pass on?"

With no lamps lit, the only light came from the fire, flickering over them both. Casting harsh shadows across their faces.

"No, they in turn become Lost Souls."

"So, their numbers would increase without your Guild knowing—if they aren't aware, say."

83

"Yes," Michael replied in hushed tones, the dread of the past two weeks threatened to cripple him.

Erica noticed his knuckles whiten on the arm of the chair.

"I requested that the other victims noted their attacks in their Loggias," he noticed her puzzled brow. "Our journals. This way The Guild should discuss them at the AGM in January. Hopefully before. In the meantime—"

"We need to keep our eyes peeled," Erica finished. Michael nodded glumly. "Who do we have who can help?"

"Ashayla, my friends Christian and Anatole, some of their friends, Lord and Lady de Temps, my former mentor Isambard and, and…" He trailed off, racking his brain for names.

"And me."

"And you? I appreciate your concern, Miss Shylocke, and you being an 'objective sounding board' but this is none of your concern; I cannot permit you to get involved."

"Michael, I've been 'involved' since you saved me. Anyway, I am a KeyMaster-in-Waiting." She ended briskly.

"You want to take up the mantle?"

"Not exactly. You could still train me though, couldn't you? That way you've got an extra pair of eyes and you won't get into trouble for being in contact with me. Once everything's over I'll pull out, that way you can carry on KeyMastering it and I can carry on, erm, studenting it."

"You're more cunning than you look, Miss Shylocke."

"Erica," she corrected him, "and I'll take that as a compliment. So, what do you say, *sensei*?"

He considered her: the slightness of her shoulders, the dark circles under her eyes and her youth. She was so young! "I cannot guarantee your safety—I don't wish to put you in danger."

"Don't worry about me. I can handle myself."

He hesitated. He really shouldn't. But there was something about her… Strength flickered deep within her eyes. That and a maturity beyond her years.

"I acquiesce, it would be an honour to be your 'sensei' and train you. You have my eternal gratitude for your help with this matter. Though, if I deem it too dangerous, you're to stop."

Erica shrugged. "Okay. This calls for a toast!" And rose her glass. "To Time!"

"To Time." His glass chinked against hers and they drained their glasses in unison.

"And, talking of time, if you permit me, it is time I accompanied you home." He rose to his feet, offering her his hand.

Taking it, she noticed the pale scars about his wrists. She looked up into his eyes, as vibrant as gemstones. *What was his story?*

"Thank you."

***

He doffed his hat in response to her wave from her window and waited until the lights in her flat went dark, only then did he feel it safe for him to leave. It'd been quite an evening. He wasn't totally sure whether he'd made the right decision, agreeing to Erica's help: for now, it seemed the best thing, but later?

He shuddered then against the memories that smothered him in their coldness. It unnerved him coming to this house on this street, no matter the years of distance.

Bracing himself, he ploughed forwards, disappearing into the night. He must go and see her: he didn't want to be late.

8
Limbo

The next day Erica kept getting transactions in a muddle, so, after the umpteenth time, Joslin banished her to shelving.

Had she done the right thing? What if she couldn't get out of being a KeyMaster? Was she now stuck to live in the shadows? It was a job, so it made sense she could resign when she wanted, right?

And then there was the growing number of Lost Souls. She tried not to think about them. The mere memory of the Wrathful bearing down on her made the hairs on the back of her neck stand on end; its Choir grated her soul. How many people had perished? How many more were going to perish? And how could she help?

"Honestly, what can I do against something like that?" she asked the spirit softly as it dusted the shelves next to her.

The shimmering spectre shrugged, equally perturbed.

***

Michael had suggested them meeting at the corner of Cheniston Gardens on Monday morning at 10 o'clock. He'd notified The Guild of her discovery in his Loggia-thingy and they needed to go and officially register her. He also wanted to give her a couple of days to mull over her decision. She was to await the periapt; whatever that meant.

Nerves were beginning to get the better of her, it all seemed very official. What if she was signing her future over after all? Michael had reassured her that he would assist with her resignation when the time came but she still felt uneasy. She couldn't deny that she was desperate to know more about The Guild, not to mention Michael.

To register, all Michael said she needed to bring was her cheque book, which concerned her as she didn't have money to pay for anything.

Seeing her unease, he'd smiled reassuringly. "Do not concern yourself."

Nevertheless, she had. Unable to sleep, she woke early Monday morning and proceeded to distract herself with chores until calling in sick to her tutor, work and Marc. She had placed the periapt on the side and kept glancing at it expectantly as she busied herself.

Lying to her tutor and HR had been easy. Lying to Marc hadn't. Which was why she'd messaged him—calling him was out of the question; he'd be able to tell she was lying. He was good like that.

"Dodgy takeout. I'm a disaster at both ends. Hopefully better to wreak havoc on Wednesday. Don't have too much fun without me X"

She hesitated: one 'X' or more? One. She sent it, grimacing at how graphic she'd been. But she was desperate for no one to come over and discover her out.

By nine o'clock she decided to get ready. Michael hadn't exactly said what would happen when she was registered—all he'd said was to 'expect the unexpected' and 'be natural', which was uselessly vague— but with everything seeming so formal, she decided to err on the side of caution. She eventually selected a fish tail skirt, tights, pretty blouse and cardigan, before finishing it off with her favourite boots and purple three-quarter jacket. She stood back to admire the affect and sighed.

"What is it?" Lizzie's voice floated up from where her phone stood perched precariously against some books. She was wearing skinny jeans, a purple crop top Erica had bought her and her statement leather jacket.

"Thighs," Erica said, smoothing her skirt to dispel their curve.

"Embrace them, Erica. You've got curves in all the right places."

87

"I can't help but embrace them—they're huge!" she muttered, reaching for her makeup.

Lizzie chortled. "Why don't you go the whole hog and wear those jeans I got you?"

"It's not really that kind of do."

"Do you still have those boots I leant you?"

"Maybe. *Ow!*"

"Have you just poked yourself in the eye with your mascara brush again?"

Erica was doubled up, hand over one eye. "Maybe."

Lizzie brushed her friend's clumsiness aside impatiently. "What kind of do is it then? Skipping work and class! It's not like you. Where *are* you going?"

She hesitated, dabbing a tissue to her eye. "I can't say. Oh bother…" She moaned, removing the tissue to reveal mascara blotches all the way across her cheek.

"Hey! It's me we're talking about," Lizzie said, brandishing her middle finger where she wore her friendship ring, a simple band with a heart.

"I know, Lizzie," Erica said, feeling the weight of her matching ring. "But you'll think I'm crazy."

"News flash, Erica, I already *do* think you're crazy!"

It was then that her periapt pulsed brightly. *"We've left and shall see you anon."* Ashayla's voice echoed.

"'Anon'?" Lizzie repeated, craning to see where the voice had come from. "Who was that?"

Erica tapped the periapt in acknowledgement before packing away her mascara and picking up the phone. "I've got to go."

"Don't you hang up on me!"

Erica looked at her friend with pleading eyes. "I promise I'll tell you everything. When I can."

Lizzie stared in disbelief as her best friend cut her off.

***

As she approached the corner of Cheniston Gardens Erica could see Michael waiting for her, wrapped up against the cold of early December. The overnight frost had mostly melted away, but the blue skies belied a piercing chill. She greeted him with a mock salute, shivering against the wind that bussed her. He smiled and doffed his top hat jauntily.

"Good morning, Miss Shylocke. And have you slept on your decision?"

She nodded, hiding her trembling hands. "I have and it's still the same."

His bright eyes regarded her. "As you wish, it'll be a pleasure working with you. However, as I said before if I deem it too dangerous your assistance will stop. I will not bring ill-fate to another."

"Of course." Her curiosity piqued. *Another?* "Where do we go to register, *sensei*?"

Michael smiled. "Limbo. The Guild is based there."

"Of course, it is."

"This way." She accepted his proffered arm and he led her up towards High Street Kensington, their breath greeting the cool air in misty plumes.

Michael stopped them in front of an iron gateway to a Victorian apartment block several metres from the hustle and bustle of the High Street. The archway to the gate was tall and made up of alternating stripes of red and white bricks fanning from its centre. Above the bricks were ornate stone corbels of scrolls, elaborate cornices, arches and a shield. Upon the shield was carved the date of the buildings' birth: 1894. A cherub looked down cheerily, an ornate pinnacle upon its head. The iron gate itself was locked.

Erica watched as Michael took out his periapt.

"For this next interlude we are best unseen. Casting Charms is straightforward, but you must be touching the stone of the periapt to deploy them. Please place your hand upon the periapt. *Actualles ignarus*," he chanted once her hand touched the central gem. A queasy sensation came upon her and she felt herself dim, fading out of real life and into nothingness. In that same instant her ears tingled and popped. She sneezed.

"The Ignorant Charm. It will keep us out of sight and sound," he said, casting the Charm on himself before pocketing his periapt. He then took out a set of ancient keys that Erica recognised from their incident at Cleopatra's Needle. "The Keys of Time. Upon inaugurating, a KeyMaster receives a set of keys, in addition to a bell, Time Piece and three periapts for a Færie of their choosing. In each set there is a key of iron, of steel, of silver, of bronze and, finally, one of gold." He showed them to her in turn. "Each was created by a different LockSmith and bears their family crest. Ultimately, each serves the same purpose, to open a Temporal Gateway, but each Gateway requires a different key. With teaching and practice you will learn which key is needed for which Gateway. We're going to open this Temporal Gateway here, but..." His professional demeanour cracked. "Would you indulge me? I should like to conduct a small experiment. Which one would you suggest? Perhaps your sensitivity to spirits will have a bearing."

He offered his keys to Erica with a boyish look of interest on his face that made her knees tremble.

She'd indulge him anything!

Taking a deep breath to clear her head, she took them. The bow of each key was decorated with fine heraldry. None 'felt' particularly right for the Gateway. She took off her gloves and held each key in turn. They were heavy, and their metallic coldness seeped through to her bones, numbing her fingers. One started to buzz at her touch.

"This one?" she ventured, holding up the silver key.

Michael looked at her intently before gesturing for her to try it. Taking a step forwards, she held the key close to the iron gate. The key quivered, first slightly, then violently. It began to shimmer, its silver tones lustrous. In that same instant there was a flash of bright light from the Gateway, cutting a doorway beneath the shield with the date: 1894. She placed the silver key in the doorway's keyhole and turned it.

"You shouldn't be able to do that, Miss Shylocke," Michael said, his face paling, wariness replacing his look of interest.

The doorway opened with a crackle of electricity. Beyond was High Street Kensington complete with the rambunctious *clip-clop* of hooves from smart private carriages, busy double-decker omnibuses and commercial vans full of goods being pulled by burly packhorses. Men in their suits were walking along with their top hats, canes in hand. Whilst street vendors called their wares from their barrows and boards. A morning fog clung to the air. Though a dimness blurred the scene, almost as if the sun wasn't working properly.

"I shouldn't?" Erica remarked absent-mindedly, too busy drinking in the scene before her. "I thought we were going to Limbo. Why are we seeing Victorian London? And could you call me 'Erica'?"

"If you're to be my protégé I must call you 'Miss Shylocke', Miss Shylocke. And no, you're not wrong. However, it's a useful lesson. This is the way we open Temporal Gateways. The Temporal Gateway for Limbo is, as you expected, slightly different."

Covering her hand, he guided her in turning the key, locking the Temporal Gateway so that Victorian London disappeared.

"For Limbo, a Temporal Gateway is needed, any to hand. And the Time Piece, but no keys." On saying, he swapped his keys for his silver Time Piece and opened it to reveal its various dials. He turned them deftly, until everything lined up to zero: the date, the month, the year and time. "Limbo is between all Times and in none. It is the beginning of all and the end. Therefore, it is nothing but remains everything: zero."

Placing the Time Piece upon the brick gateway the portal burst open with a deafening crash.

***

Before them stretched space. Or what Erica thought looked like space: a blue-black void pocked with shimmering stars and wispy nebulas in orange, green and blue.

91

Michael took off his top hat and folded it neatly away before stepping out with the confidence of habit onto the black void. Erica watched as he walked across the void from the safety of the pavement. She looked down at her feet then at the void just before their toes. She looked to where Michael stood amongst the stars.

"Really?"

"It's quite safe, Miss Shylocke. I assure you."

"How do I know this isn't just some ruse to make you smile when I fall?"

He smiled, his teeth flashing. "You don't."

Erica glared at him and swore as she took in the expanse before her: Lizzie would never believe her.

Steadying herself, she closed her eyes and took a step out onto nothingness.

***

Although she'd seen Michael walk confidently across the void before her, she was still surprised to find the blue-blackness solid beneath her footfall. Opening one eye after another, she was just taking tentative steps towards Michael, marvelling at the shimmering stars that circled her, when she felt the solidness dissolve from under her and gravity take over. She looked to Michael wildly as she felt herself plummet into the void, letting out a blood curdling scream as space whooshed past her. Arms flailing, feet kicking madly for any stronghold to stop her.

It was then that she noticed Michael standing calmly, space zooming past him, looking at her with one eyebrow raised and she realised she wasn't plummeting to her doom after all, rather falling in a controlled manner. A bit like she'd imagine freefalling to feel. She looked at the stars streaking past her and grinned wickedly.

To start with she tested her 'wings' and, moving her arms, found she could alter her course and direction. From then it wasn't long until she was twisting and turning, spinning and somersaulting her way past Michael, who remained still. One thing led to another and she found herself trying out her best Spider-man and Superman impersonations, swinging and swooping her way around Michael who seemed to be increasingly perturbed by her activities. It was then that inspiration struck.

Eyebrows raised, Michael watched as she swooped towards him at great speed on an imaginary broomstick waving an imaginary bat. It was whilst she began screaming "MIND THAT BLUDGER!" that he looked pointedly down. Following his gaze, she saw a double-walled metropolis sprawled out below them. A shimmering light emanated from it. Darkness beyond black surrounded it.

Erica swooped to stand next to Michael. He regarded her, and she beamed. "Sorry, I couldn't resist. I've always fancied myself as a Beater. Who'd think that Limbo people could be so cool as to think of freefalling?! I mean, it's genius!"

"'Cool'?" Michael looked bemused. "As in *sprezzatura*?"

"As in 'awesome'," Erica replied, looking equally bemused. "What's '*sprezzatura*'?"

"The 'cool' I'm familiar with." He cleared his throat. "There are other ways to reach Limbo."

"Better than freefalling?"

"Whether you would deem them as 'cool' as freefalling I couldn't say but I've heard there are the usual methods such as, escalators, lifts and ladders as well as slides, flumes, helter-skelters and quicksand. Though that is a bit messy."

"'Flumes'?! Oh, we're going to have so much fun!" Erica's eyes shone in anticipation.

"We are?" Michael looked down at her with amusement.

"Yes. What's that?" Erica asked, indicating to a trio of buildings that stood out amongst the bustling streets, squares, parks and boulevards that grew ever closer. The buildings were arranged in a loose triangle at the centre of the metropolis within landscaped grounds. Michael indicated to each in turn.

"In the foreground is The Guild of KeyMasters, akin to your Parliament. To the right is the University and to the left is the Library. Between all three you might just make out the Cathedral."

For the remainder of their journey Michael pointed out landmarks and sites. At first, he spoke awkwardly, but as he went on, he became more animated, leaning in close. "Limbo is encircled by two defensive walls, each over 200 feet high, like those found in ancient China. Without are the Wastelands and Claustrum, Limbo's prison. Within you'll notice that The Guild, University and Library are all Gothic in style but include domed roofs. No other buildings can be taller than The Guild. The Cathedral, though built first, is smaller—its architecture is exquisite." He trailed off to describe how Sir Christopher Wren had gifted it to Limbo in gratitude for being saved from a vicious encounter with a Virvatuli on his way home from an inn. "I suppose I should take you to see it." He ended thoughtfully.

She looked up, smiling shyly. "I'd like that."

Just then their plummet slowed, and Erica felt her weight return. Firmness reappeared beneath her feet until they were finally, carefully, deposited on the barren ground before a set of gargantuan gates.

Michael replaced his top hat. "Welcome to Limbo, Miss Shylocke."

***

The City of Limbo stretched out before them. Its primary outer wall was made from sheer stone and towered above them. An unearthly golden glow emanated from it into the black Wastelands: a beacon in the darkness.

They approached the colossal West Gate which was forty feet deep and heavily defended by countless guards. Erica had never felt so small. Halting, Michael produced his Time Piece for inspection by a guard who, after holding it with an air of consideration, returned it with a curt nod. It turned to Erica and held out its hand.

"She's with me; we have an appointment to register her at The Guild."

The guard regarded her for the longest of moments before stepping aside and saluting them. Its featureless face unreadable.

The mighty Gates opened slowly, and they passed through.

Michael explained how the Guards of the Glorious Dead were the lost souls of former servicemen and women who now policed Limbo: its gates, walls and citizens. As Lost Souls, they had no features—where a face should be there was only black swirling shadows like the Wrathful, though without any eyes. However, unlike other Lost Souls, the Guards had been Impressed and were charged with the protection of Limbo and its people, so were safe. Each was dressed in the uniform of the Guards of the Glorious Dead: black with blue and yellow stripes and white gloves. Though they were permitted to wear their service badges and medals from their previous lives.

Exiting the West Gate, they crossed over a wide moat to the secondary gate, the wall of which loomed even higher than the first, patrols of Guards walked along its battlements armed with rifles and swords. It was as they passed through the secondary gate that Michael explained how once she was registered, they'd attend the morning session where she'd be formally inaugurated as a KeyMaster-in-Waiting.

Emerging through the secondary gate, they were greeted by a market crowned with a cerulean sky. It felt like early spring with warm sunshine, fluffy clouds and only a hint of winter's chill on the breeze. Erica gasped in shock, looking back at the black skies still visible through the gate.

Expect the unexpected...

"Ready?" he asked, not noticing anything out of the ordinary. And, taking her by the elbow, they dove into the bustling market.

It was like no other market she'd ever been to. There were gentlemen and ladies in their fineries from various centuries and cultures, a dazzling cross-section of human civilization. Servants hurried along with shopping lists and baskets for their masters. Færies too, ethereal and out of place, even in Limbo, went about chores. Most were dressed in fine garments and followed their masters, some even linked arms, acting more like lovers than servants. All wore metal cuffs or slave bracelets in various designs.

The stalls themselves were like none that she'd seen in Actualle markets. For whilst there were stalls selling colourful clothing and accessories from Earth's many eras and cultures, there were also stalls selling bizarre animals from the Wastelands, weapons, quills, books, jewellery and an array of colourful bottles in all shapes and sizes—apparently containing potions and ointments. Shifty men hovered in the shadows and seemed to be tempting the well-to-do with financial newspapers: amateur and professional stockbrokers Michael confirmed. Access to financial markets from all Times was regularly abused, despite being illegal. It used to be heavily policed, though Michael said this was now no longer the case. Indeed, Erica saw no sign of the eery Guards anywhere.

Some stalls sold all manner of books, weapons and potions to equip Soul Gatherers, hunters of Lost Souls. Other stalls sold trinkets, chains and spell books for the mastery of Færies. Not to mention stalls that appeared to sell a dubious array of items. Erica stopped in her tracks at one such stall, immediately causing shoppers to bump into her.

Excusing herself, she weaved her way towards it. Upon its top were bindings and an assortment of small vials. She picked one made from purple glass and held it up to the light. A shot of dark liquid was within. Uncorking it, she boldly sniffed the contents, sneezing as its concoction of spices assailed her senses.

The stall holder greeted her.

"What's this?" she wheezed, quickly fastening the vial.

"Why, it's 'Affection' m'lady."

"And what about those?" She pointed to a collection of items made from metal, china and manmade fabric.

"That's for when the 'Affection' has worn off," he said with a wink.

Erica was about to retort tartly when Michael appeared at her side. He looked aghast. "Typical! One of the less savoury stalls; I wondered where you'd gone to. Come, The Guild expect us at half past." And, returning the vial, he firmly led her away.

Erica looked back over her shoulder at the stall, pieces falling into place. "That would explain the cuffs they all wear: the Færies, they're not servants, they're slaves." She hesitated, clearing her throat. "Is Ashayla your lover?"

Michael blushed deeply. "No! I would never dream of it. Some do, but not I."

Erica relaxed. The thought of him treating Ashayla like that made her feel sick. "I did think you two had more of a sidekick thing going on, you know like Batman and Robin." She pondered their dynamics a moment. "Make that Wallace and Gromit. Ashayla's way cooler than Robin. Anyway, slavery was abolished in 1833, so why does it still exist here?"

"Slavery of people, the Bill made no mention of Færies. But, I agree, it is archaic. Having had my own share of slavery, I happily treat Ashayla as family."

"Wait. You were a slave?!"

"Once, a long, long time ago." He nervously scratched the tip of his nose.

She stole a glance at his wrists where she'd seen scarring. He was reluctant to say anything further, so they continued through the market in silence, its scents and colours assaulting them on all sides.

"Pray, who are 'Wallace and Robin'?" Michael asked, breaking the silence. "And what's a 'sidekick'?"

"You're kidding!" She said, looking up from a bookstore she'd stopped at. "I've got my job cut out with you! When did you stop taking an interest in popular culture?"

"Erm, probably 1858."

She stopped in her tracks and began counting furiously on her hands. He watched in amusement as she ran out of fingers and gave up. "That makes you over 150 years old?!" She stammered.

He doffed his top hat in response before disappearing into the swelling crowds.

Erica watched him go dumbfounded. She had no reason to doubt him. It explained his eccentricities, but damn! He looked good for his age!

But why 1858?

9
Welcome to The Guild

They left the market, walking along a grand boulevard planted with a parade of ash, elm and oak trees. A large, intricately carved Gothic building appeared on the horizon: The Guild of the KeyMasters. Its copper dome sported a fine patina of age that stood out against the pure blue 'sky' of Limbo.

Erica was still processing the most recent revelations about Michael but was aware she was being quiet. To seem more composed she stuck to safe territory: the weather. "How come there's sky here?" Erica asked. "I mean it's lovely, but I sort of expected darkness like outside the city." She shielded her eyes as she gazed up into the deep blue.

"The inhabitants found the darkness too oppressing and charged engineers to create a sky and weather system. Now they can balance the weather to ensure crops thrive and people's spirits are lifted. They also discovered it acts as a natural deterrent to Lost Souls."

"Sounds perfect."

"As perfect as perfect is."

On approaching the humongous structure, quirky gargoyles leered out at them: keys hung from their mouths and in their hands were Time Pieces. The grand main door to The Guild was set within an ornate archivolt, a large rose window above dominated the façade. Michael explained how the main entrances to The Guild, University and Library all faced inwards, to the Cathedral, representing equality before God. All were set within beautifully landscaped grounds; verdant trees, plants and shrubs broke up the heavy architecture so only hints of the other buildings could be seen. She craned her neck—she was itching to explore.

Michael checked his pocket watch. "Apologies, but a tour will have to wait. The Registrar is expecting us."

Erica reluctantly followed him up the steps to the main door. Her heeled boots *clip-clopped* on brightly coloured ceramic tiles as she accompanied Michael across the Central Lobby and down a corridor. After the heat of the sun, The Guild was cool with its high vaulted ceilings and dark panelled walls. Fellow KeyMasters, already on official business, walked primly down the corridor. Michael nodded politely to each in turn eventually stopping at a couple of men dressed in Edwardian sack suits. He shook the hand of the older gentleman with enthusiasm.

"Michael, my good sir! What a surprise! What brings you here? It's been too long."

"I've brought my protégé to be registered. Erica Shylocke, may I present the Honourable Sir Marty Hodges, a long-serving KeyMaster of renown."

Sir Marty Hodges raised his eyebrows. "A female heir? How very unusual." He then took her hand in his gloved one and bowed, kissing it gallantly.

Erica was taken aback and bobbed clumsily in return, narrowly missing his head. "Sir Marty Hodges, it's wonderful to meet you."

"The pleasure's all mine, Miss Shylocke. I had no idea that Michael had taken on training. Congratulations!" Sir Marty then leaned in close to Erica. "Perhaps you'll be able to encourage him to attend The Guild more often."

Erica looked askance at Michael who was scratching his nose shyly.

"And this must be your nephew."

"Changing the subject, I see, Michael. Yes, this is Martin." He gestured to the young man who shook Michael's hand before planting an equally gallant kiss upon the back of Erica's hand. "His training has gone well. He should qualify in the new year, shouldn't you, my boy?" he beamed.

"I certainly hope so, uncle!" Martin replied.

"He has a good teacher."

"Flattery will get you everywhere, Michael! I shall see you later this morning. Miss Shylocke…" he said, doffing his top hat whilst his nephew bowed. In return, Michael doffed his hat and Erica gave another ill-balanced bob.

"I wish you guys would just wave or salute or something," she muttered as the two men went on their way. "I've the worst balance ever." She cleared her throat. "You never mentioned it being unusual, having a female heir."

"Female KeyMasters are not uncommon, however, it's typical for females to succeed females and males to succeed males."

"And what's this about needing to attend The Guild more? I didn't realise my *sensei* was such a renegade!" Erica tutted playfully.

"I do my quota, but I find there are more pressing matters to attend than sessions discussing the importance of whether Blood Hounds should be allowed toys that squeak when in confinement at Claustrum."

"Point taken."

She found themselves entering a stern oak panelled room and joined one of several queues at a long, tall counter. Behind the counter sat several well-dressed clerks upon tall stools. Each clerk wrote with a jaunty peacock feather quill. The scratching sound of their quills and gentle *thud thud* of stamps created a soothing backdrop. Until an unearthly screech ripped through the air.

Jumping out of her skin, Erica looked around wildly. It was then that she saw feathers wafting from behind a gentleman and a peacock strutted into view. She gaped and looked at Michael who was watching her in amusement.

Whilst queuing, Erica entertained herself by trying to entice the bird closer with some chocolate-coated raisins she'd found at the bottom of her rucksack. Soon she had it eating from her cupped hands, cooing in delight.

"Michael!"

They both looked up at the surprised voice to find a man about Michael's age leaning through the entrance. He had brown hair that curled unabashedly from under his hat and luscious brown eyes. He strode over to them and on reaching Michael, shook hands, pulling him into an embrace.

"I've not seen you in an age! Where've you been?"

"Here and there."

"Like normal, then. And who's this pretty young thing?" he asked, eyeing up Erica as she quickly wiped her sticky hands.

"This is Erica Shylocke, my protégé. Erica, this is my friend Elias Moore."

Elias took her hand and kissed it—his lips soft against her skin.

She blushed. *This, on the other hand, was something she could get used to.*

"Lovely to meet you, Erica. I see you've befriended Kevin," he said, indicating the peacock which was nuzzling her hand for more raisins.

"Kevin? Oh, yes. He's gorgeous!"

"Gorgeous and plump. He shall make someone a fine feast one of these days."

"He's joking. Elias often jokes." Michael said on seeing Erica's alarm.

"I can be serious too…" Elias said, a peevish look contorting his handsome face. "Sometimes!" And he laughed. He reminded Erica of Marc. "Well, I must dash. I shall see you in the Chamber?"

They watched him leave with a wave.

"We were on a District Council together for some years and became friends," Michael explained as he checked his pocket watch. "What's taking them so long?"

They were eventually invited to approach the counter. To her annoyance, Erica found she had to go on tiptoe to peer over the top. The clerk looked down his long nose at them. "Good morning, sir, madam." He nodded to them in turn.

"Good morning, we've an appointment with the Registrar. Mr Nicholas and Miss Shylocke."

The clerk scanned his list, scratched off their names and pointed to the office at the end of the room.

"He will see you now."

Michael touched his hat in thanks and Erica tried bobbing, which proved difficult on tiptoe, so resorted to a salute.

The clerk sneered at her.

"I think I've found a new pet peeve." Erica growled as they approached the office.

Michael knocked on the door with a chuckle.

A prim voice came from within. "Enter!"

On opening the door, the Registrar greeted them enthusiastically. "Welcome Mr Nicholas! Welcome Miss Shylocke! Sit, sit! Do sit yourselves down."

Erica took him in.

Instead of another stern face, she was greeted by a man wearing a flamboyant waistcoat and tailcoat. His red and gold striped silk waistcoat bulged under his massive girth. He wore his blond moustache and whiskers in a well-lacquered style that blended through to a sculptured fanned hairdo, suspiciously like a peacock's train.

To the side of his desk, on a small table, was a gold urn filled with an elaborate arrangement of blooms and peacock feathers. In the corner sat a peahen nestled upon a pile of velvet cushions. It cocked its head at them with interest.

Erica felt herself staring and quickly sat down in the chair indicated. The Registrar flapped about them on surprisingly nimble feet. He fetched out some documents from a filing cabinet and presented them with a flourish.

"I was thrilled to hear you had a protégé, Mr Nicholas. I wondered when you would—it's taken its time. Unusual, having a female heir, but worth the wait, I'm sure. Now, your contract. Quite simply we need a signature from you both declaring she's your protégé and vice versa. Then we can sort out finances."

"Finances?" Erica looked up, worried.

Michael signed the three documents where the Registrar indicated.

"If you please…" The Registrar tapped his finger smartly against an empty space. Erica signed with the peacock feather quill, lamenting her childish signature in comparison to Michael's ornamental calligraphy.

"Do you have your bank details, Miss Shylocke? Mr Nicholas has no doubt informed you that you will receive daily remuneration whilst you complete your training to become a KeyMaster, this will be back dated to when you took up the mantle. When was this, sir?"

"November 29th, Actualle," Michael said, referring to Friday.

"Your bank details, Miss Shylocke." The Registrar held out his hand. Michael purposely avoided her bewildered gaze as she handed over her cheque book. The Registrar nodded in thanks and proceeded to scribble out the details into a leger. He blotted the page and handed back her cheque book before getting to his feet. "You'll receive your licence, timetable, map, keys, bell and Time Piece once you're officially inaugurated. As well as your periapts—your mentor will help you with selecting your Færie. All that remains is for me to say: congratulations and welcome to The Guild, Miss Shylocke."

***

As they left the Registrar's office, they were each given a copy of the contract. Erica looked down at her copy and read her pay. She gasped as she counted the zeros. "This is too much! It can't be right!" She turned to go back, but Michael caught her arm.

"Please. There's no mistake, consider it a gift. From me, well, The Guild, for your help. It'll help you finish your degree and go on to live your life as you wish. Please."

Her lips trembled. She could give up her job and focus on her studies, her life, everything that mattered. She could do everything she dreamt of. She wiped hot tears from her eyes. "Thank you, Michael."

"No, thank *you*, Miss Shylocke. For everything."

***

Michael guided her back down the corridor to the Central Lobby and down another corridor that branched off from it. This corridor was again tiled in richly coloured ceramic tiles and panelled in dark oak. Upon its walls hung portraits of famous KeyMasters, dating back to medieval times. Whilst the majority were grim-faced men, several grim-faced women made an appearance too.

The end of the corridor was panelled and within the panelling was a double-width door, opened to reveal a large Chamber lavishly decorated. Several male Færies in red livery stood at the entrance, one taking the names of attendees to be announced and two others which oversaw the cloakroom. The glimmer of metal cuffs peeked out from under their sleeves. All shared the same glowing tattoo upon their brows: a small key.

Michael and Erica had their jackets taken in exchange for cloakroom tickets, whilst the third Færie took their names.

"Mr Michael Nicholas and his protégé, Miss Erica Shylocke." The Færie announced in a clear voice, acting as herald; same in richness to Ashayla, though different in tone. Unlike Ashayla, its hair shone a deep, lustrous gold. It looked uncomfortable and unnatural in its livery.

They walked through the double doors into the vast Chamber. Along both sides were a series of springline windows decorated with intricate stain-glass that allowed the sunshine outside to flood within, bathing the oak panelling and blue leather pews in a kaleidoscope of warm light. Looking up, Erica noticed how the ceiling was panelled with tiles decorated with heraldry. In the centre of the ceiling was a circular panel split into five sections, each depicting a key like those that Michael had shown her.

Erica realised she was gaping and made a concerted effort to look less moronic as Michael introduced her to various KeyMasters who welcomed them as they passed by. An unsettling muttering followed in their wake. Then, amongst the sea of faces, she spied Elias' smiling one and felt oddly reassured.

Michael led her to a set of pews closest to a gilded throne set up on a dais. Upon these pews sat several other KeyMasters with charges looking either excited or as overwhelmed as Erica. Michael greeted them warmly, stopping to chat with an African lady. An African girl about Erica's age sat beside her and waved at Erica who smiled weakly back, taking in the finery around her. *What had she got herself into?*

They sat down with the others and Michael scanned the Chamber as more and more KeyMasters were announced and took their seats. Just then, there was a murmur.

"The GateKeeper Zhu Yaoshi."

"'GateKeeper'?" Erica hissed, watching a petite Chinese lady walk by wearing a traditional Chinese *hanfu* suit, a white silk jacket with long, sweeping sleeves decorated in red embroidery. She wore a red silk sash tied in a bow around her slender waist. A jade bracelet—identical to Michael's—was on her right wrist and a pearl of the darkest red hung from her neck.

"They're…" He drifted off, his skin paling.

"Is everything okay?" Erica asked, turning to find a man with a mane of white hair looking murderously at Michael. The man dismissed his Færie sharply and it joined the other Færies at the back of the Chamber.

"I don't think he likes you," she hissed.

"I agree." Michael returned to face the front, his jaw set.

There was a pause.

"Well? Who is he? Why doesn't he like you?"

He cleared his throat. "His name is Reuben Wolfe and… it might be because the last time we met was in court and it was my decision that swayed the jury to sentence him to Claustrum."

"'Might'?" Erica looked at him incredulously.

Ashayla's voice suddenly appeared in his ear. *"Michael, there's something wrong with one of the Færies, though what it is, I ca—"*

The herald's clear voice rang out, cutting off Ashayla. *"The High KeyMaster The Good Sir Tresillian Wakefeld."*

A jovial-looking man with a moustache walked past them, he wore a red and black silk gown over his normal clothes. A gold chain was about his neck, its links shaped as alternating locks and keys. He stepped onto the dais and took his place behind a lectern whilst his Færie took position behind a nearby desk. A massive tome was upon it. Opening it, the Færie readied itself to take the minutes, quill in hand.

A hush of anticipation then befell the Chamber as the herald made a special announcement: *"All rise for Her Majesty the Queen."*

Erica almost fell over as she stood and craned her neck to see. She turned to Michael. "Seriously?!"

He smiled and looked pointedly at the short grey-haired lady who walked past wearing a gown that sparkled as much as her crown. The Queen stepped onto the dais and took her seat on the throne.

The High KeyMaster motioned for them all to sit.

"Your Majesty, KeyMasters, trainees, it is with great honour that I welcome you to this morning's session of governance on this fine day. Before we discuss the matters at hand, Ma'am, it is customary, at the beginning of each month, to welcome any new trainees to the family of KeyMasters. They will join us, the Children of Time, in continuing the rich and ancient tradition your forefathers created to document and safeguard Time. May they proceed forth from here with wisdom and purpose: Sachairi Bruce."

A tall boy with strawberry blonde hair rose to stand before the dais, bowing before the Queen. He wore jeans and a tweed jacket. Erica eyed his painted nails with envy; she hadn't even thought to paint hers.

"Iminathi Naidoo." The African girl took her place next to Sachairi and bent her knees in a graceful curtsy. She wore a black and white Xhosa dress with matching doek head piece, multiple piercings were in her ears.

"Tsuzuku Miyamoto." A Japanese boy stood up wearing a traditional kimono and stood next to Iminathi, bowing low.

"Erica Shylocke."

Michael smiled at her and gave her hand an encouraging squeeze as she stood up. Taking a deep breath, she went to stand next to Tsuzuku and, steadying herself, bent her knees to curtsy. It wasn't as graceful as Iminathi's, but she didn't fall flat on her face, so Erica took that as a win.

"Henrik Strøm." After a few moments, a young man appeared next to her with a set jaw. He bowed deeply before the Queen.

There was a moment of silence as the five stood together. The High KeyMaster then continued. "Now for the important part, your oath. Please respond 'I do' to the following. Do you, who stand before the Queen, promise to train in the ways of the KeyMasters, to dedicate yourselves and your talents to this craft?"

"I do."

Erica heard the other four voices and realised she'd spoken too softly. The Queen had noticed and was looking at her closely. Erica cleared her throat nervously. "I do."

"Do you promise to safeguard Time, its people and their lives from corruption, manipulation and harm?"

She was prepared, and her voice joined in with the others. "I do."

"Do you promise to forsake the lives you know, to dedicate them now to the service of Time for as long as you shall live?"

Erica gulped.

"I do."

"I hereby confirm your inauguration and wish to personally welcome you to The Guild of KeyMasters."

A resounding applause erupted in the Chamber and the Queen stood up.

"I welcome you to the fine craft of the KeyMasters, set up and preserved by my ancestors hundreds of years ago. I thank you, on behalf of the nations of the world, for your pledge to commit your lives to the service of Time, its protection and accurate documentation. To help you in your endeavours please accept these gifts traditionally bestowed, as well as one's personal thanks for your service."

The Queen motioned and five Færies came forward, each bearing a red velvet cushion with gold trim, upon which was sat a lacquered tray holding a collection of artefacts: an envelope, a set of keys, new and shining in the sunlight, a small gold bell, a Time Piece and three periapts. They bowed before each trainee and presented their gifts. Gingerly Erica curtsied and accepted the tray. The High KeyMaster motioned for them to turn, to face the

Chamber of people, and as they did there was another round of applause.

A journalist caught their attention from behind a wooden bellows camera set upon a tripod. "A photo for the Limbo Times?" He then proceeded to make some adjustments to the positioning of the camera lens before preparing the glass plate with chemicals. They stood for what seemed an age until he declared it a success.

"KeyMasters, please take your charges to the Outer Chamber." The High KeyMaster said, addressing the mentors. Raising to their feet, the KeyMasters approached their charges. Michael took Erica's elbow and guided her to turn back to the Queen.

"Take a final curtsy," he said quietly as he took a bow. Doing so, she then followed Michael, and the others, round the dais and out through a small side door.

***

She rounded on Michael. "The Queen! And you didn't tell me?!"

"What difference would it make?"

"I might've practised curtsying for one!"

"You do have shocking balance," Michael observed with a smile.

If Erica's hands weren't full, she would've flicked him. Or worse.

On entering the Outer Chamber, they were greeted by a gentleman who appeared to be in his mid-twenties, wearing a fetching double-breasted jacket trimmed with gold brocade. An emblem of a golden eagle adorned his left shoulder. He was dark haired with an easy smile and suave moustache. Welcoming the trainees each by name, he introduced himself as their Course Tutor. Whilst he shook hands with the other mentors, he drew Michael into a brotherly embrace.

"What a difference a few weeks make, my friend! You seem brighter, it's good to see." He spoke with a soft Russian accent.

Michael greeted him warmly. "Erica Shylocke allow me to introduce my good friend Anatole Orlov. He and I completed our training together."

Anatole eyed Erica brightly. Bowing, he took her hand and kissed the back of it. "Welcome, Miss Shylocke. It'll be an honour to be your Course Tutor."

"So, you guys go back some years? I bet you've got a tale or two about my *sensei*, Mr Orlov," Erica said.

Anatole smiled, a mischievous glint in his eye. "Plenty! I always relish opportunities to embarrass Michael. Like the time we—"

"Desist! At least wait until I'm elsewhere." Michael laughed.

"As you wish, my friend," Anatole said before steering them and the others towards a table laden with refreshments.

Anatole motioned to some Færies, which began circulating with trays of champagne and elderflower pressé. "My friends, welcome. I am Anatole Orlov and as I said, I shall be your Course Tutor. You can call me 'Mr Orlov', 'Sir', 'Mighty One' or 'Anatole', I don't mind which. Currently there are just over fifty KeyMasters-in-Waiting enrolled at the university, including yourselves. As you noticed with the Inauguration, it is a prestigious profession and one not everyone is capable of or selected for. But before I give your mentors time to sit, eat and gossip I'd like to make a toast." He raised his glass. "To Time!"

Everyone raised their glasses in return. "To Time!" Together they drank, though whilst everyone had a sip Anatole downed the entire glass. Surprised, the trainees looked at one another, Erica shrugged her shoulders and downed hers. Sachairi followed suit, as did the others.

"I'm now going to borrow you from your mentors. They're aware of their responsibilities so can sit and make merry." He steered the trainees towards a large table with six chairs. "Let's start! A working lunch, please help yourselves to refreshments."

Michael helped deposit her tray of gifts upon the table whilst Erica piled a plate high with sandwiches, haddock, ham, salad, cheeses, and pastries—both savoury and sweet—before taking a seat at the table. Michael eyed her plate with a smile.

"I'm hungry," she explained sheepishly.

Anatole greeted them warmly as they took their seats. "To start with, it doesn't matter if you cannot speak English. In fact, I've been speaking Russian to you the whole time." The trainees looked at one another in confusion.

"Impossible, I was about to comment on your excellent Norwegian, Mr Orlov," Henrik said.

Anatole motioned to the Færies. "Language Charm. The Charm allows everyone to understand whatever language is spoken by interpreting it automatically into your Mother Tongue. By all means, practise your language skills, though it's not necessary when the Charm is cast.

"Anyway, before we get on with particulars. Anatole Orlov, Saint Petersburg, 1858. I opened a Gateway after a particularly bad argument with my then lover. For the record, I won. Right, three things: your name, where you live, how Time discovered you. Anti-clockwise. Go."

Tsuzuku was first. "My name is Tsuzuku Miyamoto. I'm the grandson to Isamu Miyamoto." This name meant nothing to Erica, but she noticed all except Sachairi react with appreciation. "I live in Kyoto Actualle and I woke my grandfather's keys."

Anatole nodded his head, impressed. He motioned to Henrik.

"I'm Henrik Strøm, son to Aksel Strøm." Again, Erica found her and Sachairi unfamiliar with the name. They looked at one another. Were they the only ones from non-KeyMaster families? "I live in Visperud Actualle, close to Oslo. I woke my father's keys."

Erica noticed how the mentors had quietened their chatter to listen.

Sachairi was next. He cleared his throat and looked down at his nails. He spoke with a playful Scottish lilt. "My name is Sachairi Bruce. I'm studying at Edinburgh University, but I come from Dunfermline. My boyfriend broke up with me after some stupid mix-up one night in town. I was heading home down Princes Street when I opened up a Gateway."

The trainees gasped in surprise whilst Anatole whistled. "That is rare!"

A muttering floated across from where the mentors sat, like the hum of agitated bees.

All eyes then fell on Erica: it was her turn.

10
Revelations

She cleared her throat, smiling nervously. She glanced over at Michael who was watching her intently. He nodded reassuringly. *Be natural…*

But how much should she say?

"I'm Erica Shylocke. I'm studying at University College London, but my home is in Bonsall, in the East Midlands. I opened up a Gateway at Cleopatra's Needle on the Thames."

Anatole choked on a sandwich; Tsuzuku, Henrik and Iminathi gaped at her; a stunned silence befell the mentors. Even the Færies stopped what they were doing to stare at her.

She knew Michael had mentioned how Anatole would be able to help them, but she didn't want to reveal too much in front of the other trainees so had purposely avoided mentioning her perceiving Michael or her encounter with the Wrathful. Judging by Anatole's shocked expression she'd been right to be cautious.

Anatole eyes darted across to Michael for confirmation, who nodded before being rounded on by the other KeyMasters.

"A monument? Heavens!" He spluttered. "Iminathi?"

The girl was still looking at Erica in shock. "I, erh, my name is Iminathi Naidoo, I am the great-niece of Zuri Ssanyu. I come from Pretoria in South Africa and I woke my great-aunt's keys."

There was silence. Erica felt all eyes turn on her. Though Sachairi didn't fully understand the magnitude of how she'd been discovered, he couldn't fail to pick up on it. He too was looking at her.

Great, I'm a freak even here. Erica sighed, inwardly rolling her eyes.

Anatole cleared his throat. "Right. Well, erh, three Normales and two Mondials; a good mix. Three trainees from KeyMastering families and two not." He added for clarification. "Now that we've introduced ourselves, we move on to your gifts. The keys are self-explanatory. From now on, you must carry them at all times—keep them safe and hidden from Actualles, people back home. Do not lose them. If anything happens to them there will be hell to pay. Secondly," he continued more brightly, "your Time Piece. Again, this must always be kept on your person; it'll slowly attune itself to you and fast become your closest friend. The bell will be required tomorrow and will hang in the Sonnastry to announce any travel through Time that you make. Each bell will be personal to you.

"Next are your periapts; you've three for now. Once you've selected a Færie and bound it to the periapts, The Guild will take one for its archives and you will keep the remaining two. Look after them well. Your mentors are tasked with assisting you in selecting a suitable Færie by your Matriculation at the end of the week. Most Færies will be available to you, but some are deemed too dangerous to summon. Just remember that they do cost and will be with you for life, so do choose wisely. And finally, this…" he picked up an envelope. "It contains your licence, timetable, map, reading list as well as a list of required resources. The Registrar should've already given you your contract. Keep all safe."

Sachairi whistled. He had opened his envelope and was looking at the reading list and list of resources. "This is going to be expensive!"

"Which is why you're paid handsomely. You've a week to get everything in order before I start to moan. Any questions?" He looked around the bewildered faces. "Excellent." He got to his feet. "We meet here at 9 o'clock tomorrow morning. I will give you a tour and get you set up at the Sonnastry. Do not forget your bell. Dismissed!"

The trainees gathered up their new belongings before walking over to their mentors.

"Not you." Anatole growled as Erica began to head towards Michael. She stopped in her tracks, jaw clenching in anticipation.

Anatole waited until the others had left then motioned for all Færies but his own to leave.

Once they were alone, he rounded on Michael, his eyes dark. "You, my friend, have some explaining to do."

***

So, Michael told him everything.

Summoning Ashayla, who joined Vozdukha, Anatole's Færie—a tall male Færie with broad shoulders—in casting a silencing Charm over them, Michael nervously scratched the tip of his nose and told his friend all. About how he'd met Erica, how she'd perceived him, the incident at Cleopatra's Needle and how she'd chosen the correct key for the Temporal Gateway.

Anatole was quiet. His dark eyes intense as he listened to his friend. He regarded Erica with wariness.

"If everything is as you say, Michael, then Erica's path is going to be very different. I've heard of *nothing* like this. KeyMasters don't have powers, we're merely sensitive to Time but, from what Michael tells me, Erica, you're unlike any I've met before. There's been no record of a KeyMaster breaking open charms upon monuments, let alone a trainee. No one has *ever* been perceived through the Ignorant Charm. It's preserved KeyMasters for centuries. Yet for you, *puff!*" He gestured with his hands.

Erica looked from him to Michael nervously. Her stomach was churning—she really wished she hadn't eaten that last pastry.

"The Guild will find out, gossip flies, even in Limbo." He smiled sadly. "But you've nothing to worry about. You're just exceptionally talented, and we're lucky to have you with us. You'll be able to further our understanding, which cannot be a bad thing."

She looked at Michael who was watching her. *Should they tell him more?*

Michael nodded, as if reading her thoughts.

She wiped her sweaty palms on her skirt. She'd never, *ever* told anyone. Her mother's voice suddenly leapt into her head: *you can't tell them—this'll be our secret.*

114

She closed her eyes, calming her thudding heart. *She needed to. This wasn't about her. Lives depended on it.* "There's more." She stammered.

"More?" Anatole looked at her stunned.

"But you must swear to secrecy." Michael insisted, leaning forwards in earnest. "The less people who are aware, the better. Can I trust you, my friend?"

Anatole looked mildly offended. "Of course, after all these years you ask! Of course, you can!"

Michael nodded encouragingly, and she took a deep breath: she'd never said it out loud before. She looked around with unease, despite the protection of the Charm she felt exposed. When she finally spoke, her voice shook. "I'm a Medium. I see and speak with spirits."

Anatole paled and crossed himself, muttering a pray under his breath. "And you think this ability is the cause of all of this?"

Michael nodded. "I cannot think of any another explanation. But there's still more."

"What?!" Anatole looked at him now with annoyance. "More? How much have you kept from me?"

"I've kept a lot from everyone, Anatole, not just from you."

"It explains why you've been horrific company these past two weeks. Do your worst. What else is there?" he said, shoulders slumped.

"We were attacked by a Wrathful."

"And?"

Erica looked at Michael.

He leaned forwards, hunching his shoulders. "And it was unreported; the Sonnastry knew nothing of it, nor did Christian and the Soul Gatherers. And there've been other attacks by Lost Souls on KeyMasters, undetected and unknown but, as far as I know, not yet fatal. I cannot confirm if any Actualles have been killed…"

"B-but how can this be? What about the barriers?" He looked from Michael to Erica and back again.

"I don't know. Christian is none the wiser either. I've tried to ascertain a pattern in the known attacks, though so far without success. All I know is, somehow, Lost Souls are now making it through the barriers undetected. We can only assume their numbers are growing but by how much we cannot tell as the Sonnastry have no record nor are they reacting well to complaints."

"But to what end?" Anatole asked.

Michael shrugged his shoulders and, suddenly exhausted, flopped into the depths of his seat.

"I shall see the Vice-Chancellor and alter the programme to contain combat practise. It's paltry, but it's the best I can do for now, until we know more."

"What?! When did it stop?" Michael sat upright again, a look of alarm upon his face.

"Months, my friend. There've been lots of changes. If you attended more sessions at The Guild instead of obsessing over Annabelle, you'd be aware. Or even took the time to read the Minutes!" Anatole admonished, wagging his finger. Michael looked bashful, his cheeks red.

Wait, Annabelle?! Erica felt her heart plunge painfully into her stomach. She looked at Michael. She'd assumed he was single. He'd never mentioned anyone. Annabelle. *Annabelle?!* She checked his fingers: no, no wedding rings. She realised then that Anatole was watching her out of the corner of his eyes and tried to appear less flustered.

"At least you've an excuse to be more present now, having an apprentice." Anatole teased.

Michael nodded thoughtfully. "I suppose I do."

Erica smiled weakly.

***

They'd left then, fetching their belongings and returning through Limbo. Michael asked if she wanted a tour, but she really wasn't in the mood and just wanted to get home—so she politely declined saying she had work to prepare for a lecture. She tried to act normal and chatted amiably about the other trainees, as well as asking after

Anatole and their friendship. But all the time, at the corner of her mind, she kept thinking: *who the hell is Annabelle?!*

***

She suddenly found herself bidding Michael goodbye outside her flat. She really couldn't recall their return trip from Limbo. Coldness had gorged its way through the pit of her stomach. She felt sick. Unlocking the door to her flat, she reached the sofa just as her legs gave way. Bringing her knees up, she hugged them to her, burrowing her head in her lap.

After goodness knows how long, she lifted her head and stared blankly at the gifts she'd been given: her Time Piece, periapts and keys. She'd had one of the most astounding days of her life and here she was moping. She'd met the Queen for heaven's sake! And all she could think about was Michael. And Annabelle. Let's not forget her.

She impatiently wiped away tears that she'd hoped wouldn't fall.

I mean, as if he could've been interested in her. He'd been kind, yes, but he hadn't shown any signs of attraction. And who could blame him? Compared to all his years of life she was so young and silly. But she still liked him. A lot. And she'd hoped he might've grown to like her back. But if he was obsessed with this Annabelle, she didn't really stand a chance. How could she better an obsession? And one he's probably had for over 150 years?

The shadows grew in her flat as darkness fell fast. She wondered: if she were to die at this precise moment would her sorrow bring her back as a spirit or was her grudge still greater, making her a Wrathful?

She cried into her knees.

Her mobile vibrated: it was Lizzie.

"We need to talk." Her friend's voice said sharply. "About earlier."

Erica wiped her eyes. "Sure."

There was a pause. "Wait, are you crying?"

***

He waited as Erica entered her flat. He half expected her to come to the window and wave as she'd got in the habit of doing, but she didn't. He frowned. It'd been a long day; she'd done well to cope with everything. She was most likely fatigued. He thought back to his own inauguration, but he could remember little beyond the suffocating tide of grief that'd consumed him.

He shook it away.

It was earlier than normal, but he'd visit her regardless. He set off, thrusting his gloved hands deep within his pockets and hunching his shoulders up against the cold. An obsession. That was how Anatole had described her. Michael frowned again. An obsession was something bad, but Annabelle wasn't bad. Perhaps she distracted him more than she ought, but he couldn't help himself. He'd made her a promise, and he always kept his promises.

***

Dr Lennard Johnson poured himself a cup of tea out of his thermos, dunked his biscuit—a chocolate Hobnob no less—took a bite and placed his binoculars once more to his eyes. He'd been sat in the Marsh Hide at Stodmarsh National Nature Reserve, midway between Canterbury and Margate, for most of the day and had seen some magnificent birds of the feathered variety. He'd come alone but had met some other friendly birdwatchers and they'd spent a pleasant day marvelling at nature. With the reserve flooding more in the winter months there'd been plenty of wigeons, teal and geese to see. But it was the starling murmurations he was most interested in.

As a professor of Ornithology, he was recording his observations for his current article on population and behavioural ecology of starlings. As such, he had been travelling to Stodmarsh twice a week since October to study the murmurations.

When an hour before dusk approached, Dr Johnson's birdwatching companions bid him farewell: they wanted to see the murmations out near Grove Ferry. Once alone, he proceeded to set up his video equipment whilst polishing off a couple more Hobnobs.

Five minutes later, he was ready. It had dropped cooler with the setting sun and he pulled on his gloves. He began filming, stating the date, time and weather conditions, panning out over the quietening marshes.

It was a clear evening, and the dusky sky was a tonal masterpiece of colours blending from the palest peach to blue-grey then through to the deepest indigo in the zenith. Despite the encroaching cold, Dr Johnson smiled and breathed in the serenity of nature: the world was beautiful.

It was then he noticed the silhouettes of birds beginning to gather over the marshes to roost: starlings. Within a matter of seconds their numbers had doubled, then trebled until above the still marsh was a swarm of tiny black silhouettes, swooping, undulating, dancing as one. The murmuration bent and twisted this way then that, performing a mesmerising dance across the marshes; their reflection flickering upon the water's surface. In unison, the chatter of the little birds was intense, and the soft whirling of their wingbeats pulsated through Dr Johnson's veins. It was a fantastic display of nature's mystery and majesty. Sadly though, as soon as it started, it finished; with the starling's landing to roost in groups, leaving the world once more empty and dull.

Not to mention dark.

Dr Johnson noted the time and was just filming a last shot of the marsh, the first rays of the rising moon shattering in bright shards as they hit the water, when he saw it: ignis fatuus. Or, more commonly, will-o'-the-wisp.

The orb of green, blue flame was hovering just above the surface of the water. Its luminescence an eerie beacon within the dark marsh. Dr Johnson moved his video camera to film it and gazed in wonder at the luminous flames licking its surface.

He'd heard of them, everyone had, but he'd never seen one. Sightings were rarer nowadays thanks to the reclamation of swamplands. There was no actual proven hypothesis for its occurrence; scientists couldn't decide if will-o'-the-wisps occurred due to cold flames or if it was the bioluminescence of micro-organisms and insects or some other such organic decay. But folklore on them existed worldwide. Some folk tales described the light as malicious and cunning, foretellers of doom and death. Whereas some tales described them as guardians of treasure. It went by many names: Pixy-light, Aleya, ghost-lights, Min Min light, Virvatuli.

He zoomed in to focus on the greenish flames that flickered in the cold night air. It was then that it started to move.

Zooming out he followed it as it bobbed along in a slow, almost jaunty, way towards the marsh water's edge where it stopped before suddenly whizzing upwards and vanishing out of camera-sight. Puzzled, Dr Johnson looked away from the camera screen and out of the hide.

He swore. Profusely. For at the water's edge, holding the orb in its hands was a shadowy female form. It turned the orb slowly over in its hands, seemingly caressing its flames. But, whilst the will-o'-the-wisp had lit up the marsh, its light could not penetrate the shadows of the form that held it.

Dr Johnson quickly zoomed out to capture the image on his camera and watched the form bring the orb close to its face, almost as if to kiss it. The orb sparkled cheekily, and the shadowy maiden cocked its head, listening to it. It straightened abruptly and turned towards the hide. The shiver that shot through his spine was electrifying and he felt his heart skip a beat. A cold sweat broke out instantly upon his brow and he held his breath. Surely not? It couldn't know he was here.

Then, just as abruptly, it turned and began to walk away along the bank of the marsh; the will-o'-the-wisp floating before it like a lantern.

He watched it leave and quickly considered his options. To go home and tell his tale or to follow it and perhaps be the first person to firmly establish the origins of will-o'-the-wisps.

He couldn't resist the scientific breakthrough that could be associated with his name. Imagine the books, the fame, the royalties!

Munching one last Hobnob, he gathered together his rucksack and filming equipment before creeping quietly out of the hide, camera before him. Looking up he noticed the orb of light floating westwards and proceeded to follow it, carefully picking his way through the dark marsh.

He followed it for what must've been twenty minutes, across the marshes and wetlands. Many a time he found himself stumbling on the uneven ground and plunging one, or both, of his feet in the cold, dark shallows of the marsh. But he couldn't give up, the allure of the discovery was too great, not to mention he was fascinated and bloody curious. What was the form? Where was it going? And what was the will-o'-the-wisp doing with it?

It was then that he noticed the orb had stopped moving. Carefully, Dr Johnson knelt, zooming in to get a better look. The shadowy form was holding the orb once more within its hands, turned it over almost lovingly. But, in the next instance, it idly threw the orb onto the marsh's water, where it skimmed the surface like a stone; its ripples distorting the moonglade on the dark surface. Once the orb had come to a stop, the form turned away and walked towards the shadows of some nearby trees where it vanished.

Frowning, Dr Johnson refocused his camera on the ball of luminescent flames. It had come to a stop several metres from the edge of the marsh where it was bobbing slowly up and down.

He crept forwards and tore his eyes off the screen to look at the orb himself. It was quite beautiful with its greenish glow and flickering flames. Its light seemed to pulsate like a beating heart, the closer he approached, the stronger it flared in turn. He stood before it at the edge of the marsh, watching it for the longest time, marvelling and wondering at its matter and purpose: hypnotised.

There was a sudden weight between his shoulder blades, and he was pushed forwards into the marsh water. Shocked out of his reverie, he turned to see the shadowy form close to where he had just been standing, its arms raised. It had pushed him! Its swirling mass of shadows focused and concentrated about its face, peeling back to reveal a face with red gloating eyes.

Before he could react, he felt strong hands claw at his ankles and legs, pulling at him. In turning to see his assailant his balance was lost and sensing weakness, more hands then reached up out of the dark waters, grabbing his shoulders and torso, bending him back towards the water in some morbid limbo dance. The closer he got to the water's surface the more hands appeared, thrashing about until the water itself seemed alive. His knees buckled and, in his efforts to save the camera from being damaged, he fell to one knee and was immediately succumbed by the weight of a crowd of bodies as they threw themselves at him in a mad frenzy, splashing water everywhere. They stank, reeking of putrid flesh and death. As they frantically grabbed at him, pulling and scratching in their eagerness, he noticed their flesh was soft and mouldy to the touch, covered in pond weed and nibbled in places by fish and other wildlife. Their eyes, wide and urgent, were glazed and rotten within their decayed faces.

In a last effort to be free of their clutches, Dr Johnson used all his strength to kick them off and pull away from them, but to no avail. It only encouraged them, and they became desperate, yanking him this way and that between themselves until he felt his elbow and shoulder joints strain before snapping: one by one.

With that he could fight no more, and they eagerly clawed him into the cold depths of their watery tomb. The pain was intense: his vision blurred, and he was close to passing out. He tried to hold his breath and kick to stay afloat but the crowds were too powerful, and he was broken.

Looking up to the surface of the marsh, which began to grow further and further away, he cried from the depths of his soul. The light of the will-o'-the-wisp twinkled merrily as he sank. With its light, he could make out the shadowy form leaning over to watch his demise; its red eyes glowing triumphantly as it drank in his anguish, sadness and torment. Having had its fill, it dematerialised into a swirl of dark matter and was drawn into the will-o'-the-wisp which pulsed once and began to sink into the water also, illuminating the multitude of dead just below the surface.

Having learnt its secret, his final breath then left him. Water filled his lungs and the world slowly dimmed. His soul dispersed in a black flurry, floating up, up, up... Lost and confused.

The lifeless, broken body of Dr Johnson hung in the waters, trapped in its watery grave. The camera sank to the bed of the marsh still recording, its red light flashing in the gloom.

On seeing the body go limp, the crowd of Bog Dwellers lost interest. Returning to their own graves, they turned their eager eyes to the surface, waiting until another chance of escape materialised.

Dr Johnson-that-was twitched jerkily and his eyes opened, lifeless and gloopy, his skin sallow. He sank to the marsh bed and turned his face to watch the surface also.

This time, they had a new companion, perhaps they would fare better.

Sire would be proud.

11
The Sonnastry

Erica tilted her head back and screamed at her reflection: she was practising her battle cry.

She'd woken up determined not to mope, not to worry and to live. That's why they had that saying, no? Plenty more fish in the sea. Michael could carry on obsessing over this Annabelle. After all, once she'd helped him that would be it. She'd go her way and he'd go his.

She gulped and wiped away fresh tears before screaming once more—for luck—at her reflection.

To keep herself upbeat she'd chosen her rose print tights to contrast with her black skirt. Her mobile buzzed, it was Lizzie. Erica checked the time.

Yep. She was late.

***

Michael had agreed for her to meet him at the corner of Cheniston Gardens at half past eight, so they could travel to Limbo together. She could see him waiting for her as she ran up Marloes Road.

Arriving in a breathless heap Michael waited for her to compose herself with a smile upon his face. "Good morning."

Erica gave a half salute as she leaned heavily on her knees to catch her breath. "How unfit am I?! Don't answer that!" She wheezed, wagging her finger at him before he could voice any opinion.

Michael remained politely quiet, choosing to peruse the depths of his highly polished shoes instead.

Once she'd recovered, they set off in the direction of Kensington High Street, casting the Ignorant Charm as they went. Recovering from a sneeze, Erica enthusiastically told Michael of her freefalling plans for their journey to Limbo which he listened to with the patience of a saint.

On arriving at the iron gateway, Michael encouraged Erica to use her own, new, Time Piece, to open the Gateway. Fishing it from the bottomless pit that was her rucksack, she looked at it briefly, admiring its silver filigree. Upon his instruction she took off her gloves and flipped it open to reveal multiple dials in various metals, some had numbers engraved upon them. One was set with small precious stones. Each dial decreasing in size the closer towards the centre they were. In its centre was a small clock face.

"The three outer gold dials control the year; the silver controls the month; the bronze controls the day and, lastly, the time," he said, indicating the clock. "Sometimes all dials need to be manipulated, sometimes not. For Limbo—"

She cleared her throat. " *'Limbo is between all Times and in none. It is the beginning of all and the end. Therefore, it is nothing but everything: zero'.*"

Michael looked up at her then. "You have an astute memory, Miss Shylocke."

Erica waved off the compliment and, with flushed cheeks, proceeded to manipulate the dials under his watchful eye. She felt the Time Piece begin to warm up as she manipulated the final dial and placed it upon the brick gateway. An electrical surge of intense heat and power flew through her and into the Time Piece, viciously tearing open the Temporal Gateway.

They took a step back from the pulsating portal.

"I suppose I shouldn't be surprised," he said, almost to himself, as he bent tentatively towards the Gateway, examining the opening. Sighing, he straightened and looked at her. "You certainly are an anomaly, Miss Shylocke. After you…"

Fetching her Time Piece before stepping out onto the starry void, Erica rubbed her hands together. Now for some fun.

***

Freefalling proved just as entertaining the second time round and Erica was chuffed when Michael finally gave in to her pleas and spun on the spot. Not as good as her Tarzan impression, but it was something.

She noticed what appeared to be tens upon tens of shooting stars streaking their way through the starry void, like confetti. When she asked Michael, he explained how they were other KeyMasters travelling to Limbo. Some floated serenely, others plummeted wildly and some even corkscrewed down.

"Helter-skelter?" Erica surmised indicating the corkscrews. Michael nodded in acknowledgement. It looked a bit intense; her stomach lurched just looking at them. Perhaps she'd give that one a miss…

This time, on passing through the mighty West Gate, both Erica and Michael produced their Time Pieces for inspection. Once satisfied, the Guards on duty let them through and they continued, over the moat and through the secondary gate. The market was once more in session and Michael insisted on Erica leading them both out of it and to The Guild. This way he knew she'd be okay if she came on her own.

It felt more like a memory test, especially with all the distractions of the market, but, eventually, just as the clock on the Cathedral struck nine, they arrived at The Guild.

"If you need me, notify Ashayla and I shall meet you in the Central Lobby."

Erica watched him begin to walk off aghast. "Where are you going?!"

"To the Bureau before attending both morning and afternoon sessions. I've been remiss and have missed much, but not again. I believe there'll be signs I might pick up on now that I'm aware something is awry."

"What about me?" Erica stammered, suddenly realising what she'd got herself into.

"You're going to be late for your tutor if you don't hurry. Anatole and the other trainees will be awaiting you in the Outer Chamber. I shall see you anon."

She watched him walk off down the only corridor they hadn't used yesterday.

"Anon yourself," she muttered looking down the other two corridors, trying to recall their movements from yesterday. In the end, she resorted to "eeny, meeny, miny, moe" and walked down the selected corridor. On discovering it was wrong, she quickly retraced her steps and headed down the correct one, eventually arriving ten minutes late.

She apologised quietly as she took her place with the group.

"Nice to know you're human after all, Erica," Anatole said, clapping her on the back. Erica smiled sheepishly and that seemed to break whatever tension remained from yesterday. They laughed good-naturedly.

"Good morning, my trainees! What a day we have planned!" Anatole began, rubbing his hands together happily. "Firstly, I shall take you on a tour of the principal rooms within The Guild before escorting you to the Sonnastry. Who forgot their bell?"

All trainees produced their gold bells, which tinkled in merry unison. Anatole wiped his brow dramatically before gesturing for them to follow him. He took them back into the Chamber where their Inauguration was held, identifying interesting points of architecture before leading them back into the Outer Chamber.

"This is where Guild functions are held as the kitchens and Færie quarters are just yonder," he said, indicating rooms beyond the Outer Chamber.

They exited and followed Anatole down the corridor back towards the Central Lobby. He pointed out several portraits of KeyMasters and mentioned how their names would become familiar through their studies into KeyMastery, Temporal Studies, Sonnology, Smithology and Færie-Lore.

He did stop at two old portraits though: one of King Edward III and the second of a man in medieval attire with a lazy eye. A key within his hand and a fly about his head.

"This is Dilston the Inquisitive, who's considered the founding father of KeyMastery. In 1349, during the Black Death, he discovered the existence of Lost Souls, who were wandering unchecked from Limbo and terrorising Earth. They relished the pandemic, feeding off its victims and the fear, adding to the death toll. Dilston the Inquisitive worked with the King to devise the initial lock that sealed Lost Souls back in Limbo, thus KeyMastery was born."

"What happened to him?" asked Sachairi.

"He choked on a fly. Always check your soup," Anatole replied sagely.

Moving away he gestured to the second main corridor. "Down there are the offices for general administration: Finance, Lost Property, Human Resources, Periapt Store, Loggiary (where master copies of all Loggias are kept) and the Registrar. And down here," he said leading them the way Michael had gone, "is the Refectory, the suites of the Queen, the High KeyMaster, their Cabinet and Færie Clerks not to mention the Bureau, where KeyMasters work and mingle."

They walked down a wide corridor, tiled in rich ceramic tiles like the other two and similarly panelled in dark oak. However, in contrast, upon its walls hung portraits of all the different High KeyMasters dating back to medieval times.

Delicious aromas emanated from the Refectory at the end of the corridor but, just as Erica was going to ask if there was the possibility of a second breakfast, Anatole gave a holler and entered the room on their right. It was a large room with tall ceilings decorated in murals. One side housed several heavy-laden bookcases whilst the other side was bedecked with tall windows that flooded the room with warm sunlight. Around the room were many sets of desks with comfy chairs, as well as clusters of armchairs. Some were already occupied by KeyMasters busy reading and writing.

Anatole was weaving his way in and out of these desks towards Michael, who was in deep conversation with a stout grey-haired man sporting hairy muttonchops. Michael turned at his holler and they embraced before Anatole warmly shook the hand of the older man. Looking over, Michael saw Erica and smiled, beckoning for her to join them. Blushing, Erica made her way over.

"Isambard Burnside allow me to introduce my protégé Miss Erica Shylocke. Isambard was my mentor." He added fondly.

The older man shook her hand before bowing and planting a wet kiss upon the back of it. His whiskers tickled.

"It's wonderful to meet you, Miss Shylocke. I was just congratulating Michael on acquiring a protégé. Especially one so beautiful. You must do me the honour of dining with me one evening. Have you ever played Whist?"

"No, I'm afraid I haven't."

"Capital! I shall teach you, my dear."

Michael steered him away. "You shall do no such thing; I don't want Miss Shylocke influenced by your gambling."

Isambard winked over his shoulder at Erica. "For one who plays so well, you're a horrendous spoil sport, Michael."

"Someone has to keep you in check!"

Anatole gave a short bow. "Excuse me Isambard. Good to see you here, my friend. I shall see you forthwith." He began to walk away, motioning for Erica to re-join the other trainees who were waiting awkwardly in the doorway.

From there, Anatole led them back down the corridor and out through the Central Lobby. Warm sunshine greeted them, and they followed Anatole through the landscaped grounds planted with oak, ash and silver birch trees. Rhododendrons in hot and pale pinks lined the undulating path which gave way to fragrant roses and luscious hydrangeas as a large domed building appeared before them. Unlike The Guild, with its copper dome and heavy Gothic style, this building appeared like an igloo made from smooth white marble which sparkled in the sunlight. Lines of gold inlay spiralled from its crown all around to its entrance in front of them, a dainty door set at the end of a short corridor that jutted out. The sunlight caressed it, dancing upon its marble and gold in glimmering delight. It was stunning.

Anatole turned, so that he was walking momentarily backwards, and opened his arms wide. "Welcome to the Sonnastry!"

***

It was the most serene place Erica had ever visited.

Once they'd passed through the small corridor, they entered the marble dome, which made up the entirety of the Sonnastry. At its crown there was a massive skylight, from which sunlight poured in with abandonment. A series of desks were arranged in the centre of the Sonnastry directly below the skylight, and it was here a group of Færies worked, busily writing in large logbooks. All about them, hung individually upon the intrados walls, were gold bells, spiralling up the sides almost to the crown itself.

The gold bells were arranged to encircle the workers in the centre, winding round and round the dome's marble sides. The constant dinging and donging of bells echoed melodiously throughout the structure. On the back wall, more bells were arranged. One set cast in silver was arranged vertically, with its bells ranging from small to large, to very large. The smallest bell, which hung at the very bottom, tinkled continuously. Whilst another group was arranged either side of the vertical set. These bells were of the deepest black and, again, in a variety of sizes, with the largest being directly above the silver bells. Compared to the airiness of the Sonnastry, these bells stood out menacingly.

Some of the Færies looked up from their desks as Anatole led the group of trainees across the marble floor towards them. A thin, waspish lady sat on her own before the group of tables, it was here that Anatole went. She eyed him suspiciously with dark beady eyes.

"Mildrew Sterner, always a pleasure," Anatole said cheerily. "I've brought the latest group of trainees to be registered by one of your Sonnologists."

She cast her eyes over the group with a sneer. "Yophiel has volunteered to look after you."

Anatole perked up. "Marvellous!"

Mildrew's sneer grew larger.

A tall tree-like arrangement stood at one end of her desk, from it hung a selection of small gold bells. She flicked one that was close to the bottom and it chimed like starlight. Its tinkle stirred one of the Sonnologists who looked up from their desk, pupils of the palest blue appearing. It was a male Færie with pale golden hair tied up in a loose top knot. One delicate tear tattoo adorned the corner of its left eye whilst The Guild's key tattoo shone from the centre of its brow. It was wearing a head set which held golden ear trumpets to its ears, as were the other Sonnologists. On noticing Anatole, a smile lit up its face and it signed its logbook. Taking off its headset, Erica noticed it smooth down its tailored suit as it approached, adjusting its mandarin collar and pulling its sleeves firmly down over its slave cuffs. Anatole, in turn, seemed to have become suddenly obsessed with his cravat.

He took the Færie's hand hesitantly in his but, instead of shaking it, he bowed slightly over it, as if in reverence. "Good day, Yophiel."

That was it? No flirtatious remark? No joke? A smile tugged at the corner of Erica's lips.

"Good day, Mr Orlov."

They looked at one another, hand in hand.

The group waited.

Mildrew sniffed loudly and the Færie was shook from its reverie, reluctantly releasing Anatole's hand.

"Please follow me and we shall begin the registration process." It turned and led them away.

"Welcome to the Sonnastry where all movement through Time is monitored and logged. As KeyMastery developed it became apparent that travel through Time needed to be documented, as well as any alterations that might take place. We also needed to monitor the Lost Souls and their movements. Experiments led to the discovery that movement and alterations in Time created ripples, vibrations. These cannot be seen nor heard by most beings, but they do resonate. Research revealed bells to be the best at picking up these resonations and making them audible for monitoring purposes. As such, Sonnology was born." Its warm voice echoed

around them as they approached some ladders. *"How many sets of bells do you see?"*

The group looked about them.

"I can see three," Tsuzuku said.

"There are actually four, look closely at the gold bells."

He looked at the gold bells that wound their way round and round the intrados walls. Every now and then, one sounded, each with an individual chime and tone.

"They are different sizes," Tsuzuku said, realising.

Yophiel nodded. *"Very good! The smaller ones to the side indicate the year, month and time of any travelling whilst the larger ones tell us who is doing the travelling—each has its own personal chime linking it to its owner. Anyone travelling through Time needs to register for a permit and a bell: that can include any resident of Limbo, in-service and retired KeyMasters as well as Soul Gatherers. As part of your studies, you're required to learn the art of Time Travel and have been presented with a bell. It'll hang next to your mentors' as theirs hangs next to their mentors'. Without it you are not registered to legally travel through Time."*

"Why are some of the gold bells dull?" Sachairi asked, pointing out the odd gold bell that was duller than the others.

"They are for those who have passed away." The Færie said, its eyes darting briefly to Anatole.

"And what about the silver and black sets of bells?" Henrik asked, indicating the two sets on the back wall.

"The silver set is arranged vertically and is known as the Cambimetre. It measures any changes made in Time and, therefore, History. The bottom bell vibrates constantly, as History is always being written, but the ringing of any other bells indicates that dangerous changes are being made. The more dangerous the changes, the more bells in the Cambimetre ring. Never has a full set rang."

Iminathi put her hand up. "Are the black bells the Soul Bells? My great-aunt mentioned there were some bells that monitored any movement of Lost Souls from Limbo into Time. She says Soul Gatherers use them too."

"Yes, your great-aunt has taught you well."

Iminathi smiled widely, blushing.

"Now, to register you. I trust that you all have your bells?" The group produced them in a tinkling serenade. *"Wonderful! To bond with your bell, so they become imprinted with your individual chime, all you need to do is simply breathe on it and say your name. Why don't you go first?"* The Færie said gesturing to Tsuzuku.

He looked stunned and bowed deeply. "You do me the greatest honour." Doing as instructed he breathed onto his bell before saying his name. As the steam evaporated, he let out a gasp and the others crowded round to see his name left upon its golden surface.

"Now, ring it."

On ringing the bell, it no longer tinkled like it used to but instead chimed with a mellow and peaceful *dong*—like those found in Buddhist temples. Tsuzuku looked at it in awe.

Henrik then followed, imprinting his bell, which sounded stout yet cool. Sachairi's gave a chime that reminded Erica of wild hills and heather whilst Iminathi's had a regal air to it.

It was her turn. Erica breathed on hers. "Erica Shylocke," she said, feeling the gold bell heat up within her fingers and begin to vibrate as her name appeared upon it in a burning scrawl. Yophiel nodded, and Erica shook it.

A death knell sounded: deep, dark, deadly.

All the Sonnologists looked up sharply from their desks. A look of shock upon their faces.

Yophiel gave a strained laugh. *"How unusual."*

Anatole and the trainees looked at one another nervously.

Brilliant. Just brilliant. Erica grimaced.

"Now to hang them beside your mentor's." Yophiel continued, gesturing to the ladders which jerked magically to life.

One by one, the trainees told it their mentor's name and Yophiel commanded the ladder to the correct place. Magicking the air to warp and wobble until it bent to reveal more space next to the mentor's bell, as well as a handy hook for the new bell to hang from. However, the honour of climbing up and hanging the bell was left to each trainee.

Each trainee climbed the ladder, and each hung up their bell triumphantly. On descending, Yophiel shook each trainee's hand. *"Congratulations!"*

Erica felt overwhelmingly nervous when it was her turn to climb the ladder. The death knell of her bell had shaken her. Was it because she was a Medium? Was she besieged by death? Is that why she could see and commune with spirits? Growing up as a Medium helped her to no longer fear death, but it weighed her down. Like a chain round her neck. A burden that shaped her. Is that why her bell sounded a death knell?

The ladder wobbled slightly beneath her. Michael's bell was, typically, over three quarters of the way up. On approaching his, his name emblazoned upon it, she took hers and hung it on the hook Yophiel had magicked.

She felt it before it happened. A surge of energy tingling within the bell. By the time it was on the hook, it was trembling violently. Then, suddenly it was ringing, over and over with increasing force. Its tremorous chiming set off the bells to its left and right, which in turn sent palpitations through to their neighbours. Within seconds, noisy Mexican waves undulated through the sets of bells until all bells within the Sonnastry resounded in a loud, unremitting chorus. A cacophony of different *dings* and *dongs* led by her bell's death knell.

The din was excruciating. Erica pressed her hands to her ears as the *dongs* echoed relentlessly. It was so loud she felt dizzy and lost all sense of direction. She clutched onto the ladder for dear life.

The people below were looking around fearfully, wincing, hands to their ears. Yophiel and the other Færie Sonnologists were contorted in pain, hands covering their ears, seemingly more affected by the noise than the humans. Anatole was desperately holding Yophiel, trying to comfort its distress.

Finally, the bells came to a natural stop and the echoes slowly ebbed away. When able to function without shielding her ears Erica made her way back down. As her feet touched the ground everyone's eyes were on her and, instead of shock, they now held fear.

12
Dr Finnegan

"Mr Reuben Wolfe."

Michael looked up as the gentleman's arrival was announced.

"When was he released?" Michael asked, leaning close to Isambard and his whiskers.

They were in the Chamber, awaiting the start of the morning session. Men and women had been arriving in dribs and drabs the past twenty minutes, their names announced by the herald.

Isambard looked over to the sharp-eyed gentleman with the mane of grey hair. "Since appeals for crimes of Time Alteration were introduced eight months previous. On their approval, he put forth an appeal and won. He was subsequently released in August."

"No one objected against appeals for such crimes?" Michael asked, appalled.

"Not *enough* people were in session to object, my dear boy," Isambard said, correcting him. "Politics is a game, Michael, and only a few decided to continue playing it after sessions were wasted over lengthy discussions into whether Blood Hounds should be allowed toys that squeak or whether people would prefer deluxe toilet paper to be used in the Water Closets or luxury hand soap. I believe we even wasted an afternoon discussing whether scones should be served with cream then jam or jam then cream! Do you know how many KeyMasters began to send apologies for not attending morning or afternoon sessions, sometimes both? Over four fifths. Four fifths! Those loyal to the Good Sir Tresillian Wakefield remained in attendance, as well as the odd cantankerous geriatric like me, but we're outnumbered by the Good Sir's supporters. So, when serious matters are raised and questioned, our objections are overruled by the majority, his supporters."

Michael paled and held his head in his hands. He'd been amongst those absent. He'd helped make this mess and more; he was culpable. He'd been so arrogant thinking his matters were more pressing, more worthwhile, that he'd let himself be duped.

Isambard patted him on his shoulders. "Do not fret, my dear boy. You're here now, that is what matters. There's time yet to make amends."

"But not to return him to Claustrum! Did people not remember the influence he had on Time? Five bells on the Cambimetre rang. Five! The most it has ever rung! Did people not recall the work needed to combat the alterations on Time he inflicted?"

Isambard waved his hands noncommittedly. "People have short memories: the young are too self-obsessed and the old forget. Calamities, trails, mistakes they all get forgotten in the rose-tinted eyes of mankind."

There was a pause as Michael watched Reuben saunter down the aisle of the Chamber chatting amiably to fellow KeyMasters and shaking hands. He seemed quite the celebrity.

Isambard stroked his whiskers thoughtfully. "When did you say these unaccounted attacks began?" he asked quietly.

"September was the earliest," Michael replied, equally soft.

"Indeed?" Isambard sank into his seat ponderously.

They watched Reuben with increased interest. When he approached, they stood to greet him.

"Good day, Isambard, nice to see you again. And let's not forget Michael Nicholas, how are you, sir?" He growled.

They shook hands, or, rather, squeezed hands.

"Well, I thank you. How was Claustrum?" Michael couldn't help himself.

Annoyance momentarily shattered his congenial demeanour. Reuben composed himself quickly. "An enlightening experience. Thanks to you."

Michael narrowed his eyes.

"Now, Reuben, your confinement had nothing to do with Michael," Isambard said soothingly.

"It had everything to do with him. If he'd held his tongue during the trail—"

"Perhaps if you'd not sought to alter Time, I would not have ended up on your jury." Michael interrupted hotly, finding his voice.

"You missed the whole point, but then you would, wrapped up in your self-centred banal life."

"And what point was that?" Michael asked, crossing his arms.

"That Time is a mess! It needs order."

"And you were the one to order it? You cannot play God! Time cannot be ordered because the people within it cannot. Freewill comes with heartache and mess. Surely you understand that?"

"If you were less self-righteous, people would ignore you like they ought." Reuben leaned close, talking in fierce undertones. "You're a Mondial and a negro; you're no better than dirt!"

"Out of turn, sir!" Elias said, suddenly appearing between them. "Skin is of no import. Have we not moved on from such baseness? Michael is an exemplary KeyMaster. It's no fault of his if his opinion was considered. An apology is needed."

Reuben faced the three men, eyes blazing. "I will do no such thing."

At that moment, the Færie announced the arrival of The High KeyMaster. People began to hurry to their seats.

Reuben eyed Michael coolly from round Elias. "This is not over. Now, if you excuse me, gentlemen." And with that, he gave a mock bow before taking a seat close to the dais at the front.

"Thank you," Michael said, shaking Elias' hand.

"Anytime, though I think it best I sat with you. Safety in numbers," he said, joining Isambard and Michael at their pew.

There was the shuffle of feet as the High KeyMaster entered the Chamber and all rose as one. The morning session had begun.

***

After their experience in the Sonnastry, Anatole led them quickly out and across the grounds to complete their tour of the Library and University. Both of which were in the same Gothic style as The Guild, but each was adorned with gargoyles holding accessories depicting their purpose. Namely, gargoyles wearing mortar boards or carrying Loggias for the University and gargoyles reading books or going *shush!* for the Library.

They visited the Library first, much to Erica's relief. Being surrounded by books immediately soothed her nerves and she gazed around at the vaulted ceilings, stone arches and pillars in awe.

It was immense, with multiple levels and nooks and crannies filled with sturdy bookcases laden with old tomes. Spindly spiral staircases took you up through the different levels. As all the walls were crammed with shelves, the only 'natural' light came from a series of skylights in the roof. Ornate steps and ladders were dotted about to help students access the many shelves. And, amongst the bookcases, there were desks complete with reading lamps. At some of these desks were students working on assignments. A few of whom looked up with interest at the new arrivals.

"I don't think the Library requires much of an introduction. It's a Library and here you find books. And lots of them. As part of your lectures, you'll be expected to complete research for essays and assessments, so you'll become familiar with its contents very quickly."

Anatole took them to the front desk where the Librarian, Miss Rimmer, greeted them warmly. Helping them to register for their Library card, Erica was excited to find out that she could borrow a maximum of thirty books. Triple what her Actualle University allowed her to borrow! Not that she could physically carry thirty books but that didn't stop her going weak at the knees. Anatole declared her mad and, from the look on their faces, all but Tsuzuku agreed with him.

They made their way along the central aisle of the Library, past rows upon rows of towering bookcases until they reached a cordoned off area at the end of the building. This area was guarded by a set of Færies in the same red livery as with those in The Guild.

Its bookcases had decorative glass doors that were padlocked. Some even had curtains pulled shut, hiding their contents from sight. Erica's curiosity was immediately piqued.

"This is the Regulated Area. Books in this Area are heavily regulated due to their dangerous content, hence its name. Apart from accessing it with your mentor to help select your Færie for Matriculation, you'll have little reason to visit. In any case, these Færies will only permit access to those with the appropriate letters of invitation and signatures. If you don't have them, be prepared for their wrath." On saying, Anatole produced a letter sealed with wax for each of them. "This is your signed letter of invitation to research and select your Færie with your mentor. As I've mentioned once already, they are costly and yours for life, so do choose sensibly."

He began to walk back the way they'd come, beckoning them all to follow him. "Come, we'll just have time for a quick tour of the University before lunch."

***

And it was a quick tour.

Whilst the exterior of the building was identical in architectural style to The Guild and the Library, the University's interior was totally different.

Split across two floors, there were five main lecture theatres: some with built-in benches and desks, some with just chairs. All were panelled with tiered seating that circled out from a central dais where the teacher's desk and lectern were. Floor to ceiling blackboards adorned the wall behind the teacher's desk. One lecture theatre was grander than the others, with large windows and ornate arches and pillars; as such, it doubled up as the assembly hall. In addition, the University had its own Refectory, study rooms, offices, a large and busy common room and, finally, a Combat Hall.

"A what?" Iminathi spluttered as they entered the immense space. A group of Færies in red livery were hard at work, clearing out and cleaning up the space. It looked like it hadn't been used in at least a year.

"A Combat Hall. Here you will learn practical aspects for your KeyMastery and Færie-Lore modules: fencing, archery, hand combat as well as practical Færie usage," Anatole said. "When it's back up and running, it'll include a perpetually changing assault course, complete with real Lost Souls."

"Sorry, I think I must've misunderstood you. You're going to get us to *combat* Lost Souls? *Real ones?*" Henrik said, the blood draining from his face. "My father said that that was no longer the case."

"Yes, and he was correct, it wasn't, until yesterday when the Vice-Chancellor choose to re-instate it as a required part of the training programme. For those pre-19th Century, knowledge of combat is commonplace, but very few modern day KeyMasters have such experience. It's our duty to ensure you're well-equipped for whatever might come your way as a KeyMaster."

"Are you saying that KeyMasters are still attacked? My great-aunt hasn't heard of any incidents for years." Iminathi declared, arms crossed defensively across her chest.

"Officially, no, but attacks do happen. Actualles can still be attacked by Lost Souls. And you did swear to safeguard 'Time, its people and their lives from corruption, manipulation and harm'. We're guardians of Time and its people, so we must, therefore, be able to protect and attack if the situation ever arose." Anatole counted smoothly.

"I thought that was the job of Soul Gatherers?" Henrik argued, still pale.

"It is primarily their job, but you're not going to be assigned a personal Soul Gatherer to permanently hold your hand while you travel through Time. It will be just you and your Færie. Say you stumbled across a Lost Soul on your travels... Even with warning, would you know how to manipulate your Færie to attack a Wrathful without training? Would you know which Charms to use? Which would be most effective? If your Færie were destroyed—and it can happen—could you defend yourself? The former KeyMastery and Færie-Lore courses were highly academic; they didn't, however, teach you how to survive. The new will."

There was silence. Erica was glad to see that Anatole had been true to his word and had managed to change the programme so quickly, but she was as uneasy as Henrik and Iminathi. Only Sachairi and Tsuzuku looked less ruffled at the thought of combat.

"Any more questions?" Anatole looked at them in turn. "I shall take your silence to mean 'no'. Lunchtime it is then!" And he led them out of the Hall and towards the University's Refectory with a skip in his step.

***

The rest of the afternoon passed with little drama. After lunch they had their first lecture in Temporal Studies with Dr Horatio Finnegan, a short and cheery bespectacled man in a tweed jacket. Erica had half expected it to just be her course mates in the lecture theatre, but they were joined by twenty other trainees. Apparently, unless you passed each course with a Merit you couldn't qualify.

They were sat at hard wooden desks arranged in tight, steep curves that circled outwards from a central dais where Dr Finnegan stood behind his lectern. His Færie, Tempus, magicked notes upon the massive blackboard behind him as he spoke, summarising the key points. Occasionally it would get bored and begin a game of noughts and crosses, or doodle caricatures of the professor drinking too much wine in the Refectory or having a bubble bath with a rubber duck. At such moments, Dr Finnegan would be roused from his talk by giggles, turn and reprimand Tempus before continuing.

"And how many of you have travelled through Time?" The professor enquired, in an attempt to restore order after Tempus had got distracted and drawn a doodle of the Professor enjoying his trip to Limbo via helter-skelter, arms in the air and shouting *Yippee!*

All but Erica and the four other new trainees rose their hands.

"Aha! New trainees! Welcome! But it sadly looks like you all have your first homework assignment. You must travel through Time and write a report on your experience before our next lecture."

Erica and the trainees shared a look: *oh joy, more work.*

Dr Finnegan continued. "Research indicates that we humans leave traces of ourselves at all times, like a slug leaves behind a trail. You don't always see it, but you know when it's been eating your lettuce. In the same manner we shed skin cells, we also shed some of our essence: the history of our lives, actions and choices. I have named this essence: Temporal Auras. These Auras, these traces of our history and actions, weave together to create what we know as Time. Therefore, Time is fluid and needs 'pinning down', as it were. Otherwise, we couldn't travel through it, let alone study and guard it.

"In 1357, a notable KeyMaster, Suetonius Clef, discovered that artefacts, particularly dated artefacts, emitted sensory wavelengths strong enough to allow portals to form, giving access to that artefacts' history and, therefore, Time itself. Consequently, the early KeyMasters decided to 'pin Time down' to mankind's physical environment, their buildings and monuments; physical heirlooms which are passed on to future generations. Heirlooms that are readily available and which can be built on and expanded by future generations, future history-makers. And which are, therefore, eternal through all Times. Unless they're demolished. But that is for another lecture.

"The best and most precise way to pin Time to a building is to carve a date on it at its time of construction, or to have one included somewhere on its architecture. This is the same for monuments, big and small, though their gravitas and importance pulls Time naturally more to them, a date secures it. Tombstones are particularly good at pinning down Time. Though they are a somewhat macabre way to Time Travel.

"It is through these entrance points, buildings or monuments, that travel can be made through Time. Travel might consist of a direct route, from A to B, or a convoluted route, from A to B to C to D and so on. Though be warned, the more convoluted the route the more at danger you are of becoming lost in Time as you must remember your exact way back." Tempus drew a KeyMaster lost in a vortex of Time to emphasise the professor's point. Its face contorted and desperate, spiralling and spinning uncontrollably through Time. "Unless you're a GateKeeper, who are able to see Time in ways different to us. But this is not the case for KeyMasters. Many a talented KeyMaster have ventured too far to return."

There was a solemn silence. A student raised their hand. Dr Finnegan peered over his glasses at the young man.

"What happens to them when they're lost?"

"We don't know. None have ever been found. Whether they perish and are absorbed into the very essence of Time or are rejected, much like our bodies reject foreign objects, and flung out to wander one or all the many dimensions of spacetime, remain to be discovered. It's not a question I wish to use my sabbatical to research; I might be old, but I'm not suicidal."

He shuffled his notes and looked around at his students, most of whom were trying to digest the idea of being lost in Time and failing. Some had true panic upon their faces.

"But I'm sure you five will be fine." He smiled cheerily at the five new trainees.

Erica smiled weakly back.

✦✦✦

Ashayla contacted her towards the end of Dr Finnegan's lecture, informing her that they'd be waiting for her at the entrance of The Guild. Erica found them underneath the large rose window, Michael had been bidding Elias farewell whilst Ashayla was regarding those Færies dressed in livery with curiosity. (Which, in turn, were eyeing Ashayla and its cotton clothing with a mixture of envy and contempt.) Michael's face had lit up on seeing her, but Erica was trying not to let the sudden jitters in her stomach get the better of her. After all, he'd spent the day in meetings, anyone would be interesting after meetings. There was this Annabelle after all.

Erica watched Elias leave with a sigh. *One handsome hunk down…*

"And how was your first day?" Michael asked on her arrival.

"Magical."

Michael raised his eyebrows at her sarcasm. "Is this regarding what happened at the Sonnastry?"

Erica looked at him warily, she had hoped he wouldn't find out: she didn't want him to start looking at her with fear as well.

"Anatole informed me."

"Wonderful. News travels fast even here. Well, it certainly didn't help. Also, why the hell didn't you mention the possibility of getting lost in Time?!"

"Because it is exceptionally rare; I have come to no harm over the years, my mentor was fine and his before him, and so on. You might be peculiar, Miss Shylocke, but you are sensible, as such you will come to no harm."

"Thanks." *I think...* How backhanded could a compliment get? She didn't know whether she liked being viewed as 'peculiar'.

"Now, is there anything I should help you with prior to your Matriculation?" Erica produced the letter from Anatole and he scanned it, nodding. He turned to the Færie. "Ashayla, in two days we will help Miss Shylocke select a Færie of her own. I think it would be very unwise of us to select one without taking your advice into consideration also. Please spend this time reviewing possible Færies to establish which the most suitable one would be for Miss Shylocke. I emphasise the word 'suitable'."

Ashayla looked taken aback by his request but recovered itself and bowed deeply. *"You do me a great honour, Michael. Thank you."*

"Not at all. Now, is there anything else I can help you with?" he asked.

"Well, I've homework from Dr Finnegan. I need to write a report on my first Time Travelling experience. But I don't know where to go, I mean, *when*."

Michael thought for a moment. "Well, if you don't consider it forward, I'm meeting with my friend Christian tomorrow evening, I know he won't mind you joining us. He's rather curious to meet the Actualle who saw through the Ignorant Charm."

Erica looked at him expectantly. "How will visiting him help with my report?"

144

"Apologies, I forgot to mention, one can find Christian in 1935."

"1935? Cool."

"Then that is settled. Ashayla, please contact Biggleswade and inform him that 'the Actualle' will be joining me."

Ashayla bowed before closing its eyes and dissolving into a cloud of glittering mist. Erica gasped, watching it leave gobsmacked.

"Now that that is in hand, shall we depart?" He offered her his arm as if nothing out of the ordinary had happened.

Quickly composing herself, she accepted it, smiling cheekily up at him. "Yes, but the question now is, my dear Nicholas, do we take the quicksand home or the flume?"

***

"What?! You're leaving!!" Erica covered her ears against Joslin's screams. "Why?! What have we done? Is it Marc? Marc! Get your ass here now!! MARC!"

Marc came running to their desk from 'Film & TV', a look of panic on his face. "Are you two okay?! What's happened?"

"She's leaving!" Joslin pointed angrily at Erica. "What have you done?!"

"Me?! What do you mean: 'what have I done'? I haven't done anything. Right?" He turned quickly to Erica for reassurance.

"Of course not. Neither of you have done anything. And anyway, I'm not 'leaving', I'm just reducing my hours."

"That's the same thing!" Joslin rounded on her, hand on hip.

"Technically it's not." Marc interjected.

"Oh, shut up!" Joslin snapped, turning on him instead. "You're supposed to be helping me!"

There was the sound of chatter and footfall as the main doors were opened to the public below.

"This has to wait. We'll talk about things *calmly*," he looked pointedly at Joslin, "during our break. Agreed? No dramatics."

"Don't know why you're looking at me," Joslin muttered, bottom lip sticking out.

"I wonder." Marc rolled his eyes at Erica. "Anyway, I'll see you two soon. If you need me, holler, but in a more professional manner, okay?"

Joslin watched him leave sulkily and flashed Erica an eyeful of daggers.

"Come on, Joslin. I'm not leaving you. I'm just reducing my hours. Our friendship's more than a dumb shop, isn't it? Do you honestly think I'd leave you for good and never come back? You're one of my closest friends."

"I am?" Joslin interrupted. Her mascara had started to smudge, causing her to resemble an overly tall panda with lavender highlights.

"Of course!"

Joslin pulled her into a bone-crushing hug. Erica, squished awkwardly against her friend's breast, managed to release an arm and pat her on the back.

"You are silly, Joslin."

Joslin wiped her eyes on the back of her hand, sniffing wetly. "I know. So, you'll keep in touch?"

"Of course, that's why I'm still staying." And it was the truth. The money she now received from The Guild for her KeyMaster training was so much that she didn't need to work. But she valued Marc and Joslin's friendship too much to resign altogether, so she'd kept two of her shifts, her weekend ones, when they were together all day. Plus, she had a feeling she would need some normality to keep her sane amidst all the crazy things that were happening. She'd thought to wait until after Christmas to reduce her hours, but with assessments already building up from her KeyMaster course, she'd need all the time she could get to cope with the workload from both her bachelor's degree and her KeyMaster course.

Staggering under Joslin's weight, Erica smiled sheepishly at an approaching customer. They were taking the crying girl in and obviously deciding whether to pay at another till. Just then, Joslin let out a massive snort-like sob and they made their getaway.

13
Temporal Imprints

"So, your grandparents are helping?"

It was the only reason Erica could think of to explain why she would no longer need to work all the hours she could. A lie, yes but better than the truth: *I've got a paid apprenticeship with a KeyMaster and have enrolled on a course at the University in Limbo for Time Travellers.* Marc and Joslin were amazing but even they had their limits.

"Yeah, they called to see if I'd be coming home for Christmas and were shocked at how ill I was and said I must be over-worked and rundown. They felt bad and said I mustn't worry, that they knew how important my degree was so would help me by paying my rent and any course fees. Mum and dad aren't pleased but what can they do?" A tall story, gigantic in fact, but nice. Erica sighed. She wished it were true. Her family were farmers, and her studying History had never made any sense to them. History had already happened, why did it need to be researched? Which was why they'd fallen out with her when she'd mentioned her wish to apply for a PhD. Her shoulders drooped.

They were in the staffroom on their break having a coffee and sharing a cake Erica had bought as a peace offering.

"That's good, right, Joslin? She's not leaving. She's just reducing her hours. If my family could help pay the bills, I'd do the same. But they can't. Anyway, I guess this means you'll have me all to yourself."

"Heaven help us!"

"You'll miss me when I'm gone!" he said, flinging a hand dramatically to his brow.

Joslin rolled her eyes before turning to Erica. "You're still coming out for the Christmas work do, right? On the 20th?"

"And miss out on legitimately wearing my candy cane tights?!" They laughed.

Marc looked relieved.

***

Michael had arranged to call for her at eight o'clock to take her to visit Christian, which gave her several hours after work to prepare dinner, finish her preparatory reading for her lecture tomorrow and look over her notes from Dr Finnegan's lecture. The reality of her travelling through Time filled her with a mixture of dread, excitement and curiosity.

Although it wasn't a 'night out', she still wanted to make some sort of effort. To combat the cold December evening, she chose a comfy chocolate brown knitted dress, kitten heeled boots and a faux fur jacket. She pulled on some purple fishnets for good measure.

It was as she walked over to her makeup bag that the spirit appeared, right in her path. Falling through it, she cried out as freezing cold air engulfed her—its coldness burning her exposed skin instantly.

"Oh, my dear! I do apologise! I'm giving you great misfortune, I'm sorry! First your arms and now this! I feel dreadful, really, I do. I saw you getting ready for a ball and wanted to watch. Are you hurt greatly?" she said, bending to help.

"I'm fine." Erica winced as she slowly got to her feet. Her hands were already blistering, and she could feel her neck and face tightening also. She grimaced.

The spirit shimmering next to her was one of her frequent visitors. She didn't know her name, all she knew was that she used to live in the house that Erica's flat had been developed from; it appeared Erica's flat was part of her former bedroom. The woman was always seen in a smart gown of the late 19th century, with lace trimming, though never in lively hues. Her hair was piled up on her head and held in place with an array of pins and slides of precious

148

metals and stones that twinkled even in today's light. She was a striking woman, in her mid- to late- sixties but with a heavy sadness to her eyes. Since discovering Erica was a Medium, she often came for company.

"I'm so sorry! You must be getting very tired of me. I did so hope I wouldn't harm you on this occasion, especially with you on your way out for a social gathering. Do you have any of that ointment left with which you can dress your wounds?" The spirit asked in echoey tones.

"In the kitchen," Erica said as she began to make her way to her little kitchenette. She fumbled as she fetched out a pot of cream from the nearest cupboard, twisting the top off awkwardly. The cream was pungent and made her sneeze several times.

"Heavens! I hope you're not catching a chill as well!" she said, worrying her lip. She watched as Erica applied the cream to her hands. It had an instant cooling affect and Erica's skin became supple enough for her to move without pain. Quickly and deftly, she wrapped her hands in bandages from the same cupboard and proceeded to slather the cream on her face and neck.

"Don't worry. It's just the oils in the cream. How do I look?" Erica asked putting the things away and turning to face the lady.

"Much better, and the swelling's virtually gone too! You were so excited about going out, it was quite a delight to see; I am so sorry. You reminded me of my daughters preparing for a ball and I wanted to watch. It always made me smile seeing their excitement." She looked down at her hands suddenly, overwhelmed by past emotions.

"No need, just give me a bit more warning next time, okay?"

"You're too kind. Most mediums don't take kindly to burns."

"Well, they do hurt, and they aren't pretty." Erica sighed. Make-up would have to wait for another occasion. She was glad she didn't have to lie to Michael because she couldn't think of a believable excuse. She doubted 'I had the sudden urge to clean the oven whilst it was on' would've worked. "You mentioned your daughters. Did you and your family used to live here?"

"Only some of my family. Our real family home was in Regent's Park; it used to be such a happy place." A distant look appeared across her face, softening her eyes, a ghost of a smile on her lips. She looked momentarily, blissfully happy. Then the sadness returned. *"I moved here on my own with my last daughter after my husband passed away. He... he took his life, you see..."*

"I'm so sorry to hear that!" Erica said, sitting on the sofa.

The spirit sat down next to her. *"Thank you, my dear. You're so kind. He could bear it no longer... Our eldest daughter had di—"*

It was then that the periapt Erica had been given pulsed brightly.

"What a curious artefact..." The spirit canted her head with interest.

"That's my call. I have to go, but I'll be back later."

"Modern technology is a wonder. Take care out, my dear."

Erica waved her goodbyes, grabbing her handbag, gloves and keys—both sets—on her way out and locking the door behind her. Making it down the stairs she opened the main door and, turning to look back up the stairs, saw the spirit stepping through the door of her flat, her eyes watching her leave longingly.

***

"You're hurt?!"

Michael rushed forwards as soon as the streetlights fell on her face, revealing the remnants of her burns. Instinctively, he lifted her chin up with his hand, turning her face slowly from side to side. "Who did this?"

She shuddered at the warmth of his fingertips against her sore skin. "A spirit, she didn't mean it. I walked through her by accident. I'm not sure whether I should go tonight, what do I tell Christian?"

"If you hide in the shadows, he might not notice them."

She gave him a flick.

"I've applied my ointment; it's helped but I've never had burns on my face before so I'm not sure how they'll heal. The ones on my hands will take a couple of days. I'll have to go home soon I guess, my ointment's running low. My mum makes it for me."

"Your mother's a Medium also?" He took his hand away.

Erica nodded. "It runs through the female line."

"I believe you said your home was in the Midlands?"

"That's right; I haven't been back in a long time."

"They must miss you greatly. Will you visit them this Christmas?"

"I ought to." Erica tried to sound cheerful. She really didn't want to have to think about going home; she knew she needed to talk with her parents about the idea she'd had of doing a PhD or risk bearing a grudge. But she really didn't want Christmas to be filled with them moaning and arguing with her. Better that than turning into a Wrathful though.

"The burns don't pain you?" He asked, offering her his arm.

She accepted it, linking her arm through his. She loved the excuse it gave for her to lean in close. "Not anymore, they're just uncomfortable. I'll be fine. I'll have to call in sick tomorrow though." She saw his puzzled expression. "To take the day off work—there's no sensible excuse for these sudden burns. So, what's Christian like?"

"Exuberant and slightly eccentric, which is probably why we're good friends."

"'Probably'?" Erica raised her eyebrows to match her dramatic tone, making him chuckle, but regretted it immensely when pain tore through her.

"I can see we'll have to avoid sarcasm and any excessive facial gestures," Michael said.

"I'll find a way, even if I have to pass messages onto Ashayla to read out."

"Heaven forbid!"

They walked away observed from on high. The spirit's shimmering fists clenched the curtains in Erica's flat, her face grim. She looked as if she herself had seen a ghost.

***

151

The moon was high in the sky, hidden only by partial cloud. Its light cleansing in its coolness. Michael led her north towards the lively glow of High Street Kensington. Just as they wound their way right onto Wrights Lane, Michael stopped her and took out his periapt from the inner pocket of his jacket.

"For what we're going to do we need the Ignorant Charm. If you could remove your periapt, Miss Shylocke." Erica did as she was instructed. "Can you remember the incantation?" Erica looked at him blankly. "It's reassuring to know your memory is as good as the next: *Actualles ignarus*."

Erica held her own periapt in her gloved palm and looked upon its tear-shaped stone which sparkled in the streetlight. It really was beautiful. Touching the stone, she repeated the incantation. "*Actualles ignarus*."

The stone in the centre flashed, rippling out beyond its silver casing and over Erica's hands and arms until it spread up and down her body. She felt herself go dim, as if fading from real life. *Is this what dying's like?* Just then, her ears popped, and she sneezed.

Michael chuckled as he pocketed his periapt. "It is a unique sensation. In time, you'll accustom yourself to it. That is, if you do decide to stay on as KeyMaster." He added quickly.

Erica replaced the periapt and looked around her. It was as if someone had placed a filter on the world, accentuating its vivacity. Although she felt different: secondary, dim. Detached. She didn't like it.

"How can you live like this? In the background, seeing but not really seeing?" She complained, shuddering. They continued up Wrights Lane.

"It becomes second nature. Sometimes you even enjoy it, however, I admit, it has caused KeyMasters to become complacent with regards to fulfilling our duties. Nonetheless, tonight I think you'll appreciate it. Now, are you ready to see Time, Miss Shylocke?"

Erica looked up, her eyes shining in anticipation.

***

They left Wrights Lane and were faced with the colourful tumult of High Street Kensington which teemed with commuters, shoppers and tourists. Buses, taxis and cars made their noisy way along the busy road. Neon shop signs and jaunty Christmas lights lit up the winter night sky. Everywhere was light and life, laughter and chatter. It was intoxicating. Erica stopped and drank in the sights and sounds greedily, brighter and sharper than normal. She hadn't noticed how festive things were looking; she could feel herself becoming giddy with excitement like she had when she was a child. Was that a side effect of the Charm?

Michael led her up the High Street, towards Kensington Gardens. "In 1357, Suetonius Clef discovered wavelengths from dated artefacts were strong enough to allow access to Time. Although thousands of openings can, in theory, be created; Matter thins, and Time becomes distorted, consequently Temporal Gateways are restricted to dated artefacts in existence. Like the Gateway you selected the key for when you first visited Limbo." They had come to a stop outside the iron gate with its cherub still looking cheerily down. "However, our travels to Christian require an alternative route. This way!" And he walked off up the pavement.

"How come?" Erica inquired, trotting to keep up. She had thought that she would have to concentrate on weaving in and out of pedestrians, but the Charm seemed to naturally repel people.

"One can find Christian in 1935."

Erica looked quizzically at him. Unable to think why 1935 would impact so heavily on the way they travelled. Michael came to a halt and watched her. He was testing her. Erica sighed and surveyed the High Street, trying to ignore its vivacity and colour. What had Michael said, something about Gateways being restricted to dated artefacts: wells, memorials, plaques, buildings… They had stopped near the entrance to the Underground station, across the road was a McDonalds busy with customers. She ignored the interior and looked up at the carved stone plaque on the building's side; it was inscribed with a date and message. But Michael said they wouldn't be using a standard Temporal Gateway…

"Has it got something to do with the buildings themselves? I'm no expert on architecture, but if it's not the dates on the buildings is it the actual structures?"

A boyish grin played upon his lips. "A fair play, Miss Shylocke."

They continued down the High Street. "Derry and Toms began as a small drapery store in 1853, expanding by 1870 to take over the surrounding buildings. However, in 1920 it was acquired by John Barker who renovated it in the popular Art Deco style of the time, opening it in 1933." He motioned to the grand white building before them. Stiff carved columns of white stone reached high up into the night sky; striking facades, stylised carvings and ironwork winked through the spotlights on its flanks.

"So, it's a Victorian building encased in a 20th century one?"

"In a way, yes. Which can complicate matters." They paused outside the white stucco building. Michael Nicholas took off one of his leather gloves and motioned for her to do the same. "What did Suetonius Clef discover?"

She paused, caught off guard. "Erm, wavelengths from dated artefacts?"

"Correct. Wavelengths that you, as a KeyMaster, can sense if patient." With that he placed his hand upon the building's stone surface. She looked at him in disbelief.

"Seriously?"

He looked pointedly at her.

"I'll look like a tree-hugging hippy."

"I still haven't the foggiest idea what a hippy is, but it's impossible; this is a building, not a tree, Miss Shylocke. In any case, that's why you're under the influences of the Charm."

Erica sighed, took off a glove and looked down at her bandaged hand. She gritted her teeth and placed it next to his. "Fine! What do I need to do?"

"Close your eyes and concentrate. What can wavelengths create?" he asked, closing his eyes.

"Erm… Ripples? Warmth?" Erica hazard: physics really wasn't her forte.

"Precisely; it would be best if you closed your eyes to concentrate on feeling them."

She watched him with his eyes closed and sighed. She was certainly glad for the Ignorant Charm! Taking advantage, she snuck a look at him. His dark sultry skin and broad shoulders gave him a distinguished air. She noticed the elegant arch of his brow and the angle of his chin. She could see lines of grief around his eyes. *Will he ever tell me his story?*

Checking his eyes were still closed, she stole a look at the curve of his lips…

"Miss Shylocke…" his voice made her jump. His aquamarine eyes snapped open, their pupils focusing on her. "I do hope you're concentrating."

It's no wonder they say eyes are the windows to the soul.

"Of course!"

His smile reached his eyes before they closed once more.

"What am I listening for exactly?" she said, following suit.

"What is it you hear?"

Erica paused to listen. All that came to her ears were the sounds of a typical busy night in downtown London. "The usual: people, vehicles, machinery."

"Don't listen with your ears, listen with your hand. Feel it against your skin."

Erica opened her eyes and looked at him impatiently. He was still standing exactly as she had last seen him, bare hand against the stonework, patient, calm and unfathomable. He wasn't joking. She closed her eyes once more and 'listened' with her hand.

In addition to the obvious cold, she could feel the vibrations of the passing people and traffic. The slight shudders their impact made on the stonework, up and down the building. And beyond those shudders something else, something deeper.

"It's known as the Temporal Essence. To me it has always had the feeling of a heartbeat. Some KeyMasters even go so far as describing buildings as having souls. Which tallies with our personification of buildings in speech."

"If walls could talk!"

Michael laughed at her reply and she felt it ripple through the stonework and into her arm. Then she heard them: deep, powerful, steady. Two 'heartbeats', one deeper than the other, stronger, steadier. The second heartbeat was lighter, quicker, though just as strong. She then realised that the sounds she could hear and thought came through her ears were in fact coming through her hands. The deeper heartbeat carried with it echoes of horses' hooves on cobbles, the laughter of children and clatter of walking sticks, bells of a distant church, screams and tears from the dead of night—she frowned, how odd. Whereas the lighter heartbeat carried with it echoes of motorcar engines, horns and traffic, laughter and music, bomb raids and explosions. Screams and fire. She could almost smell the acrid smoke; it was so vivid.

Erica abruptly removed her hand from the stonework and stared at the wall before her, eyes wide. "Can you hear that?! The echoes!"

His eyes snapped opened. "'Echoes'? What echoes?" Erica described them quickly, the good and the bad. "Heavens, Temporal Imprints! Fascinating. I've heard of them but never had the fortune to experience them myself."

"'Fortune'? I can hear people dying!"

"And you can hear them living. What's the difference to now?"

Erica held herself as she looked around her, there were people shopping with their loved ones, but also angry people talking down their mobiles. Living, dying, happy, sad; history really did repeat itself.

"It's the unfortunate truth about humans; we neither like change nor do we change." Michael opened his jacket to produce his Time Piece from his waistcoat pocket. He flipped it open to reveal multiple dials of different metals upon its face. In its centre was a small clock face, its second-hand *ticked* merrily. "These set the year," he indicated the three slender outer gold dials; he turned one to the 19th century, the next to the 30s and then the last to 5. "This sets the month," The next dial in was silver with small precious stones inlaid on it: birthstones. He turned it so that the topaz matched up with the year. "And this one sets the day," He indicated to the next dial in, which was bronze, and had roman numerals engraved upon it: I – XXXI, one for each day of the month. He again turned it until they all matched: today but in 1935. He then placed the Time Piece against the stone wall of the building.

"When all are set correctly the Temporal Essence is sought out by the Time Piece—in this case the younger, newer one—and the correct Gateway will be opened." On saying there was a bright flash and light streaked from the Time Piece, cutting through the building to reveal a dark swirling vortex.

Michael Nicholas took away his Time Piece. "Ladies first."

14
Cerebral Projection

She looked at the vortex stretching out before her, the Gateway of light crackled, pulsating and scattering splintered shadows everywhere. Thousands of multicoloured trails spiralled their way deep into the vortex's centre. At the other end was High Street Kensington of 1935, dim and distant. Enticing.

Erica took a cautious step into the dark portal. Soundless wind buffeted her on all sides. She continued forwards. The floor was solid underfoot, despite looking like a murky winter's night. Mist swirled amidst the light trails in a corkscrew along the sides of the vortex all the way to the portal's end. She took another cautious step forward and was almost knocked off her feet by the wind that rushed from the other end. On all sides, a fleeting, scratchy haze of images whizzed by her; swirling until she didn't know which way was up or down. People walked past with their shopping, schoolchildren, mothers pushing pushchairs; then, costumes changed, and hairstyles too, as well as the shop facades, with neon signs and Christmas lights giving way to printed signage and old-fashioned streetlamps. Erica could see governess' walking with their charges and nannies pushing smart perambulators. Modern day cars gave way to vintage motorcars as the years sped by; people walked to and fro, their fashions changing constantly, as did the people: accidents, lovers, arguments, crying, laughing, screaming. She watched the constant flow of history whizz by with each step. Her head spun. It was like watching decades of footage on hyper-rewind. Her breath came in ragged short gasps: it took all her effort to focus on the end of the vortex and keep walking forwards. Michael appeared at her side.

"You don't see it? The history? The people?" Her voice was strained even to her ears.

He shook his head and, seeing her struggle, took her by the elbow and steadied her as she laboured on.

By the time they took their final step out into 1935, she felt mentally exhausted. Her knees quivered, and she stood shaking, catching her breath. "Well, that was an experience." She laughed weakly.

"I can only assume it's because you're a Medium that you—" Michael stopped abruptly. "Erica!" He sounded shocked, even alarmed. She turned to find him reaching for her face. "Your burns!"

She felt her cheeks and neck and realised there was no discomfort: no tautness nor blistering. Her burns had gone.

"Time heals all wounds…"

***

"Good evening, Mr Nicholas." Biggleswade greeted them with a pretentious sniff whilst a footman took their jackets. "Miss…" He raised his eyebrow towards Erica.

"Good evening, Biggleswade. This is Miss Shylocke. Mr Blake is expecting her," Michael explained.

"Of course. Welcome Miss Shylocke. Mr Blake will see you in the drawing room." Biggleswade turned and led them across the herringbone floor. The drawing room was at the front of the house and decorated in rich red damask wallpaper. From the ornate ceiling hung two heavy chandeliers which sparkled cheerily from the electric glow of their lights. A warm fire roared from the marble fireplace whilst two Chesterfield sofas flanked it on either side.

As soon as Biggleswade left them, Michael strode over to a sideboard and helped himself a cognac. It was then that Christian Blake II entered, smartly dressed in a tailored tuxedo and white shirt with peaked lapels. He watched as Michael took a large gulp of his cognac.

"I say, Nicholas, whatever is the matter?"

Michael pointed at Erica, who was standing close to the fire. Christian looked her up and down.

She waved back shyly. "Hello, I'm Erica. Erica Shylocke."

"As expected, I have heard much about you, Miss Shylocke." Erica looked surprised. Christian looked back at Michael. "What the blazes happened?"

Michael shook his head, finishing his drink before pouring himself a second.

Erica cleared her throat. "As you probably know, I'm training to be a KeyMaster. Michael's been teaching me how to enter Time using a building's Temporal Essence, but I ended up also seeing its Temporal Imprints. Time also ended up healing some burns I'd got. Then on our journey here I noticed a trail we'd—"

"A Temporal Aura?!" Christian interrupted sharply.

Erica nodded.

He looked at her agape.

Michael poured him a shot from the same decanter and held it out for him. Christian went over and took the proffered glass, downing it in one. Michael poured him a second.

"By Jove!" He said sitting heavily on a sofa. Michael sat down next to him, loosening his cravat in a most becoming way.

Chiding herself, Erica busied herself with getting a drink. She looked for a gin. Finding none, she then selected a red wine and poured herself a small glass. Taking a sip, she sat herself on the sofa opposite them. The two men were staring into the depths of the fire, looks of wonder and shock plastered on their faces.

"By Jove!" Christian repeated, stirring from his reverie. "First the Charm then this! I've never heard anything like it!"

"I know. It's totally unheard of."

"Totally." Christian glanced over at Erica, struggling to control his curiosity.

Erica watched him over the rim of her glass in amusement.

Michael looked up and saw him. "Christian, I brought Miss Shylocke over to introduce you to my protégé, not to run tests on her." He reminded him strongly.

"I know, my dear fellow, but a Temporal Aura!" His eyes shone brightly. "Imagine what this could mean to the field of Temporal Studies! All the theories squashed and confirmed, once and for all!"

"No. I forbid it."

"What sort of tests?" Erica asked from her seat.

"Miss Shylocke, you're not obliged to indulge him." Michael said sternly, leaning forwards.

"I know, but I don't mind simple tests. I'm just as curious. Selfishly, it might help me get some answers."

"Ha!" Christian finished his drink in one triumphant gulp and stood up. "Miss Shylocke, come with me…" He beckoned for her to follow him before disappearing out the door. Erica quickly got to her feet and trailed after him, her heels sounding primly upon the hall floor. Michael sighed and followed them down the hall to the back of the house. Christian opened a door to reveal a library, of sorts. Three of its walls were covered from top to toe with shelves upon shelves of books and journals and random artefacts. A display cabinet dominated the last wall. Within were all manner of weapons and other odd contraptions. There was a window in the far corner overlooking the dark garden. In the centre of the room were two large desks atop of which was an array of scientific equipment. A fire burned merrily in the stone fireplace.

"Is Lunita not here?" Michael asked, looking around.

"She's with the *others*," he said pointedly. "They're having their weekly meeting."

"Who's Lunita?" Erica asked from where she was browsing through the books on the nearest bookshelf.

"My girl," Christian gushed proudly. "Though old Nicholas here doesn't totally approve."

Erica glanced with interest at Michael who, avoiding her gaze, crossed the room to where a violin case sat upon a table close to the fire. Setting his glass down, he opened it, picking up the violin and its bow.

Indicating a chair close to one of the desks, she sat, placing her glass down next to her. A sombre tune started up from Michael and the violin: notes washed over her like a dull wave, full of loss and heartache.

"Why don't you play one of those nice folk songs you know," Christian suggested before turning to Erica. "I shall do some rudimentary tests to start with."

He selected a red leather notebook from one of the tables and sat in a seat opposite her. Taking a Parker fountain pen, he began to make notes. "Subject: 'Erica Shylocke', with an 'e'. Age?"

"Nineteen."

"Time and place of origin—Actualle London." He lent forwards and produced a magnifying glass, scrutinising her face with an enlarged eye. "Traces of second-degree Temporal Burns, which appear to have been healed by Time. How curious…" He made a note in his notebook.

"Now, my dear Miss Shylocke, do you have an aversion to needles at all? You see, I'd like to take a sample of blood."

"No, and please call me Erica. I keep telling Michael and he keeps ignoring me."

"It would be unseemly for a mentor to call their student by name." Michael called from where he stood, violin bow poised.

Christian and Erica shared a look. Christian chuckled. "Nicholas can be rather stuck in his ways, but he's a good egg." Michael rose his glass in a mock toast before starting a merry jig that made Erica's toes tingle.

Humming along, Christian proceeded to take a syringe from a silver box engraved with swirls of never-ending intricacy that curved in and out of themselves. Sadly, it failed to distract her from the syringe—the needle was massive. Erica gulped as she watched him remove it, sterilising its needle and unscrewing the glass syringe to add a blood sample bottle instead.

"I say, would you mind terribly rolling up your sleeve?" He could see her eyes widen in horror as she did as he asked.

"That needle is massive. I swear those back home aren't that bad!"

"Yes, it is rather large in comparison to those from your time, they are decidedly neater, what? Sadly, it's illegal to have items of one Time in another. Otherwise, Nicholas would have a rather long shopping list!"

"You're not a KeyMaster?" she asked, trying to distract herself as Christian tightened a tourniquet about her upper arm and disinfected a patch of skin on the inside of her elbow.

"What? Me? I should say not! Ha! The thought! I hunt Lost Souls. I'm a Soul Gatherer, and one of the best too, though I don't like to brag."

"You are, and you do," Michael said from where he now stood near the window, looking out on the darkened garden.

Christian laughed heartily. A look of concentration then came over him as he prepared the needle.

"Now, Erica, Nicholas, tells me you're in the process of completing a degree in History. How very enthralling, do tell me your area of preference for your dissertation."

"The Reality of the Vote in 1930s England," Erica said focusing solidly on Christian's face and not at all on the needle. Not one bit. She closed her eyes. *Why did she agree to this?!*

"How interesting. Well…" She felt the needle go in and winced. "I could take you around and show you 1935. I know of some good clubs, you and Michael could come and let your hair down whilst doing some hands-on research! Do you like the Charleston?" he asked suddenly.

"I've never tried it," she said, eyes still firmly shut.

"Even more reason to come, eh? Life isn't as fancy free as the 1920s were, bad things looming, what? But you can still have yourself a good time. Have a think. All done!" He declared loudly as he pressed a piece of cotton wool against the wound. "If you don't mind holding onto that, Erica." She placed her fingers on top of the cotton wool whilst he closed the sample bottle of blood, labelling it before cleaning and tidying away the needle and syringe back into their case.

"There's just one more test I'd like to conduct this evening, if you please, Erica."

"Sure."

Christian turned to Michael. "May I borrow Ashayla?"

Michael regarded him darkly. "I hope you're not thinking what I think you're thinking."

"You know it's totally safe, dear chap; no one should come to any harm."

"'Should'?"

***

"And you'd like me to touch Miss Shylocke?"

Ashayla had been summoned in a swirling flash of blue-white lightning and stood standing in its harem trousers, leather bodice and waistcoat. Its fine hair settled over its shoulders as the crackling lightning dissipated; bells tinkling as it landed softly upon the rug. Its eyes were forming pupils on the behest of Michael; they rested sceptically on Christian.

"Yes, I want you to place your hands upon Erica's temples and cast a Cerebral Projection for us to see."

"If that is what you wish…" Ashayla looked first at Michael, who signalled his permission with an annoyed gesture of his hand, and then to Erica who was looking nervous.

Ashayla moved gracefully to stand behind where Erica sat. Seeking Michael's permission once more, it moved to rest its fingertips upon Erica's temples.

"Without gloves, Ashayla." Christian interrupted.

The Færie looked up at the human. *"Is that wise, Mr Blake?"*

"For Heaven's sake, Christian!" Michael snapped, turning on his friend.

He held up his hands in defence. "You know it's the best way to achieve a clear Cerebral Projection, my dear fellow. Erica will come to no harm. Ashayla is strong enough to resist." Christian could see Michael was not convinced. "To see what Erica saw: The Temporal Imprints, the Temporal Auras. If we are to dispel the theories, we need clear proof. This is how to get it. Gloves get in the way. Ashayla, if you will oblige, old thing."

He indicated for the Færie to remove its cotton gloves. It looked from Michael to Christian then to Michael again before slowly removing its gloves.

"Please relax, Miss Shylocke. This might feel... odd." The Færie's rich voice said. Then suddenly, within Erica's inner ear, so only she could hear, Ashayla's voice whispered: *You can control what they see. At any time.*

Before Erica could react, Ashayla placed its fingertips upon her temples. Sharp cool pain projected through her skull as if a blunt blade of ice were being forced from one temple through to the other. In that same instant an ethereal cloud of mist ripped itself from the air before her, warping in between the space where she and Ashayla were and where the two men stood. Michael took a step forward, but Christian held him back, nodding reassuringly.

"Very smoothly done, Ashayla. Everything okay, Erica?" Erica gave a thumbs up. "Excellent! See, Michael? Nothing to worry about."

Erica could feel Ashayla roll its eyes in her mind.

Erica started. *Ashayla?!*

Ashayla smirked, mentally bowing in greeting. *Miss Shylocke.*

"Now, Erica, I would like you to think back to this evening, before Nicholas showed you Time."

Involuntary, as her mind thought back to her evening, cloudy images warped and skipped across the ethereal projection, reacting instantly to her memories. Erica faltered, stunned as her memories projected themselves so readily amidst the cloud. The memories skipped by quickly: they were from her perspective and showed her falling through the spirit, who followed her as her memory-self ran into the kitchen to apply the cream, leaving a silvery trail in its wake. Erica watched wide-eyed as the events of the evening continued to unfold. She was outside; Michael was checking her burns, tilting her face to look at them; they were walking down Marloes Road; she was applying the Ignorant Charm; then they were walking along High Street Kensington... The memories flowed out of her before she realised she'd even remembered them. It dawned on her that they would see her watching Michael, gazing at his eyes and his lips… She could feel her cheeks flush and her heartbeat quicken. Her memory-self was resting its hand upon the building, Michael at her side… She couldn't let him see that!

The memories skipped by, overlooking her eyes as they lingered on Michael's face and instead skipping onto her listening for the Temporal Essences. Erica felt Ashayla raise an eyebrow within her head. Despite Erica having averted the attention of Christian and Michael, Ashayla was aware of all memories, those projected and not. She grimaced: too late to worry about that now.

Christian was scrutinising the memories being projected upon the cloud. She could hear his exclamations of shock as he noticed the myriad colourful trails amidst the walls of the vortex and the Temporal Imprints that flashed upon it. They watched as Time healed her burns and then as her memory-self and Michael made their way to 1935. Erica leaned forwards to look more closely at the Temporal Aura, or whatever Christian had called it. Her memory-self turned around, noticed the trail following them and tapped Michael's arm, getting his attention. The Aura appeared like the trail that a snail or a slug leaves behind. But it glistened and shimmered translucently just above the ground, emitting itself from the passing of her memory-self and Michael. She noticed how each aura was coloured differently: an orange-yellow colour to the trail from Michael whilst hers was a vivid violet.

"Beautiful…."

She snapped out of her reverie on hearing his voice and focused past the ether cloud to look at Michael watching the memories. Such a look of awe was upon his face that it made her heart flutter.

In the Projection, her memory-self was watching Michael shake his head, then his eyes widen as she described what she could see, pointing. Shocked, he grabbed her memory-self's hand and pulled her quicker through the dark streets of 1935's London.

"Thank you, Erica, Ashayla," Christian said to each in turn.

It was as the memories skipped to Michael pulling the brass doorbell to Christian's home that Ashayla let go of Erica's temples and the images stretched themselves until they, and their ethereal cloud, stretched into nothingness.

There was an uneasy silence.

"Ashayla, please contact Vozdukha and request Anatole to join us. He needs to see this," Michael said quietly.

"And tell him to bring a bottle of that delicious vodka, what?" Christian added.

Ashayla dematerialised and Erica looked at Michael questioningly.

"As your Course Tutor, he needs to see this. Especially as Dr Finnegan has requested you write a report on your experiences."

Damn. Erica had forgotten about that.

***

Anatole stood agape as the Cerebral Projection was replayed before him. "дерьмо!"

Everyone looked to Vozdukha.

It smiled apologetically. *"It would be best if that remains untranslated."*

Anatole turned to his Færie: *"Lingua intellegite!* Is this what I think it is?" he asked, his Russian slurring into comprehension thanks to the Language Charm. Michael nodded solemnly. In response, Anatole opened the bottle of vodka he'd brought and began to pour out four small glasses. He handed Erica her glass solemnly. "Erica, do you realise what you've done?"

She looked at him with sudden fear. *Had she done something wrong? Weird, yes, but wrong?*

"You've proven Dr Finnegan's life work in an evening. *Everything!* All his years of research and theorising proved right in an evening." He snapped his fingers sharply together.

"Is that bad?"

"Bad? No. Highly unprecedented? Yes." He turned to the Soul Gatherer, tone serious. "What're your thoughts, Christian?"

Christian selected a slim black cigar from a silver case. He offered one to Michael who declined and then to Anatole who accepted. Tapping the cigar against its case he lit it from the palmful of red flames that Vozdukha magicked, followed by Anatole. He nodded his thanks to the Færie and leaned back against the cushions of the sofa. Christian sucked on the cigar contemplatively, flicking through his notebook. Plumes of aromatic purple smoke danced from the two cigars as a delicate whiff of lavender began to fill the air. Erica waited nervously on the edge of the chair as Christian read and re-read notes, making additions here and there.

"You're a Medium." She started at his abruptness. "We knew something was afoot—dear old Nicholas had already mentioned you perceiving him despite the Ignorant Charm—but the Cerebral Projection shows your interaction with the spirit." Christian snapped his notebook shut and leaned towards her, his eyes alight. "Temporal Imprints! Temporal Auras! It would make sense that your sensitivity could go beyond spirits!" He turned to Michael. "They are just as Dr Horatio Finnegan suggested! We leave an invisible trail in the places and times we visit and exist in. No wonder The Guild monitors one's travel so, the invisible effect of 'passing through' affects Time, even in the subtlest of ways. We leave trails wherever and *when*ever we go! Did you see those imbedded within the vortex's walls? Heavens above if major, visible effects take place in Time. It'd be catastrophic! There are no theories into an Aura having colour; I wonder if it bears any significance…" He pondered, tapping ash from his cigar into an ashtray.

"Did you see the trail from the spirit?" Anatole asked in hushed tones. "It was all over Erica's flat."

Christian nodded. "Perhaps this is what anchors them and gives them substance whilst they wait to pass on. It would be safe to assume Lost Souls leave a trail also. We'll have to conduct some experiments and catalogue our findings."

Michael leaned forwards, resting his elbows on his knees. "But what about the Lost Souls and the Sonnastry? It confuses me—the Sonnastry monitors travel made through Time by humans and Lost Souls, so how are Lost Souls now getting through? The Wrathful attacks, for example. And then the others—the Arbolis Noir and the Wistful. Not to mention the Blood Hounds! What's changed? If we impact Time in the subtlest of ways, how are these incidents now being over-looked? Someplace there's a growing army of Lost Souls which The Guild has no idea of. How? Where are they? What are their plans? Are they being coordinated?"

"I'm not sure, old boy. No one has researched Lost Soul Psychology in this way. An over-sight by the university, what, Anatole?"

The Russian shrugged his shoulders.

"An 'over-sight' seems to be putting it mildly!" Erica exclaimed, frustration boiling within. Anatole looked at her coolly. "Sorry, but I don't understand why—"

"Of course not. Why would you?" Anatole said, blowing out a plume of purple smoke. "You're young. Faced with the reality before us, it of course seems careless, but bear in mind that something like this has never *ever* happened. It has never been raised as an area requiring research. As such, there're going to be gaps in learning." He spoke tersely, the colour raising in his cheeks.

"Erica was only saying because the information would be helpful. She meant no offence to you or the University," Michael said, patting his friend's shoulder. "We just have no clue what we're truly up against."

"True. But what we do know is that something is afoot. And we now have a starting point," Christian said.

He opened his notebook and began making notes. "Orlov, you use your staff pass to access the Regulated Area of the Library. I'd eat my hat if you don't find something on the barrier. There'll be a book on its history, maybe even Charms. Nicholas, you arrange as much travel through Time as is possible with Erica. We need to document our findings to gain a clearer picture of what we're dealing with. If you run across Lost Souls along the way, even better. We need to see what sort of Temporal Aura they leave behind. I'm developing something that might help us. Considering tonight's findings, some adjustments are needed, but it should help."

The two men nodded, clear of their responsibilities.

"Erica, do you believe in fate?" he asked, turning to the girl.

Erica faltered. "I suppose so to a degree. I'm a big fan of free will though."

"Aren't we all?" Christian smiled, a twinkle in his amber eyes. "Well, here we are facing unknown foes on an unknown scale, yet we have a Medium who'll be able to perceive their Auras wherever and, more importantly, *when*ever they are in Time. I'd like to say that was Fate dealing us a good hand, what?"

15
Clash

It was late when they left Christian's and travelled back home.
On this occasion, Erica was prepared and fared better against the
onslaught of Time as she travelled through the vortex.

They were walking under the cover of the Ignorant Charm along
the High Street. Despite the sense of foreboding that had resulted
from their evening with Christian, Michael felt comforted with
Erica by his side. He wasn't used to having a companion.

"You've coped remarkably," he said as they left the High Street
in the direction of home. "Cerebral Projections are not for the
fainthearted."

"They certainly take some getting used to! I don't think I've ever
felt so exposed," she said, hugging herself against the cold.

Exposed...

He looked at her then, guilt squirming in his stomach.

"My mother was Chinasa," Michael began suddenly, his voice
barely audible. "She was daughter to King Eze Okezie, Igwe of
Nnewi in Nigeria. She fell in love with an Englishman, a Philip
Carmichael, and became pregnant—much to the horror of her father
and her betrothed. Dishonoured, her betrothed and his family
tricked her, selling her into slavery. By the time her father found
out, she was already on her way across the Atlantic to America. I
was born during the crossing. We..." he paused, unable to speak
against the sudden lump in his throat. He hadn't told *anyone* this,
not even Annabelle he realised. But he owed Erica this much,
especially after everything she'd done for him. And... it felt good
to share his truth with her. It was then he realised what a friend she
was becoming.

"We were sold into slavery. It was hard work on the plantation and my mother died from consumption when I was eight… I tried running away but was severely punished for my impudence when caught. However, fate intervened, and I caught the attention of a childless couple who were visiting the plantation, the Nicholas's. They bought me and my freedom and gave it all back tenfold. I was adopted and returned with them to England as their son. They gave me the best of new starts that anyone could wish for and were so incredibly good to me…"

Erica had been watching him with bated breath as he spoke. She hadn't dared say anything in case he stopped; and she so wanted to know his story.

His eyes were sad, his heartache plain to see.

"And what about your birth father?" she asked after a moment's pause. "Did you ever find him?"

"Yes, after many years I sought him out. You see, my mother crossed the sea believing that he'd sold us into slavery to cover up all traces of the scandal from the countess he was engaged to. A bastard child was a bind, especially one with different coloured skin. But, sometimes, she'd have hope and tell of a visiting angel who helped her believe otherwise. Nonetheless, her original fear stayed with me. Meeting him was one of the hardest things I've ever had to do. It was a good reunion, lots of truths were told… He spent months searching for us with my grandfather. But, as fate would have it, by the time they found us, my mother had died and I'd been adopted. Sometimes, I wonder what it would've been like to have him find us both in time…How different would life have been as a true family?" He cleared his throat. "But we became close. It was an honour to know him in his final years."

Erica took his hand and gave it the lightest of squeezes. "I'm glad. So sorry for everything you went through, but still glad you did find him and learnt the truth. Truth gives us hope and hope is so important. I can't imagine what it must've been like for you. Thank you for sharing it with me…"

"Bringing you into my world has exposed your truths—you deserve to see some of mine too."

"Only some?" she teased.

He flashed her a roguish smile. "Only some."

***

He looked up and watched the lights to Erica's flat turn on. She appeared at the window and waved. He tipped his top hat in reply and turned to go.

He was tired. What with Erica's discovery of Temporal Auras and the Cerebral Projection, he wasn't used to revisiting the past. He didn't regret telling Erica, but, over the years, he'd become adept at locking things away and ignoring them. He wasn't accustomed to facing them. He should really go home. He was in the wrong frame of mind to visit her. He should go home, have a bath and get some much-needed sleep.

But he would see her: a promise was a promise.

It might make him feel better.

***

By the time he opened his door, folded away his top hat and hung up his jacket—he was exhausted. He loosened his cravat and slumped into the living room. Embers glowed weakly within the grate. He threw on some paper which was welcomed eagerly, catching fire. He then fed it some kindling before adding a log. He wouldn't stay up long. He *shouldn't* stay up long.

It'd been a big week. Erica had seen more of his life than anyone had since he'd become a KeyMaster. It'd been easier than expected, in some ways. He stared into the flames, shadows flickering across his face.

He was doubting agreeing to Erica's help. Things were indeed afoot, but what and how bad he was still none the wiser. He couldn't shake the sense of unease that shrouded him. At the first sign of danger, he would forbid her to continue to help, though, truth be told, without her they would be worse off.

He could do with talking to Ashayla, but it had found the Cerebral Projection draining and was resting in the periapt. Not that Ashayla would offer much in the way of reassurance. He sighed and pinched the bridge of nose. His head ached. He hadn't been in the right frame of mind to visit her; he should've refrained from going, it had only made him feel worse. But he'd made a promise.

Unbidden, a memory filled his mind's eye. He was running pell-mell towards where crowds had gathered. Pushing through them, the first thing he saw was the blood. It was everywhere, painting the cobbles with its life-giving redness. He remembered her broken body… How she'd reached for him…

"Remember me…"

He shook his head, massaging his temples. *Why did it have to be like this?*

He rubbed away his tears and held his head in his hands. It was then that he felt it, a coolness upon his back.

"Good evening, Maria." He looked up at the fire. He didn't need to turn around—he'd been anticipating a visit ever since he'd seen the spirit in Erica's Cerebral Projection.

"Or rather 'good morning', Michael."

***

The morning had broken foggy and cold. A moody winter's morning. Erica had slept badly. She felt on tenterhooks, nervous at what lay ahead. A growing army of Lost Souls, led by a battalion of Wrathful, had threatened her dreams last night.

Christian had spoken of Fate: chance, serendipity, destiny, whatever the word the idea was the same. Had Time chosen her on purpose? Part of her felt abused. On the other hand, it was reassuring that there might be some benefits to her medium abilities. Though, beyond that she had little to offer. But where to start? She could hardly wander Time looking for auras.

Shaking herself from her reverie, she picked up her rucksack, gloves and keys. She had to go. With Time having healed her burns she had no excuse pulling another sickie. Plus, she could do with some normality: first work, then lectures. In any case, it was her last Thursday shift.

She quickly glanced at her Actualle and KeyMaster timetables to double check and froze.

There was a clash.

How hadn't she noticed?! She worried her lip, concentrating. No solution came to her. She'd have to call by and see Michael, he'd know what to do.

With that she ran out, locking the door behind her.

***

Staring up at the brick wall at the top of the steps that led to his home, she realised she still didn't have a clue how it appeared, let alone whether there was a doorbell she could ring. She suddenly thought back to the golden pentacle in the hallway and fetched out the periapt from her jacket pocket. Maybe, just maybe…

Checking the coast was clear, she applied the Ignorant Charm and walked up the steps. She'd hoped the door would materialise once it sensed the periapt, but it didn't. Cursing she was about to leave when inspiration struck. Lifting the periapt, she tapped the wall lightly. In that instant two things happened: Ashayla burst from the periapt in its elemental form and the door materialised. Erica did a victory dance only to notice Ashayla's grumpy elfin face.

"Sorry, I woke you! Would it help if I told you how cute you look like that?" Erica said crouching to speak to the pint-sized creature. Ashayla cocked its head to one side and looked at her in exasperation, its tattoos flashing.

"It's amazing how expressive you can be even without pupils!" Ashayla gave her a look of utter disdain. "See? I can tell you're pissed! It's—Oh. Sorry!"

Just then the front door flung open to reveal a dishevelled Michael half-dressed. He looked down at them. "Heavens! Is something amiss? The house was shaking!"

She blushed instantly: his shirt was unbuttoned. A toned chest peeked out from behind the cotton fabric, teasing her. Pinching herself, she tore her eyes away from the elegant curve of his torso. But not before she noticed the scars…

An image of a shackled young slave appeared in her mind's eye.

"Sorry, I didn't know how to make your front door appear." She quickly got to her feet.

"*Apparent portus* is the incantation you need. Apologies, Miss Shylocke, I should've said." For an instant he regarded her warily, then his usual bright smile erupted upon his face. "Would you like to come in?" He stepped aside.

Looking at him half-dressed, inviting her in, it took every ounce of her control not to get carried away.

"No thank you, I'm in a bit of a rush. I'm late for work but I noticed a clash with my two lectures this afternoon. I don't know how I didn't notice it before, I just assumed they were after one another." She handed Michael her two timetables. "Sorry for disturbing you." She added bashfully, stealing another look at his chest.

He yawned and finished buttoning his shirt before leaning against the door frame to look at the timetables. "It is of no import. Oh, I see where you are referring to: Evolving History and Færie-Lore…" He thought for a moment, stroking his stubble; he had yet to shave. Her fingers itched to feel its roughness. "The most straight-forward would be to forgo Færie-Lore and come back here. I can then guide you as to how to manipulate Time to attend it."

"Miss it? I've never missed a lecture in my life!"

"And you won't now, Miss Shylocke, I assure you." She hesitated. He placed his hand upon his heart. "I give you my word."

"Well, if you say so. Thanks. You look tired," she commented, taking back her timetables.

"I was tardy to bed and slept ill."

"Same, there's been a lot to digest. It's been quite a week."

He scrutinised her. "No second thoughts? I wouldn't think ill of you if you had."

Erica shook her head stoutly. "Nope, none. I promised to help and help I will. You should grow a beard; it'd suit you. I mean, you look good without one, but…" She trailed off awkwardly as he watched her with a half-smile. She cleared her throat. "Sorry, I've really got to dash. So, I'll, erm, see you here around five?"

"No need, I shall await you at the station. Remember, we must also select your Færie later. Until anon."

And with that she turned and ran down the steps, waving as she headed in the direction of the High Street and the Underground station.

Stupid, stupid! Why had she mentioned the beard?! Why couldn't she just keep her cool? Try as she might she could not concentrate on her reading during the commute to work. She kept thinking back to the line of Michael's neck and collarbone. The smattering of stubble upon his cheeks. His naked torso, its taut curve as it disappeared down... There was no stopping the burning within. So, she gave in and fell into a happy, lustful daydream.

***

"How late are you?! Oh, are you okay? You look feverish," Joslin noted when Erica finally appeared at the till.

Erica felt her cheeks—they were hot to the touch. She smiled shyly. "Yeah, I'm fine."

"Wait. You and Michael... You didn't?!" Joslin squealed, jumping to conclusions.

"Shhhh! No, nothing like that. I—"

"Glad you could join us, Shylocke," Marc said as he crossed over to their till. "I didn't think you were going to turn up."

"She was with Michael!" Joslin said, unable to control herself. Erica flicked her whilst Marc stared, his skin pale.

"I wasn't! Well, not like that. He was helping me with a timetable issue."

"Yeah, right!" Joslin teased.

"No, it's the truth. Scout's honour!" Erica said, raising her three-finger promise. "Anyway, he's got a long-term girlfriend."

"No! But I thought he was totally into you?!" Joslin looked dumbfounded.

Erica shrugged her shoulders, trying to feel as nonchalant as the gesture implied.

Marc looked relieved and noticeably perked up. "Bad luck, Shylocke. Plenty more fish and all that. Anyway, now you're here, to commemorate your last Thursday shift, and the impending joys of Christmas, I've come up with a game!"

"A game? Seriously, Marc, can't we just eat cake?" Joslin moaned.

He gave her a withering look, cleared his throat and continued. "Christmas Customer Bingo!" Proudly revealing three pieces of paper with a dramatic flourish. "We have until shift end to find all six," he said, shuffling them importantly before doling them out.

"Santa Claus doppelgänger! Novelty Christmas socks!" Joslin said, reading some of her clues out loud.

"Real-life Buddy the Elf!" Erica exclaimed looking at hers.

"Ha! I wondered who would get that one. Damn, that means I get the novelty Christmas underwear." He scratched his head thoughtfully. "Any of you ladies care to oblige?"

"Nice try!" Joslin scoffed and, taking him by the shoulders, turned him round in the direction of his department. The sounds of customers arriving were already drifting up the stairs.

"Someone else needs to verify the customer, so two ticks needed. Have fun!" He called over his shoulder as the first customers appeared on their floor.

Consequently, Erica's last Thursday shift passed quickly, with all three of them whizzing around trying to find their clues whilst serving customers and steering clear of Hincks.

By shift-end, she had managed to find all clues except one, a real-life Buddy the Elf: even the trickier Nativity donkey had been found thanks to Hincks cornering her with a Nativity scene to set out on display.

Joslin, however, had managed to find all her clues. Though, she had got some weird looks for crawling on the floor to look for novelty socks.

But the first to find all clues was Marc, despite having the tricky clue of novelty Christmas underwear. By chance, one of his customers had shopped for lingerie and when Marc had asked for inspiration for a gift for his grandmother the customer happily revealed the Ms Claus lingerie.

"I don't know how people fall for it," Joslin muttered.

"Did I forget to say that the winner gets a kiss?" he said as they checked his paper.

"You're really not my favourite gender. No offence," Joslin said with a shrug.

He sighed. "As much as it pains me to admit, this body can't satisfy all. So, how about it, Erica? *Erica?!*" He turned to find her already gone.

Joslin patted him on his shoulder. "There's always the work do."

***

Erica found herself back on the Tube heading over to uni at Russell Square and munching her lunch. She checked her watch. An hour until the clash. She'd never missed a lecture and she really wasn't chuffed to think that today might be the first. As such, she was too anxious to focus on her lecturer, everything they said just merged into one big blahblahblah.

Tick-tick-tick. She watched as the minutes closed in and two-thirty approached. Would her absence be noticed even if Time was manipulated for her to join later?

She was on tenterhooks by the time Two-thirty came and went but, finding that nothing happened, and the lecture continued as normal, helped.

Taking a deep breath, she tried to focus on the lecturer, though, try as she might, she still couldn't concentrate. She normally enjoyed this lecture; the lecturer was witty, and the topic of History's evolution fascinated her. But her notes from today were a garbled mess. Hoping for inspiration, she glanced back through her notes only to see how dull they were in comparison to those from her lecture with Dr Finnegan.

She stared blankly at them, her mind a whirl.

***

"Are you well?" Michael asked as she approached him at the Underground Station.

Erica could hardly believe that it had only been a month since they'd spoken for the first time in this exact spot. It felt like a lifetime.

"Just things, nothing important," she replied light-heartedly, waving her hand dismissively.

"If there's anything I can assist with do say—I mean that," he said, offering her his arm.

"Thank you." She took it, grateful for the closeness and warmth. He didn't realise how much he helped anchor her.

The weather had taken a turn and a cold Easterly wind blew. It carried with it a hint of frost that tickled Erica's nose and reminded her of winters back home.

When they reached the end of the Arcade, night had fallen black against the harsh glare of the streetlights and the soft twinkle of the Christmas lights. The moon peeked out from behind a passing cloud. Lots of people didn't like the cold dark months of winter, but Erica enjoyed their closeness and the way they made each light a beacon.

The High Street bustled with people returning home from work, as well as the increasing army of Christmas shoppers. Festive shop displays were dressed with enticing presents, decorations and indulgences. Erica took the opportunity to mention her Christmas work do.

"I tend to celebrate Christmas quietly," Michael replied as they walked down towards the iron gateway.

"If you change your mind, you'd be welcome."

"Thank you." He smiled at her and Erica blushed, turning away quickly.

"I would advise applying the Charm," Michael suggested as they approached the gateway.

Touching their periapts to cast the Charm, the now-familiar feeling of fading into the background washed over them. Erica's ears tingled and popped, followed by her tell-tale sneeze. They chuckled.

"Time manipulation is fairly straight forward," he began as he took out his Time Piece. He opened it to reveal its dials. "You simply alter the smallest and innermost dial—the time dial—turning it anticlockwise. Although, from time to time you might need to manipulate days, even months. On those occasions, the other dials will need altering. Though it's recommended not to alter beyond a couple of months.

"In any case, the instant that a dial is manipulated two things will happened. One, the current Temporal Plane you're on will continue, but without your current self in it. Second, you will experience Time altering. It's quite magnificent but must be done slowly. Research has shown that it's best to manipulate Time prior to entering Limbo, due to the nature of Limbo being in between all Times. Whilst it's better to manipulate Time in past Temporal Planes once they've been entered. Understood?" He looked up at her then, catching her off guard.

"I think so." She took out her own Time Piece and opened it. "So, if I need to just alter Time by a few hours I use the smallest dial. And for any further alterations I also use the day and month ones."

He nodded. "If you're altering the Time in the Temporal Plane you're in, naturally ensure you're in an alternative place or, ideally, invisible so the Actualles are not befuddled by your second self. As we're going to Limbo there's no risk. Would you like to try?"

He watched over her shoulder as she popped open the glass casing to the small clock and began to manipulate the tiny time dial anticlockwise. As warned, two things instantly happened. The Temporal Plane they'd been on was ripped out from under them and continued on its hazy way, leaving them in a shadowy reality where their surroundings were indistinct apart from the heavens high above them. And the heavens themselves began to arc and move backwards, as if on rewind.

"I would alter Time by five hours, that way you're safely on your way to your lecture and the fatigue will be bearable." He leaned in close, watching her turn the dial. She could feel his warmth through her coat.

"Fatigue?"

"You're experiencing a longer day, which can naturally be tiring depending on how much Time is manipulated as well as your general health."

Slowly manipulating the time dial, Erica found it difficult to both focus and enjoy the sight of the reversed sunset.

The inky blue-black heavens reluctantly gave way to a peek of the brave orange sunset upon which grew a bright-white halo that illuminated the inky-blueness of the night sky. Orion, Zeus' huntsman, shone bright, a stellar solo act within the cold heavens.

As the sun slowly, slowly began to re-appear on the horizon, its white brightness illuminated more and more of the heavens until there were distinct bands: orange to white to light blue to navy blue, until all melted away into blackness high above.

"Oh, glory…"

Michael looked at her and saw the heavens reflected within her wide eyes. "Majestic, don't you think?"

Erica nodded numbly, too humbled to speak.

Wispy clouds became visible and scudded across the ever-brightening sky, their constant morphing shapes silhouetted against the changing hues.

Finally, slowly, the inky blackness was banished by an icy azure blue sky that heralded the bright globe's regal return: its peach hotness licked the fluffy clouds that grew and diminished and floated back along their previous paths.

By the time Erica had finished manipulating the time dial by five hours, the sun had lifted itself back just shy of its zenith. She watched as the heavens abruptly stopped moving along their invisible arc: the sky itself was now a bright, cold blue pocked by clouds that played upon a breeze. Winter pinched her nostrils. She trembled involuntarily.

"It makes you question your place in the world, seeing such wonder." Erica remarked quietly, pulling her jacket closer and hugging herself for comfort.

"It does, especially when it's unceasing, no matter what has befallen life on Earth." Michael agreed bitterly.

She glanced across at him and saw the same great sadness that she'd seen when she awoke the Gateway at Cleopatra's Needle. She worried her lip and looked away. Tears pricked her eyes: she'd done it again. She seemed to have a knack of saying things that upset him. The palms of her hands grew hot and clammy. She angrily wiped the tears away: *I'm such an idiot!*

Just then, the Temporal Gateway to Limbo crashed open.

They looked at one another wide-eyed.

"Let me guess, I shouldn't be able to do that?" Erica whispered hoarsely.

He held up his Time Piece. "Not without one of these, no."

***

It was Erica's most solemn freefall. She knew she was different, a Medium, but why did that make her so profoundly different compared to other KeyMasters? What would others who were less understanding do when they found out?

She looked across the whizzing galaxies to where Michael stood, equally thoughtful. He'd been good to her. He hadn't treated her any different, but people had limits. He wouldn't always be this understanding.

Hell, even she had limits.

Closing her eyes, she gave herself up to oblivion.

***

Due to having already travelled through Limbo to attend sessions at The Guild, Michael decided to visit his acquaintances the de Temps to avoid his second self, promising to meet her at the Library when she'd finished her lecture.

A little nervous, Erica continued through the streets of Limbo on her own, arriving at the University with ten minutes to spare until the start of her lecture on Færie-Lore. Erica was early. Sort of.

"So, you can be early," Sachairi said tongue-in-cheek as she approached. His nail varnish today matched his blue t-shirt.

She smiled. It felt normal being teased. Normal was good. "I know, bad habit to get into, right?"

He laughed. "You like purple?" he asked, indicating her jacket.

"Is it that obvious?"

"A little. How are you finding everything?"

They were waiting outside a lecture theatre along with some other students dressed in attire from various eras. Only in Limbo could breeches, wigs and corsets be worn alongside cheongsams, saris and sherwals and not be considered out of place.

"Okay. Weird. Good, I guess. There's a lot to get my head around."

"Nice to know I'm not alone then. I was beginning to freak out when the others were talking about their families and 'awakening keys'." He ran a hand through his hair.

"Same. It really hadn't occurred to me that it could be a family-thing. But then, I suppose that's one reason why it's such a well-kept secret. The Career Advisor certainly never mentioned anything about it to me at school!"

Sachairi chuckled.

He hesitated a moment before continuing. "Bit eerie about those bells, huh?"

Erica smiled nervously. She'd hoped that had been forgotten.

Iminathi appeared wearing jeans and a bright top that matched her headscarf and showed off her slim waist. She joined them where they waited. "You're early," she commented in Erica's direction.

"I know, I was just telling Sachairi that it was a bad habit to get into to. I doubt it'll last long."

"You never know." She smiled. "Have you two got everything off the list for the 'Mighty One'?"

"Not yet, have you?"

"No, why don't we organise a shopping trip after Matriculation? I think there's a couple of hours free before our KeyMastery lecture."

Sachairi and Erica thought it a good idea, especially as they didn't have a clue where to go to buy their resources. When Henrik and Tsuzuku arrived, Iminathi mentioned it to them and they were keen too.

Just then, silence befell the crowd of waiting students.

Turning, Erica joined the students in watching a Færie walk towards them. Without a KeyMaster. It wore a simple blue linen dress and walked barefoot. Its hair was long and pale gold with matching, pupil-less, eyes. Just like Ashayla, and the other Færies Erica had seen so far, an ethereal glow emanated from its skin. It bore tattoos of dotted lines that fell like tears from its eyes down to its jaw. There were no metal cuffs about its wrists.

The students waited respectfully for it to enter the lecture theatre and, only when invited, did they follow.

16
Færie Lore

The Færie had positioned itself upon the central dais, red cushioned chairs spiralled out from it. One wall was flanked by windows that allowed the late-afternoon sun to pour in, whilst the other walls held floor to ceiling blackboards. One by one the students found a seat and took out their notebooks and pens.

With a flick of its wrist, the Færie magicked a stick of chalk to hover to the top of one of the blackboards. The chalk waited patiently for the Færie to begin, poised for action whilst the Færie settled to sit cross-legged in the middle of the dais.

"My name is…" and the Færie made a sound like one of bears fighting in a sandstorm. *"However, you may call me "Lozen." I'm not a trained academic, like your other professors, but I am a Færie, and the Vice-Chancellor sees me most capable for the delivery of this new and improved course in Færie-Lore."*

The chalk leapt into action, scrawling across the blackboard.

"This course will teach you about Færiekind, our elemental connections and talents as well as how best to use us in your work as a KeyMaster. Without us, destroying Lost Souls is difficult: your Færie will save your life." The Færie began, its voice canorous and deep.

"Each of you will create your own relationship with your Færie, but I hope to guide you in creating the fairest. Whilst it's customary for Færies to be treated as slaves by their KeyMasters, it is hackneyed and outdated. Your Færie will be at least five thousand human years of age when it's summoned and will have served multiple KeyMasters. It will have seen more of life on Earth and

elsewhere than you will ever see. Therefore, they should be treated with respect."

An uncomfortable silence befell the theatre. The Færie regarded them carefully before standing up and walking to one side.

"We Færies are elemental beings that came into existence with the beginnings of Time. In the Ancient World we lived in harmony with Earth and its creatures, freely travelling between planes and Time, but Man was born and us and our magic were feared."

The Færie rose a hand to touch its temple and conjured a Cerebral Projection for the students to see. The Ancient World, with its wild forests and seas was displayed. Elemental forms of Færies streaked about the landscape like fireflies, healing animals and helping plants to grow. The first of man appeared on the horizon, hesitant and fearful and began to attack the Færies, eventually managing to encase part of their essence within manmade objects, binding them to their will.

"Despite successfully enslaving Færies—by stealing part of their own and shackling them to Earth—Man increasingly feared retributions for their sins and banished the Færies to Utarra, the astral plane, where we stay until summoned. Not that we mind. Its essence strengthens and soothes our own befouled essence."

The scene displayed on Lozen's Cerebral Projection was a glorious skyscape of shimmering particles, soaring clouds and swirling light. Færies in their varied elemental forms skimmed the skies leaving light trails glittering behind them, twisting and turning in dances celebrating the very essence of life itself.

Erica and Sachairi leaned forwards, entranced. Out of the corner of her eye, Erica noticed some students muttering. Perhaps Lozen's candid recount of history irked them.

"As elemental beings, we are immortal and can assume whatever shape we wish. Since our magic is elemental based, the early KeyMasters found it effective in the destruction of Lost Souls. Consequently, Færies began being assigned to KeyMasters to help them in their task of safeguarding Time and its humans. Although we can freely use magic in Utarra, once summoned and bound to

Earth, charms must be employed as our freewill diminishes. I will help teach you these charms."

Lozen removed its hand from its temple and the Cerebral Projection of the resplendent Utarra faltered and vanished.

"Whilst the previous course was completely theoretical, much of this new course will be practical and held predominately in the Combat Hall. However, there will be the occasional lecture here to teach you about Færiekind. Have you any questions thus far?"

A female student rose her hand. The Færie nodded. The student spoke hotly: "Who is your KeyMaster? Why do they give you permission to lecture us?"

"I do not have a KeyMaster."

There was a stunned silence followed by the deep growl of many murmurs. Erica and Sachairi looked at one another puzzled: did it matter that it didn't belong to a KeyMaster? Iminathi and Tsuzuku were looking at one another wide-eyed. Henrik crossed himself.

"I don't understand," the student said.

"I was granted freedom," Lozen explained, displaying its cuff-less wrists before opening its palms to magic three periapts. *"I am beholden to no one."*

The murmurings increased to a heightened buzz of panic that made Erica wince.

"What's to stop you from attacking us?!" One student screamed out.

"Or bewitching us?!" Another shrieked.

"Nothing other than myself."

The Færie pressed a fingernail to the middle of its forehead and pushed deep, cutting through the flesh. A small amount of golden blood blossomed and trickled down between its pupil-less eyes. There were screams as it then 'unzipped' itself, letting its skin fall about it to reveal its elemental form that morphed and bubbled until an Apache woman knelt before them, her long dark hair covering her naked body like a shroud. She stood up and pulled the hair back from her face revealing bright war paint of dotted lines falling from her eyes. Gold blood pooled out around her, rippling underfoot.

"I am Lozen of the Chihenne Chiricahua Apache, this Færie was mine and served me magnificently, saving my life more than once. It understood my tribulations more than any human and became the dearest of friends. Before I died, I granted it the one thing Man had been too afraid to: freedom. I did this, so Man would finally see the truth about Færiekind. They are not our foes. Man is."

The lecture ended abruptly as hysteria broke out.

"Guess this means there's no homework then?" Sachairi said, trying to sound light-hearted as students ran for their lives, scrambling for the exit.

"Guess not," Erica said.

***

Michael found her in the Library bathed in the last golden rays of the day. She was standing reading a book, a look of concentration on her fine features. Dust particles danced about her as if they were entranced by her very essence. He found himself slowing to regard her, taking in the lines of her brow and cheeks. She had long lashes that framed her green eyes in a most becoming way. The line of her chin was stubborn yet her lips...

"Michael!" She noticed him then and excitedly beckoned him over. "I've been reading about Færies and their ability to weave and manipulate full or partial dominos. It's fascinating. You guys are so cool!" Erica enthused, noticing Ashayla following behind.

Ashayla looked taken aback. *"'Cool'?"*

"As in 'awesome'," Michael clarified.

"I understand 'awesome'. Thank you, Miss Shylocke, you're too kind." The Færie bowed.

Erica put the book back and the three of them walked towards the Regulated Area. The Færies on duty stood up as they approached, clapping to conjure light for them. Michael produced the sealed letter of invitation.

"We have come to select a Færie for my protégé," Michael explained as one of the Færies broke the seal to read the letter.

The Færie scanned the document before nodding to the other. They both stepped aside, letting the three of them enter.

Walking past the cordons, Erica followed Michael to the bookcase they'd been given permission to use in the letter. She was desperate to browse the books. The locked doors and curtains to the bookcases she passed only served to increase her curiosity. Finally reaching Bookcase VII, Michael flashed the letter in front of the padlock. It unlocked with a satisfying *click*! Michael undid it and set it aside, gently opening the tall glass doors.

"We are looking for *The Chronicle*. It's a large tome which has all available Færies listed."

The three of them scanned the bookcase; Erica searched the lower shelves whilst Michael climbed the ladder as high as it would go to search the upper shelves. As it was a floor to ceiling bookcase Ashayla adopted her elemental form to fly to the uppermost shelves, near the vaulted beams of the Library's ceiling.

After five minutes Ashayla's voice drifted down to them. *"Michael, I have it!"*

Both Michael and Erica looked up to see it flying down carrying a large leather-bound tome. The Færie placed it on a nearby lectern and made room for Michael and Erica, hovering at its side. The tome was shut with a metal lock. Michael presented the letter to the lock which quivered and whirled, before popping open. He stepped aside.

"As promised, Ashayla. Please show us the most suitable candidate, in your opinion."

Ashayla bobbed its head in thanks and landed, morphing back into its human form. It began to flick through the pages. Each page was elaborately decorated with illuminated calligraphy and borders depicting each Færie, its element, name, number, former KeyMasters, traits and cost.

Ashayla hesitated at a page with a sketch that closely resembled itself before eventually stopping at a page where a fire Færie was depicted. *"Færie 728. This is the Færie I would recommend for Miss Shylocke."*

Michael peered over its shoulder, reading the information on the page. "It's very inexpensive! But what's this black mark against its name? I should like to speak with it first."

"As you wish," Ashayla said, turning to Erica. *"You must summon it, Miss Shylocke. Use my periapt, but you won't have much time."*

She took out the periapt nervously. "Do I need to say anything in particular?"

"State its number and then your full name followed by the incantation 'vocavi te'."

"Right, Færie 728, my name and *vocavi te*. Got it." She took a deep breath and held the periapt in her open palm.

"If you decide to enlist it, you will need your own periapt to bind it. Once with essence, this periapt becomes the parent. The other two will in turn mirror the parent." Ashayla added, indicating for the other two to be lain on the ground.

"It will try to disarm you." Michael began as Erica sought out her own three periapts from the depths of her bag. "It will aim to scare you to assess your strength, so be firm."

"Periapts. Binding. *vocavi te*. Be firm. Got it."

Holding out her open palm, periapt flat within its centre, Erica noticed the key motif shimmering in the conjured light of the Library. She took another deep breath. "Færie 728, I, Erica Ann Shylocke, *vocavi te*." She felt her heart shuddering within her as Michael's periapt begin to quiver violently. It grew hot against her skin and, just as she was about to let it drop to the floor for burning her, the quivering stopped, and a golden orb shot from the periapt's jewel like a solar burst: hot, explosive and mighty.

The fiery orb streaked around the tops of the bookcases before crashing down before Erica. It hovered some three feet off the ground, its surface resembling molten lava.

"Prepare yourself," Michael said quietly as the orb began to revolve and grow, pulsating and burning like a fiery solar storm. Erica tried to ignore the increasing heat and held firmly on to the periapt within her palm. It was just as the heat began to scald her face that it abruptly stopped and morphed into a naked male Færie.

Raising to its full height, it looked to Ashayla speaking a word that sounded like moonlight shattering upon an icy mountainside. *"Leh-to chin-iko de?"*

Ashayla nodded and stepped forward, tears shining in its eyes.

The Færie then noticed the two humans and its eyes narrowed, the swirling tattoo in the centre of its forehead flashing menacingly. *"Lehkis zay na-saleii? En-guo na? English?"* It spoke gruffly, as if it hadn't spoken the language for many years.

Ashayla nodded. It looked at the humans again, a sneer upon its lips. Disregarding them, it turned to Ashayla. *"Where have you been, my love? I have missed not being one with you."*

"What? Wait! Ashayla, is this your lover?!" Michael rounded on the Færie red-faced.

"He's the most suitable."

"For whom? You or Erica? And what is this black mark? It says it has not been summoned since 1736. Why?"

Ashayla hesitated, eyes darting from Michael to the Færie.

Færie 728 stepped forward. *"I killed my KeyMaster."*

"No!" Michael looked at Ashayla in dismay. "I asked you to find the most suitable Færie for Erica and you recommend *this* one. Why? Out of all the hundreds, why this one?"

"Because he is strong and loyal. He will provide Miss Shylocke with the security and support she needs."

"'Loyal'?"

"I was loyal." The Færie growled, eyes blazing. *"I was loyal to him like he never was to me. He made me steal and murder. He lied and cheated and misused his social standing to abuse hundreds. He promised to free me. I did what I had to do to protect us all. No one mourned his passing."*

Erica studied the Færie, its earnest expression, its lean muscles and strength. "It's okay, Michael. I trust it. What's your name?"

Michael and the Færie turned to look at her, stunned.

"If Ashayla thinks you're the best companion for me, then you are. What's your name?" Erica repeated.

Did Ashayla just blush?

The male Færie hesitated and bowed before her. *"It is yours to choose."*

"I can't name you, you're not a pet."

It regarded her carefully. *"Nonetheless, that is the custom."*

At that moment, the periapt began to pulse brightly in her hand, like a heartbeat. Michael looked at her in earnest. "Miss Shylocke, you only have a minute left. Choose another!"

"No, I trust Ashayla, I choose this one." Erica smiled reassuringly.

"If you let her down, I will destroy you," Michael said, approaching the Færie with a growl.

The Færie bowed deeply before him. *"You have my word."*

"I have your life: the word of a murderer means nothing." Regarding him for the longest of moments, the Færie bowed again in agreement.

"Present it with your periapt, Miss Shylocke," Ashayla said, gesturing to the periapt in Erica's hands. Erica stepped forwards, offering the Færie the periapt.

"And what do you call me, ma'am?" The Færie asked, reaching out its hands to touch the jewelled centre of the parent periapt. It grimaced as some of its essence stayed in the jewel like a drop of blood, which flared golden upon its touch, the essence sinking within. The other two periapts on the ground flared in welcome of the mirrored essence.

"I don't know. What's your name?"

Taken aback, the Færie looked to Ashayla who nodded reassuringly. *"My name is…"* and the Færie made a sound that a supernova would make had it been captured within the deepest of caves.

Erica looked at him blankly. "How the hell am I supposed to pronounce that?!" The Færie shrugged its shoulders. Just then, Ashayla's periapt began to flicker wildly. Alarmed, Erica called out. "Bob! I name you Bob!"

"'Bob'?" The Færie looked at her in disbelief.

"I panicked, sorry! Okay, ignore that! Who was your favourite KeyMaster? Come on, there must have been one," she said, when she saw its look of disbelief turn to disdain.

The Færie thought for a moment. *"Xerxes."*

"The King? Wow. Okay, I name you 'Xerxes'."

Just then the pulsing periapt flashed a light stronger than any explosion, and the Færie vanished.

17
Tempus Boulevard

Guy Shylocke was walking through the village of Bonsall with his best friend Vaughn Gilchrist. It was approaching nine o'clock but already the moon was hanging high in the clear winter sky; the air was so cold it tingled his nose.

"What's wrong?" Vaughn asked as he and Guy reached Lizzie's house. They were due to meet up with some friends at the pub like usual and had promised to call for Lizzie. Like usual.

Guy was looking at the fields across the way from Lizzie's, his brow heavy. "I dunno, don't you think it's quiet?"

"It's night-time, Sherlock, it's usually quiet."

He ignored the jibe, hazel eyes scanning the snow-covered hills of the Derbyshire Dales. "I know, but it's not normally *this* quiet."

Vaughn paused to listen. He wore his hair short to hide the fact it was already receding—something he was far from happy with. A frown shadowed his fair brow. "I suppose it *is* quieter than normal. There's a family of foxes in the copse over there, isn't there?"

"Precisely my point. Where've they gone? Did Mr Tibbles ever show up?" Guy asked, suddenly remembering Vaughn's cat.

"No, he's been missing three weeks now."

"I know Lizzie said the Tea Rooms' notice board's filling up with missing pet posters. Bit odd, don't you think?"

Vaughn shrugged. "I guess. So, what's going on?"

Guy looked at him puzzled, the orange streetlight casting shadows over his caramel brown hair. He wore a leather jacket and the cold had started to settle on his shoulders. He shivered. "We're waiting for Lizzie to put on her make-up and finish talking to Erica, like we always do this time on a Friday."

195

"No, I mean between you and Lizzie. It's obvious that she likes you and you've liked her since forever. Plus, she's hot. Why don't you just ask her out?"

Guy paused as he looked up at her bedroom window, its lights were on and the curtains drawn. Lizzie's shadow passed by. "It's not that simple."

"Sure, it is! 'Hi Lizzie! I've liked you since I first laid eyes on you. You're fit, I'm fit, 'you're my lobster'. How about it?"

"Did you just quote Friends?"

"It's a classic. So, care to enlighten me why it isn't it that simple?" he asked, scratching his stubble.

Guy looked down at his trainers and sighed a soul-shuddering sigh. "I see her and I see my past, my present and my future—she's my whole life. If I tell her how I feel and she doesn't feel the same, then I'd have lost everything. I'd be left with nothing."

"Wow. That's heavy. But oh-so wrong. You wouldn't have nothing; you'd have me."

There was a pause as the friends looked at one another.

Guy smiled. "Alright, I'd have nothing *and* you."

His heart suddenly stopped as Lizzie's face peeped through her curtains. Waving shyly down at him, their eyes locked, and the familiar feeling of warmth washed over him, enveloping him. Nothing else mattered, the world faded away, and it was just her and him. She turned and, moments later, the bedroom was plunged into darkness.

"Just promise me that if things do work out between you and Lizzie, you don't forget me or the band, okay?" Vaughn said, putting a hand on his shoulder.

"Of course! Though I can't see anything happening. I'm going to die a lonely old man."

"But at least you'll have your hair," Vaughn consoled.

"Hopefully."

The front door was opened by Mrs Brennan and Lizzie appeared in the hallway pulling on her heeled ankle boots. Light spilled out onto the neat front garden.

"You're going to catch your death like that," Mrs Brennan said as she pulled Lizzie's short jacket down in an attempt to cover her exposed midriff.

"You do fuss, mother," Lizzie said kindly, bending to kiss her on the cheek. "I'll be back after last orders. Bye dad!" She shouted before pulling on her hat and scarf and walking down the path where Guy and Vaughn waited.

She was beautiful with her flowing red locks and green eyes which seemed to glow brighter the closer she got. Her skinny jeans showed off her long legs and thighs. Guy watched her mesmerised; there was no chance such a goddess could like him.

"Bring her back safely, boys." Mrs Brennan called.

He stirred from his daydream and waved up at her. "Will do, Mrs B. I'll look after her."

"I know you will. You always have." She smiled before closing the door.

The three fell in step as they turned and walked down the High Street to the crossroads and The Crown pub. Vaughn caught Guy's eye and jerked his head in Lizzie's direction.

Guy cleared his throat. "So, erm, how's Erica?"

Vaughn slapped his face, grinning stupidly when Lizzie turned to look at him, eyebrows raised.

"Still acting weird. I don't know what's got into her." She pouted sullenly. "Do you ever feel like she's hiding something?"

"Always. I've never managed to figure her out and she's my own sister! Why, do you?"

"I didn't used to. But she's become so secretive recently."

Guy looked thoughtful. "I'll give her a call. See if I can get anything out of her."

"Thank you." And she flashed him a soul-flipping smile.

He was just contemplating dunking his head in the snow to cool down when music met their ears. Looking up, he could see the lights of the pub in the distance pouring onto the street, illuminating the village cross at the top of its circular steps.

Vaughn suddenly burst into a run. "Last one there buys the first round!"

197

Guy grinned at Lizzie. "I'll give you and your heels a head start." She winked. "Always the gentleman!"

**

Thankfully, Erica's Matriculation ceremony went a lot smoother. Well, apart from the fact Xerxes ended up being summoned naked, which the KeyMasters found heartily offensive (Apparently, Ashayla 'forgot' to pass clothing on during the initial summoning). So, there it stood, in all its glory, whilst Erica signed the Matriculation Loggia with her name and its chosen one. She was told it was most irregular, which didn't bother her, as everything had been 'most irregular' ever since meeting Michael.

Once she lifted the nib of the quill, her ink signature shone brightly, updating and imprinting upon the twinned Matriculation Loggia within The Guild.

She'd dressed smartly this time, in a two-piece suit with floral lace tights. On arrival she'd been handed a black robe with white fur-trim to wear; it reminded her of a graduation robe.

"Of a sort, but you'll wear a finer robe upon graduating as a KeyMaster," Michael said as he helped Ashayla adjust the robe. "That is, if you were to graduate, of course." He added quickly.

The Matriculation ceremony had been less grand than the Inauguration ceremony at The Guild. For starters, the Queen didn't attend, nor did it take place at The Guild. Instead, it took place in the University's oldest lecture theatre, with thick stone pillars carved with various geometric designs, large windows and ornate Gothic arches. All students had been invited to attend and welcome the new trainees. One by one they had stepped onto the dais in their fur-trimmed robes and one by one they had signed their name and that of their selected Færie.

When finished they stood to the side, near to where Professor Donald Staunton, the Vice-Chancellor, stood in a silk robe of purple and yellow. His Færie collected one of their three periapts from them, placing each carefully within a purple silk-lined chest. These would then be stored in The Guild.

Professor Staunton then welcomed them officially, carrying with it his hopes for their success and contributions to the great profession of KeyMastery. There was a round of applause and another (prolonged) photograph was taken for the Limbo Times. By the end, Erica's smile had set solid, giving her lock jaw, which entertained Xerxes far too much.

A traditional afternoon tea followed in the University's Refectory, with sandwiches and fresh scones with jam and cream.

Whilst Xerxes disappeared to change into its new attire—loose cotton shirt, breeches and waistcoat—Michael approached, raising his teacup in a toast.

"Congratulations on causing another stir, Miss Shylocke."

"Why thank you, Mr Nicholas." Erica smiled, raising her teacup in reply. She hesitated before offering him one of her two remaining periapts. Having learnt their worth, she knew it wasn't merely a pretty trinket she was passing over. It meant more. "It only seems right you have the second."

Michael regarded her for a moment before bowing. "You do me a great honour." He took the periapt and placed it carefully within his suit pocket.

Just then, an elegantly dressed couple approached. The lady bent and kissed Erica twice, once on each cheek. She smelt divine, like a freshly picked rose, and wore her greying hair piled up gracefully upon her head. Erica's hand was then taken by the gentleman and kissed, his thick white moustache tickling her.

Michael took the lady's hand in his. "Miss Erica Shylocke, may I present Lord Gaubert de Temps and Lady Regina de Temps, my surrogate parents. They took me under their wing when my own passed away." He explained.

Lady Regina curtsied low, allowing her grey silk chiffon skirts to puddle gracefully about her, whilst her husband bowed grandly. Knowing she would fall flat on her face, Erica instead opted for a modest curtsy.

"Congratulations on your Matriculation, my dear. I can see why Michael speaks so fondly of you, and so often," Lady Regina said, a mischievous glint in her eyes, which were the shade of cornflowers. She took Erica's hands in hers and looked to her husband. "Gaubert? *Chéri?* May I?"

His pale blue eyes twinkled as he nodded affably.

"Each year we host the New Year Ball for The Guild in January, but we would love for you to come and stay with us prior to the Ball too, for New Year's Eve."

Erica was taken aback and blushed.

"Michael will be with us, as he is every year." Lady Regina added coyly.

Erica stammered a thank you and attempted a second curtsy.

Anatole weaved his way through the crowds towards them, his plate stacked high with scones, cream upon his moustache. "My Lord, Lady," he said, bowing at the de Temps in turn.

"Anatole, my dear, we were just inviting one of your students to stay with us for the New Year Ball. I trust you will be attending also?"

"It would be a scandal not to, milady. If you excuse me, I must borrow Erica for just one moment." And he led her away. "Let us find the others, I need to ask you all something."

Having finally gathered his students and their mentors, Anatole invited them all to lunch at a renowned restaurant. On learning that Erica and her course mates had arranged to go shopping together before their lecture, Anatole instead swapped the invitation for dinner the next day, which was gladly accepted.

With time ticking, Iminathi suggested they leave. Devesting their robes, they left to visit Tempus Boulevard, where Limbo's main shops could apparently be found. To save more time, Tsuzuku insisted on paying for a hansom cab and soon they found themselves rumbling along cobbled streets with their carriage being pulled by a horse. But not a normal horse; it was shadowy and indistinct with eyes that blazed red behind its blinkers.

Concerned, Sachairi turned to Tsuzuku who smiled and replied, in Japanese. They looked at him puzzled. Tsuzuku, realising that they couldn't understand him, tapped his periapt. *"Lingua intellegite!"* He began again. "It's a Lost Soul. All the horses in Limbo are."

Sachairi watched warily as it snorted and whinnied.

Erica leaned forwards to look more closely. "Are they safe?"

"Those Lost Souls that have been given a purpose are found to be safe, those without a purpose are not," Tsuzuku explained.

Sachairi gripped on tighter to the carriage window, apparently no more reassured.

"Can they be given bad purposes?" Erica asked, watching the powerful creature pulling its load along so effortlessly.

"It's called 'Impressing'," Henrik said. "My grandfather told me about it. All Lost Souls in Limbo are Impressed with a purpose, so they can be controlled. I'm not sure, but I suppose they could be Impressed for bad purposes, but why would you do that?"

"Oh, I'm just curious. It's all so new," she replied casually, sinking back within the cushions lost in thought.

"I can't imagine what it's like for you two," Iminathi sympathised. "We've grown up with it so it's normal, but for you, it must be so…" She paused as she searched for the right word.

"Freaky?" Sachairi offered.

"Yes, 'freaky'." She smiled.

"You could say that," he muttered under his breath, still eyeing the ghostly horse with unease.

"Thank you," Iminathi said after a moment's silence.

Everyone looked up and followed her gaze to Sachairi.

"Me? What did I do?"

"For making me realise I'm not alone. In Limbo society being gay isn't openly admittedly to and is frowned upon." She hesitated, looking down at her balled fists, white at the knuckle. "I've had to hide it for years. But you were so honest… I've… I've decided it's time for me to be honest too." She looked up then, eyes bright with determination.

"That's great!" he said, smiling as they all congratulated her.

"Are you dating?" Erica asked the girl.

"No, are you guys?"

They all shook their heads.

"Well, that has got to change! What a bunch of losers are we?"

They laughed.

Henrik cleared his throat, changing the subject. "It's rare for a KeyMaster to be discovered outside of a KeyMaster family. You must both be incredibly talented."

Sachairi and Erica looked at one another.

"Nah, not particularly."

***

Tempus Boulevard lay to the south of Limbo and had wide pavements bustling with people and Færies. Mature lime trees lined both sides of the Boulevard, magical lights within their branches. Along the Boulevard were quaint boutiques in architecture from every time and country, all displaying the best of their wares. Despite the difference in styles, the mix of architecture worked, creating its own rhythm. Today the Boulevard was busy with hansoms, omnibuses, carts, sedan chairs and other private carriages clattering along its cobblestones.

The array of shops was staggering and catered for every taste and culture, as well as every era. There were confectioners, grocers, haberdasheries, tailors and seamstresses, as well as book shops, art suppliers, tea rooms, restaurants and some department stores. Amidst the familiar was also the unfamiliar, with shops specialising in Lost Souls, Loggias, quills, weapons, Færies and their charms.

Their resource list was long and varied, with quills, Loggias, parchment and seals listed in addition to books and various equipment needed for combat practice.

As they went from store to store, it became apparent to Erica how different things were from the high street practises she was used to. In each shop they were greeted and assigned a Færie to help them with their shopping. Whilst they sat, the Færie would take their list and go and collect their items for them. Detailed descriptions and demonstrations were also given, which proved particularly useful when Erica was purchasing her combat gear: leather breeches, breastplate, vambraces and helmet. But what Erica found most fascinating was the Loggia shop.

Their resource list stated that a Loggia was required for each subject, as well as one that would be used to practise their daily log entries. Once you had selected your preferred cover colour, material and parchment, the Færie assigned to you then proceeded to Charm the parchment and cover so that they knitted together to form a completed Loggia. Watching the leaves of parchment float and come together to be finally bound within the covers of your choice was truly spectacular and Erica was glad she needed six Loggias. On completion, she gave her Færie a round of applause which surprised it greatly.

"Wait until you get clothing made," Iminathi said, chuckling to see Erica's enthusiasm.

A faraway look overcame Erica as she imagined the process. Her eyes glistened. "They're worth their weight in gold!"

"Don't be silly, they don't get paid."

"What?!"

"They're slaves, just like ours."

"Xerxes isn't going to be a slave," Erica said curtly. She really wasn't keen on the relationships KeyMasters appeared to have with Færies.

"But you still went to the Finance Office and bought it." Iminathi pointed out.

"It's not like I had much choice," Erica replied, her brow furrowing. She would need to do something if she was going to make a difference. "I'll pay it," she said, inspiration hitting her.

Iminathi raised her eyebrows. "Does it want money?"

Erica hesitated as she handed the shopkeeper a cheque for her Loggias. "I doubt it." She thought for a moment, remembering what the Færie had said about the KeyMaster it had murdered. "I'll free it."

A tiny voice whispered tentatively in her ear. *"You will?"*

***

Professor Phyllis Portendorfer stopped her rocking chair with the heel of her foot. Peering over her horn-rimmed glasses at the students, she cast off once more on her knitting needles.

"Are you getting this down?" she snapped.

The lecture hall of students looked frazzled as they furiously scribbled down their notes. Her Færie, Cecil, wiped its brow as it magicked the floor-to-ceiling blackboard to turn as if it were a page in a book: There were already two boards (front and back) full of notes before it.

"I do hate people who dawdle. There's a lot to get through, you know."

Erica clutched at her fingers as they cramped up from twenty minutes of intense writing. Professor Portendorfer liked to talk. Some of the students had muttered how she'd been known to create fifteen blackboards-full of notes in an hour, as well as finish a jumper. Apparently, she made it her mission to knit each of her students a jumper for Christmas, which would explain why Erica and the other four had been brusquely measured upon arrival.

"You haven't really left me with much time; I can't guarantee they'll be ready, but I shall do my best," she had chuntered, as the tape measure had whizzed back within its casing with a sharp *snap!*

Whilst Temporal Studies involved more physics, KeyMastery, well, the theory side to it, resembled Erica's history lectures, but with more extreme stories, dates and names. However, with Professor Portendorfer rocking backwards and forwards on her rocking chair to the soft accompanying *click-click* of her knitting needles, Erica was reminded heavily of evenings spent in front of the fire with her grandmother as she recounted weird and wonderful tales, particularly those of her great-great-great-great-great-how-many-greats-grandmother who had vanished one night without trace.

Erica shook herself to avoid falling into a deep reverie: she was tired.

"With the expansion of the British Empire, the Georgian KeyMasters also sought to expand Limbo. On doing so, they consequently refined the field of KeyMastery, which had been overlooked in favour of Smithology and Sonnology—and rightly so, if one cannot protect one's castle, what else has one got, after all? But, on turning their attention to KeyMastery, documenting its developments and those who had contributed to them, the KeyMasters discovered a link with Smithology which ruffled KeyMasters for many years." Indicating to her Færie, Cecil magicked a 3D multi-layered map of hundreds upon hundreds of lines that zig-zagged in a seemly incoherent manner. Intermitted markings and symbols appeared upon the lines.

"Routes through Time. Without these maps, KeyMasters would lose themselves in Time. Without them, Smithologists would not know which keys fit which locks nor how to repair any damages. The two are intrinsically linked, despite the majority opining that the wielder of the Keys is more important than the Keys themselves."

She paused and took a few moments to concentrate on her knitting, counting her stitches under her breath before recommencing. There were some mutterings in response to her last comment.

Noting down her stitches, she continued. "To diminish loss of life, the KeyMasters decided to continue the work of Adolphus Chance, who had documented many routes through Time before losing himself in It. By working in groups, KeyMasters were able to travel back further and create more detailed maps. However, even they had their limits and, try as they might, they could not get beyond twenty-two Gateways. Any who tried were never to be seen again."

A student raised their hand and Professor Portendorfer put down her knitting to listen. "Did they not work together, the Smithologists and KeyMasters?"

"No. Imagine how much further back one could go if they did! But teamwork was a desideratum and, nowadays, KeyMasters, including researchers, have very little need to go back any further." She nodded to Cecil, who had been enjoying a break from dictating. It magicked a brand-new board complete with their homework assignments upon it. "Which leads happily on to your homework.

One, to prepare an essay on the Founding KeyMasters and an ongoing piece, which will tie in with your Smithology course, to begin memorising the Gateway Maps."

There was a universal groan.

"I think I preferred Lozen's lecture," Sachairi muttered.

18
Summoned

The restaurant Anatole took them to just off Tempus Boulevard was salubrious with high-vaulted ceilings and voluptuous crystal chandeliers. However, the meal consisted of some quirky dishes, such as white soup, a Fricassee of Pigs Feet and Ears, Pike with Pudding in its Belly and a whole calves head. By dessert (Baked Apples, Lemon Ice, fruit Tartlets, whitedish and Sugar Plums) Erica felt quite drained and was finding her eyes becoming heavy.

"Are you quite well, Miss Shylocke? You've hardly touched your whitedish." Michael appeared next to her, taking Iminathi's seat. Looking blearily around for her, Erica found the girl attempting the spirited Barynya dance with Anatole.

"You were right." She slurred, finding her vision doubling. "Fatigue is not bearable."

His eyes narrowed as they looked her over—she was paler than usual. "You've altered Time once again."

Unable to hold back anymore, she folded her arms upon the table and snuggled into them with a yawn. "It was my last day at work, well on my old contract anyway, and Marc and Joslin wanted to go out for a meal and a drink. I mean, I couldn't say no, could I? We then went to a club. Then another one…" She trailed off sleepily.

"Consequently, you altered Time. Did you alter it to allow you rest?"

"I didn't think—"

Michael interrupted her, setting his glass down abruptly. "No, you obviously did not. Come with me, Miss Shylocke." And he hoisted her to her feet.

Bidding their party goodnight, he helped gather her things together and, supporting her, led her from the restaurant and down the Boulevard, which was now lit with magical Christmas lights that zig-zagged their way along the trees that lined the Boulevard.

Hailing down a hansom, Michael gave their destination of the West Gate and helped Erica into the carriage. The journey was a blur of unknown roads, bumpy cobbles and smudgy streetlights. By the time they arrived at the Gate, Erica was fast asleep and try as he might Michael could not rouse her. He even resorted to pinching her nose and tickling her eyelids, but to no avail. He smiled despite himself.

Paying his fee, he lifted her easily into his arms: she snuggled up against his chest before snoring contentedly.

"Ashayla, please help Xerxes to prepare Miss Shylocke's quarters," Michael said softly as he carried the sleeping girl through the West Gate, nodding his thanks to the Guards on duty.

"As you wish."

He'd decided to take the escalator up, it was slower but gentler and less likely to wake Erica.

It was as he crossed the moat that the hairs on the back of his neck stood on end and a chill ran up his spine. He shuddered involuntarily and turned to scan the towering wall behind him. *Surely not? It was out of bounds*. He paused to examine the shadowy battlements. Nothing. He hesitated: logic told him to ignore his reaction and continue homewards. He must be imagining it, though instinct told him otherwise: *how could they access the wall without the Guards knowing?*

He glanced at those Guards of the Glorious Dead which were on duty; nothing seemed out of the ordinary.

He chided himself for his poor nerves and continued towards the escalator.

***

The shadows gave up the two men from their darkest depths.

"I think we are now at the point where you come in."

"Yes, I think we are. And you shall ensure the bells sound not?"

"Leave it to us. Provided travel is random and notice is given, none will be the wiser when we visit the Sonnastry. No one has raised concerns thus far."

"Good, then I shall set to." The man doffed his hat and was about to depart when a lone figure carrying something exited the primary city wall and crossed the moat. The figure turned without warning and the man dived back into the safety of the shadows.

Waiting with bated breath, the two men watched the figure scan the battlements. After the longest of moments, the figure slowly turned and continued on its way towards the outer wall.

"Do you think they saw us?"

"Impossible."

***

Erica awoke to the distant sound of a cockerel. It instantly made her think she was home, but she knew she wasn't, she was in her London flat, not her bedroom at home. Confused, she slowly opened her eyes to find Xerxes lying next to her, propped up against one of its hands. Naked.

"So, a country girl. Good morning, ma'am. Sleep well?" It winked.

Erica sat bolt upright. "What are you doing in my bed?!"

"I'm offended you forgot. You said I was the best you'd ever had."

Erica rolled her eyes. "Ha-ha. I remember falling asleep in the carriage and…" She trailed off as she processed the fragments of memory she had. It was then she noticed she was in her pyjamas, her clothes piled neatly on a chair. "Wait, did Michael change me?" she asked, her heart growing cold.

Xerxes smiled mischievously, laughing heartily as Erica fell back against her pillows; covering her face, which burned red from embarrassment. "No, no, no, no, no!"

"You should be ashamed; your choice of pyjamas is horrifically twee. He was not impressed." Erica looked sternly at the Færie

209

which sighed: fun over. *"Fear thee not, Ashayla insisted on preparing you for bed. Mr Nicholas waited without."*

Erica pulled off the bedcovers and got out of bed. "How long have I slept?"

"Approximately twelve hours. Mr Nicholas directed me to wake you before noon—to help you re-adjust."

Erica yawned and stretched. She guessed that made sense.

Her stomach growled. Reluctantly getting out of bed, she walked to the kitchenette to start on breakfast. "I'm guessing you don't want any…"

Erica's question to the Færie turned into a torrent of expletives. "What are my tops doing in the cupboard? Why are my boots in the oven?! And what's my underwear doing in the fridge?!"

"Never leave a Færie unattended. They get bored."

Erica glared at it from the doorway. It had fluffed up her pillows and was sat propped up against them reading a magazine. "Then do something."

"I did."

"Something constructive!"

"You were asleep, what can I do when my 'master' is asleep?"

"Sleep? Clean? My homework? I don't know. You don't need to stay here if you're not needed."

"I do not?" Xerxes looked up surprised.

"Of course not, if you're not needed you have my permission to return to Utarra."

"Really!" Xerxes whipped off the covers excitedly. Erica blushed and the Færie's naked form changed into its hot elemental orb.

The orb whizzed about the room gleefully before making a beeline for Erica's periapt. Quickly snatching it, Erica hid it behind her back. The orb regarded her questioningly, its molten surface flaring hotly.

"Not until you sort out my wardrobe!"

***

In the weeks that followed, a sense of normality fell (if such a thing still existed). Erica got in the habit of lightly touching Ashayla's periapt as she left her flat in the morning so, by the time Erica had walked up Marloes Road, Michael would be waiting for her on the corner of Cheniston Gardens. Then, together, they would walk to the Underground station.

Sometimes Michael would be visible and come into town with her to sit in local cafés, the student canteen or surf the internet whilst she attended lectures, taking notes on language and habit that he'd later quiz her on. But most of the time, he'd remain invisible and watch her from the High Street as she continued to walk down the Arcade to the station. At such times Erica would see him turn back left, to attend the morning's sessions at The Guild in Limbo; although, every so often, he'd carry on down the High Street towards wherever he was going. She wondered if it was to see Annabelle. However, despite her curiosity, she felt she owed him too much to ask—after all, it was his own business.

Nevertheless, regardless which way he turned, he would be there, in the domed hall of the station Arcade, on her return at the end of the day. And, together, they would walk back to his house to continue her training.

Sometimes this would involve Time Travel, with him giving her opportunities to practise travelling in and out of different Gateways, getting used to her Keys. Not to mention, collecting data for Christian. Occasionally, a boyish sense of mischief would take over and he'd insist on them playing 'hide-and-seek' with Erica as 'it'. Whilst she counted, he would dart through a random series of doors, travelling ever deeper through Time, testing her ability to trace his Temporal Aura. Once she'd finished counting, she would follow his orange-yellow Aura through this Gateway and that, trying not to get distracted by the sights and history she walked through. To help her focus, she would count the Gateways she passed through.

There was one occasion when she counted twenty Gateways and began to get scared, frantically running after his Aura, panicking that she'd lost him to Time. On finding him through the twenty-fifth

Gateway, his grin of satisfaction turned to immediate concern as he saw her stricken face and promised not to be so foolish again.

Sometimes, he would guide her as to how to complete their Loggias. And, working side-by-side, they would fill in the required information. But, no matter how far they'd got with her training, always at ten o'clock he'd walk her back home. Then, running to her window, she'd watch him through a chink in her curtains to see him walk not back up along Marloes Road to his home, but down towards Cromwell Road. She assumed it was to meet Annabelle but, again, she was too cautious to ask.

**

On the last Thursday before Christmas, Anatole found her in the library working on some charms for her forthcoming combat practice; making notes from a small, pocket-sized book bound in burgundy leather. She was dressed in her combat breeches and simple t-shirt, having ditched the traditional loose shirt; her leather armour was stowed in the rucksack beside her.

"That will have to wait, Erica. Dr Finnegan wants to see you. Come."

"Have I done something wrong?" Erica asked, eyes wide as she gathered her things together.

"It's about the report you wrote for him. I thought it best if I were there too. I've informed Michael, but he is… detained. He'll join us as soon as he can." Anatole patted her reassuringly on the back as he saw her face pale.

She was led out of the Library and across to the University, following Anatole upstairs to the first floor where the lecturers' offices could be found. Stopping outside one, Anatole knocked on its door and opened it. Erica followed him inside, wringing her hands.

Dr Finnegan stopped his pacing at the sound of their knock and watched them enter with bright, keen eyes. She had expected to see the Vice-Chancellor there too and sighed in relief when she saw he wasn't—she wasn't being expelled. Well, not yet anyway.

"Ah, Anatole, so this is Miss, erh, Shylocke? Is that right?" he asked, checking the name on the crumpled report in his hands.

"Yes, it is. Erica, Dr Finnegan would like to speak with you regarding your report."

Indicating the chairs in front of his desk, Erica and Anatole sat down. It was a spacious office, despite the clutter and non-existent filing; piles of paper were stacked on all available surfaces. Tall windows dominated the end wall. Through which snowy sunlight filtered in, imitating the snowfall in Actualle London that morning. Winter was well and truly underway.

Dr Finnegan stood behind his desk and regarded Erica carefully for the longest of minutes. Then, suddenly unable to control himself, he flung down her report.

"Temporal Imprints, you saw them?"

She looked to Anatole, suddenly scared. He nodded. "Yes, I saw them."

"And the Temporal Auras? You saw them too? But in different colours?"

"Yes."

"How many times have you seen them? On just this occasion?"

"No. Every time I travel through Time."

Dr Finnegan hesitated then, his shoulders relaxing a little. "And the Temporal Essence—the echoes you heard in addition to the heartbeat. Was it just on this occasion?"

"Yes. But when I was writing this report, I mentioned everything to my Færie. It said that if I'd been sensitive to that building's Temporal Essence, I should be for every other building."

"And are you?"

Erica nodded, tears stinging her eyes: she wondered what it was like to be normal. "If I touch it with my bare hands, yes."

Anatole looked at her then, the coolness of the past weeks softening.

Dr Finnegan caved at the sight of her tears and sat down heavily. His stern demeanour melting away.

"I am so sorry—" Erica began.

He held his hand up, interrupting her. "My dear girl, there is nothing to apologise for. I'm not angry. I'm anything but angry. I'm just…" he searched for the right word. "Taken aback, astounded, dumbstruck. I thought you were writing a sensational report to make a fool of me."

"I wouldn't dream of it, sir!"

Dr Finnegan smiled. "I know; you're scared, I can see it in your face. It must have been an unnerving experience for you. Well, if you're happy to work with me, perhaps we can get some answers?"

"I'd like that."

Dr Finnegan turned to Anatole and smiled. "It's something to be proven right in one thing, but to have all my theories proven right is quite another! I deserve a pay rise." He chuckled.

"Provided I get a finder's fee, Horatio." Anatole smiled.

He laughed. "Why am I not surprised? Do you mind if I see them?" he asked, turning shyly to Erica.

"Not at all." Erica took out Xerxes' periapt and, once summoned, explained what was needed. Xerxes removed its gloves and flexed its fingers dramatically—making them crack—before placing them upon Erica's temples. The sharp, cool pain of her memories being cut through was a welcome distraction from her nerves.

The Cerebral Projection ripped itself from the air over Dr Finnegan's desk and Erica took him through some recent travels through Time, including the trip she wrote her report on—though, she missed out her encounter with the spirit. She didn't need that on top of everything else. She was becoming quite adept at manipulating her memories to avoid any embarrassing scenes…

At first, Dr Finnegan was speechless and looked at the Imprints and Auras open mouthed, eyes wide. "Heavens! They're… they're… beautiful…" He stammered, leaning forwards.

Then, as if shaking himself from a dream, he sat bolt upright, grabbed a piece of blank parchment and began making notes with a raven's quill. On several occasions he asked Xerxes to replay some memories—pausing and magnifying the image to let him see the Imprints and Auras more closely.

It was then that a knock sounded on the door.

"Come in, come in." Dr Finnegan called out absentmindedly, far too engrossed on the image Xerxes was replaying to be paying any real attention to the visitor.

Michael entered, still dressed in his jacket, muffler and top hat. His cheeks were flushed from the cold.

"I am extremely sorry I couldn't get here sooner, I—" He began, but Dr Finnegan interrupted him, gesturing at Erica and the Cerebral Projections.

"This is unheard of Michael!"

"Yes, I'm aware," he said, walking forwards to look at the Cerebral Projection. "I believe it has something to do with Miss Shylocke being a Medium. I believe her ability to see spirits makes her sensitive to other unseen phenomena."

Erica looked at him sharply and the Cerebral Projection stopped, exploding into a shower of sparkles.

Dr Finnegan looked aghast.

Anatole looked at Michael incredulously.

"Spirits you say?" Dr Finnegan said, regarding Erica cautiously.

On realising, Michael blushed deeply. "Oh, I, erm, apologies, Erica, I thought you'd mentioned…" He trailed off sheepishly.

Erica sighed and rubbed her temples. *Honestly, could she have no privacy?*

"Sorry, Dr Finnegan. I was waiting to see if you thought there could be some alternative reason before telling you. As you can imagine, it isn't something I blurt out to all and sundry," she said, flashing Michael a vexed look. "It has done nothing but give me grief my whole life."

Dr Finnegan regarded her carefully for a moment. "I can appreciate that." He reached for his diary. "Well, I think we need to set aside some proper time for research and tests, don't you, Erica? If we are to get those answers. What about tomorrow? First thing?"

She nodded, relieved he hadn't been put off, and he made a note in his diary.

Once outside in the corridor, she began to walk away.

Michael reached for her. "Erica, I'm sorry, truly. Please, I shouldn't have said anything."

She shook him off. "No, you shouldn't. But if you were there from the beginning you'd have known, wouldn't you?!" She shouted, surprising herself at how angry she was. "You know my dad doesn't even know? My very own father! The same goes for my brothers! They just think I'm odd. Where I come from 'this' makes you a freak! An abomination. If people found out I'd be banished, if I'm lucky! Times might have changed but people haven't. I've kept it hidden my whole life, and I was doing a damned good job until you came along!"

"That is a little harsh—" Michael started before being cut short.

"Since I've met you, the number of people who've found out have increased…" She started to count the people and Færies on her fingers, lost count and gave up. "Exponentially!"

"I can arrange for some extra maths tuition for you too, if you wish," he quipped.

Erica looked at him darkly. "I'm here because of you. Don't forget that."

"No, Time chose you."

"Yes, and I did *that* to Time, remember?" She gestured rudely. "I came back for you." And, with that, she stormed off. Hesitating, Xerxes bowed apologetically before hurrying after her.

Michael made to follow her also, but Anatole placed a hand on his shoulder. "I believe you have done enough for one day, my friend."

"I meant no harm…" He started dismally.

"I know. She knows. But it wasn't your secret to reveal. How would you like it if I told everyone about Annabelle?"

Michael looked at him, realisation dawning. He went over to a bench and sat down heavily, head in his hands.

Anatole sat next to him. "Why were you visiting her at this time of day? You should have been here with Erica. Not just me. This goes beyond the remit of a Course Tutor." He smiled weakly.

"Maria found me."

"Her mother? But she's dead."

"I am aware. She wanted me to talk to Annabelle."

"But you do…"

Michael looked to the floor, cheeks reddening.

Comprehension dawning, Anatole swore. "All this time?!"

Michael nodded bashfully, his heart aching. Anatole let out a whistle before patting him sympathetically on his back.

"So, why did Maria find you?"

"She says Annabelle is in danger."

Anatole looked at him in surprise. "And what can you do?"

"Let her go."

19
Solaris Vindictis

Erica was glad she had combat practise instead of a lecture: it provided the perfect outlet for her frustrations.

This was her seventh session of combat practise and despite never having done anything like it before, she was pleased to discover she wasn't terrible at it. Her stamina was rubbish and she had pathetic upper-body strength, so Kung Fu with the Færie Yophiel—which had apparently spent time in a Chinese emperor's court and was adept at Taichi and Kung Fu—was a struggle. And any sustained sword practise under the keen eye of Cornelius Buchanan, a Soul Gatherer with bushy whiskers, was difficult; but she was okay at her charms.

Much to her surprise Professor Portendorfer worked together with Lozen to support Charm implementation and, despite her penchant for knitting, Professor Portendorfer proved herself to be a tenacious opponent. In fact, standing in her combat breeches and leather armour, she looked quite fearsome.

"As an elemental being, your Færie has a natural preference for its element: fire, water, wood, ice, stone, electricity, air or light. Whilst all Færies can cast any charm regardless of its elemental origins, it is better to stay within your Færies' elemental strength; for example, if they are elemental beings of light then their strength will lie with light-based charms. Cecil here is an elemental being of stone, so the charms I predominately cast are those based within the element of stone. However, certain Lost Souls respond better to charms of a certain element, like Wrathfuls, who cannot abide light and are weakened greatly by light charms. Consequently, a

KeyMaster must be well-versed in all charms to ensure they are prepared for any attacks."

The students had been divided up into smaller groups and were rotating between the different tutors. Erica had been paired up with another trainee called İlkay. They'd already spent time reviewing and practising Kung Fu and had now rotated to work with Lozen and Professor Portendorfer. They would go on to sword practice last.

Erica was red-faced, sweaty and needing a drink.

"Your homework was to learn ten offensive and defensive charms from your Færie's natural element. You have twelve minutes to practise them on your own before duelling with your partner." She blew on her whistle enthusiastically.

As the trainee KeyMasters spaced out to practise their charms, Lozen and Professor Portendorfer circulated, offering advice and suggestions for improvement if needed. Memorising the charms was one thing, but Erica found implementing them sometimes cumbersome as the periapt had to be touched, at least lightly, to deploy the Charm.

"Can't we just wear the damned things?" Erica chuntered as Lozen stopped to watch her, all fingers and thumbs.

"There are accessories that you might find help, but whatever you do, do not place the periapt against your heart. To touch, we Færies find human flesh irresistible—if our periapts cover a beating heart the essence within awakens and we cannot help but possess it. Once possessed, we struggle to release it until it beats no more and is no longer of interest."

Erica turned green at the thought.

It shrugged. *"It is sad but true. Though, in that short time, the possessed KeyMaster shares our power. A worthwhile strategy if you find yourself with nothing to lose. As you were."* And it continued its stroll through the trainees.

As the twelve minutes ended, Professor Portendorfer blew shrilly on her whistle. Moving to stand with İlkay, they turned so they were back-to-back. Erica double-checked her leather helmet, ensuring the buckle was fastened tightly beneath her chin. Professor

Portendorfer then blew her whistle a second time and they began to take eight strides away from each other. Upon the eighth stride, they turned so they were looking at one another. The Professor blew on her whistle again, signalling the start of their duel. Two fingers were raised—best of two.

İlkay was fast off the mark and deployed a maelstrom that sucked Xerxes down into its watery depths, almost extinguishing him. His Færie, Aysel, landed nimbly beside him dressed traditionally in a colourful şalvar, skirt, embellished apron and contrasting long jacket. A decorative silk headdress covered its face.

If they hadn't been duelling, Erica would've laughed to see Xerxes drenched and fizzing madly in the swirling, angry water. But, as it was, she was searching mentally through the charms she'd learnt, trying to think which would best combat the attack. Finally deciding upon a counterattack, she touched the periapt but too late, Aysel launched a rip tide, jostling and battering Xerxes until his heat was no more.

She had lost.

Despite his efforts, İlkay couldn't hide his jubilation at having won the first round. He felt certain the next would also be his.

Xerxes materialised next to Erica in soggy, elfin form. *"In your own time, ma'am. Don't mind me!"* Its voice dripping with sarcasm.

"Look, I'm trying. He's just super-fast!"

"Or maybe you're just 'super-slow'?" Retorted the Færie.

"There is something called self-help!"

The Færie clanged its two thick cuffs together in one vicious gesture.

"Seriously?! You've got nothing?" She snapped.

"The joys of being elementally enslaved, ma'am. I am entirely reliant on your shrewd strategies."

"What can you do?"

It bent over and scratched its backside.

"We're screwed," she said, blanching.

"Are you ready this time?" İlkay shouted over the din of the Combat Hall to her.

220

Erica nodded brusquely. She was fed up with people walking over her today.

Nonetheless, she was just as slow off the mark and Xerxes glared at her evilly as an endless deluge of water poured onto it until it was nothing more than a blurry form.

"Monte Igneus." Erica invoked quietly, tapping her periapt.

At first nothing happened, and she could see Xerxes diminishing under the weight of the water. Then, there was a rumble and Xerxes erupted like the volcano Erica had called upon, spewing hot molten lava everywhere. The lava solidified instantly against the water that smothered it and loud hissing and steam filled the space between them.

Erica seized the chaotic moment and touched her periapt a second time. *"Solaris Vindictis."*

On uttering the charm, the hardened lava began to pulsate with increasing intensity until the newly formed shell could contain it no more and a massive supernova ripped through the stone, evaporating all water instantaneously before pulsating outwards. The nuclear eruption shook the Hall and all Færies instinctively moved as one to protect their KeyMasters as the radiation ravaged the air.

Xerxes and Erica shared a look of utter shock; it couldn't protect her with explosions continuing to emanate uncontrollably from it. As multicoloured flames headed hotly towards her, a form appeared between them: Yophiel. It instantly charmed a protective bubble to surround the two of them. From within, they watched the angry flames lick the bubble's surface as the firestorm engulfed their shelter.

After what seemed like hours the supernova finally burnt out, leaving Xerxes on all fours, drained and desperately clutching the ground.

Aysel had wrapped İlkay in a similar protective bubble and was regarding Erica coolly. İlkay looked at Erica dumbfounded.

"Are you unhurt?" Yophiel asked as their shield evaporated.

"Y-yes. Thank you for saving me," she said heart in her throat.

"But of course. Where did you find that charm?" The Færie asked wide-eyed.

"The Library…"

As people began to emerge from their Færies' protective charms, a shrill whistle ripped through the air, followed quickly by Professor Portendorfer's distinctive voice as she marched over. "These are friendly duels, Shylocke! What were you doing conjuring up a supernova?!"

The Professor was now standing before her. There was silence as all students turned to her, dusting themselves off and checking their Færies.

Erica looked around with wide eyes, the reality of what she'd done hitting her hard. Thankfully the Færies had acted quickly so there were no casualties, and the new facilities had survived with only the odd scorch mark—their protective charms had worked well. The Professor looked at her expectantly. She cleared her throat. "I didn't want to lose another round." Although she spoke softly, it still sounded loud in the silence. Loud and stupid.

"So, you conjured a nuclear explosion in a Hall full of people?! I thought you were one of the clever ones!" Despite the shouting, the Professor was ashen and clearly shaken.

Erica looked at her feet, tears in her eyes. "I didn't mean to… The book said it was just an explosion! I didn't think…"

"Clearly! You'll be lucky if you aren't expelled for this!"

Erica looked up, pained: *no*…

The Professor took a deep breath and turned to Xerxes. "Take her home."

The Færie did as it was commanded and, placing a hand on her shoulder, they were enveloped by nothingness and disappeared.

***

She was summoned back within the hour.

She'd only just dried her hair after a shower. Hastily dressing in to her ultra-sombre, black workwear she touched her periapt and felt a severe cramping sensation take hold of her; contorting her and folding her in upon herself until she was no bigger than a particle. When she felt she couldn't bear it any longer there was a loud *crack!*

Opening her eyes, she found herself back in one piece and standing under the vaulted beams of the Library in Limbo. The winter sun was finishing its arc of the sky, its light barely filtered through the skylights.

Before her, a long table had been laid out with a selection of books of various sizes under the reading lamps. Clustered at one end of the table were Miss Rimmer, the Librarian, Professor Portendorfer, Lozen, Yophiel, Michael, Anatole and Professor Donald Staunton, the Vice-Chancellor.

Erica gulped.

The Vice-Chancellor turned gravely to her. "First the bells, then this… I did not expect this this afternoon, Miss Shylocke. You have been summoned here to explain your actions before a verdict is decided: to expel you or not."

She nodded nervously, her heart beating painfully against her ribs.

The Vice-Chancellor signalled to his Færie to begin taking notes which it did, in a large red tome.

"At approximately 14:10 you began your combat session in the Combat Hall led by Cornelius Buchanan, Professor Portendorfer, and the Færies Lozen and Yophiel. You were assigned to work with a fellow trainee, an İlkay Demir, and had completed your Kung Fu with the Færie Yophiel. When the incident took place, you were duelling under the direction of Professor Portendorfer and the Færie Lozen; you had not yet circulated to train with Cornelius Buchanan." Whilst setting the scene, the Vice-Chancellor had stood still. Suddenly he began to walk along the table towards where she stood. "Can you explain what the charms were?"

Erica made to reply and found her throat had gone dry. She cleared her throat and licked her lips. "We, erh, we had been set homework to learn ten offensive and defensive charms from our Færie's natural element. My Færie's natural element is fire."

"And how did you come by your ten offensive and defensive charms?"

"From a book in the Library. From here."

"Just one book?"

"Yes, just one."

The Vice-Chancellor stepped back, as if revealing the books upon the table for the first time. "There is a selection of books on the table before you. I would like you to select the book that you used to collect your charms. You only have the one chance, so do ensure you are happy with your decision."

Erica nodded, and began to walk along the table; the book she had used had been small, but sadly the selection before her were all small. After five minutes she had whittled it down to two books, one with a cover of burgundy and another with one of maroon.

"May I?" she asked, her hands hovering just above the maroon one. The Vice-Chancellor looked to the Librarian, who nodded.

"No peeking, mind," said the Vice-Chancellor.

Picking it up, Erica felt its weight in her palms, before caressing its covers and fanning its pages, letting its aroma wash over her. She then did the same with the burgundy one.

"This one," she said confidently. Holding up the burgundy book. "Definitely this one."

"And where were you sat?"

Erica scanned the vast Library, getting her bearings. "There." Pointing to a large desk between two bookcases. "The seat to the left." Realisation dawned on her. "I left it; Dr Finnegan needed to see me, and I left it on the desk in my hurry. Sorry," she said, turning to the Miss Rimmer, who smiled shyly.

The Vice-Chancellor looked to the Librarian, who gave a small nod. "And which bookcase was it on?"

Erica went over to the seat she had sat at and looked at the nearby bookcases. Her eye had initially been attracted by a brightly bound book in purple and gold leather but had then spied the unassuming book on a shelf quite out of reach. She saw the ornate steps she had used and went to them, pointing up. "That shelf. I had to use the steps."

"I would like my Færie to perform a Cerebral Projection on you to confirm this."

Erica nodded apprehensively.

Within minutes the memories had been ripped from her mind and quivered in the air for all to see. The Vice-Chancellor watched grimly as Erica's memory-self scanned the shelves, her hand hovering over a gaudy purple and gold leather book, before the unassuming pocket-sized book caught her eye. "Bother being short!" Her memory-self grumbled as she fetched a set of steps.

"I think there is little point to go further. Well, this has proven two things: that you are astute, and you are telling the truth. You are no longer under suspicion."

The atmosphere immediately lightened, and Erica could feel the tension in her back melting away.

"But how did it get here?" The Vice-Chancellor asked Miss Rimmer sternly as Michael walked over to her.

"I told him you wouldn't have knowingly done anything wrong," he said in an undertone so only she could hear. Erica nodded, tears pricking her eyes. He put his arm around her and she let herself lean back into his chest, his warmth and strength was exactly what she needed right now.

"I don't know, sir," Miss Rimmer stammered, clearly flustered. "I checked the logbooks like you asked and it hasn't been borrowed in years."

"Is something amiss, sir?" Michael asked.

"The book, it's Regulated."

Anatole, Michael and Erica looked at each other sharply: it would appear they'd found the book.

***

It was the last day of lectures before the Christmas holidays. If Erica hadn't got her meeting with Dr Finnegan, she could've had a much-needed lie-in, especially after yesterday's ordeal. Bleary eyed and disgruntled, she looked up as the professor walked down the corridor towards her and his office.

Her wrists ached; the tray she was holding was laden with a complete china coffee service. She'd asked for coffee at the refractory thinking she'd receive a cardboard cup. More fool her.

"Sorry to keep you, Miss Shylocke. There was a queue on the helter-skelter."

She smiled. *Only in Limbo.*

He unlocked the door and pushed it open. "Do come in. We'll sit over there. I see you brought coffee, marvellous."

He walked in, indicating to two sofas arranged facing one another. Erica followed him in and set the tray down on the table between the two sofas. Sitting down she began to pour the steaming coffee. She hugged her cup gratefully—the office was cold.

Dr Finnegan came over carrying parchment and a quill and sat down excitedly, pouring himself a coffee. "I have to say, this is quite extraordinary. Never did I expect to live long enough to see any of my theories proven, let alone study them!"

She smiled over the rim of her coffee cup. Selfishly, she just wanted answers. If there were any.

"Well, if you're ready, let's set to. If you could show me some recent trips through Time with your mentor, I shall make some notes. Maybe we can start making some sense of things for you at the same time." He ended kindly as Erica summoned a tetchy Xerxes.

She grinned guiltily.

***

If you'd told Erica an hour earlier that it was possible to fall asleep whilst undergoing a Cerebral Projection, she would've laughed. But not now. Xerxes kicked her for the umpteenth time and she jerked awake.

Xerxes kicked her again.

"I'm awake!" she hissed.

"I know," it hissed back.

Sighing, she eyed the empty coffee pot before looking dully at the Projection which the professor was pouring over, manipulating

226

it to zoom in and out of details, all the while taking notes. He was flicking between five different memories, comparing the Auras that had been left behind as a permanent memento of their owner.

Erica looked at the Auras and their glistening trails, marvelling at their colours. Some Auras were a mixture of colours, whereas others weren't.

It was then, as Dr Finnegan flicked quickly between the memories, that Erica noticed it.

"What's that?" She pointed, leaning forwards.

The professor looked up from his notes and peered at where she indicated. There was an Aura in brown. "An Aura." He looked at her impatiently.

She swiped through the different memories pointing each time. Four out of the five memories contained the same brown Aura.

"Maybe it's just coincidence?" He hazarded.

Erica shook her head, suddenly awake. "I think each person secretes an Aura that's unique to them. Like a fingerprint. See?" She zoomed in to her violet Aura and Michael's orange-yellow one. "There are flecks of silver in mine, whereas Michael's has none. But the yellow in his Aura is brighter than that one." She pointed to another Aura from one of the memories.

Now interested, Dr Finnegan leaned forwards and zoomed in even more, examining the individual Auras. Each one did indeed seem to vary in strength and colour. He turned his attention to the brown one Erica had noticed—it contained flecks of black. He zoomed out and flicked through the four memories. In each instance, the brown Aura was made up of black flecks.

Their eyes met through the Projection. "You appear to be correct, Miss Shylocke. Very astute. Let's have a look at all your travels through Time."

Five minutes later and they had scrutinised each of Erica's memories: eighteen in total. Thirteen of them contained the Brown Aura.

"I think that's more than just coincidence, sir. Don't you agree?"

20
Out on the town

"You did what?!"

Erica held her mobile away from her ear as Marc squawked at her. "I invited him to join us," she said, replacing the handset to her ear.

"But why?"

Despite still being mad at Michael, after the ordeal with the book and his belief in her, Erica hadn't had the heart to not remind him of her original invitation to today's Christmas work do. She also couldn't get the feel of his arm around her—let alone the firmness of his chest—out of her head.

"He's going to be alone this Christmas, so I thought it would be nice."

"But that's why we have Christmas movies, to help cheer up those who are alone." Marc moaned.

"Stop being a Scrooge! He's going to meet us at Somerset House at nine."

"He's not coming to the meal?"

"No."

"Good."

Erica couldn't help but smile at Marc's petulant tone.

"I'll see you later then. Don't forget it's fancy dress!"

"Never fear, I've already got my tights on."

"Splendid! Can you send me a pic?"

"No!" She hung up with a laugh.

***

They piled out of the Underground train at Covent Garden hot and sweaty. Who would've thought fancy dress costumes could be so warm? Joslin, who had decided to dress as a Christmas Unicorn, was suffering more than others.

"Can we swap? This onesie is killing me!" She panted, eyeing up Erica's Ms Claus outfit enviously.

"Quit moaning, you'll be fine once we get above ground," Marc said, the bells on his elf hat jingling merrily. "You'll be nice and snug and we'll be freezing."

"I hope so!"

There was the typical queue for the lifts to the surface. Marc eyed the stairs.

"193 steps! Nah-ah! No way! This unicorn is waiting." Joslin sat down in protest.

Thankfully, the queue diminished quickly as the lifts came and went, steadily carrying passengers up to the surface.

Exiting the ticket barriers, they were faced with a large crowd bustling about a news kiosk, blocking the doors to the street beyond.

"What's the rush?" Erica asked.

"Haven't you heard? The Prime Minister's announced a state of emergency." Marc said. "It's a global pandemic: people are vanishing."

"'Vanishing'?!" Erica came to an abrupt stop and a load of people bumped into her.

Pulling her out of the way of their angry mutterings, Marc led her and Joslin away from the station. Queuing at a newspaper kiosk, Erica purchased a paper and they stepped to the side.

"When was this announced?" Erica asked scanning the front page.

"This morning. It was all over the TV. Everyone knows about it. Well, most do." Joslin flashed her a withering look. "Where have you been? Mars?"

"Not quite," Erica said. *But not a bad guess…*

Lost but not forgotten... Numbers are too great to ignore... Earliest presumed case was September... People to remain vigilant... Lockdowns likely... National and Global efforts to control the situation... Gone without trace... Dial '57' in case of emergency... Where are they?

Flicking through the pages, she came across a section filled with photos and dates and pleas. Scanning the dates, Erica noticed that the earliest went missing mid-September, with more and more vanishing towards the end of November and throughout December. All these people... There were hundreds... Pages and pages of tiny, classified ads all asking for the whereabouts of loved ones: husbands, wives, fathers, mothers, brothers, sisters, sons and daughters. Sadness overwhelmed her. All these people. All these lives. All these souls... She looked over the sea of faces, her heart numb. *This was it. The Guild couldn't ignore this.*

"I know it's really sad, but let's not let it spoil our night, agreed?" Marc said, appearing at her side and giving her a hug. She nodded and rolled up the paper—Michael would want to see it.

Taking both her and Joslin's hands, Marc led them away to Covent Garden and their restaurant. Christmas lights twinkling overhead.

***

Despite the shock of the missing people, Erica forced herself to make the most of the meal with her work colleagues. As they had (yet another) toast to peace on earth, Erica looked round the light- and tinsel-covered individuals at the table. Would one of them vanish next? Would their only legacy be a plea in the paper?

She vowed it would not be so.

They moved on to Somerset House. The streets were festive, and their rowdy laughter was not minded. Fancy dress was *de rigueur* with the occasional tourist stopping them for a photograph— especially Joslin and her Christmas unicorn.

A bitterly cold wind whipped along the streets, cutting through them without mercy. The sky was clear and bright; stars dazzled them from on-high as the moon kept guard.

"See, I told you you'd be better off in the end," Marc said through chattering teeth. Joslin laughed and posed for yet another photograph. "She's enjoying herself far too much," he muttered to Erica.

"She always does." Erica smiled, watching Joslin pose away whilst stamping her feet to keep warm. She knew she should've worn her boots and not these heels—her feet were freezing.

Taking her by surprise, Marc put his arm around her. "They do say body heat is one of the best ways to keep warm," he explained lightly.

"True," she replied, nervously. She debated whether to step away. She knew Marc liked her and she knew she liked him, but exactly how she wasn't sure. There was a twinge of guilt as she thought of meeting Michael soon. She remembered how nice it was to have his arm around her in the library. Then she remembered Annabelle and sighed inwardly, leaning closer to Marc for warmth.

Arriving eventually at Somerset House, they hired ice skates, changing in the cloakroom before venturing out to the manmade ice rink. Her stomach caved in on seeing the expanse of ice before her.

"Are you okay? You look like you're going to be sick," Joslin asked, tottering past her before launching herself on to the ice.

Erica smiled weakly. She'd never ice skated before. She was just nervous. She edged over to the ice. Music blared out over the busy ice rink, which was illuminated with cool blue lights and flanked on all sides by the Neoclassical grandeur of Somerset House. She tried to set off as confidently as Joslin had, but, instead, she watched as Deenesh, Marc and even Hincks found a gap in the crowds and leapt past her, whizzing away. The people, the music, the ice, all of it was making her dizzy. Taking a deep breath, she placed a tentative foot on to the ice and yelped as it slipped from under her. After much flailing, Erica finally found some sort of balance with the help of the handrail and shuffled along the edge of the ice rink where she was relieved to see a handful of others clinging on for dear life. She scanned the crowds for someone she recognised and saw Deenesh in his flashing Christmas jumper. Waving madly, he finally noticed her and skated effortlessly over.

"Y'alright, luv?"

"Never better. Can you, erm, help?"

Laughing, he took her hand and pulled her onto the ice rink, navigating the crowds with envious efficiency. Erica yelped and squealed with every loss of balance, finding the speed and crowds too much.

"Actually, it's ok. I'll just stay by the railings."

"What? Are you scared of the ice?"

Erica laughed nervously. "Who knew, right?" And started shuffling back to the railing, breathing deeply to calm her racing heart. She was buffeted on all sides as people whooshed by. Out of the corner of her eye, she spied a form hurtling straight for her and cowered, covering her head with her hands, bracing for impact.

Nothing happened. Puzzled, she looked up to find Michael in his Actualle clothing and wearing a Santa hat, hands outstretched. "May I?"

She accepted shyly, and he took her two hands in his. Skating backwards, he slowly led her towards the centre of the rink. "Bend you knees slightly, Miss Shylocke. Lean on your inner foot. Push off with your right. Balance, glide. Almost!" he said, catching her as she lost her footing.

"How come you can skate so well?" she asked grudgingly.

"There was much around when I was young; winters are milder nowadays."

Erica shrugged, made sense. "Nice hat, by the way."

"Ashayla noted its popularity with people and recommended I purchased one to blend in," Michael explained. Smiling, he shook his head from side to side, making its bells jingle. "I thought you would approve."

"Oh, most definitely."

"Your tights aren't purple," he commented.

"Purple isn't considered a festive colour."

He looked around. "I suppose so. Now, let's get you skating."

Following his instructions, she soon found herself able to glide forwards and began to gain more confidence as he showed her how to keep up momentum and, more importantly, how to stop.

"Though there are far too many people present for adequate skating," he murmured, as he weaved them in and out of the crowds.

"The Prime Minister's announced a state of emergency," Erica said, remembering the headlines.

"I know," he said, his voice grave. "The Guild held an emergency meeting for qualified KeyMasters. Everyone is on standby."

"Do you think it's the Lost Souls?"

"I cannot think what else it could be. The Guild have yet to confirm anything. I raised the issue of the unreported attacks, but the High KeyMaster did not take kindly to it."

"I can't see why. Surely he'd be wanting to check all angles," Erica said hotly.

She then remembered her session with Dr Finnegan. "Dr Finnegan and I discovered an odd aura."

"'Odd'? What do you mean?"

"It was repeated. It was in thirteen out of the eighteen memories we looked at."

Michael stopped abruptly and she slammed into his chest, causing them to almost fall. He clutched her to him, steadying her.

The sudden proximity was exhilarating. Catching her breath, she looked up into his eyes. They were bright with confusion. They were so close she could feel his breath on her cheeks. She was inches from his lips…

"Apologies," he stammered, blushing deeply. "You surprised me. That cannot be mere coincidence?"

"I didn't think so either."

He proceeded to skate backwards, pulling her with him as she described the aura.

"I mean, imagine someone traipsing through Time like that? Wouldn't Its matter wear thin?"

Michael averted his eyes. "In theory, yes."

"Perhaps—"

233

"Erica!"

On hearing Marc's voice, Erica turned to find him and Joslin gliding over to them.

"I've been looking for you for ages—where were you?" He eyed them suspiciously—they'd come to a standstill but were still hand in hand.

"The railings." Erica smiled self-consciously, letting go of Michael's hands. "Deenesh tried to help me but I was too chicken, then Michael found me."

"How fortunate," Marc said drily, eyeing Michael with annoyance.

Averting further tension, Joslin laughed lightly and took Marc's hand, pulling him away. "Time's almost up. Race you!"

***

Despite her odd appearance, with her lavender hair and fluffy unicorn outfit, Michael was grateful for Joslin's astuteness in defusing the situation with Marc. He failed to understand why Marc was so cool towards him, but he was grateful, nonetheless.

They'd finished skating at Somerset House and were walking from Aldwych to Wellington Street, to a bar that had been recommended to Joslin. Frost had started to form on the parked cars, glittering under the glare of the streetlights. Joslin and Deenesh were walking ahead with Marc and the others, so Erica took the opportunity to show him the newspaper.

He scanned the classifieds in shock. "So many…"

Erica nodded, her bottom lip trembling. "I just feel so helpless," she sobbed. "We couldn't do anything for them. We were too late."

He couldn't bear it. Before he even knew what he was doing he'd reached for her and pulled her into a tight embrace. If he just held her, maybe it would take the pain away.

"I know," he soothed. "I feel the same, but we're closer that we've ever been to uncovering things. The Guild will act soon." He cupped her face in his hands. His heart twisting as he took in her green eyes that werc awash with tears. "We will avenge them. All of them. I promise."

She nodded, too taken aback to speak.

He wiped away her tears with his thumb and tried to give a reassuring smile. "Come, let's catch them up before you're missed."

They had reached the bar; it was an old Victorian building on the corner with wooden panelling and original windows. Dance music blared out of its doors, which were flanked by two burly bouncers. With free entry for any in festive dress, they entered quickly, Michael watching in bemusement as the group revealed their brightly coloured outfits and Christmas jumpers from under their jackets as they gave the bouncers a twirl.

"What is the meaning behind your party's attire?" he asked quietly, eyeing Erica's Ms Claus outfit with red cheeks. He'd never seen her in such a short skirt and was unsure where to look.

"It's part of how Christmas is celebrated now, it's just a bit of festive fun."

He looked unconvinced but followed her and the others down into the basement where strobe lighting punctuated the darkness. It was as piercing as Ashayla's *Lumínate* Charm. He shielded his eyes, blinking away the spots.

There was a dance floor lit up in the centre before a small stage where massive speakers and subwoofers stood to attention. Bar tables surrounded the dance floor, whilst to the right was a bar bustling with eager punters. Michael was overwhelmed by the music that thrummed through the air, the bass reverberating through him. He sensed Erica by his side but found he could hear nothing she said. He leaned forwards and her voice broke through the noise.

"I bet you've never been to an Actualle club, have you?"

He shook his head and found he had to shout his reply. "It is very different to the clubs I'm used to." Surprising himself as he thought longingly of the armchairs and warm fires of the Intermundus Club.

A round of orders was taken, and Michael found himself being dragged towards the dance floor by Joslin. "Come on, Michael! Time to show us your moves!"

She must have sensed his unease, for Erica took Joslin's hands in hers' and pulled her into the middle of the dance floor where they proceeded to dance together. Although, it more resembled a gangly garbled mess rather than dancing.

The group dispersed over several tables, and Michael found himself alone with just his thoughts and a cognac for company. He observed how the men still preferred to watch than dance; at least some things never changed.

He was thinking back to the ball where Annabelle had worn the blue gown that was so becoming. He remembered how she'd danced and laughed, her eyes bright and her lips full, and closed his eyes against the embarrassment she had dealt.

When he opened them, Marc was before him, a drink in one hand and a sprig of mistletoe in the other. He set them down on the table.

Michael regarded his elf outfit curiously and took a sip of his drink.

"So, what's the deal between you and Erica?" Marc shouted over the music.

Michael glanced across to where Erica, Joslin and another girl now danced merrily. "We do not have a 'deal', we're not in business together."

Marc looked at him puzzled. "No, I mean what's going on?"

"Nothing, as far as I'm aware."

Marc nervously drummed the table with his hands. "Come on, man! Don't make me say it!"

"Say what?" It was Michael's turn to be puzzled.

"You know, to ask."

"Ask what?" Michael was beginning to rankle. Could Actualles not be clear in anything they said?

Marc took a deep breath. "Do you like her?"

He looked across to Erica. "Yes, she's a very pleasant person."

Marc's initial look of horror melted to one of frustration. "No, not like, I mean *like*. Do you find her attractive? Do you l-love her?" He stammered—his cheeks red even in the darkness.

Michael replied quickly and dismissively. "Of course not!"

236

"Really?!" Marc looked at him in disbelief. "What's your problem? She's amazing—funny, down to earth, intelligent, attractive… Are you gay?"

Michael frowned; this sudden turn of conversation perplexed him. "I'm not feeling particularly gay, no," he replied cautiously, certain he'd misunderstood Marc's intended meaning.

Marc rolled his eyes. "Never mind! I was going to offer you these to help you make your move." He gestured impatiently at the drink and mistletoe. "Well, your loss. I'm sure she fancies you."

"'Fancies me'?"

"Get with it, man! Where've you been these last few months? Anyway, now that's finally cleared up, you'll have no objection if I ask her out?"

"Out where?"

"Forget it!" Marc snapped, grabbing the drink and mistletoe before walking towards the dancing girls.

Michael watched as he began moving in a similar garbled way towards the three girls, who cheered and opened their dancing circle to welcome him. After a minute he shimmied over to Erica, passing her the drink. She smiled and raised it in thanks. They walked to an unoccupied table at the edge of the dance floor. Marc leaned close, speaking to her and Michael watched her laugh in reply.

Why could he hear her laughter in his own ears?

Marc produced the mistletoe and Erica blushed, looking down. Her sweeping eyelashes long and graceful. Her eyes sparkled like jewels… The elegant lines of her cheeks were high and defined. You could trace their gentle curves all the way down her neck to…

Holding it over them, Marc leaned forwards, kissing her tentatively on the lips. She didn't pull away and, encouraged, Marc caressed her cheek. Pulling her closer.

Michael faltered. He felt sick as the world darkened. The only light came from Erica. And she was being kissed by Marc. A chill like none other took hold of him, stealing the very life from him. There was an ache where his heart had been. He couldn't breathe.

How could he have been so stupid?!

He had to get away.

Scrambling to his feet, he bumped into a Pakistani girl holding up an electrical device. She was frantically showing him a picture of a young Asian man with slick hair and earrings. He leaned forwards, pretending it was the music that had prevented him from understanding her.

"Have you seen Bilal?" She shouted through the music, thrusting the device into his face. He shook his head and noticed panic setting deeper within her fine features. She turned to go but he caught her by the wrist, her long ponytail swinging.

"When did you see him last?"

"He got in a fight and stormed out about fifteen minutes ago. Now, he's not answering his phone." Her lips wobbled, tears spilling down her cheeks. "He'd never leave me alone in town."

Michael felt sure it would be nothing but thought it better to check. In any case, he would be happy to leave the scene before him.

Following the girl, she guided him through the crowds to a corridor that led to the toilets and fire exit. Weaving in and out of those loitering in the narrow space, there remained one final person in their way. A good-looking Korean leaned against the wall, cigarette in hand. He was wearing a tight sleeveless top, black jeans and ankle boots; the garish light of the 'exit' sign picked out the curve of his biceps and pectorals. Four large tattoos—a Chinese dragon, the Yin and Yang symbol, a phoenix and a kumiho—dominated his left arm and neck. Whilst scribbles littered every other space from his hand up to his jaw, some larger than others. He was staring at the scribbles on his inner wrist, a wistful look in his eyes.

"I didn't realise you had tattoos. Wait, are those names?"

The man looked up at the sound of Michael's voice, pitch-black eyes dancing in amusement. They glanced at their matching jade bracelets.

Taking a final drag on his cigarette, the man flicked the stub to the ground before stepping on it. "There's a lot you don't know about me, Michael," he said, blowing the smoke away. "So, what brings you here? You're the last person I expected to see. Nice hat." Despite all the years, there remained a slight accent to his English.

"I could say the same about you, Nathaniel. Hungry?"

"Hardly, I like the music." Nathaniel then noticed the Asian girl looking at him shyly from behind Michael's broad shoulders. She seemed quite enamoured by him. He flashed her a dazzling smile. "You sly dog! I didn't think you had it in you."

"This lady's companion has vanished. She's growing worried." He said giving Nathaniel a look.

"Tad boring, Michael. I was expecting something more risqué. Well, we'd better take a look outside then," he said, opening the fire exit.

They were greeted by a blast of freezing cold air that sent Michael's and the girl's teeth a-chatter. Nathaniel stepped out without seeming to notice the temperature change. He glanced up and down the alleyway before drawing up sharp and raising a hand.

Michael joined him at his side and immediately noticed how saturated by shadows the cobbled alleyway was. Not to mention, how much darker and denser the shadows appeared. They looked at one another: Shadowlings.

Nathaniel turned and gestured for the girl to go back inside. "Telephone the police and stay inside. Tell them it's a code '57'. We'll take a closer look." On mentioning the code from the news, the girl cried afresh but nodded and brought the device to her ear, making the call.

Once the door had closed behind her, Michael fetched out his periapt and applied the Ignorant Charm to both him and Nathaniel. He then summoned Ashayla, which materialised in elfin form beside the two men. It stopped and gaped at the shadows: it had never seen such a concentration of Shadowlings.

"A young man has gone missing," Michael explained, tapping Xerxes' periapt. "We will do our best to find him alive whilst Xerxes gathers Christian and as many other Soul Gatherers as he can. The Police have also been called." Xerxes appeared in its elemental form, which flared worryingly at the sight of the writhing mass of shadows before it.

"When you have notified Christian and Erica is no longer… *detained*, ensure she and her friends get home safely. Stay in the light."

The molten orb bobbed in acknowledgement, weighing Nathaniel up before morphing into elfin form. Drawing Ashayla into an embrace, it reluctantly let go before disappearing in a solar flare.

"Erica? As in Erica Shylocke?" Nathaniel asked abruptly.

Michael removed his Santa hat, letting it fall onto the cobblestones. "Yes. How do you know her?"

"It's complicated," he said, his lips set in a tight line.

Eyeing the vampire, he turned to Ashayla. "Are you ready?" he asked, fastening a vambrace to his wrist. He slotted in its periapt.

Ashayla nodded brusquely, poised for action.

Nathaniel flexed his neck, his jaws unhinging to reveal long fangs. His nails, red-black in the moonlight, grew to talons.

Michael smiled darkly. He was looking forward to the fight. A recklessness had befallen him—he finally realised that only now did he have nothing to lose.

"*Ferrum vocaví.*" On uttering the charm, a golden sword materialised before him, decorations etched upon its blade with an equally decorative knuckle-bow. Plucking it from the air, he adjusted its weight with the ease of familiarity.

Sensing an attack, the Shadowlings gathered before them; pairs upon pairs of red eyes turning on them malevolently.

They set to, Nathaniel a blur as he dove into the shadows, ripping and shredding any Soul in his path. His eyes burning crimson.

"*Lunae Lumen!*" cried Michael, casting a charm that caused the moonlight to flare and burn into the shadows. Ashayla channelled columns of light to burned through the Souls, their screams resounding through the alleyway.

Souls dispersed in their wake, swirling in black flurries before succumbing to the wintery breeze.

21
Homeward Bound

Thirteen hours later, Erica found herself seated on a train hurtling towards the North. Grey, bleak suburbs eventually gave way to quaint towns, rolling snowy hills and frosted hedgerows; icy mist hugged the ground. Winter had truly set in.

She gazed out at the passing countryside unsure how she felt. It had been almost a year since she'd last returned home; she'd missed the countryside but not her parents' moaning.

Getting out her sandwiches and book, she couldn't resist tapping her periapt again. "Any news?"

"For the hundredth time, ma'am. I will let you know when I hear from Ashuylu. Now will you please let me rest? I have quite the headache." Its voice snapped in her ear.

She bit into her sandwich glumly. Where was Michael? What was he doing? And what had happened?

Thankfully, by the time Xerxes had appeared in its human form everyone was far too drunk to worry about the ethereal glow that emanated from its skin and hair, or its gleaming tattoo, or the cuffs about its wrists. Instead, they'd welcomed it warmly, but it was in no mood for frivolities and, once it had finally convinced them that they needed to leave, the long journey home began with much singing, dancing and merriment. When they eventually reached Erica's flat, after Xerxes had got everyone home safely, it was gone six in the morning. By which time, frost had settled thickly upon the cars. They'd had a couple of encounters with Shadowlings but nothing serious.

Erica had dismissed the Færie to Utarra whilst she took a hot shower and had finished her packing.

With her train home leaving St Pancras just before midday there had been no time to sleep, not that she could. Try as she might, she couldn't resist checking with Xerxes whether it had heard from Michael or Ashayla. Though with little joy.

Her mind was reeling. Somehow things had shifted between her and Michael, but where to, she wasn't entirely sure. And then there was Marc's kiss. The mistletoe had taken her by surprise and, although it really wasn't what she'd wanted, she'd felt unable to decline such a festive frivolity, though she knew it meant more for Marc. Sure, she liked Marc, but whether it was as much as he liked her, she didn't know. She didn't like leading men on. It wasn't her style; hearts were too fragile to treat so lightly.

She sighed into her packet of crisps.

It wasn't long before she found herself at Derby train station waiting for her connecting train to Matlock. It was sleeting and much colder than London, being further north. When the two-carriage train finally appeared, Erica was glad to get into the warmth, finding a seat close to a radiator.

She was beginning to get nervous; she hadn't spoken with her parents for months and the last phone call had ended in yet another argument. The only person she'd spoken to recently was her brother Guy and that had been strained with him asking her a load of questions she couldn't answer. She wasn't even sure if they'd got her voicemail to say that she was coming home for Christmas.

She put her head in her hands. How could life get so complicated?

Try as she might to distract herself with her book, it remained untouched. The only thing that seemed to calm her increasing nerves was the view out of the window.

Suburbia gave way to snowy hills and valleys as the train thundered along into the depths of the Peak District. Following alongside the Cromford Canal and occasionally criss-crossing over the River Derwent before diving into the depths of an old tunnel. Bursting back into the feeble winter sun, the train clattered along, passing by Victorian mills, remnants of the Industrial Revolution that had shook the world. The next station was her stop: Cromford, home of the world's first water-powered mill, developed by the renowned Richard Arkwright.

Gathering her rucksack and giftbags as the train screeched to a stop, she alighted along with several others onto a quaint snow-covered platform. Intricate iron pillars held up a large wooden shelter. Walking under it and through the rail station, Erica headed to Mill Road and her bus stop. Her feet crunching through the crisp snow. Although the snow ploughs had cleared the roads, the pavements remained buried under snow, four feet in some places—the snow drifts were the worst she'd seen in years. Sadly, she'd packed light, planning to rely on her remaining clothes at home so only had her ankle boots with her. By the time her bus came her feet were soaked through and frozen.

The bus trundled along the windy country lanes, eventually turning right at the Clatterway Bed & Breakfast and making its slippery way up the icy Clatterway to the heart of Bonsall, her home. Normally she would've stopped off at the Tea Rooms to see Lizzie, but the snow drifts were even worse here thanks to the steep hills that the village clung to. Instead, she remained on the bus, holding on for dear life as it slowly climbed the precarious Abel Lane. Thankful to alight, she waded through the snow drifts, slipping and sliding to her home at the end of the lane: Birchdale Farm.

Struggling to open the gate, she hoisted up her skirt and clambered over it instead, landing in a massive snow drift in the farmyard.

Cursing and even more cold, she reached the doorstep. Her gloved hand hovered over the old brass doorbell. She bit her lip. *What if they didn't want her to stay?* But she didn't have much choice as she could no longer feel her feet—sighing she pressed the bell.

After a few moments, she heard footfall in the hall and the door creaked open. Out of the gloom stepped her father. He looked at her in shock before his emerald eyes narrowed, flashing ominously; a stubborn line settled upon his lips. Erica smiled weakly. Suddenly, her mother with her caramel brown hair and hazel eyes peeked round and, on seeing her, pushed past to open the porch door. Pulling her into her arms, she gave her the biggest of hugs.

"You're home! Oh, my darling! You're home! I didn't dare believe you'd actually come!"

Taken aback by her mother's embrace and kisses, Erica couldn't stop the tears from flowing. "I-I'm sorry, I shouldn't have fallen out with—"

Her father cut her off. "Bloody right you shouldn't! And now you come here—"

Her mother cut him off in turn with a sharp glare. "Now is not the time and here is not the place. You're frozen, Erica. Come inside. We'll talk later." And Erica was ushered through, past her grizzly father and across the flagstones to the toasty kitchen where the stove was stoked high.

She sat and took off her icy boots, placing them by the hearth. An awkward silence ensued as her parents looked at her.

"Where are Cole and Guy?" Erica asked casually. She could see through to the living room and noticed no Christmas tree. How odd.

"They're in the fields, checking on the livestock." Her father growled.

"I'll go and change and see if there's anything I can do to help," she said, getting up to go to the door that led to the back hall and stairs to the first floor.

"You'll help with dinner?" Her mother asked, eyes hopeful.

Erica smiled. "Of course."

The stairs squeaked familiarly as she ascended, passing through a random nook that her and her brothers had made into a small playroom complete with sofa, TV and games console. A bookcase full of books and board games lined the end wall. They'd spent many a happy evening chatting and playing here.

Walking past her two brothers' rooms, she climbed a quirky set of stairs into the attic where her bedroom was. Opening the door, she was greeted by her small but cosy bedroom. As she changed, she eyed the periapt and was tempted to disturb Xerxes once more, then decided against it: she daren't risk its wrath.

Finally togged up in much more suitable clothing, she pocketed the periapt and grabbed a walkie-talkie from the dock in the kitchen, tuning into Channel 3. "Break 1-9, Optimus, Barbie, have you got your ears on? Over." Erica smiled on saying the handles she'd given them all, inspired by their favourite childhood toys.

There was a crackle over the radio, then her brother Cole's voice erupted from the small speaker. "Copy that. Barbie has its ears on, I repeat, Barbie has its ears on. Nice to hear your voice, sis. Over."

"Affirmative. The Bookworm has landed."

"Copy that! Optimus hearing you loud and clear. Bookworm, can you bring us a flask of tea? I'm freezing my na—"

Erica laughed, cutting him off. Typical Guy. "Copy that, Optimus. Come and pick me up in five. Over."

It was good to be home.

***

Standing in the middle of the farmyard, armed with a flask of tea, Erica laughed as she watched both her brothers race each other over the fields home. They rode quad bikes which they'd adapted for the snowy weather, adding snow ploughs and chains to the tyres.

Both brothers had stayed local on finishing school. Guy was the middle child and had taken on an apprenticeship at the local garage as a mechanic, helping on the farm when able. Whilst Cole, the oldest, worked full-time on the farm. He had green fingers and had helped the farm expand into arable farming as well as livestock. Erica had been the odd one out. Although she loved being on the farm, she'd wanted to pursue her love of history, ending up at university. Whilst her parents had been proud, the reality of her moving away, the expense, all for studying history, made no sense to them. An opinion they regularly voiced. Especially when Erica started expressing an interest in continuing her studies with a PhD.

On reaching the farmyard, Guy and Cole proceeded to do doughnuts round her, spraying her with snow. Erica laughed as she shielded her head.

"Enough! Or the tea gets it!" She threatened, opening the flask.

Cole was the first to slow down, stopping beside her. Taking off his helmet he got off the quad bike and enveloped her in a massive bear hug. Whilst she adored both her older brothers, Cole was a better listener and it was him she'd turned to when deciding to go to university.

Guy was more carefree, performing wheelies much to the bemusement of the horses looking over the stable doors.

"Good to see you, sis," Cole said looking her up and down—they shared the same black hair and green eyes. "You've grown. The Big Smoke treating you okay?"

Erica nodded and began pouring them a cup of tea, they sipped from it in turn, enjoying its warmth.

"The farm's looking good," Erica commented, as they looked out over the neat fields, tidy outbuildings and restored polytunnels.

"Can't take any of the credit, it's all down to, Barbie," Guy said, lifting the cup in Cole's direction, who blushed graciously.

"Thanks, it's all dead now though. You'd have to come back in the spring to see it at its best."

"It's not dead," Erica said, "everything's just gone away on holiday."

Her brothers laughed. "You always did see things differently."

"No problems then?"

"Not really, though some cattle's gone missing. Same with the neighbours. They probably got lost in the snow—it's been really bad this year. We never did find them."

"How come there's no Christmas tree up?" Erica asked casually, helping them clean and lock up the quad bikes.

"Because of you, silly. *'No tree! It isn't Christmas until the family's back together!'*" Guy said, doing his classic impression of dad.

"Dad said that?"

"He's more sentimental than he lets on. You really hurt him, and mum. They've both really missed you," Cole, over his shoulder.

Erica looked at her feet her cheeks reddening. "I know. I'm going to make it right."

"Of course, you will," Guy said, waving his hand dismissively. "Now, more importantly, are you helping mum with dinner?"

Erica nodded.

The brothers high-fived enthusiastically. "The Yorkshire puddings are saved!"

***

Within the hour they were sat all around the dining table, a steaming dinner of roast beef with onion gravy and Erica's homemade Yorkshire puddings. As they helped themselves to roast potatoes and vegetables, Erica noticed that the Christmas decorations had been fetched from the loft.

Looking at her dad, she saw him avert his eyes quickly. Mustering all her courage, she held up her glass of wine. "A toast. To families."

Each of them rose their glass in turn. Taking a big swig for luck, Erica cleared her throat.

"I wanted to apologise. I know I upset both you and mum, dad; I'm sorry." Her father looked up at her. "I never meant to. I was just upset myself and annoyed. But I was wrong to not call back and sort things out. I'm sorry."

In her mind's eye, she was going to sullenly wait for an apology from them but given the reality of thousands of people vanishing and, most likely, being turned into Lost Souls, as well as how stubborn her father was, time might be against her. Pride was one thing, but she didn't want to risk anyone's soul over an apology.

Her father cleared his throat but floundered, unable to speak. Her mother touched his hand reassuringly. Stealing a look at Cole, he rose his glass in approval.

"Thank you, darling. We appreciate that. We've missed you terribly, both of us. And we're sorry too, aren't we, dear?" She looked to her husband, who nodded stiffly. "If you really want to do a PhD, we will naturally support you, however we can, won't we, dear?"

Erica smiled at her father's hesitant nod. "That means the world to me, thanks. But you don't need to worry. I got a new job, so I can pay for everything."

Her father spluttered. "What?! Everything! What sort of job?" His eyes widened as his mind went through the types of jobs that a young woman could do to bring in such money. "It's, erh, not street-based, is it?"

Guy and Cole guffawed into their wine glasses, spluttering wine everywhere, whilst their mother kicked at their legs under the table.

"Of course not!" Erica replied blushing deeply.

Once composed, Guy helped himself to seconds. "Now we've established Erica's not a hooker and we're all happy families, can we please put up the Christmas tree?"

Erica held her head in her hands: it was times like these when she wished she were an only child.

Their mother laughed. "Provided you boys do the washing up!"

***

It was late by the time they'd finished decorating the house and tree for Christmas. She was glad she'd come home; it hadn't even occurred to her that her father wouldn't celebrate Christmas without her. She smiled to herself—he really was a softy.

Having just showered, she towelled her wet hair and sat on the bed, touching the periapt to summon Xerxes in a blaze of hot sparks. Unaware of its new surroundings, its elemental orb ricocheted off the sloping ceilings of the attic, splattering against the wall.

"QuiTé! A little warning next time, ma'am!" The Færie growled as it morphed into its cantankerous self, rubbing its head.

"Sorry. Any news?"

"None," it replied glumly, sitting down on the edge of her bed. *"Where on earth are we?"*

"Home. Welcome to Bonsall."

"Charmed, I'm sure."

Erica studied it as it took in her bedroom. It looked exhausted with its ruffled golden hair and tired eyes. "You really love Ashayla, don't you?"

It regarded her carefully, before fiddling with the cuffs about its wrists. *"Yes, I do. We Færies are attracted by each other's elements—"*

"But you and Ashayla have different elements."

"Who says they have to be the same? Differences can attract. And sometimes your differences make you stronger together and your offspring more beautiful." The Færie sighed deeply, its eyes overwhelmed. *"It is not customary for Færies to mate with just one, but we have. We have been together centuries. I have missed it; there is none like Ashayla. My world would end if harm befell it."*

Xerxes words struck a chord. Although she knew Michael wasn't interested in her, she knew she would be devastated if he were hurt, or worse. Scared of giving away too much, she busied herself with changing into her pyjamas: wriggling about under the bed covers much to Xerxes' amusement.

"Shadowlings aren't bad though, are they?" Erica asked, finally changed and propped up against her pillows. Thinking back to her Sonnology lectures with Dr Coons, as he regularly talked about the different Lost Souls in relation to the vibrations they made in Time.

Xerxes sat cross-legged on the bed. *"All Lost Souls are dangerous, in particular Wrathful and Strigoi. Whilst Shadowlings are regarded as less vicious, no Lost Soul should be underestimated. If the shadows are dense, the concentration of Shadowlings high, then they could be quite devastating..."*

Erica twiddled her fingers nervously. Trying not to think of Michael and Ashayla surrounded by thick hordes of Shadowlings. "Where do they go?" she asked, more to keep her mind off her worry.

Xerxes looked at her scornfully. *"They transcend the planes heading to Limbo, obviously. They're lost."*

"No, I mean, do you know where Lost Souls go once they've been 'dealt' with? What happens to them in Limbo? And why are they lost? Where are they trying to go?"

The Færie looked at her blankly. *"I have to say I don't know. The Guild has never properly considered it."*

It was Erica's turn to look scornful. "I know they haven't. Anatole's already given me a lecture. But what do you Færies care about what The Guild thinks is worth consideration? I somehow thought you guys would've had more of a clue than us humans."

It shifted uncomfortably.

Erica shook her head, raising a hand to her temple in disbelief. "So, Færies *and* The Guild accept Lost Souls flitting between all planes of existence? You happily lock them up in Claustrum and attack them, but don't think to find out where they go or why they're lost?!"

"You put it so succinctly."

Erica tried to process this fact, too stunned for words.

"To my knowledge," Xerxes said, *"the only human who might be able to help is the GateKeeper Zhu Yaoshi."*

22
Christmas Eve

It was Christmas Eve. Erica had still not heard any news from Michael. Nothing! Part of her was relieved (no news was good news, right?) and part of her swung between being sick with worry to wanting to punch his face for being so inconsiderate.

She had whiled away the time helping with the usual Christmas baking: mince pies, shortbread, mince pies, gingerbread men, mince pies, Christmas cake and more mince pies. Her mother had left her in charge of decorating the Christmas cake, so she'd invited Lizzie over for an afternoon of icing and hot chocolate. Lizzie was still annoyed with her, but they'd come to a truce when Erica explained how she hadn't told anyone what was going on.

"I wish you would," Lizzie had muttered with a moody bottom lip. "I mean, how weird could it be?"

Unable to adequately describe just how weird her life currently was they'd settled with the promise that when she could, Erica would tell her all.

"So, are you going to reply?" Lizzie asked as she crafted a snowman from the regal icing.

She was referring to Marc's message that Erica had received that morning. "Of course, but I don't want to appear eager; I'm not sure how I feel about things yet."

"It was a mistletoe kiss, Erica. Don't get too heavy about it. You'd have been a Scrooge to say no. Anyway, he sounds nice; why wouldn't you want to date him?"

Caught off guard, Erica didn't know where to look, let alone what to say. Lizzie gave a yelp of excitement and grabbed her. "Who is he then?!"

"Who?" Erica asked innocently as she put the finishing touches to the Christmas tree she was moulding out of icing.

"Don't give me that! I know you, Shylocke. Who is he?"

Erica hesitated. If she revealed it was the same guy who'd made her cry Lizzie would call her a fool.

"Wait, don't bother, I'll get it out of you later," Lizzie said.

She was referring to the pub crawl that was happening that evening before Midnight Mass. Even though there were only two pubs in the village, Lizzie had proved remarkably skilled at extracting information on such occasions in the past. Either that or Erica was a light weight.

Erica let out a groan as her iced Christmas tree fell over.

"Timber!" Guy chuckled as he appeared at the doorway. Lizzie and he shared a look before he cleared his throat. "You still going out tonight, Lizzie?"

"Of course! Erica's Christmas Day hangover doesn't happen all by itself, you know."

Guy laughed before blushing heavily, his hazel eyes dancing. He ran a hand through his hair. "Well, erh, I'll see you later then?"

Lizzie nodded, smiling like the Cheshire Cat, a dreamy look in her eyes as she watched him leave.

Erica poked her with a rolling pin. "This is getting boring—do something! I'll get *you* some mistletoe if you want."

"You will?"

Erica looked stunned—she'd been kidding. "I thought you said mistletoe kisses weren't that 'heavy'."

"Exactly. He'd be a Scrooge not to. I should've thought of this sooner! Erica, you're a genius!" she exclaimed, giving her friend a big hug. "You'll get me some?"

"I'll ask Cole, I'm sure he knows where to find some."

In any case, she had a favour of her own to ask.

***

The Inspector bent and picked up the device from the cobbles, blood and blackness splattered its screen. Peering at it, he noted 47 missed

252

calls. A photo of the missing man, Bilal, with an attractive Asian woman stared back at him. He placed it into a bag and labelled it. He then looked at the band of misfits before him with their leather coats and weapons. It really was too early for this.

"Due to the nature of this incident, I've been told to ask you to remain until MI5 arrives. They won't be long," he said. Not that he felt like anyone was listening to him.

Several of the Soul Gatherers who'd answered Michael's plea were huddled together in a group, wiping down swords, staffs, daggers and axes.

"I hope you've got licences for those," said the Inspector.

The group shot him a mixture of incredulous looks and he backed down—he'd let the Organisation talk to them.

Michael sat on the kerb nursing a broken sword arm.

They hadn't discovered any remains, common in attacks by Shadowlings which absorbed all but the soul of their victims. It was safe to assume that Bilal had been overcome by the Shadowlings before Michael and Nathaniel, or any of them, could get to him.

"We did our best," said Nathaniel, patting his arm before walking over to talk to a tall African with glowing silver hair and eyes: Amberson Solway, a Fæ. A Doberman Pinscher was sitting by his feet. Lunita joined them, her glowing connate nipping playfully at the nervous Inspector before bounding over to the Doberman Pinscher which greeted it with lots of tail-wagging.

"Are you ready, Michael?" Ashayla asked as the Færie prepared to set his arm. It was exhausted and looked drained enough without having to perform more magic. But the sooner the arm was set the better.

Michael had been drinking from a bottle of Pisco Lunita had passed him: it'd already started to work, numbing his aches and pains, numbing his mind. He nodded tersely.

Christian, who also looked worse for wear, offered him a bite stick from a small medical pouch. "I know you're half-cut, old chap, but you'll be needing this."

Michael accepted it gladly and bit down on it, nodding again to the Færie.

Ashayla hovered its hands over Michael's skin, veins glowing. An extreme coldness began to emanate from them causing the air to crystallise. *"I shall count to three. One…"* The magic neatly snapped the arm back into place.

Michael's muffled curses made the other Soul Gatherers look up. Nathaniel took the opportunity to pocket some papers that Amberson was passing him. Nodding his thanks, he then walked into the shadows and vanished.

"We tend to at least count to two, old girl," Christian said with a wry smile as Lunita re-joined him.

The battle had been brutal. All had suffered injuries, some minor, others severe. Beyond his broken arm, Michael had sustained a cut to his temple which seeped blood down his face and into his eye, blurring his vision.

"I say, Ashayla, I should return to your periapt and rest. You look peak," Christian said gently—the Færie's glow was weak. "Don't worry. I'll look after him."

Ashayla looked to Michael, unsure: it didn't want to leave him. Michael smiled, reassuringly. "Rest. Do not fret yourself, Ashayla. And thank you."

It nodded and fell into the periapt exhausted. Shimmering, the stone welcomed the Færie's return.

Michael passed back the brandy to Lunita who took a swig before offering it to Christian who accepted it with thanks. Pocketing the periapt, he held his hand over it protectively.

"I owe it my life."

Christian patted his shoulder. "And Ashayla would've gladly died for you. Now, though your arm is mended, it will be sore for a good few days. You might find you need a sling. Let's have a look at your eye," he said, producing a needle and thread from his medial pouch.

"I have never seen such an infestation. Not in all my years," Lunita murmured almost in awe.

With dawn peeping its head over the rooftops, it'd been agreed that the Soul Gatherers would work with the special forces to start collectively combing the streets, eliminating as many Lost Souls as possible. They feared by the time The Guild acknowledged the situation it would be beyond control.

"You fought differently," Christian commented quietly, stitching Michael's cut.

Michael grunted in pain. "Pray tell."

"As if you didn't care whether you would live, old chap." Christian watched him carefully.

Michael averted his gaze. "Like a fool, I realised something too late."

Christian waited expectantly.

Michael hesitated. "I will tell you, my friend. But I must do something first."

"Have a bath?" Christian chortled, tying off his stitches.

Michael thanked him and stood up. "That and something else: I need to see Annabelle and bid her farewell."

Christian watched him leave, stunned. "By Jove! Michael, are you sure?"

He turned back. "Maria advised me to let her go and I couldn't, but this…" He indicated the remains of their battle. "Spirits are as much at risk as humans. I cannot risk this befalling her because I couldn't let her go..."

"If you're sure, dear boy? There'd be no going back."

Michael looked down the alleyway, where more and more Soul Gatherers gathered, answering the call to arms. He nodded, "I am. I should've done it long ago. I should've been less selfish."

Christian patted his shoulder kindly. "You missed her, old chap, that's all. Only natural, what?"

Michael nodded, guilt suddenly clenching his heart: *he had missed her, but not anymore.* For the first time in over 150 years, it didn't hurt to think of her. It was as if a shroud had been lifted.

"I wonder if this has something to do with a certain green-eyed beauty?" Christian said with a crooked smile. Lunita nudged him in the ribs, and he held up his hands in defence. "I'm just saying! He's been half-decent company since she walked in on his life."

Rolling her eyes, Lunita pulled Michael into an embrace. "*Te acompaño en este momento de dolor*. I am with you in this moment of grief. I know very well what it's like to have to say goodbye to a loved one. But it's a good sign that you feel able to love again," she said, voice thick with emotion.

"Thank you…" he said, his heart heavy but renewed.

He turned to leave.

"Oh, and Michael!" Christian called for his attention once more. "Talking of green-eyed beauties, I finally got the results from Erica's blood test. On the surface, totally normal, but when exposed to temporal energy, the red blood cells light up like you wouldn't believe. Temporal Cells, all of them. That's why it took me so long, difficult to identify, don't you know."

"I fail to understand you."

"Meaning she has a natural predisposition to temporal activity. She's a GateKeeper, old boy."

***

She found Cole in his bedroom. Knocking, she entered to find him furtively hiding textbooks under his bed covers.

"Erica, hi, it's not time to go out yet, is it?"

It was a decent sized bedroom for a cottage, with black beams crossing the white ceiling and a window overlooking the old farmyard. She sat on the edge of his bed. "We haven't eaten dinner yet, silly." She pointed out.

He laughed sheepishly. "Oh yeah, so, erm, what's up?"

"Two things, Lizzie would like some mistletoe, do you know where we could get some?"

"'We'?" He smiled. "I'll sort some out for later, I know where there's some. And what's the second thing?"

"I need some waders."

"Waders? For a pub crawl?"

"They're for after the pub crawl."

"Sure. How drunk are you planning on getting?" He laughed.

"Not very. And, erm, if I vanish, don't worry, okay?" Without giving him opportunity to question her she carried on. "Are you going to tell me what the textbooks are for?" Erica asked, dragging a book out to have a nosey despite his protests. *Business Studies for Dummies*. "You're not going to leave the farm, are you? Dad would be mortified."

"You can talk! No, I'm, erh, I'd like to expand and establish a nursery and show garden."

"That sounds like a great plan!" Erica enthused.

She could see him visibly relaxing and he proceeded to fetch out a notebook. "The only problem is," he began, as she flicked through his sketches and notes, "I'd need to attend a college course. I haven't got a clue where to start with setting up a business, marketing and everything. I need to learn if I'm going to do it right."

"If you put forward a business plan, dad won't mind losing you for a day or two if it helps the farm in the long-term. Put it like this, he can't disapprove, it's not a history course!" Erica smirked.

"You know, you're really something. Carrying on with your plans even when none of us supported you, it can't have been easy."

"You've always supported me."

"But I should have stuck up more for you with dad. I'm sorry."

She gave him a hug. "Doesn't matter, you believed in me, that was enough."

"And are you liking it? Still happy with your PhD plans?"

Erica hesitated. "Truth be told… I'm not sure anymore."

***

Little Reggie had been her best friend since she learnt to walk. They would play ball together, hide-and-seek, tag, hopscotch, all the usual childhood games. Erica didn't think anything of it. He helped her with her counting, he read to her, listened to all her secrets and was always there, no matter what. He was the perfect friend. So long as you ignored the fact he was dead.

She was only aware that things were different when she was four. She'd stopped to play marbles with Little Reggie whilst her mother chatted with Mrs Ford. He was sat as usual on the steps of the village cross opposite The Crown Pub. Her mother's conversation was boring, so she'd walked over to join him. They'd played and chatted for a good five minutes when her mother had suddenly yanked her to her feet, face pale, eyes blazing. Scolding her, she had dragged her home, muttering the whole way.

"You can't do it, darling. You just can't! Not in public. I don't know what they'd do but they'd have you, call you a witch and all sorts."

It was only when they'd reached the brow of the hill that she'd stopped and pulled her into a tight bear hug.

"But Little Reggie…" Tears had choked her then—her little world was crumbling.

Her mother had looked heartbroken and had taken her hands in hers. "Little Reggie is, is dead, sweetheart. He's a spirit."

"But, but he's my best friend!" Erica remembered wailing.

"And he still is, darling. But he's got to be a *secret* best friend. No one else can know." Her mother had said, cupping her face gently, eyes insistent.

"But why? Cole doesn't hide his friends. Guy doesn't neither."

"Either, darling." Her mother had corrected, wiping away Erica's tears with her thumb. "Because… no one else can see him, darling."

Erica was dumbstruck. "But what about Mrs Ward?"

Her mother had nodded.

"Albert the Shepherd?"

Her mother had nodded again. "And Margaret Tatlow, Molly Mayhew, Geoffrey Brassington, the friar… They're all spirits, darling. That's why, when you hold their hands, it burns."

Realisation was dawning. "And you can see them?" Her mother had looked around then, just to check they were still alone. With the coast clear, she had nodded, very slightly.

"And daddy? And Cole? And Guy?" Her mother had shaken her head, again very slightly.

"And they mustn't know," she had replied quietly, getting back to her feet and continuing their journey home. "You can't tell them—this'll be our secret."

Our secret.

And it had, until she met Michael…

Erica sighed and nursed her mulled wine. She was sat on the steps of the village cross waiting for Little Reggie. Scanning the shadows, she looked at her wristwatch. He was late.

Guy had insisted they made the most of the snow and proposed they sledged down to the Dripping Rabbit, the first in Bonsall's two-pub pub crawl. After a hair-raising sledge ride down the steep and windy village lanes they had arrived, snow-chilled but happy and ready for a drink. Lizzie met them there and Erica had slipped her the sprig of mistletoe Cole had fetched for her. Giddy with excitement, Lizzie quickly hid it in her handbag.

The Dripping Rabbit was a quirky pub that clung to The Dale and was home to the Harknesses and their famous Hen Racing. After a few drinks and several rowdy carols, the four continued to The Crown, on Yeoman Street, where the village cross was located. Guy and Cole pulled the girls in the sledges, racing one another along the snowy lanes which were busy with carol singers and other festive merriment.

Being closest to the church, The Crown was the final stop for many before Midnight Mass, which was well supported by the villagers. It was eleven o'clock and the pub was already busy inside and out: fairy lights, candles and music created a festive atmosphere that Lizzie quickly took advantage of. Feigning interest in a poster about the Christmas Quiz, she lured Guy over before producing the sprig of mistletoe and smiled mischievously. Initially taken aback, he gazed at her, eyes burning before pulling her to him, cupping her face and kissing her deeply in front of everyone. Cheers erupted around them and Erica and Cole looked at each other in shock.

Well, that definitely went to plan.

Spying friends, Cole quickly made his excuses, leaving Erica alone. Taking one last look at the Lizzie and Guy—who still hadn't come up for air—she seized the opportunity and left to meet Little Reggie at the cross.

Discovering she could see spirits had shocked Erica as a young child and to cope she'd turned to history. Somehow, learning about their lives made the spirits less frightening. (She never asked about their deaths though, that would've just been rude.) And the more she delved into their pasts, the more she wanted to know about the past of everything. This desire led her to college, then to university and then to Michael.

She frowned into her wine glass. *Do you believe in Fate?* Christian's question floated up from her memory. Was there such a thing? Could everyone's lives be structured so? Even loosely? But what if freewill was strong enough to let you change it?

She felt a coolness next to her and looked up as nonchalantly as she could. It was Little Reggie. She let out a sigh of relief. "Everything okay getting here?"

The spirit shook its head, looking about it nervously. He was a fourteen -year-old evacuee from London with a waistcoat and jacket and a smattering of freckles upon his nose. He had arrived in Bonsall in September 1939, staying at The Lodge with the Bennetts, caretakers to the Miller family. *"There are some shadows about, but I know all the hidey-holes better than them. They… They got Molly though. She got scared and wouldn't listen. But…"* He gruffly wiped his tears away. *"It's good having so many people about, they're staying away. Seems like they don't want to make themselves known just yet. So, will you help?"*

Erica looked at him, her first friend, and noticed his fear. It was selfish to make him stay. "Of course, I will. I'm sorry I reacted so badly—it was too much…"

Togged up in every woolly garment imaginable, Erica had taken one of her usual night-time walks the previous night, hoping to find Little Reggie or the other spirits at the cross, their favourite haunting place. She'd sat on its steps for a good half an hour and was just about to head home when there was a *psst!* from behind a wall. Thinking Little Reggie was playing a game, she'd started to berate him for leaving her out in the cold when he'd shushed her, pulling her behind the wall. It was then that he'd told her about the shadows and how they'd been taking the spirits—he and Molly were the last remaining. Quickly establishing that he was describing Lost Souls in the nearby woodland: Arbolis Noir, Bloodlings and Strigoi, Erica was shocked to hear that spirits were being targeted as well as humans. If so many thousands, dare she say millions, of humans had gone missing worldwide, what about spirits? How large was this army?!

"Will you help me?" he'd asked, realising that the only way for him to avoid being taken was for him to pass on.

Shamefully, Erica had screamed at him then. Unable to face the prospect of her first friend leaving her for good, she'd stormed off home. He wasn't supposed to leave. He'd promised to haunt her forever.

She gulped and wiped away tears.

Little Reggie looked away then, trying to hide the tears that warmed his eyes. *"I know…"*

She placed her gloved hand on his comfortingly. "But I'd rather you be safe than be turned into a shadow."

Out of the corner of her eye, she noticed two young men look up in her direction. Damn! It was Billy Derbyshire and Craig Stanley, two school 'friends'. Billy had never let her forget that she was considered a 'freak' by most of her year group when at school.

"Let's go," she whispered, finishing off her mulled wine and getting to her feet. "The waders and metal detector are on the sledge."

"You brought a metal detector?!"

"Yeah, it's my dad's. It's waterproof. He won't notice it's gone—he hardly uses it."

Hurrying past as casually as possible, Erica cursed again when Billy spoke to her. "Still talking to spirits, Shylocke?"

"Hi Billy, hi Craig," she greeted them in turn, ignoring his comment. "Merry Christmas to you both."

He seemed disgruntled at her not raising to his bait and reluctantly raised his pint glass. "Home for Christmas then? How's the Big Smoke? Lots of spirit friends keeping you company?" The two boys smiled at each other.

"You have no idea," she quipped, unable to resist. Seeing their stunned faces, she quickly diverted conversation to safer ground. "Big, unsurprisingly. Anyhow, I've got to go."

"So soon? Stay, I'll buy you a drink and we can laugh about old times."

Erica didn't know what to do without drawing too much attention to her and what she was about to do. Just as she started to panic, Little Reggie spooked a load of snow from the neighbouring table and begin building a miniature snowman. Billy and Craig watched in petrified silence as the spirit dramatically rolled the body, then head before picking up discarded straws for its arms. For his finale, Little Reggie blew on the remaining snow, causing it to flurry poetically.

Rushing to their feet, the two pushed their way inside the pub.

Erica chuckled, and high-fived Little Reggie. "Neat. Thanks! Now, let's get you out of here."

She stopped in her tracks when she noticed the girl. She was only about twelve years old and staring at her with big blue eyes. It was Tiarella Harkness, the daughter of the proprietors of The Dripping Rabbit. She was holding a wire-haired dachshund in her arms.

"You didn't see *anything*, understand?" She warned in hushed tones.

The girl nodded tersely, before hurrying away in the opposite direction.

Satisfied she wasn't being watched, Erica stopped to collect her bundle from the sledge before walking up the hill of Church Street and along to The Lodge and its well.

They had a necklace to find.

23
Little Reggie

"Got it!" groaned Erica as she emerged wet and cold but triumphant from the well.

They had sneaked into the gardens of The Lodge through a small side gate. Keeping in the shadows of the expansive garden, Erica and Little Reggie had made their cautious way to the well that Little Reggie had died in. The light and laughter that had echoed from the house felt a million miles from the task that was before them. To save Little Reggie he needed to pass on. To pass on Erica had to not only locate the lost necklace but also return it to Ms Miller.

"How the hell did it end up at the bottom of a well?" Erica had muttered grumpily as she had pulled on the waders.

"Some local boys had stolen it to frame me. They threw it down this well to hide it. They wanted me sent back to London," he'd explained sadly. He hadn't wanted to be there anymore than Erica. *"Gwendolyn liked me and they didn't like that."* He'd rubbed his neck awkwardly.

"Ms Miller? She liked you!" Erica had chuckled before realising that Ms Miller had once been a young woman, like her, with the same loves and dilemmas. She'd cleared her throat. "Did you like her?" she'd asked carefully whilst she'd assembled her father's metal detector.

Little Reggie had been eyeing the foliage, spooking at the slightest rustle. *"I climbed down the well to retrieve the necklace—what do you think?"*

Erica had then stood at the edge of the well and had dropped a small stone down into its watery depths. She had counted four seconds before there'd been a satisfying *plop!*

She'd looked at her friend then, his small scruffy frame, freckles and bright eyes. She couldn't imagine him not being here. But she couldn't bear the thought of him being turned into a Shadowling or Arbolis Noir or any other Lost Soul. She didn't want him to become some *thing* bent on bringing about the downfall of any that crossed its path just to satisfy its own insatiable loss.

"How did it happen?" She'd asked gently.

Little Reggie had also been staring into the depths of the well, horrific memories swimming up before his eyes. *"I managed to get down with the help of Tommy and I eventually found the necklace, but the rope frayed on my way back up…"* He'd nursed the back of his head absentmindedly. *"I drowned."*

Erica had looked up at the dark heavens to stop the tears. A wintery moon hung above them, branches from a nearby tree cast their scratchy shadows over its celestial orb. Would this have been like his last sight of earth as the waters slowly filled his unconscious self?

"I dropped the necklace when I fell. By the time Tommy got help it was too late…"

She'd looked at the climbing rope and harnesses she'd packed and had changed her mind, summoning Xerxes instead. Little Reggie had looked at it in awe as Erica had explained her plan.

"You would like me to magic you down, stand guard and keep the well alight?" Xerxes had asked, seeking confirmation. Erica had nodded. *"All for this little waif?"* It'd mused, squatting to regard Little Reggie with its gold, pupil-less eyes. *"You humans are odd creatures."*

"Takes one to know one. Right, wish me luck! And keep an eye out!"

The way down hadn't been as bad as she'd feared but that was mostly due to Xerxes magicking her down with the utmost care. Although it had 'somehow' lost concentration the last few feet causing her to plummet noisily into the freezing water.

"You did that on purpose!" She'd shouted up, her echoes bouncing around the narrow space. Xerxes' silhouette had shrugged indifferently and disappeared, leaving her alone in Little Reggie's watery grave.

The waters had lapped just above her waist, she had been glad for the waders, though they hadn't kept the icy cold out. Quickly turning on her father's metal detector, she'd set to work. Within minutes she'd found all manner of bottle tops, cans, buttons, coins, buckets and horseshoes but no necklace. Her teeth had started chattering. Stamping her feet for warmth, the silt under her left foot had given way and she'd stumbled—she had just caught her balance before she'd gone under. The metal detector had then started beeping angrily. Delving in the water she'd fished out a chain, its diamond breaking the inky surface. Wiping it clean of grime, it had twinkled in Xerxes' light.

"I've got it!"

Xerxes and the spirit leaned gingerly over the edge of the well.

"What was that? Are you alright?" Little Reggie called down. He then saw the twinkling of the necklace and gestured for Xerxes to magic Erica back up.

Arising triumphant, it was whilst they were distracted that the Arbolis Noir attacked. Swiping Erica aside with one of its heavy branches as its tentacles grabbed at Little Reggie, intent on getting their prize. The spirit dodged it as best as it could, but there was little room to run, let alone places to hide in the garden. The malevolent tree swung at them, bashing them with its branches and causing its roots to knife through the ground at them. Spying a gap, Little Reggie made a dash for a forest path that led up into the woodland beyond the garden and Erica seized her chance.

Or she would've done, had she not had problems reaching for her periapt.

Swearing, she glanced up in time to see tentacles slashing down on her. Dodging one successfully, she let out a cry as several others cut and sliced her. Her vision blurring from the pain. Fumbling within the depths of the waders for her periapt she failed to dodge a root that had appeared and fell forwards. Straight towards the well opening. At the last minute, Xerxes grabbed her ankles.

"Use the periapt!" it hissed, shielding her.

"I'm trying!" she grunted in frustration. Finally feeling the cool edges of the periapt against her fingertips as she clutched it within her palm.

"*Fulgur impetum!*" she cried, conjuring a lightning attack that struck the possessed tree repeatedly, splintering it in two. Its final screams shattered the black night, resounding out over the snowy hills.

***

Christmas morning broke with the usual tradition: hot chocolate and muffins. Erica couldn't stop yawning and had black shadows under her eyes, but she enjoyed watching her family open their Christmas presents. With her new income, she'd decided to spoil them with silk scarves, fur-lined gloves, branded goods, wallets, perfumes, colognes, books, chocolate and alcohol.

"I hope you're no getting into debt with such extravagance!" her mother exclaimed.

Erica waved her hand dismissively. "We only live once, right?"

Normally, Christmas Day was a pyjama day with lots of food, drink, TV re-runs and perhaps a board game or two. But, when Guy announced that he'd invited Lizzie over to have lunch with them, hysteria descended the Shylockes as everyone took dibs on the bathroom, with Guy sneaking in first. Having had tonnes of sleepovers, Erica wasn't bothered if Lizzie caught her in her pyjamas and had gallantly volunteered to be last in the bathroom stakes.

Left alone and in charge of getting Christmas dinner started, she took the opportunity to check her wounds. Besides a sore ankle, she'd got cuts on her waist and elbow. Throwing the bloodied bandages into the bin, she proceeded to dress them afresh before checking her pocket for the antidote that Xerxes had fetched; it was bitter, but it had saved her. She'd ensure she always had a bottle on her from now on.

When the doorbell sounded, she naturally assumed it was Lizzie and thought nothing of answering it in her purple checked flannel pyjamas and fluffy slippers. Opening the door, she was stunned to find Michael on the doorstep, wrapped up against the cold in his Actualle clothing, tight jeans and reefer jacket.

On seeing her, a redness warmed his cheeks, although he hadn't yet clocked her outfit. When he finally noticed her pyjamas, he averted his eyes and blushed more deeply.

"I… erh, apologies. I thought that perhaps you would be dressed, Miss Shylocke. Is now a bad time?"

Despite now wishing she had taken dibs on the bathroom; she couldn't hold back her anger at his radio silence. Stepping forwards, she planted a short sharp slap on his cheek. "That's for leaving Xerxes and me in the lurch!" Gasping, she looked at him, stunned at what she'd done. "Sorry, it's just that we've been worried sick about you and Ashayla. Where've you been? I've heard nothing since Friday!"

"I thought you'd be too 'occupied' to notice," he replied tartly, nursing his cheek.

"Don't be ridiculous. I've been beside myself with worry!"

Realisation flared in his eyes and he looked at her, eyes bright with something she hadn't seen before. Hope? "I suppose I deserved it then. I'm sorry."

Studying him, she noticed his exhaustion, the dark shadows under his eyes and how wan he looked, the stitches at his temple and his arm in a sling. "What happened?!" she whispered reaching for him.

He briefly closed his eyes against her touch and when he opened them, they burned. "I was foolish and let myself be disarmed by a Shadowling. Ashayla saved my life."

"Is it okay?"

He nodded, tapping his breast pocket. "It's resting."

"And where have you been since?"

He hesitated. "I will explain myself. I promise I'll tell you everything. It's the least I can do. But, not now, not today, please?"

Erica looked him up and down. She was desperate to know but he was here and he was alive. That was enough for now. "Okay. But later, you promise?"

"I promise." He let out a shaky sigh. "Talking of today, I was wondering if you would be free late afternoon?" He scratched the back of his head nervously.

"Yes. You came all this way to ask me that? Why didn't you just ask Xerxes?"

"I also wanted to give you this," he said, handing her a parcel wrapping neatly in brown paper and tied with a red ribbon. A sprig of holly adorned it. "Merry Christmas," he murmured and, leaning forwards, planted a lingering kiss upon her cheek. Frissons ran down her spine.

He turned to go.

"Wait! Stay for lunch. We've already got one extra guest; another won't be a problem."

"I do not want to intrude on your family Christmas. I shall—"

"You won't be," interrupted Erica. "I can't have you wandering around in the cold."

He avoided her eyes. "Are you certain?"

"I insist, Michael."

He looked shyly up at her. "Then I cannot but acquiesce."

Wrapped up against the cold, it was then that Lizzie appeared behind him on the path. A wry smile on her lips. "I hope I'm not interrupting anything?"

Michael blushed graciously.

"Not at all. This is my friend Michael. Michael, this is my best friend, Lizzie."

He gave a little wave, wishing her a 'Merry Christmas'.

"So, this is The Michael!"

"Lizzie, be nice!" Erica ordered.

"Of course, I'll be nice." She rounded on him, poking him in the chest. "If you ever hurt her again, *ever* make her cry again, I'll rip your balls off and feed them to my dog. Got it?" She turned back to Erica. "Nice enough for you? Is Guy in?" she asked voice changing to its normal bright tones. She walked past and entered the hallway.

"She's joking," Erica said hurriedly, smiling nervously. "She doesn't have a dog."

"I made you cry?"

268

She blushed at her feet.

"I never meant—"

"I know," she said, looking up to find his eyes filled with shame.

It was then that Guy appeared on the stairs, sporting a goofy smile and a Santa hat. "Mum! Dad! Lizzie's here! And, we have another visitor! I think Erica needs next dibs on the bathroom!"

***

Showered and dressed in a black dress with glittery tights, she hid her wounds with a red cardigan and, spritzing on her favourite perfume, went downstairs nervously, carrying her gift for him.

"Come to think of it, it wasn't really on the skin, was it?"

She walked into the living room to find Michael in a Christmas jumper surrounded by her family. He was perched on the edge of the sofa, a photo album on his knees. Her mother was looking particularly chuffed and was happily sat next him pointing out photos, whilst the others eyed him with intrigue. Apart from her father, who sported a frown. They all looked up when she entered; Michael visibly relaxed making her brothers wink at her impishly.

Lizzie was sat with Guy, leaning into his chest with his arms about her. They looked the happiest she'd ever seen them. She was glad.

"What's that?" Erica asked, setting his gift aside and sitting down.

"The scar you had when you were born. It wasn't really on your skin, was it? More like in your veins," Cole repeated thoughtfully, looking closely at a particular photo.

"I wouldn't know, I can't remember," she replied with a half-smile. "I thought the nurse said it was from the forceps."

"Didn't Guy have one too?" Cole asked, looking at his parents for confirmation.

"No, he's just got that birthmark on the back of his neck," said their father.

"What, here? Where your hair's white?" said Lizzie as she turned to look.

269

"Yeah…" Guy said shyly.

"That's so cool! I've got one on my—"

"Yes, well, enough of that!" said their father as Lizzie made to lift up her top.

"Aw, our little miracle baby," said their mother—she was still cooing over photos, a soppy smile on her face.

"What do you mean?" Erica asked.

"Well, you totally surprised us coming so soon after Guy. It was as if you just appeared one day. Very odd—your father had had the snip, you know."

"Ursella, really?!" cried her father, turning the shade of a beetroot whilst Lizzie choked on a mince pie. Michael quickly turned another page in the album, making some random comment about an outfit whilst Erica leapt to her feet.

"I'll go check on dinner!"

"Good idea, I'll come with you. Boys, you sort out drinks for everyone," her mother said standing.

Leaving Cole and Guy rolling about in laughter, her mother followed her into the kitchen.

"Where've you been hiding him!" she whispered, checking the oven.

"We work together. It's this new job I've got, he's a colleague from there," Erica replied, busying herself with the batter for the Yorkshire puddings.

"So he said. A *very* nice colleague too," she smiled cheekily.

"Don't you go meddling! Anyway, he's got a girlfriend."

She raised her eyebrows in surprise. "Are you sure? He doesn't strike me as the kind of man to abandon his girlfriend on Christmas Day."

Erica faltered, breath catching. There was some truth in what her mum said. A warm tingle ran through her. Suddenly, she felt massively self-conscious and began to fidget with her hair.

"You look beautiful," she said, catching her hand. "Michael certainly doesn't seem disappointed!"

Erica smiled up at her. "Thank you. Just make sure you behave then, please, mum."

"I'll try, promise."

Lunch was a merry affair with plenty of wine to accompany the goose and festive trimmings. Erica couldn't remember a happier Christmas. Her parents were thrilled to have Lizzie and Guy finally together and whilst she was no clearer of Michael and his intentions, she was glad he was there. He entertained with witty jokes and interesting anecdotes and gave as good as he got from Cole and Guy.

As her father lit the rum-soaked Christmas pudding to a round of applause, Michael looked at her through the blue flames. There was a lightness to him that she'd never seen before, as if a burden had been lifted. His smile revealed a new tenderness that made her heart ache.

Her parents insisted on clearing up, leaving the youngsters to themselves. Excusing themselves Guy and Lizzie went upstairs to the nook and Cole left for his bedroom, leaving Michael and Erica alone in the living room.

There was a brief, nervous silence.

"A member of the family served in the army?" Michael asked at length, breaking the silence.

Erica looked up to where he indicated, at the golden sword and scabbard that hung over the sofa.

"Yes, it was my great-great-grandfather's. He served in World War I."

"He must have been a brave man."

"He won a few medals before going missing in action."

Spying her gift that she'd left so that she could get ready, he passed it to her again. "I hope you like it."

"Let's open them together," she suggested.

They sat together on the sofa and she passed him his gift. He accepted it humbly. They then opened the presents to reveal a purple silk scarf from Michael and homemade one from Erica. They chuckled: *great minds*...

"I was unaware you could crochet."

She laughed. "It's my first attempt."

"Then I am especially honoured," he said proudly. Standing in front of the mirror, he proceeded to try to put the grey scarf on. Seeing him struggle with his injury, she got up and helped him. He regarded her intently through his thick lashes as she wrapped it gently round his neck; his gaze caressing her. This close, she could feel his warm breath on her cheeks and shivered.

Returning reluctantly to her seat, she began to unfold the scarf, admiring its purple swirls. "It's beautiful!"

"I noticed how much you liked wearing purple…"

A soft leather vambrace and small dagger fell out onto the rug. The dagger was bejewelled and housed in a decorative sheath.

"And I overheard Xerxes complain how much you struggle to fight with your periapt. This vambrace can be worn on either wrist and allows for one or two periapts to slot safely here within easy reach," he indicated a casing on both the dorsal and ventral sides. "It makes combat more efficient. I don't like to think of you fighting, but I would rather you be well prepared if it does befall you. The dagger will be a useful letter opener if anything. Which arm would you like the vambrace on?" She raised her left arm and he gently pulled up the sleeve to her cardigan, the touch of his fingertips was electric.

On seeing her wounds, his worried eyes flicked up at her face.

With her help, he pulled the vambrace on like a glove and fastened the buckles round her thumb and wrist. "The soft leather means that it's not only supple, but it can also be stowed with ease."

"Thank you! I could've done with this last night," she said and quickly described her encounter with the Arbolis Noir.

"That explains your injuries. Why were you out at such an hour? Especially in the current climate! You acquired the antidote without problem?" he asked quickly.

She nodded, and, in hushed tones, proceeded to tell him about Little Reggie, the well, the necklace, the attack and how Xerxes had fetched the antidote for her.

"They're vicious Souls!" She finished as she slotted in her two periapts, pulling down her sleeve to hide it.

"They are. Superficially placid, but, in truth, deadly. Most attacks end with fatalities. Their poison can turn you into a Soul if an antidote isn't administered promptly. I'm grateful Xerxes looked after you so well. How is your ankle?"

"He's scared of you, that's why!" Erica laughed. "It's just sore, nothing serious."

"Good. If anything were to happen to you, I'd never forgive myself." He glanced up, his eyes tinged with anguish.

She bit her lip. Her heart was thudding so loud she was sure he could hear it. "I've never seen a spirit pass on before." She continued nervously, changing the subject. "It was quite beautiful, if it's not wrong to describe something like that as beautiful." And she described how Little Reggie had appeared before Ms Miller when she'd returned the long-lost necklace.

"I knew it wasn't you," Ms Miller had whispered, voice choked by tears on seeing the young boy she loved. "I knew it." She had reached for him then, caressing his face and he had covered her hand, keeping it there for the longest of moments.

"I stayed for you, Gwendolyn. To be near you. But... I've got to go now." He'd admitted tearfully.

She had nodded, tears trickling down her cheeks. "Wait for me?"

He had smiled, planting a delicate kiss upon her lips. *"I've never stopped."*

With that he'd blown apart, like golden blossom scattered by a sudden breeze. His soul had shimmered around them, enveloping Ms Miller in its warmth before drifting up to the heavens.

***

"It is beautiful. You're right to describe it as so. But then it should be, to honour the life that has passed, don't you think?" Michael said quietly, eyes distant.

"You've witnessed it?"

"Once. It's quite unforgettable. Especially when it's someone you once cared about."

There was a silence. Erica watched him gazing into some private reverie, but, for once, didn't feel the wave of melancholy crush him.

"UK Soul Gatherers are now working with the secret service to comb the streets for Lost Souls," he said, changing the subject.

"What's The Guild saying?"

"Nothing official, but the High KeyMaster is an attendee at the Prime Minister's current COBRA meeting. He shall call a meeting at The Guild tomorrow."

"Are Prime Ministers aware of Limbo?" Erica asked.

"Not normally, as their terms in office are short. However, in emergencies, such as this, people who need to know are informed."

"Bet that's a shock for them," she smiled.

He wavered before continuing. "And... Martin Jenkins was killed last night."

Martin Jenkins? Martin. She'd met a Martin recently...

"Sir Marty Hodges' nephew. We met them at your Inauguration," he prompted.

The jovial young man floated up in her memory. "Oh no! Was it... an attack?"

Michael looked grim. "No, not like you think. He was murdered by an armed burglar. Sir Marty is quite devasted, Martin was his last living relative."

"We'll have to visit him."

Michael smiled at her then. "You're very kind. We'll call on him when we're with the de Temps for New Years."

What with everything that had happened, Erica had forgotten the invitation by Lord and Lady de Temps. "I've never stayed with a Lord and Lady before, let alone gone to a Ball."

"You shall be fine. In any case, I shall be there to laugh at you if you're not." He eyes glinted mischievously.

"How reassuring!"

The clock on the mantel piece chimed three times. Michael looked up with a start. "I'm forgetting myself. I have one last gift for you; although, it will involve some 'travel'. If your ankle permits."

Catching his drift, she got up. "It certainly does! I'll go get ready!"

***

Having changed into her leather combat gear and boots, they wrapped themselves up in each other's scarves before excusing themselves—much to her mother's delight—and Michael led her down through the village. Passing by the village cross and up Church Street towards St. James the Apostle's Church.

"And how is Marc?" he asked casually, but his tense shoulders said otherwise.

"I don't know. He messaged me yesterday and I replied but I've not heard from him since."

Michael looked at her sideways. "Really?" He cleared his throat, a fresh bounce in his step. "I hope you don't find it too grisly if we use the graveyard? Some find them gruesome as means of Travel, but they do expedient the search for appropriate dates."

"You're asking a person who's first friend was a spirit." Erica laughed.

A wintery dusk was quickly settling. Snow was beginning to fall, covering the snow-covered ground afresh, quickly hiding all blemishes and scars.

Reaching the graveyard, Michael made a beeline for a particular gravestone close to the church door. It was a stepped plinth made from orange stone, a gothic cross upon its top. Lichen grew in places, but the name could still be made out 'George Brooks' As well as the date of his death 'September 1874'.

"This is the one. 3:45," he said, noting the time. "Best not to be seen from now on: *Actualles ignarus.*" He incanted, conjuring the familiar fading sensation of the Ignorant Charm.

Following suit as Michael fished out his keys and unlocked the Temporal Gateway, Erica felt the electrical surge as the Gateway opened, humming and crackling. The soundless wind of the vortex buffeted them, tousling their hair.

"Ladies first," he said, holding out his good hand.

24
Blood Spilt

They found themselves in a bitterly cold and very snow laden Bonsall of 1874.

Once the vortex closed behind them, Michael checked his watch before removing his Time Piece. Smiling sheepishly, he asked for her assistance in adjusting the time dial causing the temporal planes to split and the sky to arc, lightening the crisp winter sunset. "Adjust it only a little, please. There's a cart I wish us to catch. We should have time now." And, taking her hand, led her down the hill of St James' Church, along winding footpaths trodden within the deep snow of the hillside which Erica recognised as being the ancestors to those paths she knew so well from her time. Although, whereas those of Actualle Bonsall had steps and railings, these had nothing.

After much slipping and sliding, they reached Yeoman Street. The Street had been roughly cleared to allow people and carts passage. The cart that Michael led them to was laden with lead. Sneaking on the back, they held on tightly as it made its slippery and rickety way down the Clatterway to the Via Gellia Road. Huddled together, their breath came in icy plumes.

Although quiet, there were some people out, dressed warmly and making social calls. Lush evergreen wreaths decorated most doors, and candles were alit in many windows—the only lights for Michael and Erica as they made their bumpy way down the Clatterway. At its end, the Via Gellia Mill loomed before them in all its Georgian brilliance. The mill still bustled with workers despite it being Christmas Day.

As the cart pulled to a stop, Michael helped her down and led her over a stye and through some trees. Leaving the trees behind,

Erica was greeted by a frozen pool that glistened in the setting sun. Excited, Michael scampered ahead, brushing snow off a bag that he must have hidden prior to visiting her.

With her assistance, he opened the bag to reveal two pairs of ice skates. "Would you join me in some ice-skating, Erica?" he asked with a coy smile.

Once changed into her skates, she helped him into his and he let her clutch at him as she waddled over to the frozen pool's edge. Erica was relieved to notice that the ice was several feet deep. Gingerly she stepped on with his help and she watched as he whizzed gracefully away, circling the pool effortlessly.

"Show off!" She laughed, edging forwards as best as she could. The fact that there were no railings around the pool's edge disconcerted her a great deal. He chuckled and returned to her. Wincing as he removed his injured arm from its sling, he shyly offered her his gloved hands. This time, taking them felt different, special, intimate. Eyes meeting, he smiled and, holding her hands, he skated backwards, gently guiding her along.

Following his instructions, she found herself relaxing. It certainly helped having no crowds whizzing by. A winter moon swung up slowly in the early evening sky as stars came out against an inky blackness; their starlight harsh and dazzling in their coolness, bathing them and the pool in their celestial light. The trees that encircled the pool were frozen, their petrified branches and icicles twinkled with the brilliance of the moon whilst the ice beneath them sparkled like stars.

Succeeding in not falling over increased Erica's confidence and, with Michael's encouragement, she let go of one hand and they skated hand in hand round the pool—the shimmering lights enveloping them. It was exhilarating to feel the cool air against her skin: it heightened her senses, making her feel giddy. It was a joy to be alive, to be here, in this moment.

Without thinking Erica tested herself, coming to a sudden stop. Having failed to tell Michael, he lost his balance and fell onto the cold ice with a bump.

"Sorry! I got carried away!" she cried ruefully, trying to pull him to his feet by his good arm. Failing, she fell also, landing next to him. "How's your arm?" she asked with apprehension.

"I have a confession to make... I shouldn't though... I don't deserve anything..." he said, voice husky and tremulous.

Looking up, she found her face inches from his, the warmth of his breath thrilling her—his eyes drank her in hungrily.

"And what is that, Mr Nicholas?" she purred, relishing his closeness.

"I care for you, greatly... You mean the world to me..." He hesitated, self-control visibly weakening. Tentatively, he touched her face and a heat like no other exploded deep within. Caressing the line of her cheek down to her chin he lingered near her lips; shivers ran through her like electricity. "I'm falling for you." Tilting her chin upwards, he leaned forwards... "In fact, I think..."

But before his lips could touch hers, an almighty explosion splintered the sky. Lights pulsed and flared like sheet lightning, the ground shook—deep cracks appearing within the ice. Michael scrambled to his feet, pulling her with him, ignoring the searing pain in his arm. On reaching solid ground, Michael held her behind him, scanning their surroundings in anticipation. Everything seemed normal, in fact none of this Time's people seemed concerned in any way.

"What was that?!" she whispered, doubling over. "It feels..." She tried to explain the agony deep within, as if someone was twisting her very soul. She felt fragile and tainted all at once. Her blood tingled and her skin crawled. She clutched her chest; it hurt, like she'd been kicked by a mule.

"Erica?!" He held her close, checking her for any injuries.

"It hurts... What happened?" she asked again, bracing herself against the pain.

"Time. Someone's tried to manipulate Time. As KeyMasters we can sense the ruptures, whereas the Actualles here cannot."

"'Tried'?"

"If they'd succeeded, things would be a lot worse. Are you well enough to travel? I fear we must leave straight away."

***

They rushed back as quickly as they could, altering Time to account for their absence. Despite Erica pleading to go to Limbo with him, Michael insisted she stayed with her family.

"If I'm not needed, I shall return. If that doesn't inconvenience you?" he added, taking her hand in his.

Erica smiled shyly. "I'd like that."

"And you're feeling better?"

"Yes, I've no idea what it was, but I feel fine now."

He looked at her thoughtfully.

The sun was setting when they reached the farm. They found Erica's mother standing with Cole in the farmyard, binoculars fixed firmly to her eyes. Cole had one of the hunting rifles in his hands.

"Mum! What's happened?" She called as Michael helped her over the gate.

Her mother spun round her face ashen. Relief flooded her features on seeing them. "Thank goodness you're back! Guy checked in on the walkie talkie—Lizzie's been attacked! Your father's gone to fetch them."

"What do you mean Lizzie's been attacked? Where did they go?" Erica asked, panic gripping her.

"I don't know, Guy was babbling on about the trees at the copse," she replied, turning once more to face the copse of trees they were talking about. It was three fields away, the trees thick and dark. Guy's quad bike lay abandoned nearby.

Michael and Erica looked at one another: Arbolis Noir.

"He was taking her to see the old tree house," Cole explained grimly.

Erica rolled her eyes: *I bet he was…*

"I shall go and assist, Mrs Shylocke," Michael said, taking a step towards the fields. "What are you doing?" he asked, seeing Erica join him.

"Take a quad bike, it'll be faster," she said, indicating the shed.

"But you know I cannot drive."

"I know," she said with a sly smile. "I'll just have to come along, won't I?" She saw his worry. "She's my friend, I can't stand by and do nothing."

"This is no game. It's dangerous. It could be deadly... I don't want to lose you."

"And I don't want to lose you," Erica said crossing her arms. "We appear to be at a stalemate. So, where do we go from here?"

He smiled a lopsided smile and sighed, raising his hands. "I yield. You win. If I cannot stop you then you *must* listen to my instructions. If I say run, you run, understood?"

She nodded and they turned to leave.

"Erica! What are you doing?!" her mum screamed, watching her dash to the kitchen and fetch the keys.

"I'll be okay, I promise! We'll take the last quad."

"We don't know what's going on or how dangerous it is. It should be me going," Cole said stepping forwards.

"You need to stay with mum," said Erica.

Cole looked from his mother to Michael, torn between his responsibilities.

"I shall keep her safe, I promise," Michael said.

"You'd better, mate, or I'll be coming for you!"

Michael nodded, eyes darting nervously to Erica who shrugged. "He is my big brother."

Directing them to the shed, Erica leapt on the quad bike and turned the key. The engine roared into life.

Michael reached inside a pocket and produced a vambrace like the one he'd bought her. Wincing, he undid his sling, tucking it in his pocket and attempted to fasten his vambrace to his injured wrist. Seeing him fumble, Erica leaned over to help, securing the two Færies' periapts.

"Ready?" She looked up.

He was watching her with a smile on his lips, his eyes ablaze.

"What is it?" she said, passing him a helmet.

Crossing the space between them, he lifted her chin and kissed her gently, breaking away before she had time to register or react.

"Never stop amazing me." He breathed, their foreheads touching, before climbing on behind her and pulling down his helmet.

Heart thumping, she blushed, putting on her helmet before revving the engine. Holding her around her waist, they lurched out of the shed across the yard and through the open gate into the first field. Their shadows scattering across the snowy valley. Despite the darkening sky, they could still see the tracks from two quad bikes, one taking leisurely twists and turns, with several doughnuts here and there, and the other taking a determined straight route towards the gate and the second field beyond. In the distance they could see Erica's father entering the third and final field. Switching gears, the quad shot forwards.

He leaned close. "The problem before us is that we cannot use the Ignorant Charm—I think seeing you vanish wouldn't go down well with your mother, let alone Cole. Ashayla or Xerxes will have to apply it. Can Xerxes be subtle?"

"I'll ask," Erica said as she navigated the ruts and bumps of the field.

Moments later, they'd summoned the two Færies, which both materialised in their diminutive forms.

"Can I be subtle?" Xerxes chuntered, as it cast its own Ignorant Charm flying to the right of the quad bike.

Ashayla followed suit, flanking them on the left.

"Ashayla, please alert Christian and ask him to rally whomever he can," Michael instructed.

Bowing, the little Færie vanished in a swirl of matter.

They were just over a field away now. For ease, they followed in the wake of the other quad bikes, using the paths that had already been cut through the deep snow. All the while, keeping a keen eye on the copse and Erica's approaching father. He was just over half a field away.

Hearing the engines, Guy emerged from the undergrowth waving his arms madly. A snow shovel in his hands. Having caught his father's attention, he then disappeared.

The copse of trees shuddered as one before exploding in a fury of tentacles and fighting branches: Arbolis Noir. Guy frantically burst through the undergrowth, this time dragging Lizzie's limp body, shielding her and batting away the Arbolis Noir with his shovel. They were not going to relinquish their prey so easily and several tentacles caught hold of Lizzie's hands and feet and neck, lifting her up in some sick parody of life.

Erica let out a primal scream and gunned the engine: *subtlety be damned!*

***

Erica's father stopped his quad bike where he was and took aim with his hunting rifle, firing round after round at the branches and trunks. Roosting birds rose from the trees' shadowy canopies, but instead of fleeing, they flew with unnatural precision, as if they shared one conscious. Swooping round, they flew straight for Erica's father who crouched, covering his head as they dove.

Their eyes gleamed red.

The shadowy birds circled and dove again, a hundred daggers falling from the sky. Erica's father howled as their beaks and claws met their mark.

Seeing the chaos erupting before them, Michael and Erica drove through the gate that Erica's father had left open in his hurry, scattering the snow as they tore through the drifts.

"Bullets will have no effect. Xerxes, *calidaté pluvat!*" Michael shouted, and fire began to rain down on the trees, melting the snow that remained. The fire storm grew stronger and stronger until the snow had evaporated entirely, exposing bare branches which dried instantly to burst into flames. The shrieks of the Arbolis Noir echoed across the valley.

Fire-rain fell onto the birds, their burning bodies lighting up the dark sky as charred corpses rained down, dispersing their souls in thick plumes of black blossom.

They finally reached the writhing form of Erica's father. Diving off the quad bike, Erica scrambled to him, cradling him in her arms. Both his eyes had been gouged out and stinky black blood oozed down his cheeks. He was scratched to pieces—chunks of skin were missing from his face, neck and hands. He was howling against the pain, holding his head in his hands. Overwhelmed, she hugged him to her, rocking him in a vain effort to comfort him.

"Administer the antidote! His wounds could be infected!" Michael shouted, leaping off the vehicle and continuing on foot towards Guy who was hacking at the tentacles, screaming viciously.

Summoning his sword, Michael plucked it from the air with his injured arm. He grimaced as the pain took his breath away: *not good*. Brushing it aside, he took his place next to Guy and began attacking the tentacles that held Lizzie.

Then, in a flurry of light, Ashayla reappeared in its elfin form.

"What the hell?!" Guy cried, jumping back. "What is that?"

"A Færie. Its name is Ashayla."

"I have notified—oh glory!" It exclaimed on seeing the bedlam before them.

The remaining Arbolis Noir began to uproot themselves in their effort to get their prey and more.

Slicing through the last remaining tentacles, Michael assisted Guy and, together, they half-carried, half-dragged Lizzie away from the advancing trees.

"*Lumínate concallus!*" Michael incanted and Ashayla plunged its tiny fists into the snowy ground. Light tore through the ground in a mighty explosion, streaking its way towards the Arbolis Noir, creating a chasm in its wake.

Guy swore vehemently, eyes wide with shock. He looked at Michael—he'd turned a shade of green. "What did you say you did again?"

"It's complicated."

The Souls shrieked as the light burned their roots. Unable to cross, the trees threw out their tentacles, slashing at the humans and Færie in frustration.

Then they paused.

Shuddering as one there was a moment of uneasy silence before a distant rumble sounded, growing louder with each passing second.

From the dark undergrowth a sick menagerie of Bloodlings emerged: foxes, badgers, cattle, cats and dogs, frothing at the mouth, eyes glowing blood-red, fangs bared.

Michael's eyes widened in fright and he spun round. "Erica! Run!!"

Hearing him, she quickly replaced her vial of antidote and looked up, cursing as she saw the angry pack advancing, finding their way across the chasm. Some faster than others. All hellbent on soul-lust. Scrambling to her feet with her father in tow, she stumbled to the quad bike shouting orders to Xerxes which promptly began aiming fire balls at the malevolent Souls.

Bending, Michael fetched out a small black vial and tipped a few drops of its contents down Lizzie's throat. She was covered in lacerations; many were inches wide and deep. Blood oozed out relentlessly, soaking the snow. Her breath was ragged and shallow.

"Wait! What's that?"

"It's an antidote for the poison."

"'Poison'? Those things are poisonous?!"

"Yes, you should take some too, just to be safe." He looked at Guy anxiously. "You need to go. She's weak—take her to safety. We shall hold them off." He proceeded to take his stance, studying the advancing animals and calculating his best move. Ashayla appeared by his side, teeth bared, tattoos flashing, its hands flaring hotly.

Guy looked down at Lizzie's battered body, anger filling his soul. "Like hell you are. Give me your sword!" he growled.

Michael regarded him in surprise. Seeing the hatred in Guy's eyes, he wavered: if he succumbed, he'd become a formidable Soul... He looked back at the Bloodlings hurtling towards them. "*Defendí!*" And he waved the periapts over Lizzie—a wall grew up from the ground, surrounding her, setting solid. "I can do better, but you *cannot* die! *Ferrum-avi vocaví!*"

A thrumming filled the evening air, getting louder and louder by the millisecond. Just as the closest Bloodling hurtled towards them, a sword flew straight through it, annihilating it, its soul dissipating in a flurry of black petals.

284

The sword came to a stop before a dumbfounded Guy.

He recognised it as that of his great-great-grandfather that had hung in the living room. All these years and he'd never noticed the markings upon its blade—like rays of sunlight. A tiny sun motif was nestled at the base of the sword's hilt. Shaking off his surprise, he snatched it, vaguely noticing a surge of power as it moulded to his grasp before lunging into the midst of the Bloodlings, hacking and slicing. Souls evaporating blackly in his wake.

He was too engrossed to notice the blade's glow, as bright as the morning star amidst the darkness.

Michael faltered. He'd heard legends of DawnBringer blades but never believed them to be true. *What was this family? First Erica, then Guy…*

Sensing his distraction, a nearby Bloodling dove on Michael's injured arm, leaping up to bite and tear it. Headbutting it away with his helmet, he deftly countered their attacks but not without being manoeuvred backwards to the chasm. "Ashayla!"

Looking up from where it guarded Lizzie, the Færie charmed a storm of lightning bolts, flinging them at the Souls and incinerating them there and then.

Waving his thanks, Michael went after Guy, Ashayla providing cover whilst it continued to protect Lizzie—its essence seething.

More and more Bloodlings emerged from the burning Arbolis Noir, driven by soul- and blood-lust. The phantom trees shuddered in unison one last time, and as they succumbed to the magic fire, they relinquished their darkest secret.

Seeing the escaping shadows swoop out of the flames' way, Michael blanched, cursing loudly.

"What?!"

"Strigoi!"

Guy looked up, puzzled. Seeing a shadow flying towards him with red eyes and vicious fangs, he understood: vampires.

Rooted to the spot, he watched as lightning streaked to meet the Strigoi head-on, dispersing the Soul in the ensuing explosion.

He turned to thank the little Færie, but it was pointing frantically at the other advancing shadows. *"Later!"*

With the airborne Strigoi joining forces with the Bloodlings, the three closed ranks, covering each other's backs, all the while protecting Lizzie in their centre.

***

Encumbered with her unconscious father, Erica was making poor progress—she really needed to work on her upper body strength.

Finally yanking her father onto the quad, she was just getting on herself when a Blood Fox leapt over the wall knocking her to the ground. Remembering the dagger Michael had given her, she unsheathed it from her boot and slashed at the Lost Soul. Growling through barred teeth, it swiped at her with sharp claws. Only to have her blade find its mark in its chest. It exploded over her, engulfing her in black petals as another Bloodling leapt over the wall, then another.

Xerxes landed next to her and cast a shield around the quad bike, protecting her father. "*Flammaté!*" Erica screamed, and Xerxes directed a twelve-foot flame at one Bloodling then immediately at another. But it was no use. More and more appeared until they were surrounded. Xerxes cast a second shield over the two of them, but it was weak and flickered whenever a Soul threw itself against it. Noticing, some of the Bloodlings began to throw themselves at the shield protecting Erica's father, which also flickered weakly.

"*I cannot hold two shields at maximum strength, ma'am!*" Xerxes apologised.

Erica took a deep breath: one would have to go. "*Grandis,*" she murmured, and watched as the charmed dagger grew until it was the size of a sword.

She nodded to the Færie. She was as ready as she'd ever be.

Just then, several things happened all at once. Xerxes lifted the shield and the Bloodlings pounced. As the Færie prepared a firestorm, the shadows beside them wobbled and bulged and, with a squelching sound like that of a boot being pulled from the deepest, muddiest puddle, Christian leapt out, his long leather coat billowing after him, wearing a pair of goggles, swords in hand. A woman with flowing black hair followed him, then a copper wolf, a blur, a boy looking utterly bewildered and a tall African man with a Doberman Pinscher at his side; its ears erect and fangs exposed.

Christian's twin sabres found their mark in the nearest Souls, whilst the African stabbed others with his bladed cestus; a Tomahawk was strapped to his back and a pair of short swords hung from his belt. Slicing a nearby Bloodling in two, he lifted a flaring palm to blast another to smithereens with a jet of hot light. Fixing its gaze on a Lost Soul, the Doberman Pinscher pounced, shredding it with ease.

The woman flung herself at the copper wolf, merging with it to solidify into a dark, hairy mass with eyes that blazed copper. Striding through the hoards, the over-sized wolf cut through the Bloodlings, taking them in its jaws and biting down to scatter the Souls in a whirlwind of black blossom.

Then they heard Michael's cry.

"Strigoi!"

All watched in horror as several soul-thirsty shadows hurtled across the fields straight for them.

Instinctively, Xerxes directed its firestorm at the Lost Soul aimed for Erica, destroying it. Whilst a second lunged at the Færie, forcing it to the snowy ground. The Færie struggled to fight it off as teeth gnawed at it. Swiping it with its metal cuffs, the Soul hissed and flashed its claws.

Erica shouted profanities as she dove at the shadow, hacking at it with her sword. Xerxes let out a cry as the Soul bit it before turning to grab Erica by the throat and squeeze.

Just as Erica's vision darkened, blades sliced through the Strigoi's neck, taking off its head. Black petals exploded from it in a flurry. Looking up, Erica was startled to find herself reflected in the silver pupil-less eyes of the African. His short curly hair was silver and glowed like a Færie's. Black matter dripped from his cestus to the snowy ground.

"Thank you," she stammered, massaging her throat.

"You're welcome," he said, helping her to her feet. His voice was low and gravelly with a soft American drawl. "Stay down!" He suddenly shouted. Ducking, Erica watched wide-eyed as he clanged together his cestus to produce a lightning bolt that ruptured a pair of advancing Souls.

"Who are you?!" Erica asked, looking at him and the others, taking them in. The blur had stopped to reveal itself to be a short East Asian man with a pale, creamy complexion. He was raking a hand through his glossy black hair which he wore in an undercut style and was sporting a peevish frown as he spoke heatedly with the young boy. A Lost Soul careered towards them—sweeping the boy behind him, the man grabbed at the Soul and literally tore it apart with his bare hands, snarling to reveal sharp fangs. It was then he stilled. Turning abruptly in her direction, nostrils flared, he paled even more. Their eyes locked and something inside her faltered.

"I'm Amberson Solway, a Soul Gatherer," he said, drawing her attention back. "We answered Ashayla's call. Though 'we're having a little bother in Bonsall' doesn't quite cut it!" He turned to Christian. "We'll need reinforcements!"

"There aren't any! They're all busy!" he cried.

The group turned to face the advancing hoards, weapons and claws at the ready.

***

Cole and his mother watched with unease as the situation before them worsened. Letting out a scream when she spied her husband attacked through the binoculars, Erica's mother threw them to Cole.

"I'll go!" he said, readying his rifle.

"If they're what I think they are, bullets aren't going to do anything," she cried, disappearing inside.

Cole followed her into the kitchen. He could hear her footsteps on the stairs. "Mum! MUM! What are you doing? What do you mean bullets won't help? How do you know? What are they?"

Silence answered his frantic cries. He ran a hand through his hair as he paced the kitchen: he had to do something! Just as he'd made up his mind to go after Erica, his mother appeared in the doorway carrying an old, lacquered box. Scattering its contents on the kitchen table, she searched frantically before grasping a small silver tear-shaped medallion in triumph.

"What's that?"

"Our last hope," she said, racing back into the yard.

On her heels, Cole watched as his mother rubbed the medallion like an Aladdin's lamp. They both jumped when the precious stone at its centre shimmered and a streak flew from it—bright and cold.

"Do as you were charged! Protect my family!"

***

There was a sound like that of a comet splintering the night sky and an ice blast exploded out from the farmhouse, its icy shockwaves advancing across the fields.

Before Erica could process what was happening, the air temperature plummeted drastically, freezing the ground and Bloodlings upon it instantly.

They watched as the icy storm flooded the valley, rolling in like fog, causing ice crystals to form and grow jaggedly on the dry-stone walls and gates before speeding towards any fleeing Bloodlings or Strigoi.

The ice storm overwhelmed them and, as the Souls froze, collapsing icily in on themselves, their essence floated away in thick black flurries.

A form emerged from the freezing fog.

A Færie: tall, cold and ancient.

They were saved.

Epilogue

The Wastelands stretched out dark and barren before her. She walked without destination but most definitely with purpose. The Lost Souls would find her wherever she was—they couldn't resist, she was a DawnBringer.

Not that she was one to sit idle and wait.

The sword hanging from her chatelaine glowed from within its scabbard. Frowning, she drew it a little way. The gold blade was bright with renewed lustre, its metal core alive.

"Its twin... Someone has awoken its twin?"

She looked up to scan the horizon, as if expecting to see whoever it was there. *Could it be starting?*

An ice-cold orb hovered next to her as if observing the blade, before floating away. It was the only light for miles within the gloomy Wastelands. Streaking this way and that, it never strayed too far, always returning to lighten her footfall. Though she had wandered the Wastelands for many, many years, there were still dangers even to one like her.

In the never-distance she could make out a moving shadow, lost and scared.

"Over yonder," she said to the orb, pointing gracefully from the thick cloak she wore.

The orb halted abruptly and spun, flaring frostily, regarding the distant shadow in apprehension. Was it ready to submit or would it need encouragement?

Just then something happened that took them by surprise. A tingling sensation gripped the Færie, overpowering it.

"Mistress, I am being summoned?!"

The lady looked up then, her hazel eyes alight from under the hood of her cloak. She pulled back the hood to reveal ashen hair, pale and flecked with gold. It glowed almost like that of a Færie's in the dark Wastelands.

She'd been right. It was starting.

"It is time! You are dismissed. Guide them to me! I shall gather the others—await us at the valley!"

The Færie could resist no longer. *"But mistress!"*

"I shall be well, fear ye not," she said, and from her robes she unsheathed her sword. It was dainty yet didn't lack substance. "I look forward to your return and… thank you!"

The lady watched the Færie vanish in a flurry of ice crystals that sparkled as they floated down to the dusty ground.

She was alone.

Of a sort.

***

To start with, no noise reached her ears. There was just movement and shouting but no sound. The first thing she was aware of was the moon, big and bright overhead. It bathed her and everyone in its pale goodness. Then, a dull ringing started followed by vibrations through the frozen ground. Blinking, Erica's eyes began to slowly make sense of the muffled chaos before them. The tall African with glowing hair and eyes was reaching a hand down to her. Accepting it, he hauled her to her feet and her ears were bombarded with a cacophony of noise, shouts and wails. Losing her balance, he held her as she gathered her bearings.

"What happened?" she asked, voice hoarse—her throat still hurt from where the Strigoi had grabbed her.

Amberson looked over to the Færie standing amidst the dissipating fog. It was watching them with interest before suddenly transforming into an icy orb that whizzed back over the fields to the farmhouse. "I'm not sure."

Erica squinted, just making out a running form with bundles under its arm: Cole. He was followed close behind by the Færie in its icy elemental form.

Instinctively, Erica tightened the grip on her sword and checked on Xerxes and her father. Both were losing a lot of blood—Xerxes' gold staining the snow beneath it—but they were breathing. That was something.

"Can you help them?" she asked, tears blurring her vision.

"Already on it," Amberson said as he knelt next to the Færie. He'd fetched rags out of a pouch on his utility belt and was passing them to Xerxes. "Here, staunch the flow with these."

Obediently, Xerxes pressed the rags to its neck and watched as the man's veins began to pulse with light down to his palms which flared hotly. Raising two fingers, he pressed them against the bite before massaging the Færie's neck and shoulders with quick, sweeping gestures. The Færie visibly relaxed as if its discomfort had been washed away.

"It's safe for you to touch Færies *and* humans? What are you? You can do magic but you're not a Færie."

"A Fæ, half-human, half-Færie."

"That explains the eyes. And the hair."

He smiled. "I guess it does. Is he your father?" he asked, indicating the slumped form on the quad bike.

"Yes, this is my Færie Xerxes and that's Cole, my brother," she said, pointing across to the figure that was still a field away. The orb was following behind him at a safe distance.

"By Jove, that was close. What do you think it could be, Solway, old chap?" Christian asked, walking over. He pushed his goggles to the top of his head.

Extracting herself from the wolf, the curvaceous woman took her place next to Christian. The copper wolf padded over to the Asian man and boy—well, teenager, really—watching Cole and the orb approach with wary eyes.

"I'm not sure. But whatever it is, that was old magic."

Christian went to Erica's father and felt his pulse. "He's out cold. We need to take him to the farmhouse and get him cleaned up before there's any infection." He turned to Erica. "I might be able to make him something to help him see again."

"Y-you can do that?" she asked, kneeling next to her father and smoothing the hair from his face. She bit back tears at the sight of the bloody holes where his eyes had been.

"I'll certainly try."

"Thank you," she said, swallowing against the sudden lump in her throat.

Cole finally arrived. He ran over to his father, falling to his knees next to Erica. "Dad!"

"He'll be okay. He's just—"

"He's lost his eyes?!"

"Yes, but he's alive."

Cole threw a blanket to Amberson, he then turned to Erica and poked her in the chest. "What the hell is going on?! Guy and Lizzie getting attacked is one thing, but… trees coming alive? Crazed animals and those swoopy things? Then mum grabs this old box and fetches out some sort of medallion and this thing comes out like a firework!" He jerked his thumb in the direction of the orb.

"I can explain—"

He suddenly noticed her sword and grabbed it off her. "Where did you get this? You could get hurt!"

"You know the pandemic they're talking about?" Christian said, coming over. "This is it."

"Who are you? How did you get here?! I could get you arrested for trespassing, you know!" Cole said, eyes furious as he pushed Erica behind him and pointed the sword at Christian.

"Christian Blake II, Soul Gatherer. It's technically called 'Umbrageous Teleportation', but Nathaniel prefers to call it 'Shadow Jumping'." He indicated to the Asian man. "Can only be done on the same temporal plane, don't you know."

Teleportation? Erica noticed the man watching her with eyes overflowing with heartache. Almost as if he knew her…

Cole ran a hand through his hair. Erica didn't think she'd ever seen him so agitated—she felt a pang of guilt and reached for him.

"I know it's crazy, but it's okay."

"'Okay'?! How can *this* by anywhere near 'okay'?" He gestured to the chaos around them.

She winced. He had a point.

"So, people aren't vanishing, they're being killed by those things?" he asked, turning to Christian.

"'Lost Souls'," Christian offered. "Yes, that's right. And we stop them with the help of Færies." Here he pointed at the orb which seemed to be watching them with interest. "And quondams, also known as Dæmons." Indicating Lunita and Nathaniel.

"'Quondams'? I didn't know about them. Cool!" Erica looked at them with renewed interest.

"Which is why Michael used to disapprove of Lunita, with her being a Dæmon and all."

"Yes, I can imagine," Erica said, realisation dawning.

"Right, okay. I think I've got all of that, as crazy as it seems," Cole said, lowering the sword. "And where's Lizzie?"

As if doused in cold water Erica started and looked across the fields to where huddled forms knelt: o*h no*…

***

"I'm sorry, Ashayla, but we really need you to focus," Michael prompted softly, removing his helmet.

The Færie was looking across the field to where the others were gathered, its eyes searching for one in particular… Finally, resting on one that glowed, relief washed over it.

"Xerxes will be okay. Look, Amberson is with it," he said.

Indeed, at that moment, heat burned in the veins of one of the forms.

Nodding, the Ashayla reluctantly turned its attention to the bloody form before it.

Cradled in Guy's arms, Lizzie was barely breathing. Bruises, cuts and burns desecrated her pale skin. Blood streaked with black poison soaked the ground around her.

Raising its hands, its palms flared hotly and the Færie began to move them up and down Lizzie's arms, hands, torso and legs, hovering just centimetres from her clothing and exposed flesh. Soothed by the magic, a ghost of a smile appeared on Lizzie's lips.

"Yes, it's an emergency!" Guy was on his mobile. He'd called for an ambulance and was alerting them to the attack.

"Tell them it's a Code '57'," Michael said.

Glancing across at him, Guy relayed the message on.

The tone of the voice on the other end of the line suddenly changed. "A Code '57'? There'll be someone with you ASAP. Two ambulances are on their way. Leave the victim where they are. Don't touch anything."

"But they'll freeze!" Guy cried as the line went dead. "Why a Code 57? Is this something to do with what's on the news?" he said, turning to Michael.

"Yes, if you'd not fought back, they would've taken you both without trace."

Guy paled, clutching Lizzie to him even harder.

Looking up, they saw Erica running over with Cole and Christian. The cold orb streaked after them, staying close to Cole.

"Lizzie! NO!"

At the sound of Erica's screams, Michael leapt to his feet, holding her back.

"Do not crowd her," he said as her tears began to fall at the sight of her friend. Checking Erica for any signs of injury, he noticed the marks on her throat.

"I'm fine," she said. "Amberson saved me."

"I owe him a lifetime of thanks," he said, crushing her against his chest.

Ashayla looked at them in surprise.

"Have you given her the antidote?" Christian asked as he and Cole wrapped Lizzie in blankets.

"Yes, a good fifteen minutes ago. I did it as quickly as I could," Michael replied.

The two friends shared a brief look.

"She'll be okay?" Erica sobbed, wringing her hands. She felt utterly helpless.

"We can but pray," Michael said.

Cole threw Erica Lizzie's leather jacket. It was splattered with blood and black gloop. Lizzie would be fuming if she saw it now.

"You'd better look after it for her."

Erica nodded numbly. "I'll clean it up."

The party glanced at the orb that hovered nearby.

"Any clearer what it is?" Michael asked Christian in an undertone.

"No, not a sausage. Amberson said it was old. It's being controlled by someone at the farm," said Christian, eyeing the orb thoughtfully.

"Cole said mum fetched a 'medallion' out of an old box," Erica said, flashing them a knowing look.

They shared a look of surprise: a periapt? What did it mean?

"Can we move her? I can't leave her here. She's so cold…" Guy said, voice breaking, eyes looking up at his big brother.

Cole glanced at Christian and Michael who nodded.

"Okay, let's take her to the stables and keep her warm."

"Wait, isn't that great-great-grandad's sword?" Erica asked, suddenly noticing the weapon on the ground by Guy. "How did that get here?"

"He summoned it," Guy said, nodding in Michael's direction. He passed Lizzie's bundled form to Cole before getting to his feet. "Could you carry it back for me?"

"Sure," Erica said, glancing at Cole for approval who shrugged in annoyance at his thwarted efforts.

"You never told me he could do magic," Guy growled.

"Technically, it's Ashayla who does the magic and it's not really something that comes up naturally in conversation."

"Guess not. At least we know why've you been so secretive recently. You've got some explaining to do! You've put us all in danger!"

Erica paled.

"Now, Guy, none of this is Erica's fault. It's that pandemic-thing. How about I fill you in on the way back?" Cole offered, patting his brother on the shoulder.

Guy nodded. Suddenly overcome, he wiped away tears before taking Lizzie from Cole. Then, cradling her in his arms, the two brothers carefully set off, taking it in turns to carry her. Erica could see Amberson and the others already on their way to the farmhouse.

"Go to it," Michael said, noticing Ashayla's agitation. "And thank you."

"Daité puluh-so," it said with a quick bow. And, leaping into the air, it transformed into its elfin form before flying past the two men and hurtling towards Xerxes.

"Well, we know one thing," Christian said with grim satisfaction, breaking the silence.

"We do?" Michael asked.

"They're waiting. They've been waiting here for goodness knows how long feeding on anything that unwittingly stumbled their way. If Guy hadn't had his wits about him, they'd have killed them both before returning to their waiting game."

A coldness washed over Erica as she thought of the countless Lost Souls hiding in the shadows all over the world. The sea of faces from the newspaper bombarded her; she felt sick.

"They were in a frenzy..." Michael said thoughtfully.

"I don't think they'd had access to human souls yet—I can imagine they 'taste' quite different to animals. Guy and Lizzie were too good to resist."

"But what were they waiting for?" Erica asked.

"A sign. We can safely presume they've been Impressed—they're being controlled somehow, and I doubt whoever's controlling them will be pleased that the Lost Souls here blew their cover. There'll be repercussions when they find out. Are you cold, *querida*?" He turned suddenly to Lunita, putting his arm around her. Her connate nuzzled up close to her.

"It's just too much... So much loss," she said, burrowing her head in his chest.

Christian looked over to Michael and nodded to the farmhouse: they'd see them there.

Michael and Erica watched them leave, Lunita's glowing connate walking beside her.

Turning her attention back to the sword, Erica wiped blackness away from the blade with the sleeve of her jacket. It was old, with nicks along its edge. Markings of the Royal Artillery had been crammed next to the sun motif on its hilt. She looked up to find Michael's eyes on her.

"Any reaction?" Michael asked.

"How do you mean?"

"It glowed. When your brother took it, it reacted to him."

"It 'glowed'? What does that mean? It's just a sword."

He shook his head and pointed to the small sun motif. "I think it might be more."

Her mind was reeling. "I don't understand…"

"But I think your mother does."

They looked towards the farmhouse and its lights. People were busying about in the yard, there was a wail as her mother ran to her father's limp form carried by Nathaniel. Guy and Cole had almost arrived with Lizzie. Ashayla had transformed back into its human form and was helping Amberson with Xerxes.

A sadness gripped her heart, sadness and fear, ice-cold fear. "Everything's changed…"

"Yes," said Michael, reaching for her free hand and taking it in his. "It has."

**To be continued in Book 2 of the Soul Dominion series:
Keys of Fate**

It would mean the world to me if you could leave some stars or a short review on the page you bought the book or on Goodreads. Reviews help new readers find the books and your help in spreading the word is gratefully appreciated.

Acknowledgements

A massive thank you to Chloe, Bethan, and Sarah, my amazing Beta Readers, for taking the time to read through the draft and send me feedback. Your enthusiasm for the story was overwhelming! Thank you for your help, it was invaluable and it was an honour working with you all again! You're all stars! An extra special thank you to Sarah for helping right up until she gave birth! Welcome to the world, baby M! Congratulations to you all! A big thank you to my parents for their constant support. You've always been there cheering me on, and for that I'm profoundly grateful. Thank you to my editor for your help, support and suggestions—not to mention, patience! A special shoutout to my mum who was my Alpha Reader and the first person on earth to *ever* read this book. I'd have published it without your approval, but your love and passion for the story makes it that much easier. (I love the fact that you ended up reading it within days because you couldn't put that down! I count that as a win!) Thank you to Carin and the team at GetCovers for creating such a gorgeous cover—you're awesome! To T, thank you for inspiring me to dust off the original manuscript. I'll follow my dreams if you follow yours. Last but by no means least, the biggest of 'thank yous' to my husband. Thank you for helping me realise my dreams. Your belief and support mean everything to me. Sorry it doesn't have any pictures.

Georgiana Kent

Keys of Fate

Fate can be cruel.

Left devastated by the attack, Erica is thrown ever deeper into the shadows of Limbo society. And she is in danger. Someone is hunting GateKeepers like her, hunting and killing them.

Though, that is the least of her problems. The army of Lost Souls, led by their mysterious commander, is preparing to strike. Can she and Michael put their differences aside in time to save mankind?

Welcome to *Keys of Fate*, Book Two in Georgiana Kent's *Soul Dominion* series, where KeyMasters, quondams, and Faeries collide in mankind's fight for survival. Perfect for fans of epic urban fantasies!

Coming Summer 2022

Pre-order your copy below!

~ Keep checking as more stores are added ~

https://bit.ly/KeysOfFate

Georgiana Kent

Enjoyed Keys of Time?

Want to know what happened when Michael met Annabelle? Sign up to my mailing list and receive your bonus chapter, *Letting Go*:

Letting Go is the hardest of things. Especially when it comes to your first love.

Annabelle Williams has it all: she is beautiful, of high-standing and the most desired debutante of the season. However, whilst most young ladies would be happily chased by every eligible bachelor, Annabelle is not. She wants to turn heads and live life! That's when she meets Michael Nicholas, an up-and-coming gentleman who is making his way in Victorian society, proving there is more to him than his heritage. But will Annabelle's father, Sir Geoffrey Williams, Chairman of The East India Company, approve?

Probably not!

From their first meeting until their last, read Michael and Annabelle's tragic love story.

~ This bonus chapter fits in after the Shadowling attack and Christmas Day in Keys of Time and follows Michael on his timeline ~

https://bit.ly/KoTBonus

Georgiana Kent

About the Author

Georgiana Kent has worked as a cleaner, software tester, waitress, translator and MFL teacher (in no particular order). She has had a lifelong love of languages and cultures and has spent much time in the Far East. She is fluent in Mandarin Chinese and considers Beijing a second home.

Having always been creative, she originally focused on Manga before turning to writing. She has always adored fantasy and is currently working on two young adult series set in her *KeyMaster Chronicles* universe: *KeyMaster Origins* and *Soul Dominion* are urban fantasies on an epic scale.

Georgiana is a Christian and lives in Derbyshire with her family and, when not working, enjoys exploring the Peak District, sneaking in an ice cream when she can. As a Hufflepuff, she has an eclectic tight collection, gets excited by anything kawaii and is slightly obsessed with miniature Dachshunds.

Want to know more about Chinasa and Philip? Curious how Michael met Christian? And what really did happen between Anatole and Yophiel? Check out Georgiana's FREE prequel novella *Inner Demons* and keep up to date with writing news, behind the scenes exclusives and releases:

https://bit.ly/GeorgianaKent

Georgiana Kent

Urban Myth Publishing

An independent small press focused on providing gripping YA Urban Fantasy fiction on epic scales.

Urban Myth Publishing is proud to present Georgiana Kent's first two series: *KeyMaster Origins* and *Soul Dominion*. *Keys of Time* is Book One in her debut *Soul Dominion* series and is available at your favourite digital store. Whilst *Inner Demons*, Book One in her prequel series *KeyMaster Origins*, is currently FREE on her Patreon page. (Available here: https://bit.ly/GeorgianaKent)

If you enjoy stories driven by diverse, strong characters filled with suspense and adventure you've come to the right place! Georgiana's *KeyMaster Chronicles* books weaves together the mystery and pace of Urban Fantasies with supernatural thrills, a smattering of romance and a host of characters for you to fall in love with. Perfect for fans of epic Urban Fantasies!

Visit her website here: http://bit.ly/keymasterchronicles

Georgiana Kent

Keys of Time